STAR WARS®
The New Essential Guide to Vehicles and Vessels

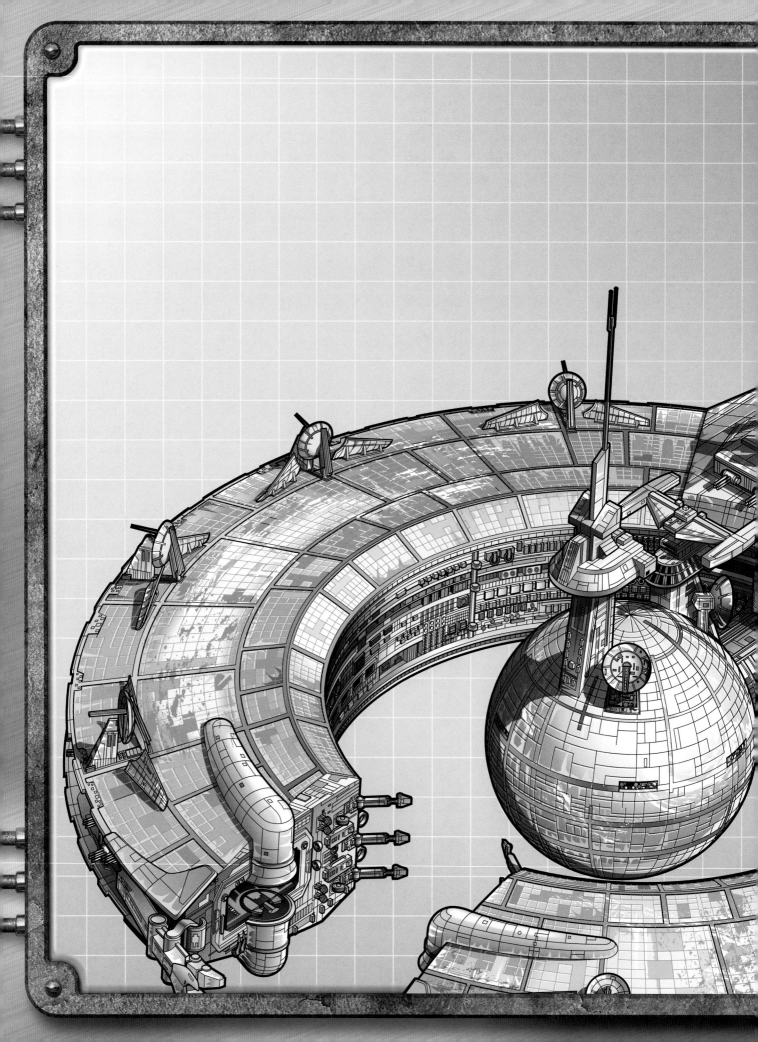

STAR WARS®
The New Essential Guide
to Vehicles and Vessels

W. Haden Blackman

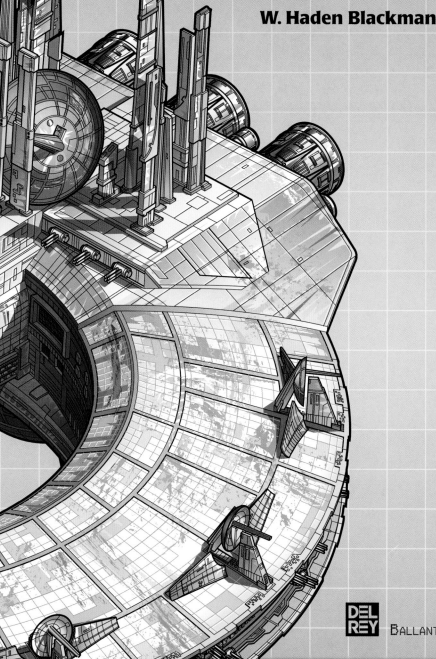

BALLANTINE BOOKS ■ NEW YORK

Author Acknowledgments

I would like to thank Steve Saffel and Kathleen O'Shea David at Del Rey for their patience and keen insight into the *Star Wars* universe; Jonathan W. Rinzler, Lucy Autrey Wilson, Leland Chee, Sue Rostoni, and Iain Morris at Lucasfilm, where that universe is kept in good hands; and Camela McLanahan at LucasArts for pulling me into the *Star Wars* universe in the first place. This book would not have been possible without further aid from Dan Wallace, Allan Kausch, Chris Cerasi, Jon Knoles, Kevin Schmitt, Mike Gallo, Ryan Kaufman, Clint Young, Tim Longo, and Justin Lambros—thank you all for your help and extensive *Star Wars* knowledge.

I would also like to thank all the novelists, game designers, comic book writers, artists, and other creative folks who have contributed to the *Star Wars* mythos. Of course, all things *Star Wars* start and end with George Lucas, but those who labor to grow the *Star Wars* universe only make it a better place in which to play. I would especially like to laud the contributions of Bill Smith, Doug Chiang, and Troy Vigil, who collaborated on the first edition of this book.

Finally, to my wife, Anne-Marie, who always puts everything back into perspective.

Artist Acknowledgments

Illustrating this book has been a challenge, at times demanding, but above all memorable.

My thanks go to fellow illustrator Paul Bates; also to Rob Garrard and John Hawes for their input.

A Del Rey® Book
Published by The Random House Publishing Group

Copyright © 2003 by Lucasfilm Ltd. & ® or ™ where indicated.
All Rights Reserved. Used Under Authorization.

All rights reserved.

Published in the United States by Del Rey Books, an imprint of The Random House Publishing Group, a division of Random House, Inc., New York, and simultaneously in Canada by Random House of Canada Limited, Toronto.

Del Rey is a registered trademark and the Del Rey colophon is a trademark of Random House, Inc.

www.starwars.com
www.delreybooks.com

A Library of Congress Catalog Card Number is available from the publisher

ISBN 0-345-44902-9

Cover illustration by Steven D. Anderson
Cover design by David Stevenson
Interior design and art direction by Michaelis/Carpelis Design Associates Inc.

Printed in China

9 8 7

**To my great-grandmother,
who only went to one movie a year
and loved *Star Wars*.**

Contents

INTRODUCTION

My favorite moment from the entire *Star Wars* saga comes when Han Solo, Princess Leia, Chewbacca, and C-3PO are preparing to escape Hoth in *The Empire Strikes Back*. As Imperials advance on the *Millennium Falcon*, the starship's engines fail and the lights in the cockpit flicker. Frustrated, Han smacks the cockpit wall, and suddenly the *Falcon* comes back to life.

This moment gives the film a certain verisimilitude and connects that fantastic galaxy with a very real, true-to-life experience (I once had a television that would conk out until it received a good smack to the side...). It also helps to develop the *Falcon* as a character possessing a real personality and a well-defined relationship with her owner.

That the vehicles of *Star Wars* are able to engender emotion is part of the saga's tremendous appeal. Boba Fett's *Slave I* is menacing, reflecting his disposition; Imperial Star Destroyers display the Emperor's power with a single visual outline; and the *Falcon* is a crucial member of the heroic home team. All these vessels linger in our minds because we connect to them as more than just plastic models or computer-generated images; they *feel* real.

This book is meant to serve as an overview of the many vehicles that populate the *Star Wars* universe. They are drawn from the films as well as the comic books, role-playing games, novels, concept art, and video games. Each is more than just the sum of its parts; they all have specific roles to fill within the greater mythos.

TIMELINE

This book is written as if during the height of the Yuuzhan Vong invasion, as described in the current New Jedi Order series. The Yuuzhan Vong invasion begins about 25 standard years after the Battle of Yavin, the conflict depicted in *Star Wars*: Episode IV *A New Hope*. Although every effort has been made to keep this book up to date, the Yuuzhan Vong invasion is still ongoing as of this writing. In addition, there are key events that will be explored in Episode III that obviously can't be addressed here.

VITAL STATISTICS

Each major entry includes a list of vital statistics, which are interpreted as:

SIZE: The height and/or length of the vehicle, listed in meters or kilometers.

MAXIMUM SPEED: For ground-based vehicles, the maximum speed (in kilometers per hour, or kph) over open ground; for atmospheric craft, the maximum airspeed in normal atmospheric conditions; for starships, the maximum acceleration attainable in space, followed by hyperdrive class (if any), and finally airspeed in an atmosphere.

PRIMARY MANUFACTURER: The company most responsible for designing and building the vehicle.

AFFILIATION: The group or individuals with which the vehicle is *most often* associated. Some vehicles are used by multiple organizations or characters; this section lists only the most prominent of these.

Schematics Color Key

- Weapons
- Defenses, physical ship components
- Communications, sensors, controls, commands, etc.
- Power sources, engine technologies

A Layperson's Guide to Technology

Each vehicle used throughout the galaxy is, in many ways, a mechanical marvel composed of dozens of truly miraculous components and systems. Whether a planet-bound airspeeder capable of floating above the ground, or a battleship able to hop between star systems in an instant, these craft utilize astonishing technological advances such as the repulsorlift engine or the hyperdrive.

Yet many galactic denizens take technology for granted. The hyperdrive has been a part of their daily life for eons, and the airspeeder is treated as a common tool. This casual attitude, coupled with the complex vocabulary employed by persons who deal in galactic technology, can lead to confusion among laypeople and outsiders encountering the galaxy's vehicles for the first time. The following should serve as an introduction to concepts and common terms used across the galaxy.

Vehicle Classes

Capital Ship

A capital ship is any large starship, specifically those vessels designed for deep-space warfare. Capital ships begin at roughly 100 meters in length, and the class includes everything from Imperial Star Destroyers to Mon Calamari star cruisers and the Yuuzhan Vong's miid ro'ik warship. Often used as the primary attack vessels in a fleet, capital ships boast powerful deflector shields along with numerous weapons emplacements where a wide range of ion cannons, turbolasers, and laser cannons are located. Many capital ships are also responsible for transporting starfighters, shuttles, and support craft into battle. Given their sheer size, capital ships require large crews, often numbering into the hundreds or even thousands. At 1,600 meters long, an Imperial Star Destroyer requires a crew of 37,000 and supports more than one hundred weapons emplacements.

Repulsorlift Vehicle

Perhaps the most common vehicles in the galaxy, repulsorlift craft are equipped with engines that produce an antigravity field. When a repulsorlift engine is engaged, it allows the vehicle to hover above the ground. Even the most primitive propulsion system can move a repulsorlift vehicle forward, and some craft are capable of attaining speeds in excess of 1,000 kilometers per hour. Most repulsorlift vehicles have limited altitude capabilities, with flight ceilings ranging between two and fifty meters. More powerful repulsorlift craft, such as Cloud City's twin-pod cloud cars, can attain low orbit. Landspeeders, snowspeeders, Podracers, speeder bikes, and even AATs are all repulsorlift vehicles.

Speeder

Speeder is a generic term often applied to any high-speed ground vehicle equipped with a repulsorlift system. Speeders range from the civilian XP-38 landspeeder to the T-47 snowspeeders favored by the Rebel Alliance.

Starfighter

While capital ships provide heavy firepower during battles, the smaller starfighters are a fleet's staple attack craft. Designed to carry out precision strikes, protect capital ships, and participate in atmospheric combat, starfighters are generally sleek, agile, and very fast. Starfighters may be heavily armed and armored, like the Rebel Y-wing, or lightly protected and designed to attack in numbers, as is the case with the Imperial TIE fighter.

Star Yacht

Typically regarded as a symbol of wealth, a star yacht is a large pleasure vehicle used for intergalactic travel. It is likely to boast luxurious quarters, a spacious cargo hold, and a variety of creature comforts. Those travelers who explore more dangerous portions of the galaxy arm their yachts with weapons and shields.

Transport

A transport is any starship meant to carry cargo or passengers. The term is usually reserved for nonmilitary starships, including small light freighters, passenger liners, and even massive container ships such as those used by the Trade Federation. Because they tend to favor safe and well-established trade routes, transports are rarely armed or shielded. They also tend to be slow at both sublight and hyperdrive speeds. A transport's modular nature makes it very easy to modify, however, and many smugglers, pirates, and Rebels have converted these otherwise unremarkable craft into exceptional combat vessels. The *Millennium Falcon*, originally a stock Corellian YT-1300 transport, was modified to include a Class 0.5 hyperdrive, twin quad laser cannons, an advanced sensor suite, and formidable deflector shields.

Engine Technologies

Hyperdrive

A vital component on many starships, the hyperdrive is responsible for accelerating a vehicle for faster-than-lightspeed velocities and propelling it into the dimension known as hyperspace. While in hyperspace, a vehicle can cover huge expanses of space in an instant.

The hyperdrive is often credited with allowing the Old Republic to explore and colonize the galaxy. Despite its wide use, however, hyperspace travel remains dangerous, because objects in "realspace" often cast "mass shadows" into hyperspace. Colliding with a mass shadow can destroy a starship. In order to avoid these hazards, hyperdrives are generally equipped with precise navigational computers that determine safe routes around stars, planets, asteroid fields, and stellar debris. Most pilots also travel established hyperspace lanes to further increase their odds of survival.

Hyperdrives are categorized by "class," with lower classes denoting faster speeds. Class Three hyperdrives are common among civilian craft; Class Two or Class One hyperdrives transport most military vehicles throughout the galaxy. Class 0.75 or 0.5 hyperdrives are rare, and usually the result of exceptional modifications to existing engines.

Hyperdrive Classifications

Class 4 TIE Advanced, Rebel transport

Class 3 Sith Infiltrator, Yuuzhan Vong miid ro'ik

Class 2 Imperial Star Destroyer, Rebel blockade runner, (B-wing, Droid Control Ship, E-wing, *Eclipse*, *Executor*, *IG-2000*, Interdictor cruiser, Rebel cruiser, Republic cruiser, TIE defender)

Class 1.8 Naboo Royal Starship

Class 1.5 Solar sailer, Yuuzhan Vong worldship (Chiss clawcraft, CloakShape, *Havoc*, *Hound's Tooth*)

Class 1 X-wing, Imperial shuttle (A-wing, Imperial landing craft, Jedi starfighter with hyperdrive ring, *Lady Luck*, Mon Cal cruiser, N-1 starfighter, *Slave I*, *Virago*, *Wild Karrde*, Y-wing)

Class 0.8 *Inferno*

Class 0.75 *Outrider*

Class 0.7 Naboo Royal Cruiser

Class 0.6 Republic assault ship, *Sharp Spiral*

Class 0.5 *Millennium Falcon, Jade Shadow*

Class 0.4 *Jabitha*

Ion Engine

A propulsion system found on virtually every starship, the ion engine is a standard component of the sublight drive responsible for nonhyperspace space travel. An ion engine is powered by local power cells, liquid reactants, or onboard generators. The device uses an internal fusion reaction to produce a stream of charged particles, which is then channeled through the engine's exhaust ports to provide forward movement.

Repulsorlift Drive

The repulsorlift drive is an extremely common propulsion unit used by land, atmospheric, and spacecraft. The system utilizes a fusion generator to produce an antigravity field, which in turn enables a vehicle to hover anywhere between a few centimeters and several hundred meters above a planet's surface. Repulsorlift drives are often the primary engine system on a vehicle, as is the case with airspeeders. Starships and starfighters also make use of repulsorlift engines to travel or land inside an atmosphere. Specialized repulsorlift drives can be integrated into flying droids, hovering cargo containers, and even floating cities.

Sublight Drive

Sublight drives maneuver vehicles through realspace, and usually employ one of several engine technologies, including ion drives. Sublight drives are almost always engaged upon leaving a planet's atmosphere and during space battles. Most sublight drives also project varying gravitic effects to protect pilots and passengers during sudden changes in sublight acceleration.

Weapon Technologies

Blaster Cannon

Also known as the "flash cannon," the blaster cannon is a limited-range heavy artillery weapon that fires bursts of energy. Though not as powerful as the laser cannon, blaster cannons are nonetheless quite effective during atmospheric combat and can be devastating when used against ground troops or military structures. They can be found mounted on many repulsorlift craft and other ground vehicles.

Hyperdrive

CONCUSSION MISSILE

Similar to a proton torpedo, a concussion missile is a projectile that travels at sublight speeds and can cause damaging shock waves upon impact with its target. Concussion missiles are especially effective against large, stationary targets, and they are quite capable of penetrating the heavy armor used on capital ships.

Concussion missiles were originally developed by pirates and mercenaries to combat starfighters, and were later adapted by the Empire to use aboard bombers. Ironically, the Rebel Alliance used concussion missiles to destroy the second Death Star.

ION CANNON

Considered by many the most important weapon in the galaxy, the ion cannon is capable of disabling enemy starships without causing any lasting damage. The most common ion cannons, such as the Y-wing's ArMek SW-4, fire powerful bolts of ionized energy designed to overload a target's systems or fuse mechanical components. During the Galactic Civil War and other conflicts, warring factions used ion cannons to capture cargo, prisoners, and highly prized vehicles while keeping them intact.

LASER CANNON

The laser cannon is the dominant weapon in the galaxy, found aboard all military craft and many civilian vehicles as well. Essentially large and powerful blasters, laser cannons fire bolts of concentrated energy in order to damage their targets. Starfighter pilots frequently rely on laser cannons because of their incredible range and rapid recharge rate. Laser cannons have also become popular among civilians because they are light, easy to install and modify, and relatively inexpensive.

Laser cannons are almost always complemented by computerized targeting systems that provide increased accuracy and advanced cooling systems that prevent overheating. Laser cannons can draw power directly from a vehicle's generator, although many rely on dedicated power sources. Laser cannons are quite effective against most structures, small ground- and aircraft, and starfighters, but they lack the ability to penetrate the thick armored hulls and deflector shields used to protect most capital ships.

PROTON TORPEDO

Common concussion weapons found aboard modern starfighters and capital ships, proton torpedoes are high-speed projectiles fired from specially designed tubes. When a torpedo impacts its target, the weapon's high-yield warhead detonates, releasing a devastating wave of protons. Proton torpedoes bypass standard deflector shields and can be stopped only by complete particle shielding.

Starfighters can carry a limited number of proton torpedoes, so pilots must deploy them wisely, but a well-placed torpedo can seriously cripple even large capital ships. Miraculous shots are not uncommon: proton torpedoes seek out their targets with the aid of advanced guidance computers, and the margin of error for even the most basic torpedo is less than three meters. Only the fastest and most maneuverable vehicles, piloted by the most competent space jockeys, can dodge a proton torpedo.

Proton torpedoes are far less accurate against smaller objectives, such as the two-meter-wide exhaust port that Luke Skywalker successfully targeted in order to destroy the first Death Star.

Variations on the proton torpedo include the proton bomb, which can be dropped on targets, and the expensive proton hydrotorpedo used during nautical battles.

TURBOLASER

While starfighters tend to rely on standard laser cannons, capital ships, military installations, and space stations can support the much larger and more destructive turbolaser. The energy blasts produced by a turbolaser can tear through armored starships and demolish entire starfighter squadrons. A turbolaser's effective range is between double and triple that of a laser cannon, and many capital ships carry turbolasers capable of targeting planetary structures.

This increased power comes at a significant cost: turbolasers recharge slowly and require dedicated turbines, multiple capacitor banks, and expensive and high-maintenance independent cryogenic cooling systems. Trained crews must often be assigned to turbolasers to carefully monitor energy flow, in the hope of avoiding explosive power surges. Because of their low

Turboblaster

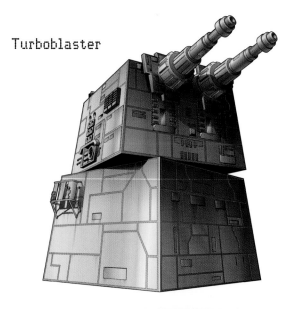

rate of fire and slow rotation speeds, turbolasers can be dodged by skilled pilots.

Turbolaser placement is extremely important. When installed haphazardly, as is the case on the Trade Federation's battleships, turbolasers do not provide complete defensive coverage, and small starfighters can slip through the large openings between turbolaser emplacements in order to attack the capital ship. Aboard well-designed capital ships, including Imperial Star Destroyers, turbolasers are organized into banks. Computerized fire-control systems synchronize each bank, ensuring sustained barrages that are far more difficult to avoid. Turbolasers may also be controlled by trained live gunners located in protected stations.

OTHER EQUIPMENT TECHNOLOGIES

ASTROMECH DROID

An astromech droid is a general utility droid, often designed to aid in the upkeep and use of vehicles. The various astromechs are grouped into series, ranging from R1 to R7. Each series exhibits different capabilities and programming, although most are able to calculate coordinates for hyperspace jumps, aid in navigation, and make repairs. Many starfighters are manufactured to carry astromechs in a specialized socket, which allows the droid to interface more efficiently with the starship. Larger vessels have secure droid holds that may release a squad of astromechs when a mechanical emergency is detected.

R2 units, such as Luke Skywalker's R2-D2, may be the most versatile of all astromechs. When used aboard a starfighter, an R2 unit evaluates flight performance and makes necessary adjustments to increase the vehicle's efficiency. It can also identify, isolate, and repair malfunctions, and can store up to ten sets of hyperspace coordinates.

Astromech
Droid

CLOAKING DEVICE

Extremely rare and notoriously difficult to acquire, cloaking devices render starships invisible to electronic detection systems. All starships emit electromagnetic waves, which can be identified by a variety of sensors; a cloaking device functions by disrupting these waves, preventing the ship from appearing on scanners.

Cloaking devices, such as the one found aboard Darth Maul's Sith Infiltrator, were traditionally powered by stygium crystals. Mined only on the volatile Aeten II in the Outer Rim and prone to burnout during use, stygium crystals existed in increasingly limited numbers throughout the galaxy in the waning years of the Old Republic. At the time of the of the Empire's rise, Aeten II's cache of crystals had been all but depleted, making the manufacture of new stygium-based cloaking devices a near impossibility.

During the Galactic Civil War, Emperor Palpatine aggressively researched new cloaking technologies, seeking alternatives to stygium-powered devices. Although most experiments were unsuccessful, the Emperor's researchers did produce at least one working prototype. Years after the Battle of Endor, Grand Admiral Thrawn discovered this nonstygium prototype in one of the Emperor's hidden storehouses. Unfortunately, all modern, nonstygium cloaking devices are bulky and require sizable independent power sources, limiting their use to larger starships.

DEFLECTOR SHIELD

The deflector shield is vital to survival aboard nearly every starship. Deflector shields surround craft in two protective force fields: ray shielding and particle shielding. Ray shielding, also known as energy shielding, is designed to absorb radiation and raw energy, including laser cannon fire. Particle shielding, in contrast, repels solid objects such as concussion weapons and space debris. Ray shields are engaged during combat, while particle shields are generally kept activated at all times to defend against accidental collisions and micrometeor impacts.

A deflector shield's power source determines the strength of the shield, the shield's radius, and the amount of damage it can absorb. Civilian-grade deflector shields usually burn out after absorbing a significant amount of damage, while military models recharge over time. Some ground vehicles can be equipped with weak deflector shield generators, but only starfighters and other starships carry the power sources necessary to support high-end shields.

ESCAPE POD

Space travel is undeniably dangerous. Starships encounter a wide variety of hazards, ranging from

Escape Pod

pirates to asteroid fields. In the event that a starship is disabled and left unable to continue on its journey, passengers and crew may board escape pods: space capsules equipped with fundamental life support and survival supplies. Escape pods range from small, one-person lifeboats to the expansive, environmentally sealed salon pods found aboard Republic cruisers.

Once launched, an escape pod will scan the surrounding space in search of a suitable planet. A very rudimentary sublight drive system then points the pod toward this safe haven. A repulsorlift engine equipped with maneuvering jets aids in a soft landing. During flight, passengers are strapped into padded g-couches for their protection.

Nav Computer

The key component of any navigational system, the nav computer (or "navicomputer") works in conjunction with the hyperdrive and sensor systems to calculate light-speed jumps, as well as realspace trajectories and travel routes. Most nav computers are programmed with hundreds of astrogation charts, any of which can be displayed as two- or three-dimensional projections for pilots to study. Nav computers are usually designed to interact with astromechs and other droids. Ground vehicles and planetary aircraft also make use of nav computers, with complex mapping functions used for determining safe routes over land or in an atmosphere.

Sensor Array

While traveling through the galaxy, starships are constantly gathering information from the space around them. Starship pilots need to identify and locate other starships, stellar hazards, planets and moons, and galactic anomalies. Planetary vehicles need to collect similar data, including updates relating to the terrain and weather. The sensor array on any vehicle scans the area and sends this information to onboard computers,

which then display updates for the pilot and crew.

Passive-mode sensors, the most basic scanning devices, evaluate only the area directly around a vessel. More powerful scan-mode sensors can actively gather information in a much wider range; and search-mode sensors are programmed to actively search for information in specific directions. Finally, focus-mode sensors can closely study a small area of space or an environment to collect a massive amount of data.

Scanners utilize a variety of sensors to gather and evaluate data. The most common include: electro-photo receptors (EPRs); full-spectrum transceivers (FSTs); dedicated energy receptors (DERs); crystal grav-field traps (CGTs); hyperwave signal interceptors (HSIs); and life-form indicators (LFIs).

Targeting Computer

Nearly all weapons systems, and particularly laser cannons, are complemented by targeting computers designed to acquire and track fast-moving objects, such as an enemy starfighter. Targeting computers communicate with a starship's nav computer and sensor array to identify all possible targets within range of the vehicle's weapons. With the aid of these other systems, the targeting computer can also calculate trajectories to determine attack and intercept courses. Aboard larger vehicles, independent combat computers control turret servos to make constant, minute adjustments, improving firing accuracy throughout a battle.

Targeting computers are powerful tools, but could never replace a competent pilot or skilled gunner. Unlike a sentient gunner, targeting computers can't predict the unexpected movements of a creative enemy or react intuitively to new situations.

Tractor Beam

Tractor beams are modified force fields capable of immobilizing and moving objects in space. Essential tools for large capital ships and space stations, tractor beams are most often used to guide incoming starships into landing bays. Other craft deploy tractor beams to move salvage or cargo, retrieve stranded vehicles or pilots, and reposition space stations and orbital structure. Imperial Star Destroyers, however, rely on tractor beams to capture enemy vessels, which can then be boarded or destroyed by turbolasers.

Like many large starship devices, tractor beams require a great deal of onboard space, maintenance, and power. The largest tractor beams, including those installed aboard Star Destroyers, demand crews of ten technicians and operators and are dependent upon a bulky reactor. The tractor beams aboard the original Death Star were coupled to the main reactor, which provided a constant flow of energy.

Major Manufacturers

Vehicles are an integral part of life in the galaxy. Whether the craft is a beat-up landspeeder used for travel between desert towns on Tatooine, or a modified Corellian transport piloted on long-distance trips from Coruscant to the Outer Rim, vehicles are a necessity for most sentient beings. As a result, literally thousands of companies design, manufacture, modify, and repair all manner of craft. Thousands more create vehicle replacement parts, modification kits, weapons, and other equipment.

Nearly as diverse as the craft they create, the galaxy's major manufacturers range from small, independent operations to huge galactic corporations with hundreds of factories spread across dozens of systems.

During the height of the Old Republic's power, large-scale armed conflicts were extraordinarily rare, and even the Republic had no need for a standing army. Most manufacturers focused on civilian craft rather than military vehicles. As the political climate changed after the Battle of Naboo, however, many companies adopted new strategies and began producing increasingly more dangerous craft.

Aratech Repulsor Company

Aratech is dedicated to the design and manufacture of speeder bikes. Well established long before the Battle of Geonosis, Aratech was one of the first companies to pledge support to the Republic in the war against the Confederacy of Independent Systems. As the Republic assembled its clone army, Aratech provided a fleet of its notable 74-Z speeder bikes for use in the ground battle on Geonosis. Aratech managed to survive well past the Emperor's reign, with its 74-Z becoming a staple of both Imperial and New Republic forces.

- Speeder Bike (74-Z Military Speeder Bike)

Baktoid Armor Workshop

Prior to the Battle of Naboo, Baktoid Armor Workshop was a Trade Federation–owned design firm that specialized in developing rugged all-terrain ground vehicles for use by civilians. A Baktoid design tended to be heavily armored, with delicate or important components placed in secure, well-protected areas near the rear of the craft. Early Baktoid vehicles were rarely manufactured with weapons, but they did possess standard weapons emplacements, allowing combat modifications to be made after purchase.

In order to build its secret army, the Trade Federation provided Baktoid with funding for a complete line of ground assault vehicles and transports. It is also rumored that the Trade Federation arranged a merger between Baktoid and Haor Chall arms merchants, although Baktoid representatives denied this claim. Nevertheless, with the Trade Federation's support, Baktoid began work on several new craft, including the fearsome AAT battle tank and the nearly unstoppable MTT. During development of these vehicles, the company made a conscious effort to adhere to a unified design style, resulting in a line of vehicles reminiscent of large and dangerous animals.

After the Battle of Naboo, the Trade Federation tried to distance itself from the Baktoid Armor Workshop, which was accused of providing the front-line assault vehicles used in the capture of Theed and other settlements. The Trade Federation dramatically dissolved Baktoid, only to quietly transfer many of the company's manufacturing facilities and designs to other Trade Federation subsidiaries.

- AAT
- Commerce Guild Spider Tank (Homing Spider Droid)
- MTT
- STAP

Bespin Motors

Widely recognized as the galaxy's leading manufacturer of cloud cars, Bespin Motors was originally a subsidiary of Incom Corporation. The company was founded specifically to create Cloud City, the massive mining facility suspended in the atmosphere above Bespin. When it became apparent that the Empire would nationalize Incom, Bespin executives arranged a buyout of Bespin Motors, which then broke away from its parent company. With Bespin Motors autonomous, the company began research and development of the high-altitude cloud cars.

- Cloud Car

Chiss

The Chiss are a species of blue-skinned humanoids well known for their self-control and intelligence; these traits have translated into a series of well-designed and innovative starships. In order to travel through hyperspace, Chiss starships rely on a series of navigational anchor points that spread out from their homeworld of Csilla. This system allowed the Chiss to explore the galaxy methodically, but kept them from encountering other cultures until early in the Emperor's reign. After a Chiss named Thrawn made contact with the Empire, the species began producing hybrid starfighters, such as the Chiss clawcraft, that combine Imperial and Chiss technologies. Due to the secrecy with which the Chiss cloak their internal affairs, outsiders know very little about individual Chiss manufacturers.

⌗ Chiss Clawcraft

Corellian Engineering Corporation

Possibly the most prolific and widely known starship manufacturing company in the galaxy, Corellian Engineering Corporation (CEC) has built its reputation on fast, durable, and easily modified commercial vehicles. Unlike its two primary competitors, Kuat Drive Yards and Sienar Fleet Systems, CEC has long relied on civilian sales rather than military contracts. Among its most successful civilian products have been its modular freighters, which can be upgraded for combat duty using both legal and illegal modification kits. The company's freighters range from the YG series first produced centuries before the Battle of Yavin to the VCX series manufactured shortly before the Yuuzhan Vong invasion. CEC also produces reliable long-distance starships such as the Republic cruiser, light warships like the Corellian corvette (or Rebel blockade runner), and even escape pods.

CEC's success may be related to its location: the company's orbital shipyards are based in the Corellian system, whose worlds produce an unusually high number of skilled starship engineers and designers.

⌗ *Hound's Tooth* (YV-666 Light Freighter)
⌗ *Millennium Falcon* (YT-1300 Transport)
⌗ *Outrider* (YT-2400 Freighter)
⌗ Rebel Blockade Runner
⌗ Republic Cruiser
⌗ *Wild Karrde* (Action VI Transport)

Cygnus Spaceworks

One of several companies tied to the Empire, Cygnus Spaceworks is a relatively small manufacturer of military starships. The corporation relies on a strong connection to Sienar Fleet Systems (SFS), which has provided Cygnus with numerous components and subcontracts, and funding from the Imperial Navy. Even after the rise of the New Republic, Cygnus remained fiercely loyal to the Empire. About half of Cygnus's designs are simply modifications to existing vehicles, as is the case with the Sentinel-class landing craft, which is a variant of the

SFS Lambda-class shuttle. The rest of the Cygnus line exemplifies the other extreme: cutting-edge vehicles such as the Alpha-class Xg-1 Star Wing assault gunboat used by the Imperial Navy.

⌗ Imperial Landing Craft (with Sienar Fleet Systems)

FreiTek, Inc.

Founded by the former Incom Corporation designers responsible for creating the X-wing starfighter, FreiTek, Inc., rapidly became a major supplier of military starships. FreiTek openly supports the New Republic; in fact, its first design was the powerful E-wing starfighter used in the conflict against Grand Admiral Thrawn. With the success of the E-wing, FreiTek rapidly expanded its operations and continues to research the latest in starfighter technologies. The company subsidizes its R&D efforts by producing upgrades for numerous older starfighters.

⌗ E-Wing

Gallofree Yards, Inc.

Another casualty of the fiercely competitive starship market, Gallofree Yards, Inc., was a smaller company that produced transports and freighters. Not nearly as innovative as Incom or as reliable as CEC, Gallofree Yards eventually suffered bankruptcy and vanished shortly before the Battle of Yavin. However, many of the company's starships remained in active use as part of the Rebel Alliance's fleet.

⌗ Rebel Transport

Haor Chall Engineering

One of the galaxy's more unusual manufacturers, Haor Chall Engineering was founded by the fanatical Xi Char, a religious order devoted to high-precision manufacturing. The insectoid Haor Chall zealots worked tirelessly in cathedral factories on Charros IV, producing a number of experimental starfighters and engine technologies. The Trade Federation contracted the Xi Char to manufacture the droid starfighters and C-9979 landing ships used during the invasion of Naboo, and Haor Chall continued to work closely with the Trade Federation well into the early days of the Confederacy. Acting on orders from the Republic, however, a clone army led by Jedi Knights eventually invaded Charros IV and destroyed the Haor Chall factories, crippling the company. Sienar Fleet Systems absorbed what remained of Haor Chall Engineering, including its patent on Haor Chall Ring Drive Jell.

⌗ Droid Starfighter
⌗ Hailfire

Hoersch-Kessel Drive, Inc.

A successful and respected starship design firm during the days of the Old Republic, Hoersch-Kessel Drive, Inc. (HKD), was actually a subsidiary of the Trade Federation. Originally owned by Neimoidians, HKD produced many of the Trade Federation's cargo vessels, including the massive craft later converted into battleships for the invasion of Naboo. After the Trade Federation's defeat at Naboo, HKD was sold first to Duros investors and then, during the Clone Wars, to a Nimbanese clan. In an attempt to make it more profitable, the Nimbanese gutted the corporation, closing down hundreds of factories and entire design divisions. This drove many designers and engineers away from the company, further weakening its ability to create quality products. Ownership of HKD changed several times between the Clone Wars and the rise of the New Republic, but the company has managed to cling to life. By the time of the Yuuzhan Vong invasion, HKD returned to its roots, manufacturing large transports and container vessels. The company is still unprofitable and builds fewer than one hundred starships each standard year.

⌗ Droid Control Ship

Huppla Pasa Tisc Shipwrights Collective

The Huppla Pasa Tisc Shipwrights Collective is a Geonosian-owned and -operated company responsible for manufacturing vehicles specifically for use by Geonosians. The design firm's most visible success has been the Geonosian Beak-Wing. Huppla Pasa Tisc is virtually unknown outside the Geonosian system because its vehicles rely on the Geonosians' unique physiology and senses, making them virtually useless to all other species. The Geonosians are also fiercely isolationist. However, Huppla Pasa Tisc did agree to manufacture a remarkable solar sailer for Confederacy leader Count Dooku.

⌗ Geonosian Beak-Wing
⌗ Solar Sailer

Incom Corporation

Established several millennia before the rise of the Empire, Incom was a high-profile manufacturer of starships and personal transports, successful with both civilian craft, such as the T-16 skyhopper, and starfighters like the Z-95 Headhunter. During the early days of the Empire, when many starship companies were rallying around the Emperor, the fiercely independent Incom attempted to remain neutral. Meanwhile, the Empire imposed greater controls on non-Imperial starship designers. Frustrated with the oppressive Imperial controls, several leading Incom engineers fled to the Rebellion, taking with them all designs for the state-of-the-art T-65 X-wing starfighter. Many Rebel pilots credit the X-wing with saving the Rebellion and allowing the Alliance to eventually defeat Palpatine's regime. As a direct reaction to this defection, Palpatine personally nationalized Incom. The company quickly faded in prominence, creating only a handful of new craft and instead focusing on modifications and limited-run specialty vehicles for the Imperial Navy.

After the Battle of Endor, Incom slipped free of Imperial control and could again concentrate on starfighter design. Ironically, the company's next milestone was the I-7 Howlrunner, introduced shortly after the Emperor's return and used almost exclusively by the Empire. Again trying to remain neutral, Incom continued to offer starships to both Imperial Remnant and New Republic forces, with mixed results. The stigma of long years under Imperial control has kept Incom from becoming one of the New Republic's favored manufacturers, while Imperial commanders still remember the "X-wing defection."

⌗ Howlrunner
⌗ Skyhopper (T-16 Skyhopper)
⌗ Snowspeeder (T-47 Airspeeder)
⌗ X-Wing
⌗ Z-95 Headhunter (with Subpro Corporation)

Koensayr

Koensayr executives enjoy reminding the galaxy that nearly one-fifth of all starships in operation have been touched by the corporation. In fact, Koensayr produces remarkable component technologies, including advanced weapons, powerful engine systems, a wide range of shields, and versatile sensor suites. At the time of the Yuuzhan Vong invasion, Koensayr continued to rely on component sales for nearly 80 percent of its revenue. For the record, Koensayr is also responsible for its own vehicles, including the Y-wing starfighter favored by the Rebel Alliance, and the *Sigma*-class shuttle.

⌗ K-Wing
⌗ Y-Wing

Kuat Drive Yards

While companies such as Incom struggled to find their way under the Emperor's rule, Kuat Drive Yards (KDY) recognized the potential of completely aligning itself with the Empire. Throughout the Galactic Civil War, KDY was the top supplier of Imperial starship hardware. Before that, KDY had diversified by developing local manufacturing firms such as Rothana Heavy Engineering, the company responsible for building the majority of vehicles used by the Republic during the Clone Wars.

Equal in power and prestige to CEC and Sienar Fleet Systems, KDY began secretly experimenting with massive battleships and planetary weapons even years before the start of the Clone Wars. High-ranking KDY officials were also members of the Trade Federation Executive Board, and it seemed as if the company would almost certainly aid Count Dooku's Separatist movement. That changed, however, when Neimoidians took control of the Trade Federation by murdering top Kuati executives at the bloody Eriadu Conference a decade before the Battle of Geonosis. KDY turned its back on the Trade Federation and its allies, and quickly joined forces with the Republic. In anticipation of the coming war with the Separatists, KDY continued to manufacture its newest military designs at well-protected facilities, such as factories on Rothana.

When the Republic finally assembled an army to battle Count Dooku's secessionist movement, KDY and its subsidiaries were able to provide a number of vehicles, including large troop transports and agile starfighters. KDY remained one of the Republic's principal suppliers for the Clone Wars.

After the Emperor seized power, KDY was immediately granted many of the most important Imperial contracts, including the Star Destroyer, a descendant of the *Acclamator*-class Republic assault ship, and the much more destructive Super Star Destroyer. Upon the Empire's collapse, KDY lost much of its financial support, yet continued to work almost exclusively for Imperial Remnant forces. In the era of the New Republic, KDY engineers produced the terrifying *Eclipse* Star Destroyer and the Imperial A-9 Vigilance starfighter.

Throughout its history, KDY has been considered extremely predatory. The company constantly consumes other manufacturers. Perhaps KDY's most famous acquisition was Core Galaxy Systems. One of the original starship manufacturers, Core Galaxy Systems was founded during the earliest days of the Old Republic. The company produced a staggering array of starships, including its own version of the heavily armed Dreadnaught. However, 5,000 years before the Battle of Yavin, Core Galaxy Systems found itself in vicious competition with Kuat Drive Yards. Constant price wars, acts of industrial espionage, and unexplained accidents at various manufacturing facilities resulted in a rash of financial losses for Core Galaxy Systems. When Core was forced onto the auction block, KDY immediately purchased the company. Soon after, the Core Galaxy Systems name and logo were retired.

- ⊞ AT-AT
- ⊞ AT-PT
- ⊞ AT-TE
- ⊞ *Eclipse* Star Destroyer
- ⊞ *Executor* (Super Star Destroyer)
- ⊞ Juggernaut
- ⊞ Rebel Cruiser
- ⊞ Republic Assault Ship
  (through subsidiary Rothana Heavy Engineering)
- ⊞ Republic Gunship
  (through subsidiary Rothana Heavy Engineering)
- ⊞ SPHA-T
- ⊞ Star Destroyer

Kuat Systems Engineering

Spawned from the much larger Kuat Drive Yards, Kuat Systems Engineering (KSE) was founded shortly before the Clone Wars in an attempt to diversify the Kuat brand. KSE produced the CloakShape fighter, the Delta-7 starfighter, and a small fleet of experimental Firespray patrol and attack craft, all viewed as engineering marvels among the starship design community. Unfortunately, KSE's inability to develop a commercially successful vehicle frustrated KDY officials, who brought the subsidiary back under their direct control. KSE provided aftermarket upgrade kits until shortly before the Emperor's death, when the company was purchased by a mysterious group of Vaathkree merchants. KSE's new owners had strong ties to the Rebellion and, after the fall of the Empire, KSE became a major supporter of the New Republic. KSE products are costly, but they are often worth the extra credits due to the Vaathkree's stringent quality-control standards.

- ⊞ CloakShape Fighter
- ⊞ Jedi Starfighter
- ⊞ *Slave I* (*Firespray*-Class Patrol and Attack Ship)

MandalMotors

One of several companies that attempted to capitalize on the exciting reputation of the Mandalorian warriors, MandalMotors was allegedly founded by a retired Mandalorian officer. Though this story can be neither confirmed nor denied, MandalMotors has established itself as a leading designer of military starships. During the Clone Wars, MandalMotors was accused of supporting a "mercenary mentality," because the company supplied weapons and vehicles to both the Republic and the Confederacy. Under the Emperor's control, MandalMotors was blacklisted until the company agreed to install Imperial "advisers" on its executive boards. Once the Empire fell, MandalMotors ousted its

Imperial managers and became a reliable developer for the New Republic.

⋕ *Virago* (*StarViper*-Class Attack Platform)

MOBQUET SWOOPS AND SPEEDERS

A subdivision of the Tagge Company, Mobquet Swoops and Speeders manufactures a variety of repulsorlift vehicles, including airspeeders and landspeeders. Its most successful vehicles have been swoops such as the Nebulon-Q racer and the advanced Flare-S. The company regularly sponsors champion racers in Core swoop-racing leagues.

⋕ Swoop (Flare-S Swoop)

MON CALAMARI

The Mon Calamari is an amphibious species native to a world of the same name. The species is known for its ability to engineer some of the most impressive starships in the galaxy. Mon Cal vessels are handcrafted, ensuring that each starship is unique, although all Mon Cal vehicles share an organic appearance marked by curves and domes.

The first Mon Cal starships were designed for exploration and long-distance travel. After encountering Imperial hostility, the Mon Cal began designing new combat-ready vessels, complete with heavy armor and multiple large weapons emplacements. They also converted most of their surviving fleet into battle cruisers. The Mon Cal warships remained in orbit around Mon Calamari until Admiral Ackbar joined the Alliance and convinced his people to aid the Rebel cause. The Mon Cal donated their existing starships to the war against the Empire, and constructed advanced orbital shipyards above their homeworld to design and produce new vessels.

⋕ Mon Cal Cruiser

NUBIAN DESIGN COLLECTIVE

The Nubian Design Collective is a loose coalition of designers, engineers, and laborers who colonized the planet Nubia 300 years before the Battle of Naboo. The Nubian Collective is actually composed of numerous spacefaring species, including humans, Bith, Zabrak, and Sullustans. After claiming Nubia as its own, the collective began accepting small contracts from wealthy clients, including the Naboo. The Nubians produced much of the technology used for the Naboo N-1 starfighter and the Queen's Royal Starship.

At the time of the Battle of Naboo, Nubian technology was used throughout the galaxy and could be easily acquired on most Republic worlds. When the Empire rose to power, the collective went underground in order to keep its more experimental designs out of Imperial hands. The company continued to produce innovative technology and resurfaced with a full catalog of new devices and systems shortly after the Battle of Endor.

⋕ The *Havoc* (Scurrg H-6 Bomber)
⋕ Naboo Cruiser
⋕ Naboo Royal Starship

OTOH GUNGA BONGAMEKEN COOPERATIVE

Gungan engineers are well versed in both technology and biology. Nowhere is that more evident than among the designers at the Otoh Gunga Bongameken Cooperative on Naboo, the company dedicated to producing bongos and other transports for the Gungans. Located on the fringes of the city of Otoh Gunga, the cooperative grows bongo hulls in expansive underwater farms. The skeletal structures are harvested, then fitted with a combination of Gungan and Naboo technology. Each bongo is individually crafted and designed, but while no two vehicles look alike, certain designers do have signature styles.

The Cooperative survived the invasion of Naboo, and soon thereafter began experimenting with larger designs fit for use as starships. The company suffered a major setback when the Empire established a presence on Naboo; fearing Imperial capture, the Gungans went into semiseclusion and the cooperative cut its production output. The cooperative enjoyed a huge resurgence after the Empire's defeat, when the Gungans finally began traveling in much larger numbers, both across Naboo and throughout the galaxy.

⋕ Bongo

RENDILI STARDRIVE

Although not nearly as well known as Kuat Drive Yards, Rendili StarDrive was no less important to the rise of the Empire. When the Old Republic sought larger versions of its military assault ships, Kuat Drive Yards contracted Rendili StarDrive to manufacture the first Victory-class Star Destroyers, which set the standard for all Imperial starships to come. Rendili StarDrive was founded alongside the Old Republic, but enjoyed its greatest success shortly after the rise of the Empire. Aside from the Victory Star Destroyer, the company produced the Dreadnaught heavy cruiser and the Mandalorian dungeon ships.

Although the Empire made constant use of the Victory Star Destroyers, Rendili did not receive any notable military contracts during the Galactic Civil War, and remained underutilized well into the era of the New Republic. However, Rendili is constantly researching new technologies and designs, which has attracted interest from New Republic and Imperial Remnant leaders.

- Star Destroyer (*Victory*-Class)

SANTHE/SIENAR TECHNOLOGIES

Santhe/Sienar Technologies is actually an umbrella company encompassing several different manufacturers, including Sienar Fleet Systems, Republic Sienar Systems (RSS), and Sienar Design Systems. Founded and owned by the powerful Sienar family, Sienar Technologies and all of its subsidiaries produce a wide range of vehicles, but are especially well versed in dangerous starfighters.

The original Sienar company, known as Republic Sienar Systems (RSS), provided numerous starships for the Old Republic for more than 15 millennia. During the Clone Wars, RSS produced numerous vehicles for the Confederacy of Independent Systems, earning the disdain of the Republic Senate. Shortly before the Emperor took control of the galaxy, the Senate ordered the dissolution of RSS. The company's holdings were absorbed by the Republic Navy, but RSS was soon resurrected by direct order of the Emperor. Renamed Sienar Fleet Systems (SFS), the company was placed under the control of Raith Sienar and quickly became one of the Empire's most prolific manufacturers.

While under exclusive contract with the Empire, SFS perfected a new generation of powerful twin ion engines, which in turn allowed the company to develop the agile TIE fighter. Based on the TIE fighter's success, SFS went on to produce the TIE interceptor, TIE defender, TIE bomber, and the TIE/D fighter. The company is also responsible for the *Sentinel*-class landing craft, *Lambda*-class shuttle, and other transports, along with the Scimitar assault bomber and the Interdictor cruiser manufactured after the dawn of the New Republic.

Also worth mention is Sienar Design Systems (SDS), a short-lived division of RSS that focused on experimental technologies and unique starship designs for a wealthy clientele. SDS, which was considered Raith Sienar's pet project, operated in complete secrecy, conducting research in laboratories hidden across the galaxy. Nearly all of SDS's craft were one-of-a-kind vehicles, many of which have never been identified. In fact, of the several dozen starships allegedly designed by

SDS, only one—Darth Maul's deadly Sith Infiltrator—has been recovered. When the starship was captured by the Republic after the Battle of Naboo, SDS denied any involvement in creating the vehicle and its powerful cloaking device, but the close scrutiny caused Republic Sienar Systems to close down the "outlaw" operation.

Ironically, several years later, Raith Sienar formed his Advanced Projects Laboratory, a firm very similar to SDS. Sienar Advanced Projects led the design efforts for many prototype vehicles, including Darth Vader's TIE Advanced starfighter.

- Imperial Landing Craft
- Imperial Shuttle
- Interdictor Cruiser
- Sith Infiltrator
- TIE Advanced (Darth Vader's TIE Fighter)
- TIE Bomber
- TIE Defender
- TIE Fighter
- TIE Interceptor

SLAYN & KORPIL

One of the Rebel Alliance's greatest strengths was its ability to attract valuable allies in the fight against the Empire. Like the Mon Calamari and defecting Incom engineers, Slayn & Korpil falls into this category. A Verpine hive colony located in the Roche asteroid field, Slayn & Korpil joined forces with the Rebel Alliance shortly after the Battle of Yavin. With the aid of then-commander Ackbar, Slayn & Korpil designers conceived the B-wing, one of the Alliance's most heavily armed starfighters. The B-wing became a major component of the Rebel starfighter fleet and was integral to the Alliance's victory at the Battle of Endor. Although small, Slayn & Korpil has managed to produce several advanced B-wings as well as the New Republic's V-wing combat airspeeder.

- B-Wing
- V-Wing

SOROSUUB

A massive Sullustan corporation, SoroSuub's central business venture is mineral processing. The company also has numerous divisions and subdivisions, undertaking everything from energy mining to food packaging. SoroSuub's technology divisions develop weapons, droids, and, of course, starships and other vehicles. Of particular note are the company's civilian landspeeders, such as the resilient X-34 owned by Luke Skywalker and the more fashionable XP-38 Sport landspeeder.

SoroSuub employs roughly half the population of the planet Sullust and, in fact, took control of the Sullustan government during the early days of the Galactic Civil War. To protect its holdings, SoroSuub declared allegiance to the Empire, an act many Sullustans opposed. After enduring great political dissension on Sullust, SoroSuub's savvy leadership wisely decided to support the Rebel Alliance shortly before the Battle of Endor. After the Empire's defeat, SoroSuub played a role in creating the New Republic's government and has remained a staunch ally ever since.

- Flash Speeder
- Gian Speeder
- *Jade Shadow* (*Horizon*-Class Star Yacht)
- *Lady Luck* (Personal Luxury Yacht 3000)
- Luke Skywalker's Landspeeder (X-34)
- Lars Family Speeder (V-35 Courier)
- XP-38 Sport Landspeeder
- *Sharp Spiral* (Cutlass-9 Patrol Fighter)

Subpro Corporation

A fairly large starship manufacturer based in the Inner Rim, Subpro is responsible for the Z-95 Headhunter, among other starships. Unfortunately, buyers in the Core Worlds often consider Subpro's vehicles to be of lesser quality simply because they are manufactured far from the center of the galaxy. More knowledgeable pilots recognize that Subpro produces superior vehicles, usually for far fewer credits than its competitors. As a result, Subpro craft are a common sight in the Outer Rim, where they are used by enterprising merchants, smugglers, and others who know a good value when they see it.

- Z-95 Headhunter (with Incom Corporation)

TaggeCo (The Tagge Company)

Few companies are as powerful, as diversified, or as well connected as the Tagge Company (TaggeCo), a megacorporation that has been successful in virtually every type of manufacturing. Because TaggeCo is owned by the House of Tagge, an extremely influential political family based on the planet Tepasi, the company has been able to maintain close ties to various planetary and system governments.

Shortly before the Battle of Naboo, TaggeCo formed a partnership with the Trade Federation, whose Executive Board included several House of Tagge loyalists. However, the Executive Board was rocked by betrayal when Neimoidians assassinated many members of the ruling body in order to take complete control of the Trade Federation. While the House of Tagge did not suffer any losses during this coup, the political family realized that they could never trust the Trade Federation again and severed all ties to the group. The House of Tagge remained largely neutral throughout the Clone Wars, but readily allied with the Emperor after his rise to power. TaggeCo joined the Empire's stable of manufacturers and achieved unprecedented Imperial support, largely due to the fact that several House of Tagge members were also Imperial officers. TaggeCo suffered a brief decline following the Battle of Yavin, but rapidly regained its strength and has remained one of the leaders in the galactic economy.

TaggeCo produces a number of vehicles, including the Air-2 Swoop, and also owns other vehicle manufacturers, such as Mobquet Speeders and Swoops, Tagge Industries, and Trast Heavy Transports.

- Swoop (Air-2 Swoop)

Theed Palace Space Vessel Engineering Corps

The Theed Palace Space Vessel Engineering Corps is one of literally thousands of small, well-educated design firms spread across the galaxy. Like others of its kind, the Theed Palace development group produces craft for its homeworld, in this case Naboo. The engineering corps designed the Naboo N-1 starfighter and the Queen's Royal Starship, both of which utilize systems and components from the Nubian Design Collective. The Theed Palace engineers are dedicated to creating vehicles that are both aesthetically pleasing and ecologically sound. They pioneered the elegant spaceframe used by the N-1 and modified the starfighter's Nubian engines to produce fewer emissions. Among the Theed Palace Space Vessel Engineering Corps, being selected to design a Royal Starship—each of which is unique—is considered the highest possible honor.

- Naboo Cruiser
- Naboo Royal Starship
- Naboo Starfighter

Trilon, Inc.

While Corellian Engineering Corporation and other large companies develop starships from scratch, smaller specialty manufacturers, like Trilon, Inc., find greater success in reusing existing technologies. Trilon, Inc., purchases nearly all of its vehicle systems, including weapons and engines, from larger companies such as Kuat Drive Yards, which allows Trilon to assemble starships using the best possible components and create vehicles exactly to a buyer's specifications. Most of Trilon's starships are generic transports, but the company also created the *IG-2000*, an assault starfighter used by droid bounty hunter IG-88.

   # *IG-2000* (Aggressor Assault Fighter)

UBRIKKIAN

Ubrikkian is an established manufacturer that has gained a foothold in the repulsorlift market. The company produces sail barges, civilian and combat landspeeders, cloud cars, speeder bikes, and skiffs. Ubrikkian also developed the HAVr A9 floating fortress, a repulsorlift weapons platform used by the Empire.

   # Desert Skiff
   # Sail Barge

YUUZHAN VONG

The first invaders from outside the galaxy to threaten the New Republic, the Yuuzhan Vong is a terrifying alien species with incredible technology. Rather than rely on mechanical devices, the Yuuzhan Vong has mastered bioengineering. Its weapons, vehicles, and equipment are almost entirely organic. Vehicles, in particular, are designed by shapers, who then oversee hundreds of slaves responsible for tending to the craft during its development. The Yuuzhan Vong's bioengineered vessels are more resilient than standard durasteel craft used by the New Republic, and their organic nature often results in a fearsome appearance.

   # Coralskipper
   # Vangaak
   # Yuuzhan Vong Transport Carrier (Yorik-Trema)
   # Yuuzhan Vong Warship (Miid Ro'ik)
   # Yuuzhan Vong Worldship (*Koros-Strohna*)

ZONAMA SEKOT SHIPBUILDERS

Zonama Sekot was a mysterious world far from the Core, where master shipbuilders created truly unique vessels for wealthy clients. A Sekotan ship was an organic vessel produced through a strange combination of technology and agriculture. Such a vehicle possessed a resilient cellular structure capable of supporting metals and polymers, enabling the shipbuilders to integrate engine systems and other devices purchased from outside manufacturers such as Haor Chall Engineering.

Potential owners of Sekotan ships had to prove themselves to the shipbuilders. Those who managed to pass the tests received one of the fastest starships in the galaxy. Each owner developed a strong bond with the living craft, so a Sekotan ship separated from its owner would eventually die. Anakin Skywalker and Obi-Wan Kenobi forged a strong relationship with their own Sekotan starship, the *Jabitha*.

Sadly, not a single Sekotan starship remains in existence. Production of the vessels ended when Zonama Sekot fell under attack by then-commander Tarkin three years after the Battle of Naboo. To escape the assault, the planet fled into hyperspace. Upon losing contact with their homeworld, all Sekotan vessels already in operation throughout the galaxy quickly sickened and died.

   # *Jabitha*

OTHER MANUFACTURERS

 ALDERAAN ROYAL ENGINEERS

 ARAKYD INDUSTRIES

 BYBLOS DRIVE YARDS

 CORE GALAXY SYSTEMS

 CORELLIA STARDRIVE

 DAMORIAN MANUFACTURING CORP.

 HAPAN CONSORTIUM

 OLANJII/ CHARUBAH

 PANTOLOMIN SHIPWRIGHTS

 REPUBLIC ENGINEERING CORP.

 REPUBLIC FLEET SYSTEMS

 SEDRIMOTORS LTD.

 SSI-RUUVI

 SURRONIAN

 TENLOSS SYNDICATE

 TRANSGALMEG INDUSTRIES, INC.

 ULSHOS MANUFACTURING

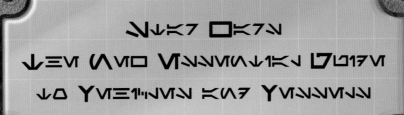

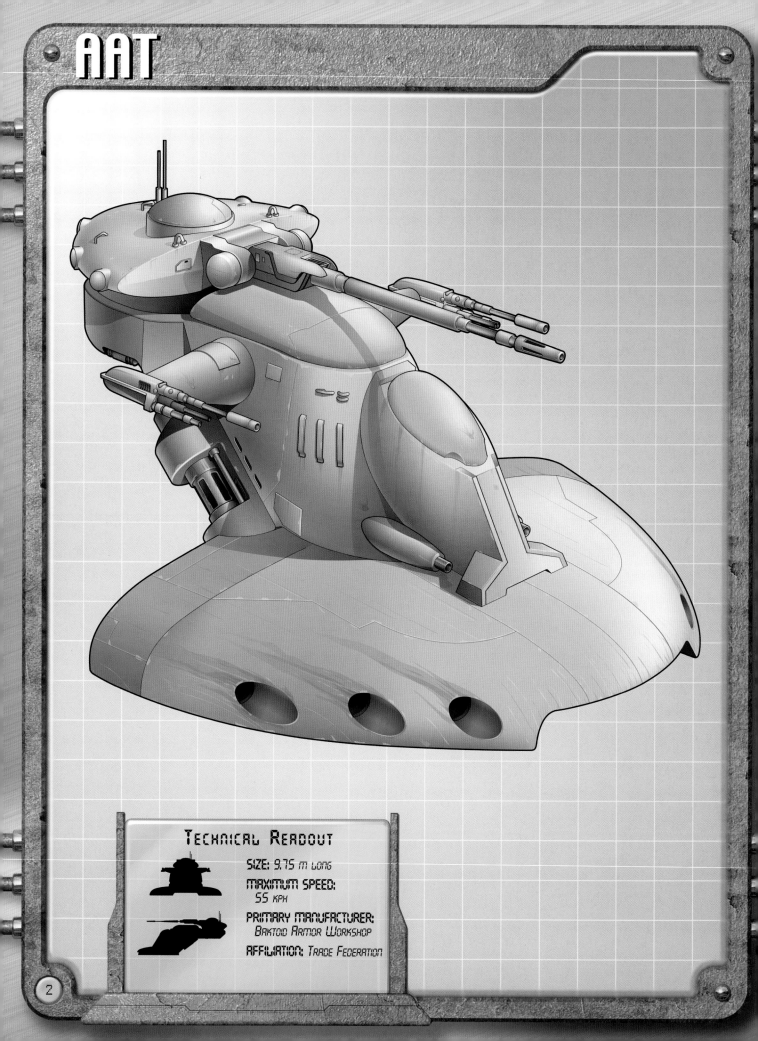

TECHNICAL READOUT

SIZE: 9.75 m long

MAXIMUM SPEED: 55 kph

PRIMARY MANUFACTURER: Baktoid Armor Workshop

AFFILIATION: Trade Federation

Trade Federation Armored Assault Tank

The AAT, or "armored assault tank," is a battle tank commissioned by the Trade Federation for use during the invasion and occupation of Naboo. It is one of the most heavily armed and armored vehicles ever produced by Baktoid Armor Workshop.

Intended for frontal assaults, the AAT's primary weapon is a turret-mounted laser cannon designed for long-range strikes. Secondary laser cannons enable targeting of smaller vehicles. Finally, a pair of short-range antipersonnel blasters located near the foot of the tank concentrate on enemy troops.

The vehicle is equipped with six launch tubes that fire standard high-energy shells. Armor-piercing antivehicle shells and explosive "bunker busters" designed to level buildings are often standard. Fired shells are encased in plasma in order to increase both speed and penetration. AATs can typically carry up to 55 shells, but when this payload is depleted, the vehicle must return to a Trade Federation landing ship, battleship, or base, where reload stations remove the lower portion of the tank and install a fully loaded replacement.

For protection, the AAT is covered in thick armor plating and sports a reinforced nose ram. As with many Baktoid designs, all sensitive components and systems—including the AAT's main reactor and power converter—are located near the rear of the craft for additional protection.

The AAT's crew consists of four battle droids. A droid pilot and two gunners occupy a small cockpit in the heart of the tank. The droid commander sits just behind the primary laser cannon, surrounded by battlefield sensors, a communications array, and secondary control systems. Both the pilot and commander have access to a stereoscopic cam and periscope scanner, and can plug directly into the AAT's central computer in order to receive detailed information downloads. The pilot can also open a front hatch for direct visual sighting. Handholds on either side of the tank allow the vehicle to carry up to six additional battle droids.

Before the invasion of Naboo, the Trade Federation tested its AATs on remote Outer Rim worlds, pitting the battle tanks against one another. For a more realistic assessment of the vehicles, the Trade Federation also deployed the tanks to fight pirates on Lok in the Karthakk system. These conflicts were fierce, ensuring that many of the AATs were battle-scarred by the time they reached Naboo.

After the Battle of Naboo, the Trade Federation continued to use AATs on Lok and other worlds. Baktoid went on to produce a number of specialized AAT variants boasting increased mobility or dedicated deflector shields.

"Ouch Time ..."
—Gungan reaction to seeing AATs

1 **AAT Primary Laser Cannon:** The tracking hardware built into the AAT laser cannon enables it to acquire small, fast-moving targets, including Naboo starfighters attempting to escape the Theed hangar.

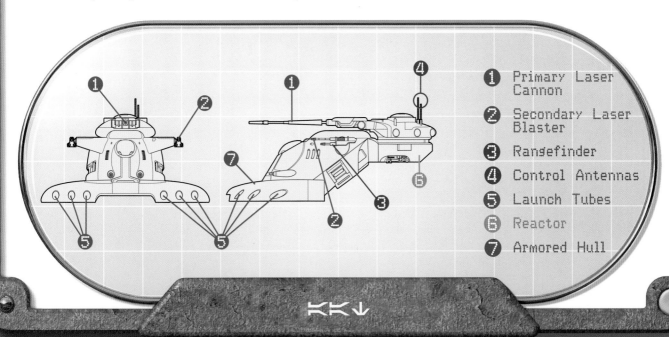

1 Primary Laser Cannon
2 Secondary Laser Blaster
3 Rangefinder
4 Control Antennas
5 Launch Tubes
6 Reactor
7 Armored Hull

Anakin's Airspeeder

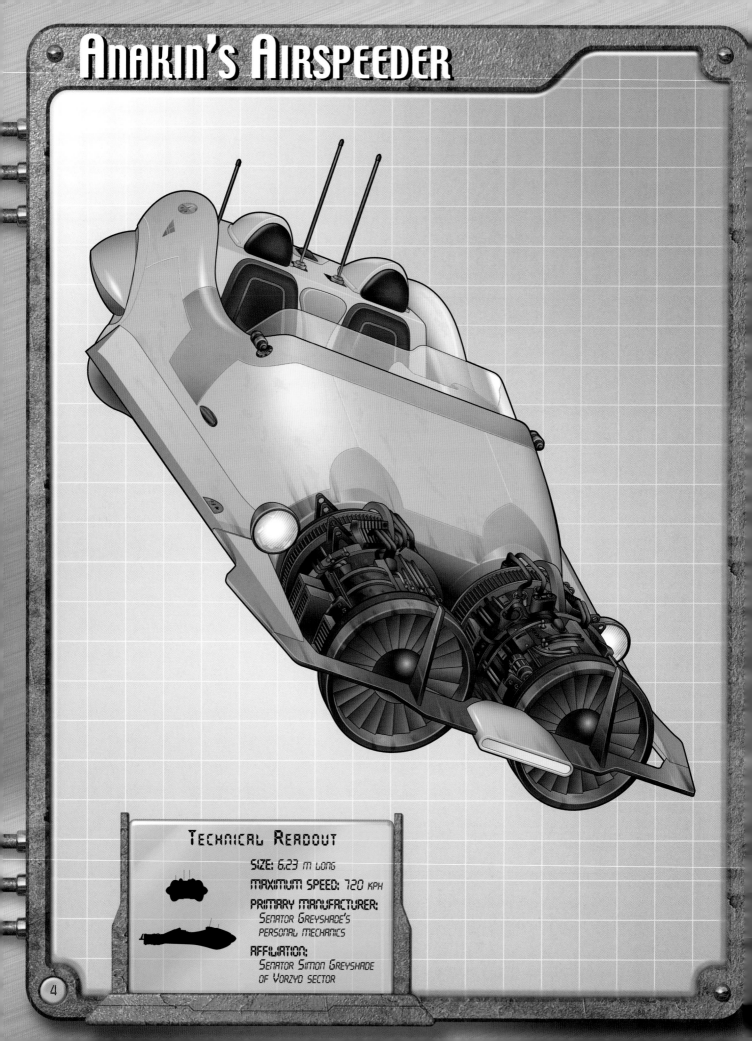

Technical Readout

SIZE: 6.23 m long

MAXIMUM SPEED: 720 KPH

PRIMARY MANUFACTURER:
Senator Greyshade's
personal mechanics

AFFILIATION:
Senator Simon Greyshade
of Vorzyd sector

Custom-Built Narglatch XJ-6

Airspeeders are a specific type of repulsorlift vehicle widely used throughout the galaxy as personal transports. On congested Coruscant, airspeeder use is so common that traffic must be tightly constrained to rigid skylanes that weave between and through the massive buildings.

A typical airspeeder is a small, wedge-shaped vehicle with powerful repulsorlift engines and limited life support capabilities. Airspeeders are generally designed to fly within a planet's lower atmosphere, although some can reach heights in excess of 250 kilometers and travel at speeds of up to 900 kilometers per hour. Civilian airspeeders are sold without weapons, although blaster cannons can be easily added to many models. Nearly all airspeeders have very simple and non-species-specific controls, making them accessible to a wide range of consumers.

> **"Oh, you know, Master, I couldn't find a speeder I really liked, with an open cockpit... And with the right speed capabilities... And then, you know, I had to get a really gonzo color..."**
>
> —*Anakin Skywalker*

Beyond their basic capabilities, no two airspeeder models are alike. They range from single-occupant speed demons to sluggish family transports with enclosed canopies and HoloNet transceivers.

Coruscant's air taxis are indicative of standard airspeeder technology. Air taxis utilize robust repulsors located beneath the craft, enabling them to levitate more than three kilometers. The repulsorlift engines are designed for maximum efficiency and can travel up to 210 kilometers before refueling. The primary repulsorlift engine is supported by several smaller antigravity devices that interface with nav computers to avoid collisions with buildings and other craft. An array of docking repulsors provides gentle landings on air taxi pads located throughout the city. Air taxis are primarily open-air craft, although an electromagnetic generator envelops each vehicle in an electrified field that protects passengers from insects, debris, and the elements. Advanced receivers provide the pilot with the latest information from Coruscant Air Traffic Control.

Air taxis, like many speeders, are easily modified after purchase. They can be retrofitted with canopies and life support systems to accommodate a wide range of alien species. An air taxi can also support small blaster cannons, although such upgrades are illegal on Coruscant.

As exemplified by the air taxi, the airspeeder has a wonderfully generic design. This accessibility has given rise to an entire subculture built around airspeeder modifications. Young pilots frequently install more powerful engines for atmospheric races, and a heavily modified airspeeder is viewed as a status symbol on some worlds. In the waning days of the Old Republic, a group of young Senators led by Simon Greyshade formed a clique devoted to air speeders. Greyshade and his cohorts

7 Open Cockpit: During Anakin's pursuit of Zam Wesell, the airspeeder's open cockpit allowed the Padawan to catch his falling Master, Obi-Wan Kenobi, and later to leap onto the bounty hunter's own vehicle.

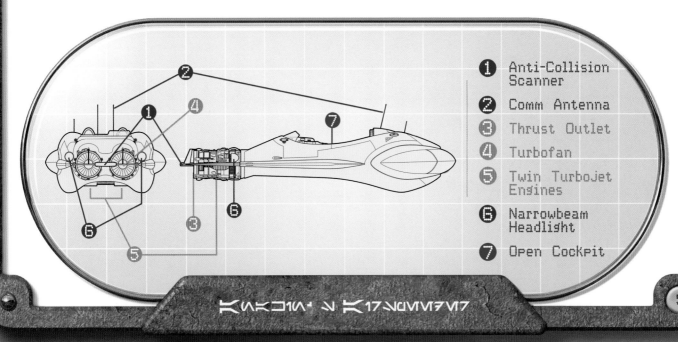

1. Anti-Collision Scanner
2. Comm Antenna
3. Thrust Outlet
4. Turbofan
5. Twin Turbojet Engines
6. Narrowbeam Headlight
7. Open Cockpit

used their great wealth and power to acquire a number of custom-built airspeeders, which they proceeded to pilot recklessly through Coruscant's crowded skylanes.

Greyshade's personal airspeeder became part of galactic history when Anakin Skywalker "borrowed" the vehicle in order to pursue bounty hunter Zam Wesell. As Anakin quickly discovered, the bright yellow speeder was the ultimate high-performance vehicle. Twin turbojet engines installed near the front end of the vehicle achieved speeds of 720 kilometers per hour, while electrogravitic gyro flywheels near the rear of the craft enabled turns, dives, and steep ascents.

> **"My speeder might be built like a dung beetle, but it could survive an acid storm on Mordis VI."**
> —*Zam Wesell*

During that dramatic chase through the skylanes of Coruscant, Zam Wesell piloted a *Koro-2* Exodrive airspeeder. Manufactured by Desler Gizh Outworld Mobility Corporation, the *Koro-2* is designed to function on wasteland worlds with very thin or corrosive atmospheric conditions. The craft is self-contained, with an enclosed cockpit and robust life support systems allowing trips on low-oxygen worlds. In order to ensure that the *Koro-2* can travel in a diverse range of conditions, the standard repulsorlift system is complemented by electromagnetic generators located in the vehicle's forward mandibles. The electromagnetic field charges the air particles surrounding the airspeeder; these charged particles are then shuttled between the mandibles and toward the rear of the vehicle, creating forward thrust.

Zam stole her *Koro-2* from a mining colony on an Outer Rim world controlled by the Mining Guild. She planned to add a concealed blaster cannon to the vehicle eventually, but the trip to Coruscant delayed any work on the airspeeder. Zam's *Koro-2* was badly damaged when it crashed onto a Coruscant street, but this didn't stop a group of thieves from quickly stealing the vehicle's most valuable components. By the time Republic authorities arrived on the scene, only the stripped hull remained.

6 **Canopy:** The airspeeder's canopy automatically tints to conceal the occupant's identity and activities.

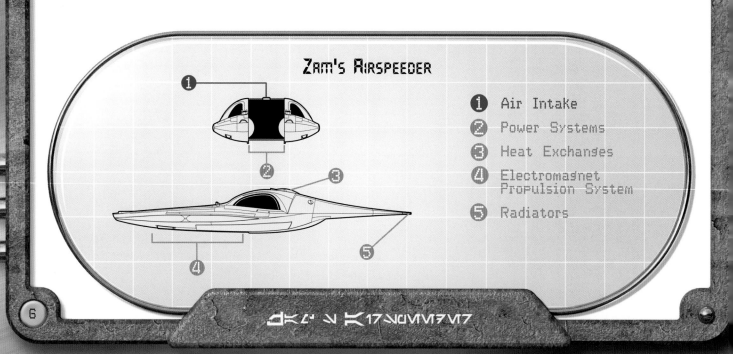

ZAM'S AIRSPEEDER

1. Air Intake
2. Power Systems
3. Heat Exchanges
4. Electromagnet Propulsion System
5. Radiators

AIRSPEEDER CLASSIFICATION

V-Wing Airspeeder

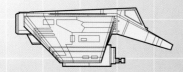

Zam's Airspeeder

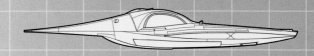

T-24 Airspeeder

Anakin's Airspeeder

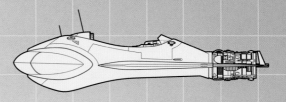

Talon I Combat Cloud Car

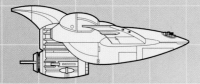

J12 Twin-Pod Airspeeder

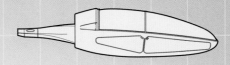

Utilitech Metrocab

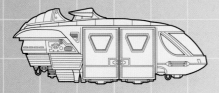

M31 Airspeeder

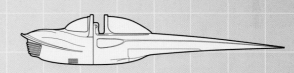

TaggeCo. Cargohopper

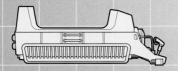

T-77 Airspeeder

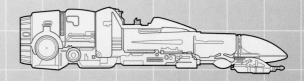

Gaba-18 Airspeeder

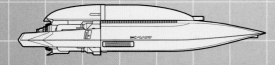

Tsik Vai (Yuuzhan Vong Flier)

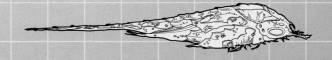

AT-AT

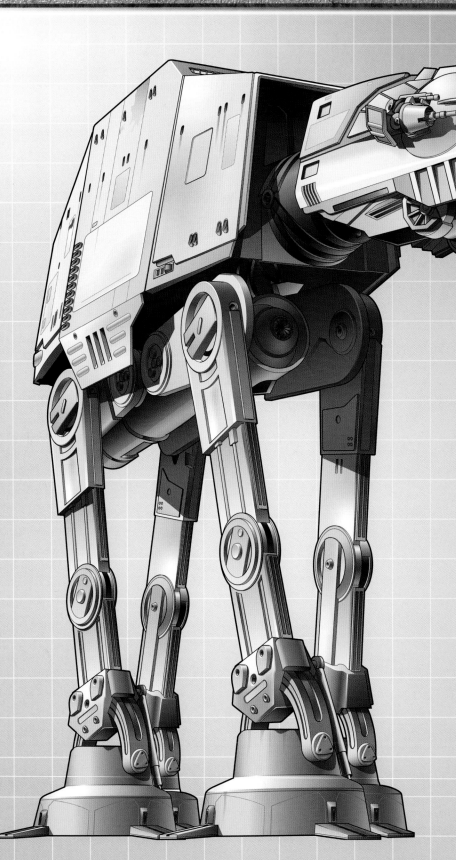

TECHNICAL READOUT

SIZE: 15 m tall, 20 m long

MAXIMUM SPEED:
60 kph (overfalt terrain)

PRIMARY MANUFACTURER:
Kurt Drive Yards

AFFILIATION:
Galactic Empire

Imperial All Terrain Armored Transport Walker

Possibly the most formidable military vehicle ever assembled, the All Terrain Armored Transport (AT-AT) was designed by Imperial engineers to move troops into occupied areas and inspire fear in enemy forces. The AT-AT's history began during the Clone Wars, when the Republic experienced success with the AT-TE, the AT-PT, and other "walkers." Years later, Commander Maximilian Veers resurrected the AT-AT concept, and the vehicles became a staple of the Imperial Army. Veers went on to lead Blizzard Force, a unit of modified AT-ATs used at the Battle of Hoth.

During the height of the Galactic Civil War, the Empire produced hundreds of AT-ATs. Components for these vehicles originated with numerous companies, but assembly of the vehicles was carefully monitored by Imperials at secret Kuat Drive Yards factories. The New Republic later destroyed AT-AT facilities on Kuat, Carida, and Belderone, but other installations survived to supply new AT-ATs to Imperial Remnant forces.

The awe-inspiring AT-AT stands more than 15 meters high and can carry up to 40 stormtroopers, 5 speeder bikes, and a variety of heavy weapons. In order to release troops, an AT-AT kneels to within three meters off the ground and lowers a rear assault ramp. AT-ATs can also be configured to carry two AT-STs. The command crew consists of a pilot, gunner, and commander located in the vehicle's "head."

The AT-AT boasts both long-range heavy laser cannons and short-range medium blasters. The laser cannons serve as the primary assault weapons, while the blasters, which can rotate independently, are designed to provide covering fire for ground troops. The AT-AT's swiveling head can swing up to 90 degrees left or right and up to 30 degrees up or down, creating an impressive field of fire. The gunner controls all four weapons, assisted by a 360-degree holographic targeting system. Many AT-AT pilots also use the walker's heavy feet to crush enemy units and buildings.

The AT-AT's armored hide and powerful drive motors make the vehicle virtually unstoppable. Most conventional weapons, including blaster cannons and antivehicle shells, are incapable of penetrating an AT-AT's thick shell. Two drive motors accelerate to 60 kilometers per hour over flat terrain and can function even after sustaining massive damage. To make AT-ATs even more effective, the Empire often equipped them with special components for specific environments. So-called dune walkers, for example, incorporate Sienar z23 heat dissipation units to allow long marches on hot worlds.

Typically the first Imperial vehicles into battle, AT-ATs are transported from Star Destroyers to combat zones via short-range landing barges. As they approach, AT-ATs pummel enemy forces, clearing paths for smaller vehicles and troops.

> **"We had the Battle of Gormen won, until the AT-ATs arrived. They came out of the fog and ripped apart the front lines. The locals ran in terror, but the experienced soldiers surrendered. We knew that you can't outrun an AT-AT."**
>
> *—Major Bren Derlin,*
> *Rebel Alliance field commander*

7   Soft Spot: Where the AT-AT's "neck" connects to the passenger compartment is the transport's only weak spot. After Wedge Antilles used a snowspeeder's tow cable to topple an AT-AT at the Battle of Hoth, the transport was destroyed by a well-placed shot to this unarmored area.

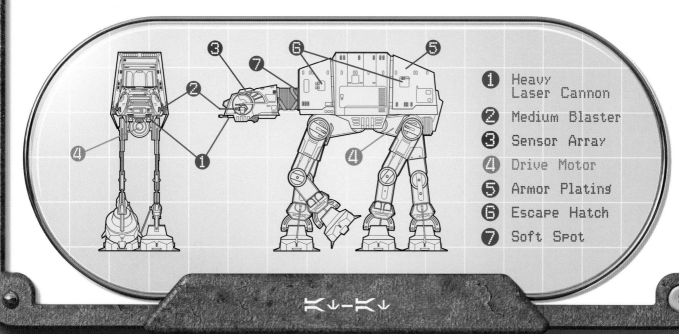

1 Heavy Laser Cannon
2 Medium Blaster
3 Sensor Array
4 Drive Motor
5 Armor Plating
6 Escape Hatch
7 Soft Spot

Technical Readout

Size: 3 m tall

Maximum Speed:
60 kph (over flat terrain)

Primary Manufacturer:
Rothana Heavy Engineering
(Kuat Drive Yards)

Affiliation:
Old Republic

Republic All Terrain Personal Transport

During the Clone Wars, the Old Republic was forced to fight on numerous worlds. Planets with high or low gravity, magnetic fields, or other conditions proved the most difficult arenas because they prevented the use of standard repulsorlift vehicles. To overcome this obstacle, the Republic embraced the walker designs produced by Rothana Heavy Engineering, a subsidiary of Kuat Drive Yards. As the war intensified, the Republic saw the need for a smaller walker that could be used as a mobile weapons platform, and soon after the AT-PT was born.

The AT-PT is meant to carry a single trooper into intense combat situations. At three meters tall, it provides the pilot with a fair view of the battlefield. The modular weapons emplacements typically hold twin blaster cannons and a concussion grenade launcher.

The walker's design is relatively simple, with a central command pod suspended between two flexible legs. The AT-PT's legs feature independently adjusting suspension, allowing the vehicle to cross most terrain, including shallow water, mountain regions, jungles, and cities. The AT-PT can also climb inclines of up to 45 degrees and step over obstacles that would hinder repulsorlift or treaded vehicles.

The armored command module houses the cockpit, which can be accessed through a side entry hatch. Once inside the vehicle, the pilot is completely safe from small-arms fire. The command pod can also be raised to provide increased visibility, or lowered to

> **"Sure, they don't look like much. But when you're trapped on Eos, where the electromagnetic fields keep 'advanced' airspeeders grounded, you'll wish you had a whole fleet of AT-PTs."**
>
> *—Imperial commander Brenn Tantor shortly before the Battle of Eos*

ensure greater stability while moving. The cockpit is cramped, however—able to carry only one additional passenger in an emergency—and the pilot must rely on a very primitive sensor suite for navigation.

When the AT-PT walkers were first introduced, the Republic planned to form entire AT-PT platoons. Equipped with long-range comlinks and able to cover ground at speeds nearing 60 kilometers per hour, AT-PTs were deemed perfect for reconnaissance and patrol duty. But the Republic never built more than a small fleet of experimental AT-PTs, most of which were aboard the *Katana* Dreadnaughts when that fleet vanished. Funding and support for the vehicle soon disappeared as well, but the basic design philosophy behind the AT-PT resurfaced several years later when the Empire began developing AT-ATs and AT-STs. In addition, New Republic forces eventually recovered the *Katana* fleet and the lost AT-PTs, which were used in the campaign against Grand Admiral Thrawn.

❻ Emergency Flare Launcher: When an AT-PT becomes disabled or separated from its squad, the emergency flare launcher allows quick retrieval.

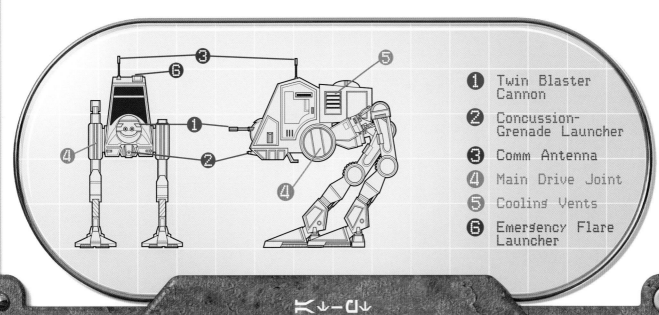

❶	Twin Blaster Cannon
❷	Concussion-Grenade Launcher
❸	Comm Antenna
❹	Main Drive Joint
❺	Cooling Vents
❻	Emergency Flare Launcher

AT-ST

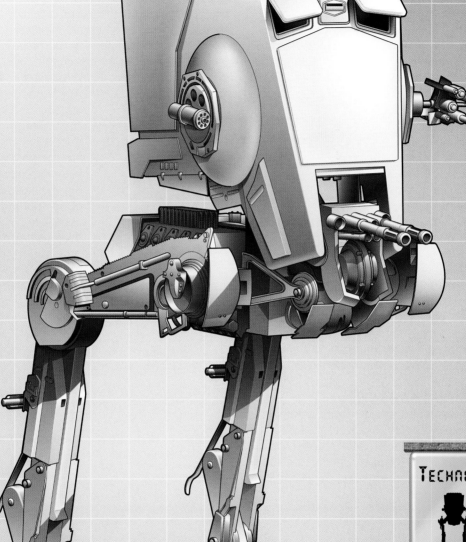

Technical Readout

SIZE: 8.6 m TALL

MAXIMUM SPEED: 90 KPH

PRIMARY MANUFACTURER: Imperial Department of Military Research

AFFILIATION: Galactic Empire

Imperial All Terrain Scout Transport Walker

Designed to fill a valuable role as a support and reconnaissance vehicle, the All Terrain Scout Transport (AT-ST) is a highly mobile, two-legged walker capable of going head-to-head with many Rebel ground vehicles. Fast, maneuverable, and precise, the AT-ST is valued by Imperial tacticians for its ability to make swift attacks against ground troops and repulsorlift vehicles. They are also excellent patrol vehicles, and were used during the Battle of Hoth and the Battle of Endor.

The AT-ST is the descendant of the Old Republic's AT-PT, and the two vehicles are remarkably similar. Like the AT-PT, the AT-ST's design consists of a pair of flexible legs and an armored command module. The AT-ST's legs are longer and thinner than the AT-PT's limbs, making the scout walker faster but more unstable than its predecessor. The AT-ST can reach speeds of 90 kilometers per hour across open ground. A single drive system powers the legs, while an advanced gyro system provides balance.

To improve upon the AT-PT, Imperial engineers positioned the AT-ST's armored command module *atop* the legs, allowing this "head" to rotate nearly 240 degrees. The command module carries both a pilot and gunner, who use viewports and a 360-degree holographic targeting system to navigate a battlefield. The cockpit is accessed via a small hatch atop the command module.

The AT-ST's mission profile includes reconnaissance, perimeter defense, and support for troops and AT-ATs. It performs these duties with the aid of chin-mounted twin blaster cannons with a range of two kilometers. Twin

> ## "AT-STs will no longer be deployed on planets with an abundance of trees or other known obstacles such as rock-wielding primitives."
>
> —*Excerpt from the Imperial AT-ST manual, updated shortly after the Battle of Endor*

light blasters and a concussion grenade launcher provide additional firepower for close-quarters combat. During invasions, the AT-ST's clawed feet can also be used to cut through fences and defensive structures.

The AT-ST's design isn't without flaws. The vehicle's gyro system, located beneath the command module, is easily damaged. Unlike the AT-PT or the much later MT-AT, the AT-ST is not well suited for steep terrain, because it can become caught in pits or crevices; it can also be hindered by dense foliage. After the Battle of Hoth, Rebel tacticians learned to foil AT-STs by using hidden trenches to trap the vehicles. Once an AT-ST was immobilized, Alliance sharpshooters could destroy the gyro system with a well-placed rifle shot, toppling the scout walker.

The first AT-STs appeared during the Clone Wars. The original prototype was known as the AT-XT (all-terrain experimental transport), but the Old Republic embraced the vehicle, and, after slight modifications, it became known as the AT-ST.

The AT-ST has inspired a few variants. A ten-meter-tall version of the AT-ST, known as the "assault walker" or AT-ST/As, sports a single heavy blaster cannon beneath its command module, along with a more advanced and better-protected gyro balance system and reinforced leg braces to prevent collapse.

7 Hatch: The AT-ST's entry hatch is meant to be inaccessible to enemy forces. However, Chewbacca and his Ewok allies managed to reach the hatch by using Endor's tall trees to descend onto the vehicle from above.

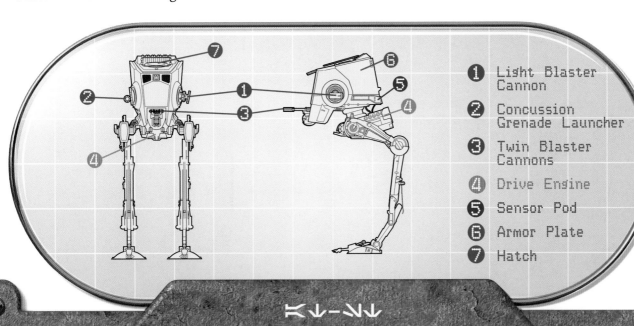

1 Light Blaster Cannon
2 Concussion Grenade Launcher
3 Twin Blaster Cannons
4 Drive Engine
5 Sensor Pod
6 Armor Plate
7 Hatch

AT-TE

TECHNICAL READOUT

SIZE: 5.02 m TALL,
12.4 m LONG

MAXIMUM SPEED:
60 KPH

PRIMARY MANUFACTURER:
Rothana Heavy Engineering
(Kuat Drive Yards)

AFFILIATION: Old Republic

All Terrain Tactical Enforcer Assault Walker

The Battle of Geonosis marked the first major conflict between the newly formed Confederacy of Independent Systems and the Old Republic. Although Count Dooku and his allies had some understanding of the Republic's military capabilities, the Confederacy was still unprepared for the onslaught of clone troopers, starships, and military vehicles that accompanied the Republic's invasion. Among the many craft deployed at the Battle of Geonosis was Kuat Drive Yards' experimental All Terrain Tactical Enforcer, the first military vehicle to utilize a six-legged walker configuration.

The AT-TE is a multipurpose tactical assault vehicle. Its mission profiles range from standard transport to full-out attacks on enemy installations. The AT-TE is also ideal in support roles, providing covering fire for ground troops while protecting larger, slower-moving vehicles.

Few ground vehicles have ever achieved the firepower of the AT-TE. The assault craft's primary weapon is a large, turret-mounted heavy projectile cannon designed to accommodate a wide range of ordnance, including explosive bunker busters, heat-seeking projectiles, and sonic charges. The cannon's tremendous range enables it to destroy buildings, artillery, or troop formations before the enemy can react.

The central cannon is flanked by six antipersonnel laser cannons, all mounted on swiveling turrets. The four forward-mounted laser cannons clear deployment zones before troopers are unloaded, while two rear cannons protect the AT-TE from ambushes. When the AT-TE falls under attack by smaller units, the troopers are responsible for defending the vehicle's flanks.

Two troop compartments, located in the front and rear of the vehicle, each hold up to ten armed clone troopers, who can be moved into nearly any type of terrain. The AT-TE's six legs allow it to climb slopes and step over obstacles, while the vehicle's low center of gravity provides a great deal of stability. It is vulnerable to mines, and its short legs limit the gunners' field of view; Kuat Drive Yards would later erase these design flaws with the much taller AT-AT.

Due to its size and complexity, the AT-TE requires a large crew consisting of a pilot, a spotter, and four support members to operate the laser cannons and serve as technicians. A seventh crew member controls the projectile cannon from an external firing chair. Most AT-TEs also keep an IM-6 battlefield medical droid on board.

The AT-TE can be transported through space aboard any number of large transports, but they require specialized barges or attack ships to actually land on a planet's surface. During the Clone Wars, AT-TE walkers were carried into an atmosphere and across battlefields in LAAT/c cargo gunships, modified versions of the standard Republic gunship.

After the Clone Wars, Palpatine decommissioned many of the AT-TEs in favor of newer and more destructive ground vehicles. Those AT-TEs that were not destroyed eventually saw action on remote Outer Rim worlds during the Galactic Civil War. Because each AT-TE relied on a cargo gunship for planetary transport, many of the vehicles were eventually abandoned.

> **"These weapons of war would be awe-inspiring, if they were not so terrifying."**
> *Supreme Chancellor Palpatine*
> *to KDY executives after the*
> *official unveiling of the AT-TE*

5 Gunner: During the Clone Wars, the projectile turret gunner was a clone specially trained for this dangerous duty.

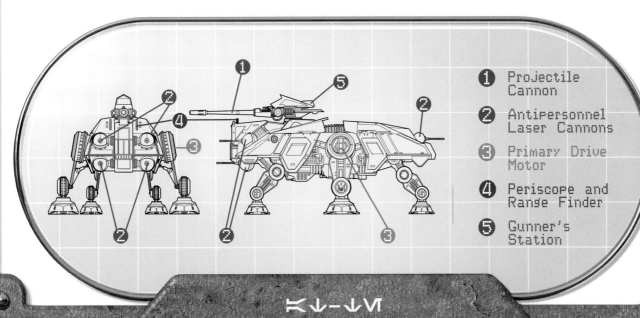

1. Projectile Cannon
2. Antipersonnel Laser Cannons
3. Primary Drive Motor
4. Periscope and Range Finder
5. Gunner's Station

A-WING

TECHNICAL READOUT

SIZE: 9.6 m LONG

MAXIMUM SPEED:
5,100G/CLASS-1
HYPERDRIVE/1,300 KPH

PRIMARY MANUFACTURER:
ALLIANCE UNDERGROUND ENGINEERING

AFFILIATION:
GALACTIC EMPIRE

Alliance RZ-1 A-Wing Starfighter

By far the fastest starfighter used during the Galactic Civil War, the compact A-wing was a Rebel Alliance response to the Empire's growing number of TIE fighters and TIE variants. Realizing that the Rebels needed a craft capable of outrunning these enemy fighters, General Jan Dodonna joined forces with engineer Walex Blissex, originator of the Delta-7 starfighter, to create the A-wing shortly before the Battle of Endor. Because of its speed, the A-wing excels at hit-and-run missions, long-range patrols and reconnaissance, and surgical strikes against large starships. A trio of A-wings single-handedly destroyed the *Executor*, Darth Vader's personal Super Star Destroyer, at the Battle of Endor.

The A-wing's speed is provided by two powerful Novaldex J-77 "Event Horizon" engines. A combination of adjustable thrust-vector controls built into each engine and thruster-control jets located between the engines supplies the vehicle's famed maneuverability. During atmospheric flight, the craft's flight path is controlled by making small adjustments to the stabilizer wings. Unfortunately, the A-wing's controls are notoriously sensitive, and few pilots can handle the craft at top speed.

The A-wing relies on its speed and agility in combat. Its armament is relatively weak, consisting of two wing-mounted blaster cannons. These cannons pivot as much as sixty degrees up or down for a greater field of fire, and each has its own power supply. Modified A-wings occasionally possess an additional rear-mounted blaster cannon. Concussion missile launchers are far more common and have become a standard component on New Republic A-wings. Although they have a relatively short range, an A-wing's concussion missiles are much more dangerous than the starfighter's blaster cannons.

In order to achieve the A-wing's remarkable speed, Blissex discarded anything that would draw energy away from the engines. As a result, the A-wing has weak armor plating and only a very small shield generator. In addition, the position of the cockpit exposes the pilot to enemy fire. After some debate, Blissex also decided against including an astromech droid, which might provide in-flight repairs and flight adjustments on other starfighters. Powerful avionics, including a power-jamming system that allows pilots to blind enemy targets prior to attack, compensate somewhat for these weaknesses.

A-wings require constant maintenance, and the Alliance found it extremely difficult to keep a squadron of craft operational for any length of time. Despite this, the A-wing has remained one of the New Republic's most prominent interceptor fighters.

> **"Any pilot who volunteers to fly an A-wing better be brave or crazy. Probably helps to be a little of both."**
> —*New Republic general Han Solo*

7 Front Wedge: The A-wing's wedge-shaped design and explosive fuel system allow it to cause tremendous damage when it collides with another ship. A-wing pilot Arvel Crynyd used this "tactic" to bring down the *Executor* at the Battle of Endor.

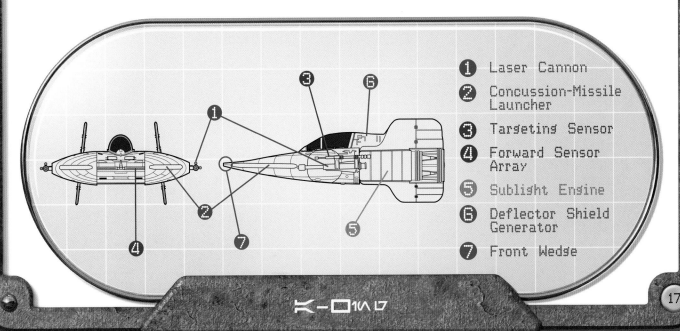

1. Laser Cannon
2. Concussion-Missile Launcher
3. Targeting Sensor
4. Forward Sensor Array
5. Sublight Engine
6. Deflector Shield Generator
7. Front Wedge

Bongo

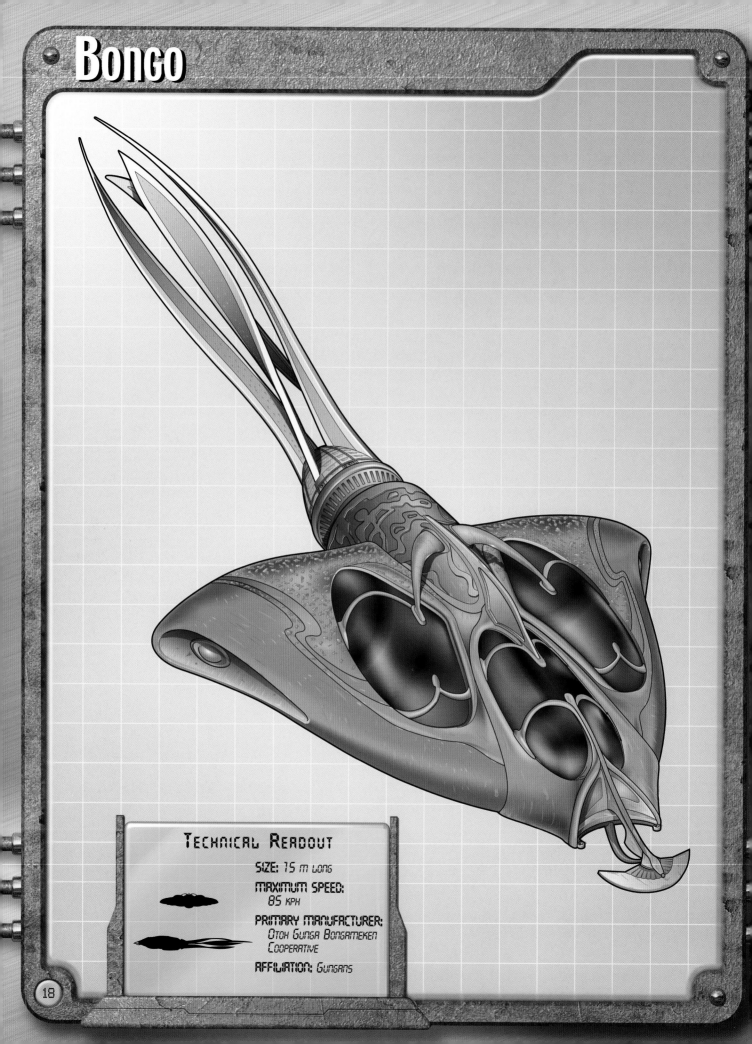

Technical Readout

SIZE: 15 m long

MAXIMUM SPEED:
85 kph

PRIMARY MANUFACTURER:
Otoh Gunga Bongameken
Cooperative

AFFILIATION: Gungans

Tribubble Bongo Sub

In order to navigate the watery depths of Naboo, the Gungans rely on unusual, organically engineered submersibles known as bongos. Bongos range from small, single-occupant craft to the huge "heyblibbers" used for long journeys. Jedi Master Qui-Gon Jinn and his Padawan Obi-Wan Kenobi piloted a tribubble bongo through Naboo's core.

Bongos are handcrafted, ensuring that each is unique. A bongo is built around an organic coral-like skeleton grown in specialized underwater harvest fields by Gungan designers. This skeleton forms the hull of the craft, which is exceptionally strong, though still susceptible to damage by sea monsters encountered in deep waters. The hull is equipped with an electrical power plant, guidance system, and passenger seating. Aesthetically, most bongo designers are inspired by creatures from the seas around them. As a result, many bongos resemble squid or other animals.

Although bongo engineers have experimented with a variety of propulsion systems, the most commonly used system relies on long, aft-mounted tentacles that rotate to push the craft forward through the water. The tentacles are powered by an electromotive field motor. Bongos also have repulsorlifts for entering and exiting specially designed bongo bays connected to most Gungan cities.

Bongo passengers sit in small compartments covered by bubblelike canopies. These canopies are actually hydrostatic fields, similar to those used to create the buildings in Otoh Gunga itself. Gungans generate hydrostatic fields by channeling energy between two opposing poles. In the case of the bongo, energy moves between a positively charged prong jutting out over the cockpit and several small, negatively charged receptors located around the passenger compartment. Once activated, the field keeps air in and water out.

Perhaps the most complex aspect of the bongo is its buoyancy system. Spongelike hydrostatic chambers are spread around the perimeter of the sub. In order to dive, heavy oil is released into the chambers; the sponges absorb this oil, changing density. When surfacing, the chambers are purged of oil, forcing another density shift. The oil is recycled throughout the system.

While Gungans produce much of the technology necessary for bongo creation, some electronics and specialized equipment, such as metal cargo containers, must be acquired from the Naboo. Gungan traders living on the fringes of Gungan society procure such items from the Naboo in exchange for foodstuffs and medicine.

Bongos are incredibly versatile and can be built for almost every function. Cargo bongos feature cargo holds instead of passenger modules. A Grand Army transport bongo—much larger than the tribubble bongo—can accommodate at least five armed passengers. Gungans also produce monobubble racing bongos. Bongo technology has even enabled the Gungans to build starships, with which they've colonized the Naboo moon of Ohma-D'un.

> **"Wesa give yousa una bongo. Da speedest way tooda Naboo tis goen through the planet's core. Now go."**
> —*Boss Nass*

4 Cockpit Bubble: An access panel is located under the cockpit bubble and allows temporary repairs to the steering systems. A mechanically minded pilot, such as Obi-Wan Kenobi, can also rig the wires to jump-start a floundering bongo.

1. Drive Fins
2. Engine
3. Navigational Lights
4. Cockpit Bubble
5. Diving Plane
6. Cargo Bubbles

B-WING

TECHNICAL READOUT

SIZE: 16.9 m LONG

MAXIMUM SPEED:
2,390G/CLASS 2
HYPERDRIVE/950 KPH

PRIMARY MANUFACTURER:
SLAYN & KORPIL

AFFILIATION: REBEL ALLIANCE

Slayn & Korpil B-Wing Starfighter

The B-wing was the Rebellion's most formidable assault starfighter, armed with an array of weapons and unique cockpit and wing designs. Integral to the Alliance's victory at the Battle of Endor, the B-wing continues to be an essential component of the New Republic's fleet.

The B-wing is essentially a long wing with a pair of folding airfoils studded with weapons emplacements. The craft's eight weapon-mounting emplacements are entirely interchangeable, allowing Alliance mechanics to easily reconfigure the starship's armaments based on a pilot's preferences or a mission's profile. A standard configuration consists of twin auto blasters on the cockpit, two proton torpedo launchers at the craft's midsection, ion cannons at the tip of each secondary wing, and an ion cannon, laser cannon, and proton torpedo launcher at the base of the central wing. An advanced targeting computer aids the pilot in combat by linking the ion cannons and proton torpedo launchers for full-out assaults on starships. The B-wing also features a weak targeting laser for gathering range and vector data.

Because of its heavy armament, the B-wing's primary mission profile includes attacks on much larger Imperial ships. Utilizing ion cannons and other unusual weapons, the B-wing is capable of quickly disabling these targets. Secondary missions include assault strikes on orbital and ground-based Imperial facilities, and escort duty for X-wing and Y-wing fighter squadrons.

The B-wing's cockpit is perhaps the craft's most unusual feature. The cockpit is surrounded by a unique gyrostabilization system, which ensures that the pilot always remains stationary, even as the rest of the ship rotates during flight. Due to this radical design and the starfighter's numerous weapons, however, the B-wing is extremely difficult to handle. B-wing pilots, such as the pilot Ten Numb, are infamous for becoming personally attached to their ships, participating in every repair, modification, or upgrade.

The B-wing was personally designed by Commander Ackbar, with the aid of Verpine shipbuilders at Slayn & Korpil. The starfighter's incredible performance played a part in Ackbar's promotion to admiral.

After the Battle of Endor, Ackbar led the design of a more advanced B-wing, the B-wing/E2 or "Expanded B-wing." This model incorporated an elongated command module, allowing for a gunner seated directly behind the pilot. The addition of the gunner has relieved much of the burden of combat duties from the pilot, resulting in much higher kill ratios for the B-wing/E2. The fighter is also more durable and faster than the original, but less maneuverable due to its larger cockpit.

> **"You're among the best pilots in the galaxy. You'll have to be if you want to control this starship."**
> —*Admiral Ackbar, briefing B-wing pilots before the Battle of Endor*

❼ Gyroscopic Cockpit: The B-wing's unique cockpit allows it to rotate with the craft. Unfortunately, if the gyros are damaged, the starship will spin out of control.

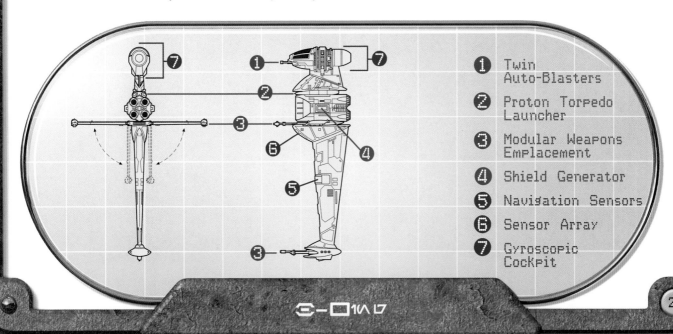

① Twin Auto-Blasters

② Proton Torpedo Launcher

③ Modular Weapons Emplacement

④ Shield Generator

⑤ Navigation Sensors

⑥ Sensor Array

⑦ Gyroscopic Cockpit

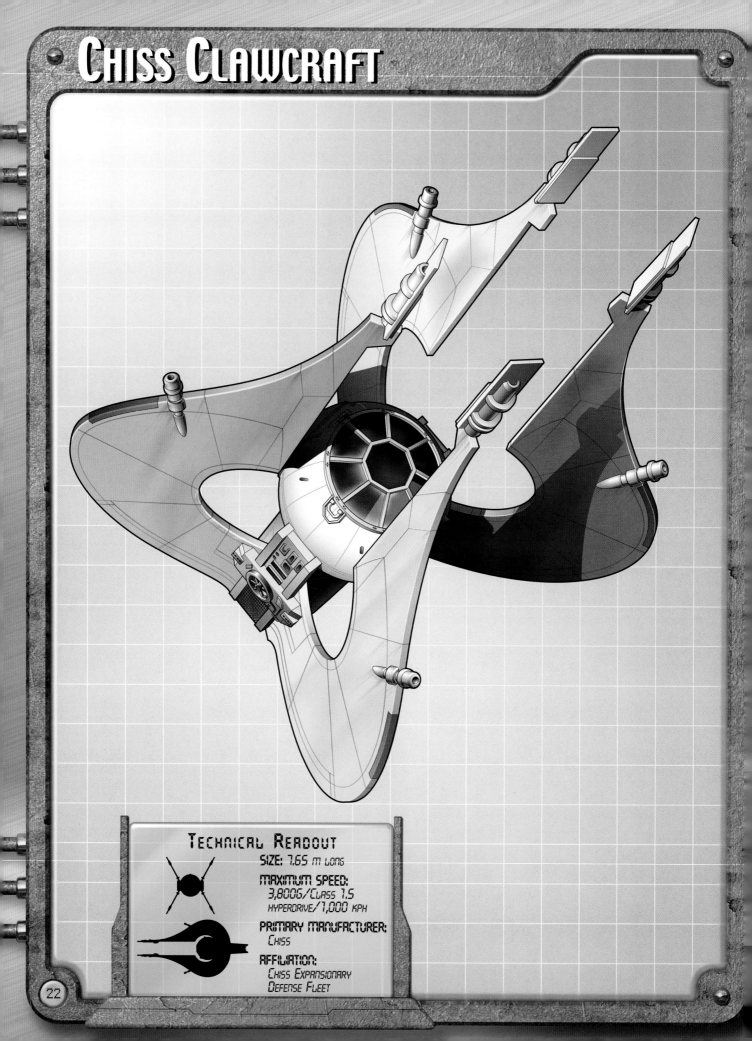

CHISS CLAWCRAFT

TECHNICAL READOUT

SIZE: 7.65 M LONG

MAXIMUM SPEED:
3,800G/CLASS 1.5
HYPERDRIVE/7,000 KPH

PRIMARY MANUFACTURER:
Chiss

AFFILIATION:
Chiss Expansionary
Defense Fleet

Chiss–Imperial Hybrid *Nssis*–Class Clawcraft

For centuries before their first encounter with the Empire, during which they resided in isolation from the rest of the galaxy, the Chiss created a variety of advanced technologies. Having developed an analog to the hyperdrive engine, the blue-skinned humanoids set out to methodically explore the galaxy. Eventually, a Chiss named Thrawn made first contact with the Empire and later joined the Imperial ranks. Using Thrawn's growing understanding of Imperial starfighters, Chiss engineers designed the Chiss clawcraft, an ingenious hybrid of Chiss and Imperial technology.

The Chiss clawcraft can be easily recognized thanks to its round cockpit, which is actually a modified version of the TIE fighter's ball cockpit. Like the TIE fighter, the clawcraft has twin ion engines, located in a pod attached to the rear of the cockpit. The Chiss aesthetic is plainly evident in the four curving weapons arms that sprout from the vehicle. Each arm is capped by a modified Sienar Fleet Systems L-s7.2 TIE cannon. Stealing a bit of the X-wing's design, the fire-linked cannons are arrayed to provide the greatest possible field of fire. The weapons arms also double as control vanes; even minute adjustments to the position of a single arm will result in sharp turns and other sudden maneuvers. During combat, many Chiss pilots have learned to launch the clawcraft into a frightening spin while firing all four laser cannons simultaneously. This tactic creates a barrage of laserfire that is nearly impossible to dodge.

While the Empire uses expendable TIE fighters to overwhelm opponents, the Chiss prefer to out-think their enemies, and they consider each clawcraft an important asset. The clawcraft is therefore equipped with a modest deflector shield generator and heavier armor than the TIE fighter. Both of these additions put greater burden on the ion engines, making the clawcraft slightly slower than the standard TIE fighter at sublight speeds.

The clawcraft is used primarily to patrol the borders of Chiss space. Clawcraft also participated in New Republic battles, such as the Battle of Kalarba. In order to reach trouble spots, the clawcraft is equipped with life support systems and the Chiss equivalent of a Class 1.5 hyperdrive. Like all Chiss starships, the clawcraft's hyperdrive relies on a network of hyperspace anchor points spread throughout Chiss territories. These anchor points broadcast a signal that Chiss spacecraft can follow through the maze of hyperspace.

Because the Chiss rely on these hyperspace beacons, however, nav computers are uncommon aboard the clawcraft. Without a nav computer, travel beyond Chiss borders becomes extremely dangerous. In order to strike out into new territory, the Chiss must install nav computers aboard a lead starship, which then guides wingmates via a homing beacon.

> ## "You have to admire the Chiss. They don't just steal your technology—they make it better."
>
> *–Anonymous Imperial engineer*

1   **Hyperspace Beacon:** Chiss rely on a unique nav beacon system to travel through hyperspace.

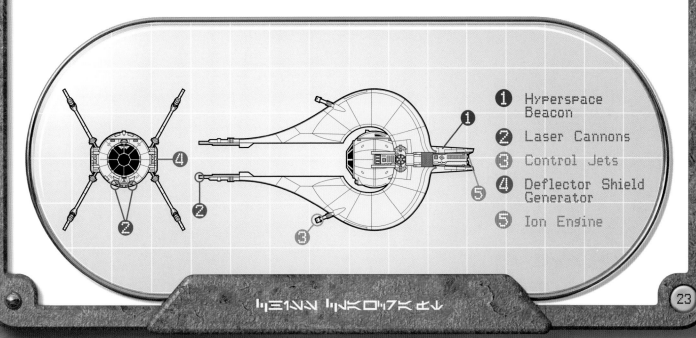

1 Hyperspace Beacon
2 Laser Cannons
3 Control Jets
4 Deflector Shield Generator
5 Ion Engine

CloakShape Fighter

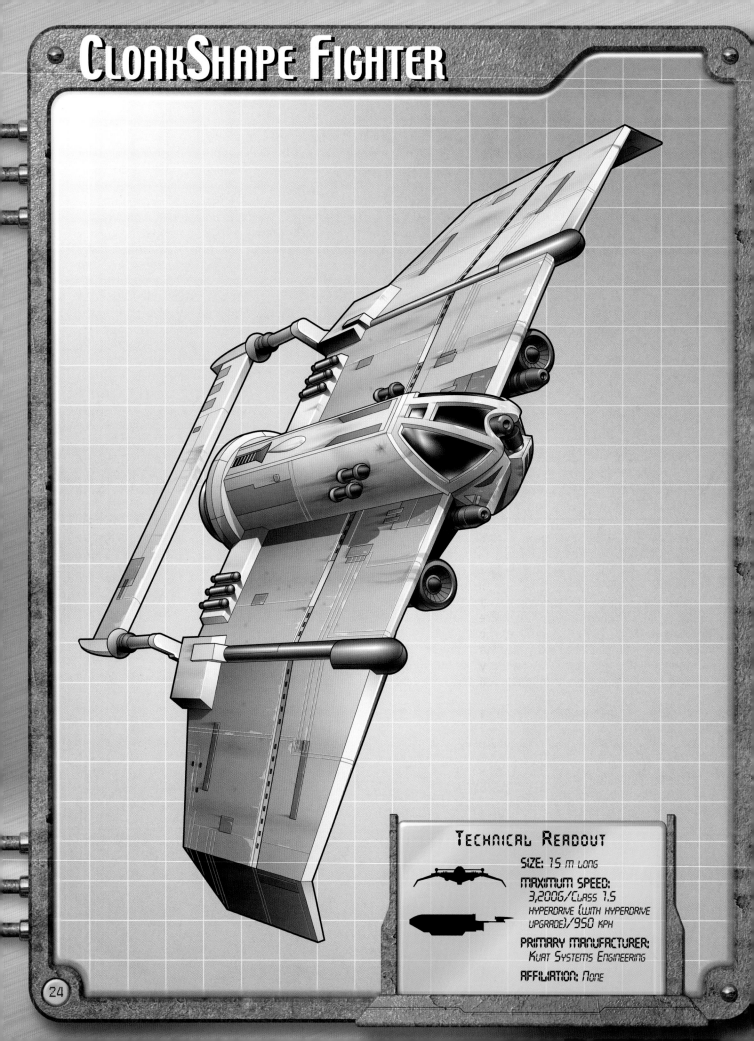

Technical Readout

SIZE: 15 m long

MAXIMUM SPEED:
3,200G/Class 1.5
Hyperdrive (with hyperdrive upgrade)/950 KPH

PRIMARY MANUFACTURER:
Kuat Systems Engineering

AFFILIATION: None

24

Kuat Systems Engineering CloakShape Fighter

First developed decades before the Clone Wars, the CloakShape fighter was originally intended for atmospheric combat and short-range space travel. Although no longer considered cutting-edge technology, the CloakShape remains in active use throughout the galaxy because it is remarkably easy to modify and upgrade. This versatility makes the CloakShape especially attractive to pirates and smugglers. During the last days of the Old Republic, the Jedi Jaizen Suel piloted a modified CloakShape called *Dawn Raider*. Years later, CloakShapes were used by bounty hunters who pursued Han Solo to Nar Shaddaa.

When first produced, the CloakShape fighter was considered a competent assault starfighter perfect for planetary defense. The starfighter became a component of many local militias, and was integrated into several corporate and private security forces. The CloakShape proved very effective in this role, largely due to its thick hull and resilient onboard systems.

Han Solo and others who have been caught by the CloakShape's targeting computer can attest to the strength of the starfighter's weapons. Laser cannons on either side of the cockpit soften targets, which are then destroyed by a series of concussion missiles.

Because the original CloakShape fighter was never intended for front-line combat duty or extended flight, it lacks deflector shields and a hyperdrive. In addition, the relatively small power generator cannot keep the starship running at maximum efficiency for prolonged periods of time, especially during battles when both the engines and weapons are drawing massive amounts of energy.

Nearly all discussion about the *original* CloakShape is academic since very few of these craft remain true to the stock specifications. At the most basic level, CloakShapes can be upgraded using several aftermarket modification kits produced specifically for the starfighter. The most popular kit provides a rear-mounted maneuvering fin to increase turning radius and improve handling. A self-powered hyperdrive sled, similar to the hyperdrive ring used by the Delta-7 starfighter, is also available. Both kits were in use by Nebula Front CloakShapes during the attack on the *Revenue* at Dorvalla. Still other kits provide an advanced sensor suite, upgrade the targeting computer, or convert the cockpit into an escape pod for emergencies.

The CloakShape is so easy to modify that entire systems can be torn out and replaced. Even a novice mechanic can replace the power generator with a more robust power supply or affix additional weapons to the craft. It is not uncommon to find a CloakShape with completely redesigned engines and thrusters, or even a deflector shield generator.

> "I once had a guy come in here looking to buy an 'original' CloakShape. I just laughed and told him that there's no such thing as an 'original' CloakShape."
>
> —*Mechanic Shug Ninx*

3 Maneuvering Fin: Maneuvering fins are such a common addition to CloakShapes that many pilots believe they are part of the original design.

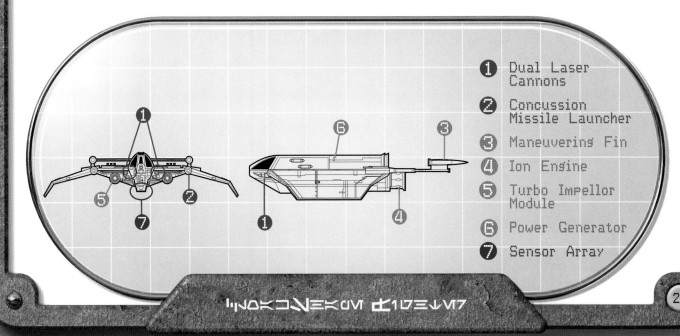

1. Dual Laser Cannons
2. Concussion Missile Launcher
3. Maneuvering Fin
4. Ion Engine
5. Turbo Impellor Module
6. Power Generator
7. Sensor Array

Cloud Car

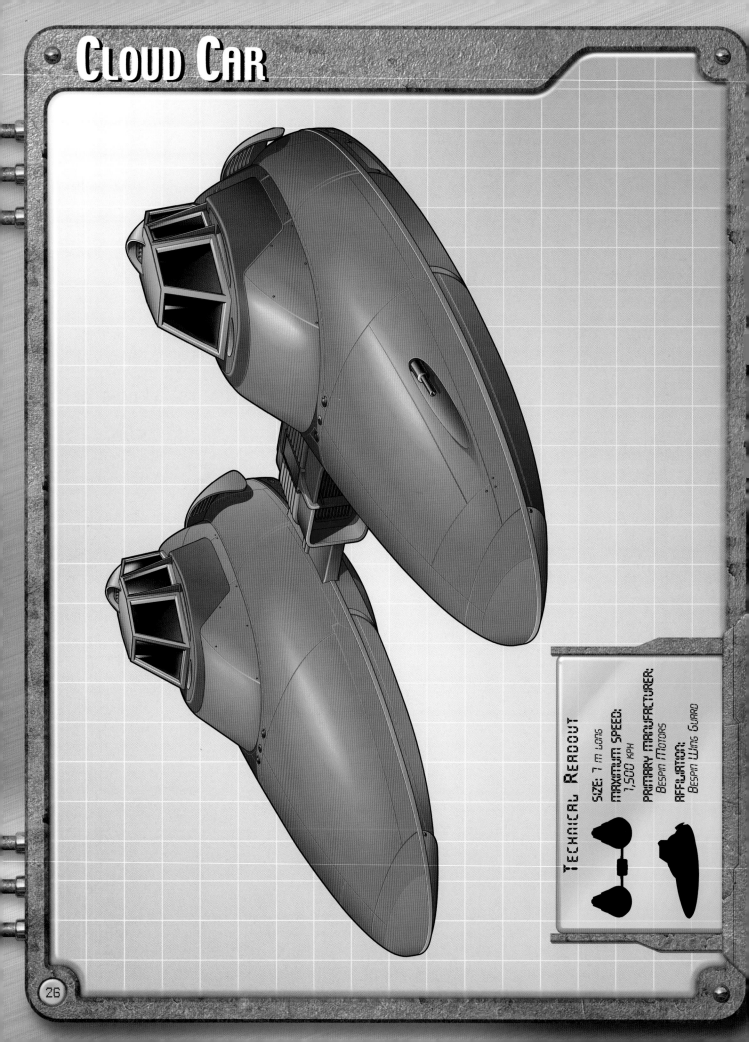

Technical Readout

Size: 7 m long

Maximum Speed:
1,500 kph

Primary Manufacturer:
Bespin Motors

Affiliation:
Bespin Wing Guard

Bespin Motors Storm IV Twin-Pod Cloud Car

While the term *cloud car* has come to denote any high-atmospheric craft, the vehicle that originally bore this name first appeared in the skies around Bespin's Cloud City. Designed by Bespin Motors as a patrol vehicle for the floating mining colony, the first cloud cars consisted of two armored cockpits connected by a sturdy engine block. Bespin's Wing Guard pilots still utilize Storm IV cloud cars to greet incoming vessels, investigate disturbances, inspect outlying mining facilities, and defend Cloud City. Civilians use the cloud cars for sight-seeing and travel around Bespin.

Each of Bespin's cloud cars sports a pair of twin blaster cannons, which can be controlled by a gunner stationed in the starboard pod. The weapons emplacements are modular, but the original cloud car's small power generator prevents the vehicle from supporting anything more powerful than blaster cannons. Some industrious mechanics, however, have replaced the vehicle's sizable sensor suite with miniaturized Fabritech devices, creating more room for a larger power generator that can, in turn, support true laser cannons.

The pilot, seated in the port pod, has access to advanced navigational systems and a communications array. Designed primarily for atmospheric flight, cloud cars generally lack advanced life support systems, but the cockpits are pressurized for high-altitude flight. Most cloud cars can reach low orbit.

The small but powerful ion engine serves as a cloud car's primary propulsion system. The vehicle can reach speeds in excess of 1,500 kilometers per hour using the ion engine alone. The secondary repulsorlift drive aids in complex maneuvers and increases the vehicle's speed. Both engine systems are open to the air for cooling. Small maneuvering jets, mechanized flaps, control vanes, and rudders all also enhance speed and control.

When the Empire took control of Cloud City shortly after the Battle of Hoth, Bespin Motors began selling its cloud cars to other markets. Competing manufacturers also adopted the basic cloud car design to produce a staggering array of similar vehicles. Cloud cars have become widespread throughout the galaxy as both personal transports and military vehicles, the latter used most often for atmospheric patrol and reconnaissance.

Among the most successful cloud car variants is the "combat cloud car," a more advanced military version of the standard cloud car. Upgrades to hull armor and weapons emplacements—notably the addition of high-powered laser cannons—allow these vehicles to face freighters and starfighters. In addition, many combat cloud cars are well suited to low-orbit missions: the Talon I, for example, has a maximum flight ceiling of one hundred kilometers and a dedicated life support system.

> **"If you can bribe a member of Bespin's Wing Guard into taking you on a spin around Cloud City, you won't regret spending the credits. The views are stunning."**
>
> —*Excerpt from* Ullok's Underground Guide to Bespin

❶ Blaster Cannon: Although relatively weak compared to the advanced weapons on modern starfighters, the cloud car's blaster cannons are sufficient to keep starships such as the *Millennium Falcon* in line.

❶ Blaster Cannon
❷ Sensor Suite
❸ Engine Block
❹ Armor Plating
❺ Gunner's Pod
❻ Pilot's Pod
❼ Cockpit

Commerce Guild Spider Tank

Technical Readout

SIZE: 7.32 m tall

MAXIMUM SPEED:
90 KPH

PRIMARY MANUFACTURER:
Baktoid Armor Workshop

AFFILIATION:
Confederacy of
Independent Systems

Baktoid Armor Workshop Homing Spider Droid

While it's true that the Old Republic turned out to be especially well prepared for the Battle of Geonosis, historians sometimes overlook the fact that the Confederacy of Independent Systems possessed its own army as well. The combined forces of the Commerce Guild, InterGalactic Banking Clan, Techno Union, Trade Federation, and Corporate Alliance provided Count Dooku's new army with a host of weapons, including battle droids and droid-controlled vehicles.

The spider tank, more accurately known as the homing spider droid, was developed by Baktoid Armor Workshop prior to its dissolution shortly after the Battle of Naboo. During the company's final days, Baktoid tried to sell many of its unproduced designs, and the Commerce Guild purchased several droid models, including the homing droid. Like the Republic's self-propelled heavy artillery units, the homing spider droid was designed to transport a large and devastating weapon throughout a battle zone.

The core component of the homing droid is a laser emplacement mounted beneath the droid's round body. The circular dish fires a precision homing laser that can be maintained until the droid's internal power supply is depleted. This sustained firepower enables the homing droid to wear down shields, bore through armored vehicles, and sweep troop formations to cut down enemy soldiers. The droid's antipersonnel cannon is activated for close-quarters combat, while a retractable ion cannon can be extended to disable starships or other valuable vehicles.

The spider tank's weapons systems are conveyed

> **"It is fortunate that these clone troopers know no fear."**
> *—Jedi Knight Ki-Adi-Mundi,*
> *upon first seeing the homing spider*

into battle by four long, hydraulic all-terrain legs originally designed to travel over rugged and roadless mining worlds. Because of the drive unit's great height and extendable hydraulics, the tank can position its homing laser above enemy targets or move to higher ground to blast atmospheric craft. The legs are susceptible to damage, and if just one hydraulic support is disabled, the entire vehicle will crash violently to the ground.

Homing spider droids are designated by number alone and do not have developed personalities or long-term memory modules. They do possess an internal logic processor and military protocols for prolonged missions, but the droids are often configured to receive orders directly from a central control computer.

In many large battles, homing spider droids also work in tandem with the Commerce Guild's much smaller burrowing spider droid, which serves as an armed scout, wielding a powerful blaster cannon as it explores battlefields. Infrared photoreceptors and high-definition scanners enable the droid to survey the terrain and relay targeting data back to the homing droid. When the burrowing spider identifies a prime target, it sends a tracking message to the homing droid, which then ambles toward the signal to deliver the killing blow.

④ **Armored Core:** The homing droid's core holds a volatile reactor. If the core is breached, the reactor violently explodes.

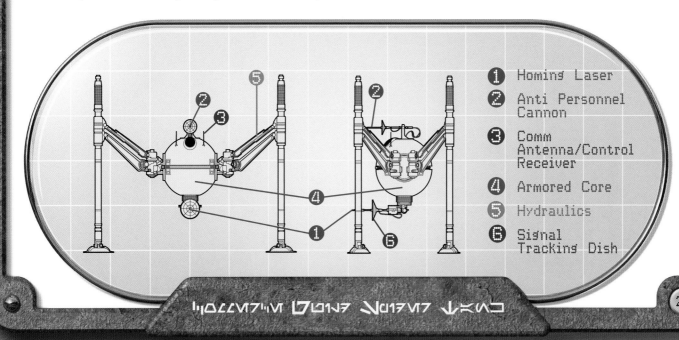

① Homing Laser
② Anti Personnel Cannon
③ Comm Antenna/Control Receiver
④ Armored Core
⑤ Hydraulics
⑥ Signal Tracking Dish

CORALSKIPPER

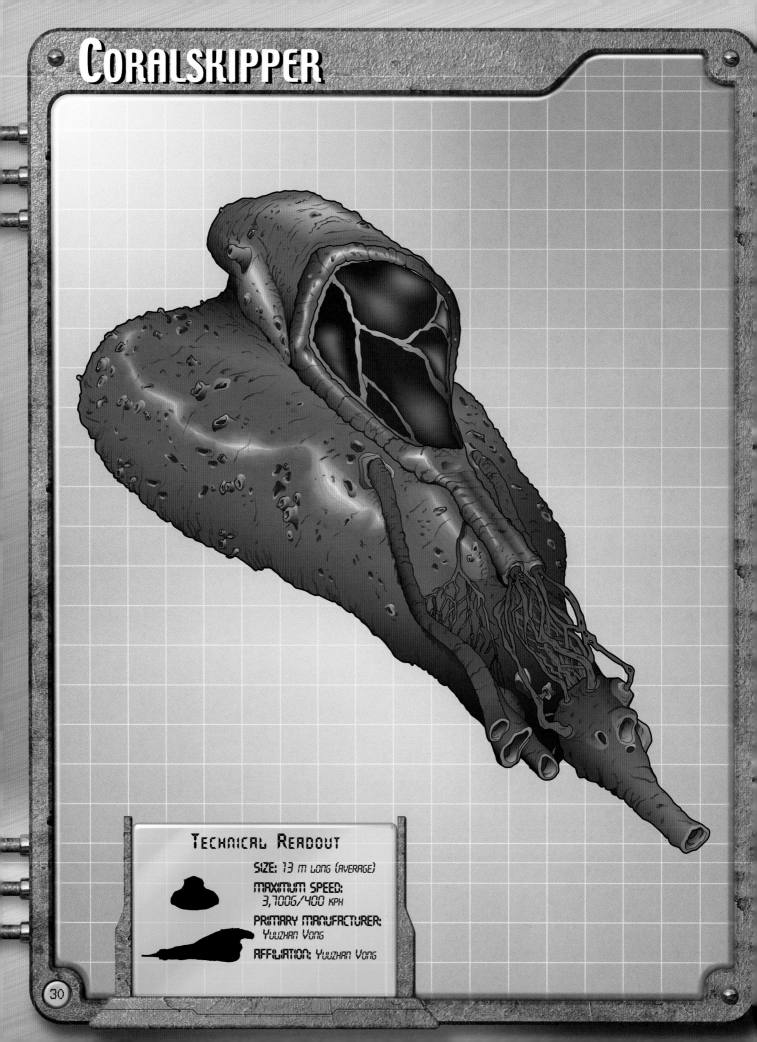

TECHNICAL READOUT

SIZE: 13 m long (average)

MAXIMUM SPEED:
3,700G/400 kph

PRIMARY MANUFACTURER:
Yuuzhan Vong

AFFILIATION: Yuuzhan Vong

Yuuzhan Vong Yorik-Et

During their invasion of the galaxy, the Yuuzhan Vong unleashed a host of dangerous bioengineered vehicles on the unsuspecting New Republic. Among the most pervasive of these is the coralskipper, the invading army's answer to the standard starfighter.

A living vehicle, the coralskipper is largely composed of organic yorik coral. A coralskipper "nursery," like the one discovered by Luke Skywalker and Jacen Solo on Belkadan, consists of a mass of leafy vines surrounding dozens of growing starfighters. The vines redirect solar energy and nutrients to the coralskippers. Because they are grown rather than manufactured, no two coralskippers look exactly alike. All coralskippers, however, share some basic features, including a tapered nose, dark canopy, and aerodynamic, triangular body.

The coralskipper's weapons system is unique. When the Yuuzhan Vong pilot fires on an enemy, a small appendage on the front of the vehicle releases a flaming, molten rock. When this mass strikes a spacecraft, it can burn through armor plating and cause irreparable damage. The same mechanism propels the starfighter, as the opposing force of the magma release pushes the vehicle through space. A coralskipper is both rearmed and refueled by consuming rocks, small asteroids, and stellar debris.

Barely visible on the front of a coralskipper is a small "dovin basal," which resembles a pulsing, invertebrate creature. Although unassuming, the dovin basal is possibly the coralskipper's most formidable component. It functions much like a miniature black hole, creating a tremendous supergravity field when activated. This field can be directed at an enemy starfighter in order to overload its shields. It can also act as the coralskipper's own shield by intercepting laserfire and proton torpedoes.

Fortunately, New Republic pilots learned several methods for defeating the dovin basal. By boosting the sphere of a New Republic starfighter's inertial compensator, a pilot can adjust for gravity wells and prevent a loss of shields. The coralskipper's own "shield" can be kept occupied by a series of low-power laser blasts, which force the dovin basal to draw energy away from other systems, including weapons and engines.

Coralskippers are strictly space vehicles and do not perform well in gravity. In addition, they aren't designed for long-range travel, and must rely on massive carriers to transport them across the galaxy.

After Lando Calrissian captured a coralskipper, following the attack on Dubrillion, the New Republic learned that Yuuzhan Vong pilots actually communicate with their living starships via special masks called cognition hoods. This hood is, in fact, part of the coralskipper, which can understand and speak the Yuuzhan Vong tongue.

> **"In the yorik-et, two minds become one."**
> —*Yuuzhan Vong pilot's creed*

❶ **Yuuzhan Vong Mask:** The mask worn by a coralskipper pilot is actually part of the starship itself and enables the pilot to communicate directly with the ship.

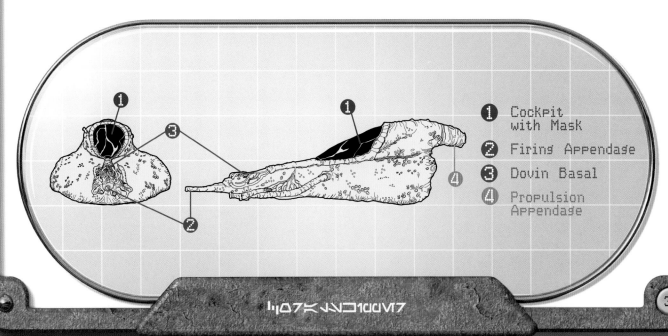

❶ Cockpit with Mask
❷ Firing Appendage
❸ Dovin Basal
❹ Propulsion Appendage

CORPORATE ALLIANCE TANK DROID

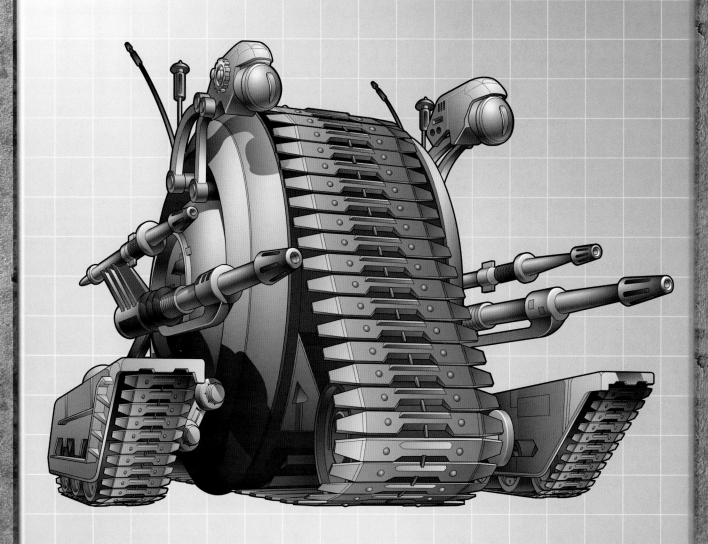

TECHNICAL READOUT

SIZE: 6.2 M TALL
(7.5 M WITH CONTROL RECEIVER)

MAXIMUM SPEED:
50 KPH

PRIMARY MANUFACTURER:
CORPORATE ALLIANCE

AFFILIATION: CONFEDERACY OF
INDEPENDENT SYSTEMS

Corporate Alliance *Persuader*-Type Droid Enforcer

Even before joining the Confederacy of Independent Systems, the Corporate Alliance frequently resorted to violence in order to achieve its goals. When local populations on Outer Rim worlds opposed the Corporate Alliance's development plans or complained about unfair business practices, the organization deployed massive tanklike droid enforcers to protect its interests.

The *Persuader*-class droid tanks produced by the Corporate Alliance stand well over six meters tall and use a single, treaded drive motor for locomotion. A pair of large outrigger arms connected to either side of the drive motor can be armed with virtually any known weapon. During the Clone Wars, the Corporate Alliance equipped the droids with a combination of conventional ion cannons and homing lasers. For specific missions, the ion cannons or lasers could be replaced by concussion missile launchers, homing missiles, dumbfire torpedoes, and even thermal grenade launchers.

The tank droid offers slow acceleration but a fairly solid maximum ground speed of 50 kilometers per hour. When cruising at top speed, the vehicle usually extends a pair of stabilizing outriggers for added support. These outriggers are also used during combat to prevent the vehicle from being knocked over by collisions or enemy fire.

Because of its size and speed, the tank droid is sometimes used as a short-range reconnaissance vehicle. The tank droid's stereoscopic visual scanners can quickly evaluate enemy fortifications or terrain elements even as the vehicle rushes to attack. Tracking transmitters on the tank droid allowed

Corporate Alliance Clone Wars commanders to monitor the vehicle's every movement, and orders could be sent directly to the droid's command control receiver.

Throughout the Clone Wars, tank droids were used to complement larger units that included such vehicles as the homing spider or hailfire. In many battles, the tank droids worked in pairs to protect a homing spider's flanks from enemy attack, although it required three tank droids to adequately protect a single hailfire.

While tank droids weren't suited to many types of terrains, including ice planets or forest worlds, they were often deployed in urban areas, where their sheer mass permitted them to break through walls and topple buildings.

Of all the Confederacy vehicles, tank droids were among the most feared by civilians because of their power and relentless nature. While homing droids might ignore unarmed civilians and hailfire droids carried limited payloads, the tank droids simply crushed everything in their path and fired their weapons with wild abandon. Late in the Clone Wars, the Corporate Alliance began equipping the tank droids with voice modulators, which served to make the vehicles even more terrifying.

> ## "These are automated agents of evil!"
> *—Jedi Master Plo Koon,*
> *rallying clone troopers on Geonosis*

6   **Control Receiver:** Like many droid units in the Confederacy's army, the tank droid was able to receive orders from a Droid Control Ship. It also utilized backup processors in the event the Droid Control Ship was destroyed.

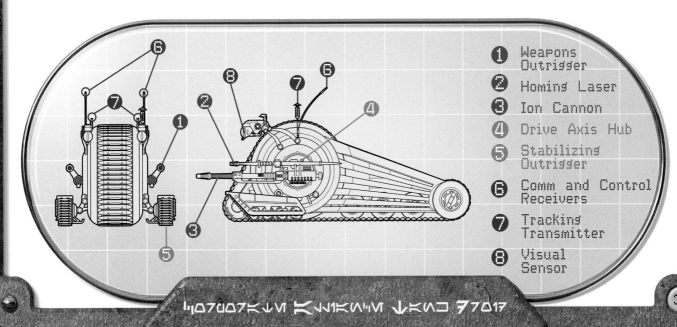

1. Weapons Outrigger
2. Homing Laser
3. Ion Cannon
4. Drive Axis Hub
5. Stabilizing Outrigger
6. Comm and Control Receivers
7. Tracking Transmitter
8. Visual Sensor

DESERT SKIFF

TECHNICAL READOUT

SIZE: 9 m long

MAXIMUM SPEED:
250 KPH

PRIMARY MANUFACTURER:
Ubrikkian

AFFILIATION:
Jabba the Hutt

Ubrikkian Bantha II Cargo Skiff

Skiffs are general repulsorlift utility vehicles easily modified for a broad range of industrial uses in a variety of planetary environments. The basic skiff design features an open deck with a very simple control station located near the rear of the vehicle. A repulsorlift engine allows the craft to hover up to 50 meters above the ground, while thrust nozzles propel the vehicle forward at speeds nearing 250 kilometers per hour. A pair of steering vanes provides maneuverability.

Skiffs are well suited for cargo transport and are often found in warehouses and spaceports across the galaxy. Most mass-produced skiffs possess retractable magnetic lifters engaged for transporting cargo modules onto the vehicle's deck. Once aboard the skiff, the modules are restrained by magnetic fasteners and traditional cargo straps. A typical skiff can carry more than 100 tons of cargo. Alternately, up to 16 seats may be installed on a skiff's deck, transforming the vehicle into a mass transit vessel, personal transport, or pleasure craft.

The skiff's proliferation is due, in part, to its ease of use: skiffs can be piloted even by relatively unskilled laborers. Skiffs are also very inexpensive, allowing the most destitute worlds to purchase at least a handful for public uses.

Often, skiffs must be modified for local conditions, but this is a fairly easy task. The most common modification is the addition of an enclosed deck and piloting station, which protects the passengers and crews from the elements. Water skiffs boast retractable rain screens and upgraded repulsorlift engines for crossing oceans or rivers. Desert skiffs, such as those used by Jabba the Hutt on Tatooine, are fitted with sand filters and enhanced engine cooling systems.

Skiffs make poor combat vehicles. A basic blaster can easily damage a skiff's steering vane or repulsorlift engine, making the vehicle very unstable. A sudden shift in weight or a sharp turn can completely topple a damaged skiff.

Despite the skiff's drawbacks, Jabba's crew used a fleet of desert skiffs to raid nearby settlements, escort the Hutt's sail barge during pleasure cruises, and battle the forces of rival crimelords. These desert skiffs were bolstered by light armor and portable laser cannons. Jabba also ordered that his skiffs be equipped with extendable gangplanks; enemies forces to "walk the plank" usually found themselves in the gullet of the mighty Sarlacc. Such modifications proved ineffective, though, against Luke Skywalker and his allies.

> ## "A skiff so easy to pilot, even a labor droid can handle it!"
> —*Ubrikkian advertisement*

7 The Plank: Jabba often forced his enemies to "walk the plank" right into the Sarlacc's beaked mouth.

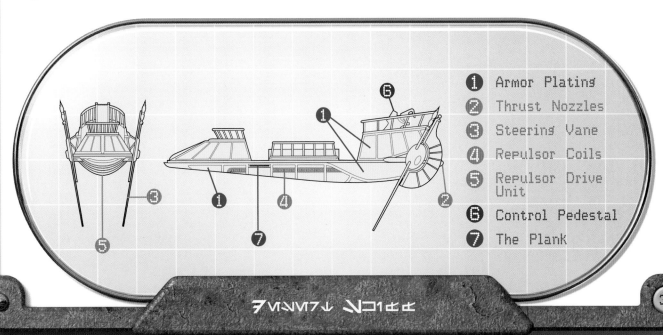

1. Armor Plating
2. Thrust Nozzles
3. Steering Vane
4. Repulsor Coils
5. Repulsor Drive Unit
6. Control Pedestal
7. The Plank

DROID CONTROL SHIP

TECHNICAL READOUT

SIZE: 3,170 m DIAMETER

MAXIMUM SPEED:
3006/CLASS 2
HYPERDRIVE/500 KPH

PRIMARY MANUFACTURER:
HOERSCH-KESSEL DRIVE, INC.

AFFILIATION:
TRADE FEDERATION

Modified HKD *Lucrehulk*-Class LH-3210 Cargo Hauler

When the Trade Federation began creating its secret army, the Executive Board knew they would need stellar cruisers to transport their weapons of war throughout the galaxy, battleships to defend against starfighter attacks, and—most important—flagships for controlling their legions of mindless battle droids. Reluctant to spend the credits necessary to construct a fleet of military starships, the Trade Federation opted to convert existing *Lucrehulk*-class cargo freighters into versatile warships.

The Lucrehulk, originally manufactured by Hoersch-Kessel Drive, is a massive starship more than 3,000 meters in diameter. The Trade Federation began transforming these leviathans by installing a network of laser cannons; a typical Trade Federation battleship was equipped with 42 quad laser emplacements. Each battleship also carried a small army consisting of 6,250 tanks (ATTs), 550 large transports (MTTs), and 50 landing ships. When attacked, a Trade Federation battleship could unleash a horde of 1,500 droid starfighters.

The Droid Control Ship was simply a modified version of the Trade Federation battleship. The most important addition was the central control computer, located in the heart of the vessel and programmed to create protocols for the Trade Federation's various droid units, including battle droids and droid starfighters. These commands were broadcast via transmission towers mounted on the vessel's centrisphere. The Trade Federation droids, in turn, sent battlefield updates and other information back to the control ship's array of 16 signal receivers. The control computer used this data to quickly evaluate the most current

> ## "Their deflector shield is too strong! We'll never get through it!"
> *—Ric Olié during the attack on the Droid Control Ship*

protocols and make adjustments as necessary. Of course, commanders on the Droid Control Ship could override any order and issue commands of their own, although these, too, had to be relayed to the battlefield by the control computer.

Despite the countless modifications made to the cargo vessels, it is plainly evident that the haulers were never designed for war. The weapons emplacements, installed along the equatorial band, provided limited coverage. During space battles, enemy pilots could exploit this weakness by flying extremely close to the battleship's surface. In addition, the battleships had extremely volatile reactors, as Anakin Skywalker discovered at the Battle of Naboo.

After the Battle of Naboo, the Republic ordered the Trade Federation to dissolve its army. The Trade Federation pretended to comply with this decree by seemingly disassembling many of the battleships, only to transform the centrispheres into detachable core ships that were used at the Battle of Geonosis and throughout the Clone Wars. When in retreat, the core ships were found to be able to reenter space and reattach themselves to the outer ring. After the Clone Wars, the few Trade Federation battleships and core ships that remained found their way into the Corporate Sector or were purchased by wealthy merchants.

6 Hangar Entrance: Anakin Skywalker flew into one of the Droid Control Ship's unshielded hangars and blasted the starship's core reactor to end the Battle of Naboo.

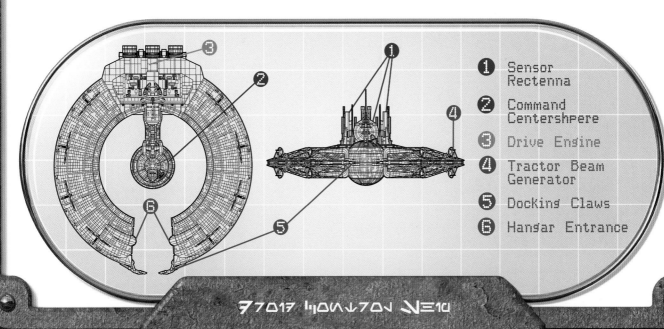

1. Sensor Rectenna
2. Command Centersphere
3. Drive Engine
4. Tractor Beam Generator
5. Docking Claws
6. Hangar Entrance

DROID STARFIGHTER

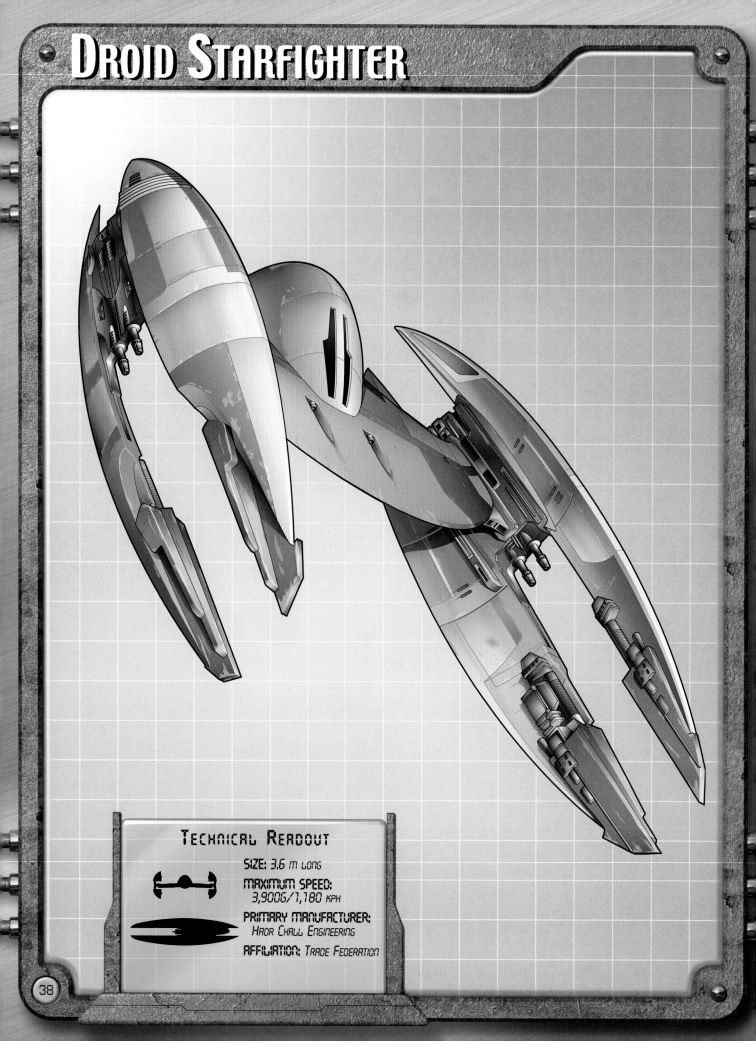

TECHNICAL READOUT

SIZE: 3.6 m LONG

MAXIMUM SPEED:
3,900G/1,180 KPH

PRIMARY MANUFACTURER:
Haor Chall Engineering

AFFILIATION: Trade Federation

Xi Char Variable Geometry Self-Propelled Battle Droid, Mk. 1

During the Battle of Naboo, the Trade Federation Droid Control Ship was tightly protected by what seemed to be an endless swarm of fast, merciless droid starfighters. The agile starfighters, equipped with droid brains to ensure that they acted in concert and would sacrifice themselves without thought, overwhelmed the Naboo pilots and nearly secured victory for the Trade Federation.

Designed by the fanatical Xi Char engineers, the droid starfighter was produced in massive numbers shortly before that battle. The starfighter represents classic Xi Char design: a compact body that offers only a small target, sports multiple weapons emplacements, and has an odd, insectlike appearance. The vehicle excels in both atmospheric and space combat.

The droid starfighter's primary weapons system consists of four blaster cannons arranged two to a wing. The laser cannons have great range, although they are relatively weak even when compared to the weapons on the Naboo starfighter. In standard flight configuration, the starfighter's wings are collapsed, concealing the laser cannons. When combat is imminent, the wings separate to reveal the weapons. The laser cannons are complemented by two energy torpedo launchers that soften targets before the starfighter closes to deliver a laser cannon barrage.

The Xi Char viewed the droid starfighter as a short-range combat craft that would attack in giant flocks to quickly eliminate opponents. The starfighter's fuel system relies on unconventional, solid fuel-concentrate slugs that provide thrust when ignited. Because the fuel slugs deplete rapidly, droid starfighters must frequently return to hangars or space stations for refueling.

Droid starfighter squadrons consist of hundreds of individual fighters, all programmed to attack in unison, with frightening efficiency. The starfighters lack deflector shields and are easily destroyed, but reserve units are continually launched to bolster thinning squadrons.

The droid starfighter's most unusual feature is its ability to transform into a walking configuration. The vehicle's wings become four legs, allowing the starfighter to patrol captured sites during planetary occupations.

Like the AAT and other Trade Federation military vehicles, the droid starfighter endured rigorous testing before its deployment during the invasion of Naboo. The starfighters saw combat during raids against Degan pirates in the Elrood sector and were instrumental in defeating Nym's army on Lok. The Naboo first encountered the droid starfighters when Echo Flight pilots led by Essara Till ran afoul of the machines during an assault on Station TFP-9, only a few weeks before the Trade Federation's full-scale attack on Naboo. After the Battle of Naboo, droid starfighters remained in operation as part of the Trade Federation "defense fleet," participating in the invasion of Zonama Sekot and the occupation of the Karthakk system.

> **"Droids don't talk back, they don't questions your orders, and they never complain when you send them on suicide missions."**
> —*Trade Federation tactician Rune Haako*

5 Sensor Eyes: The droid starfighter's sensor eyes are designed to efficiently collect combat data—and to give the vehicle a sinister appearance.

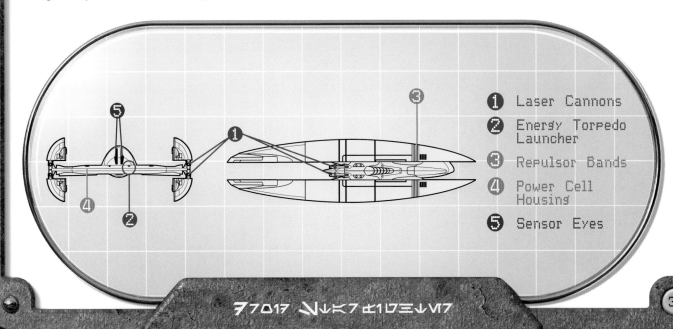

1 Laser Cannons
2 Energy Torpedo Launcher
3 Repulsor Bands
4 Power Cell Housing
5 Sensor Eyes

ECLIPSE STAR DESTROYER

Kuat Drive Yards *Eclipse*-Class Super Star Destroyer

Emperor Palpatine's plan for galactic domination revolved around inspiring terror in all of his would-be subjects. This philosophy resulted in the creation of the huge Star Destroyer, which was soon followed by the even larger Super Star Destroyer. When the Emperor was reborn in a clone body six years after the Battle of Endor, he continued to sow fear through the *Eclipse*, a starship more than 17 kilometers long.

The jet-black leviathan was a powerful weapon of psychological warfare. It terrified enemy forces and scattered fleets before a single shot could be fired. It quickly became the Emperor's personal flagship, only increasing its terrible reputation.

Once it entered combat, the *Eclipse* proved that its reputation was well deserved. It boasted 500 heavy laser cannons and 550 turbolaser batteries, making it one of the most heavily armed starships of all time. In addition, the *Eclipse* concealed a superlaser capable of cracking a planet's crust. Heavy armor and powerful shields allowed the *Eclipse* to ram virtually anything that stood in its way, while ten gravity-well projectors ensured that enemy vessels could not escape into hyperspace.

The *Eclipse* also served as a carrier, transporting starfighters into battle. Its docking bays held 600 TIE interceptors divided into 50 squadrons, and 96 TIE bombers organized into eight squadrons. These starfighters alone could take on almost any New Republic fleet.

> ## "The hyperspace tunnel opened and this black *thing* came crawling out from between the stars....We thought it was a ghost ship, until it opened fire."
> —*New Republic information officer Nara Dun*

While its primary mission profile involved engaging enemy space fleets, the *Eclipse* was quite capable of launching ground assaults. The starship accommodated five prefabricated garrison bases, 100 AT-AT walkers, and 150,000 stormtroopers. Due to its tremendous size, the *Eclipse* required a crew of more than 700,000 trained personnel.

The *Eclipse* could have enabled the clone Emperor to crush the New Republic if not for the efforts of Luke Skywalker and Leia Organa Solo. While over the Pinnacle Base, Emperor Palpatine began generating devastating Force storms. In order to stop the Emperor's advance, Luke and Leia combined their own Force energies. The Jedi overwhelmed Palpatine, and the Force storms raged out of control. Luke and Leia escaped, but the Force storms destroyed the *Eclipse*.

Undaunted, the Empire built a second *Eclipse*-class starship, dubbed the *Eclipse II*. This vessel was destroyed, however, when R2-D2 placed it on a collision course with a superweapon called the Galaxy Gun high above the planet Byss.

1 Superlaser: The *Eclipse*'s superlaser was designed to penetrate a planet's crust, making the starship nearly as powerful as the original Death Star.

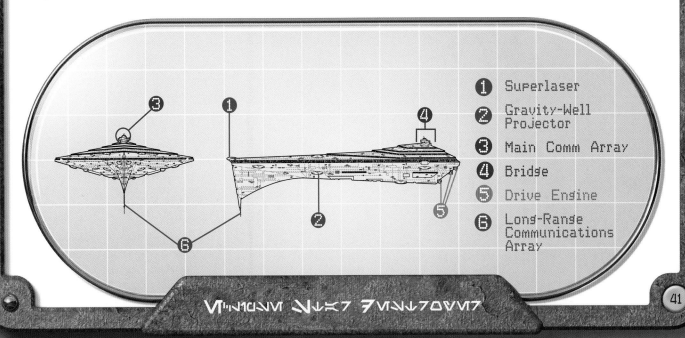

1. Superlaser
2. Gravity-Well Projector
3. Main Comm Array
4. Bridge
5. Drive Engine
6. Long-Range Communications Array

E-Wing

Technical Readout

Size: 11.2 m long

Maximum Speed:
4,200g/Class 2
Hyperdrive/1,300 kph

Primary Manufacturer:
FreiTek, Inc.

Affiliation:
New Republic

FreiTek, Inc., E-Wing Escort Starfighter

During the early days of the New Republic, the fledgling government faced countless threats. Among the most dangerous of these was Grand Admiral Thrawn, who rekindled the Galactic Civil War. Out of this conflict arose the E-wing, a powerful starfighter designed to protect New Republic convoys from Imperial raids.

Developed by the same engineers who created Incom's X-wing starfighter, the E-wing is, in many ways, an improvement over the "state-of-the-art" A-wing. While not as fast as the A-wing, the E-wing can keep pace with TIE interceptors, and is better armored than other New Republic starfighters, including the X-wing. Its armaments are rivaled only by the B-wing's arsenal.

The E-wing's primary weapons are three fire-linked laser cannons, one located at each wing, with the third installed directly above the cockpit. Sixteen proton torpedoes allow devastating attacks on capital ships and military installations. Because of its great firepower, the E-wing often doubles as medium-range assault craft.

While most starfighters gain maneuverability through movable wings equipped with flaps and steering vanes, the E-wing utilizes a pair of fixed wings. Maneuverability is provided by miniaturized flaps located in the exhaust nacelles, designed to redirect the engine's ion streams. In order to further increase efficiency, FreiTek engineers ensured that everything aboard the vehicle—from engine components to cockpit seats—would be totally modular.

The E-wing was designed for a single pilot, aided by a targeting computer and astromech droid. However, the E-wing was too advanced for the R2 units commonly used aboard X-wings and Y-wings, so the New Republic championed the creation of the R7 astromech, a droid designed specifically for use in the E-wing. The astromech is housed in a sealed compartment, where it regulates power, operates the hyperdrive system, and monitors damage. The R7 can also perform rudimentary maneuvers such as takeoffs and landings, and can even pilot the starfighter or serve as a gunner during emergencies.

Although considered exceptional, the E-wing is still a work in progress. When it was first introduced, the E-wing's laser cannons were powered by synthetically spin-coiled Tibanna gas. The gas deteriorated too quickly, greatly reducing the cannons' effective range. As a temporary fix, the New Republic modified the fighter to accept triple the normal power feed, resulting in the "Type B" E-wing. The Type B's weapons had greater range, but would occasionally overload.

After the defeat of Thrawn, FreiTek developed the Series 4 E-wing, which utilizes more stable blaster gas and has a secondary power generator dedicated to the weapons system. The new E-wing's astromech requirements have also been adjusted, allowing R2 units to serve aboard E-wings.

> **"I say let the Imperials keep coming, because every time a new admiral crawls out of the Outer Rim or some Imperial goon finds a lost superweapon, Rogue Squadron gets a new starfighter. Seems like a good deal to me."**
> —*General Wedge Antilles*

7 R7 Astromech: The E-wing's astromech is kept in a sealed compartment to protect it from being destroyed by enemy fire, a common fate for astromechs aboard X-wing and Y-wing fighters.

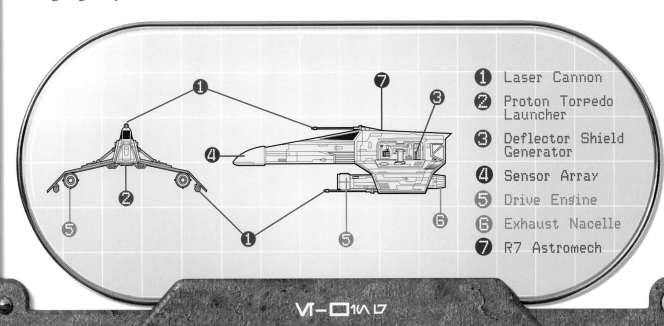

1. Laser Cannon
2. Proton Torpedo Launcher
3. Deflector Shield Generator
4. Sensor Array
5. Drive Engine
6. Exhaust Nacelle
7. R7 Astromech

EXECUTOR

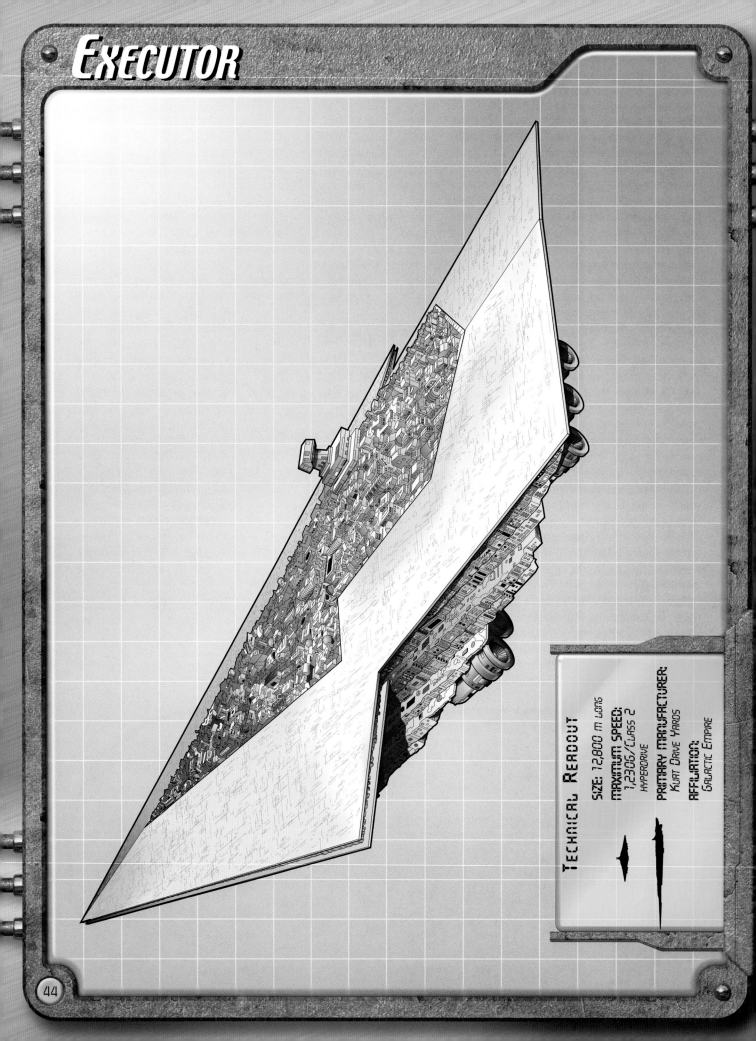

TECHNICAL READOUT

SIZE: 12,800 m LONG

MAXIMUM SPEED:
1,230G/CLASS 2
HYPERDRIVE

PRIMARY MANUFACTURER:
KUAT DRIVE YARDS

AFFILIATION:
GALACTIC EMPIRE

Kuat Drive Yards Super Star Destroyer

During the height of the Galactic Civil War, no enemy was more feared than Darth Vader. Emperor Palpatine's personal enforcer, Vader relentlessly pursued the Rebel Alliance. To aid in this hunt, the Sith Lord acquired the *Executor*, the first in a new line of Super Star Destroyers designed to crush the Emperor's foes.

At 12,800 meters long, the *Executor* was the largest military starship of its time. Its size flaunted the Emperor's power and seemingly unlimited resources, making the Super Star Destroyer an effective deterrent against insurrection before a single shot had been fired. For space engagements, the *Executor* wielded more than a thousand weapons, ranging from standard tubolasers and ion cannons to more specialized concussion missile tubes designed for attacks on space stations, and tractor beam projectors for capturing enemy vessels.

Starfighters were in large supply aboard the *Executor*. The vessel originally carried 144 TIE fighters split into two full wings. By the Battle of Endor, the starship's starfighter fleet included a mixture of TIE interceptors, TIE bombers, and generic TIE fighters. Secondary docking bays held up to 200 additional support starships.

For ground campaigns, the *Executor* held a full stormtrooper corps equipped with a wide range of weapons, vehicles, and terrain-specific armor. The army's vehicle pool consisted of two dozen AT-ATs and their accompanying landing barges, 50 AT-STs, and a small armada of speeder bikes, landspeeders, and AT-PTs. Three prefabricated garrisons and 38,000 additional ground troops completed the starship's massive army.

Built in secret at the starship yards of Fondor, the *Executor* was designed by Lira Wessex, the famed visionary responsible for the original Imperial Star Destroyers. Upon its completion shortly before the Battle of Hoth, the *Executor* became Darth Vader's personal flagship and the headquarters from which he continued his search for Luke Skywalker and the Rebel Alliance. Although Admiral Ozzel initially commanded the vessel, Vader grew disgusted by the Imperial officer's incompetence and eliminated Ozzel. Admiral Piett immediately assumed control of the starship.

By the Battle of Hoth, the *Executor* and three other Super Star Destroyers were in operation, with several others under construction. The exact number of Super Star Destroyers completed by the Battle of Endor remains unknown, but a handful of these vehicles have since resurfaced under the control of various Imperial Remnant leaders and rogue warlords. The *Executor*, however, did not escape the battle. After a disabled A-wing starfighter crashed through the starship's bridge, the wounded destroyer spun out of control and collided with the second Death Star, exploding upon impact.

> ## "With the *Executor* under my command, *I* will be the ultimate power in the universe!"
> *—Admiral Ozzel, only moments before he is killed by Darth Vader*

5 Meditation Chamber: Darth Vader's personal quarters aboard the *Executor* included a special meditation chamber, from which he reached out with the Force in an attempt to track down Luke Skywalker.

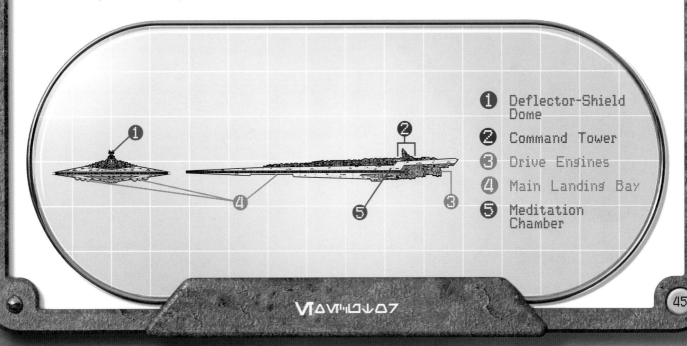

1. Deflector-Shield Dome
2. Command Tower
3. Drive Engines
4. Main Landing Bay
5. Meditation Chamber

FLASH SPEEDER

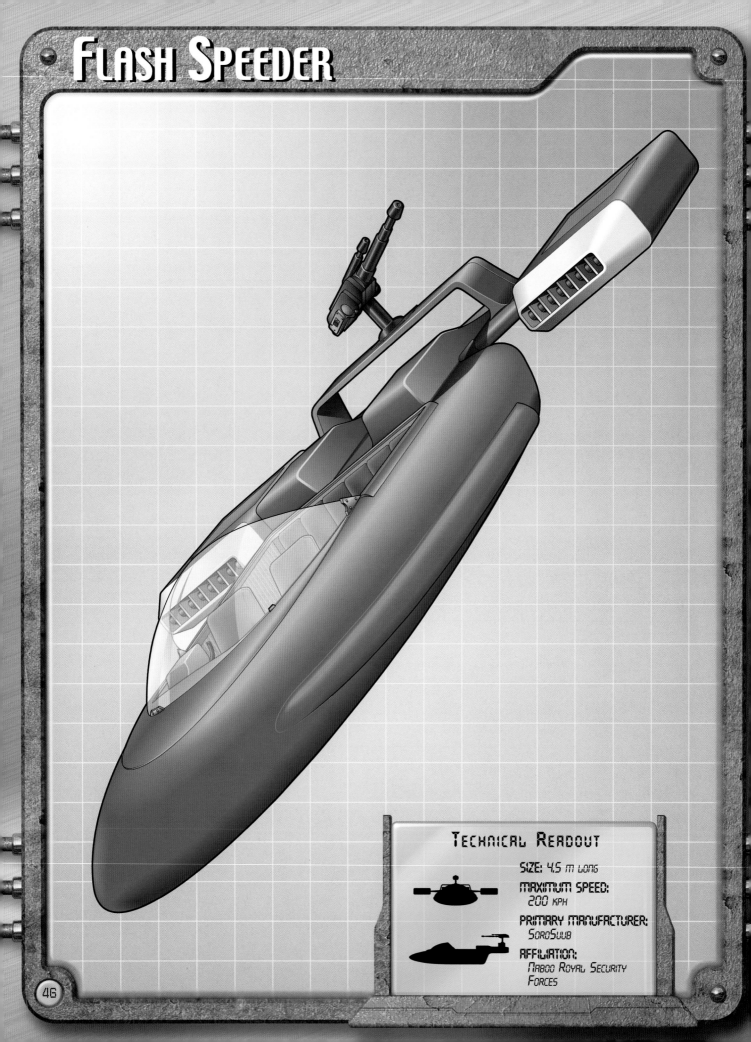

TECHNICAL READOUT

SIZE: 4.5 M LONG

MAXIMUM SPEED:
200 KPH

PRIMARY MANUFACTURER:
SoroSuub

AFFILIATION:
Naboo Royal Security
Forces

Modified SoroSuub *Seraph*-Class Urban Landspeeder

The Naboo Royal Security Forces, a law enforcement branch tasked with protecting Naboo's populace, makes use of several modified vehicles in their mission to keep the peace. Like many small planetary defense groups, the RSF favors landspeeders, which allow rapid response to crisis situations. The Flash speeder, the fastest ground vehicle in the RSF fleet, is a compact and agile landspeeder outfitted for light combat duty.

The Flash speeder was first introduced three decades before the Battle of Naboo, when the RSF's Palace Guard requested a small landspeeder to complement the larger and less maneuverable Gian speeder. After testing numerous designs, the RSF engineers settled on the Seraph, a vehicle well known for its speed and solid handling.

Originally designed as an urban transport for civilian use, the Seraph could easily carry two armed RSF officers to virtually any location in Theed within minutes. Repulsorlift engines provided speeds in excess of 200 kilometers per hour as the vehicle moved over smooth Naboo city streets, although the craft became unstable when traveling over rocky or rough terrain. With minimal effort, the Seraph was equipped with a rotating pursuit and defense blaster for combat encounters.

The Flash speeders were well received when they reached Theed and were soon adopted by Keren and other Naboo cities. The Flash speeder allows authorities in these cities to patrol narrow streets, chase down criminals, and quickly respond to a variety of emergency situations.

Prior to the Battle of Naboo, Flash speeders saw very little combat action. On rare occasions, the vehicles were used to corral gunrunners in the employ of Borvo the Hutt or frighten away dangerous wild animals that had strayed too close to city limits. The Flash speeder's role changed dramatically when the Trade Federation invaded. After the capture of Theed, members of an RSF underground resistance used Flash speeders for reconnaissance and to relay messages between rebel cells spread across the planet.

> **"I always thought the Flash speeders were only good for joyriding. Then the Trade Federation invaded and I found out why we keep these green genies around. I just closed my eyes, and next thing I knew, I was ten kilometers away from Theed."**
>
> *—RSF lieutenant Gavyn Sykes*

Flash speeders also allowed Queen Amidala and Captain Panaka to reach Theed's secret tunnels without arousing suspicion.

Many of the RSF's Flash speeders were destroyed by Trade Federation forces during the Battle of Naboo, but the RSF quickly commissioned an even larger fleet that included more heavily armored versions of the vehicle. Flash speeders continued to be an important component of the RSF motor pool.

During the early days of the Galactic Civil War, several RSF Flash speeders mysteriously disappeared, only to resurface later in the hands of the Rebel Alliance.

6 Streamlined Body: The Naboo favor the Seraph in part because it shares design elements with their own vehicles, which are typically streamlined with gentle curves.

1. Blaster
2. Engine
3. Drive Turbine Air Intake
4. Thrust Pod
5. Power Generator
6. Streamlined Body

Geonosian Starfighter

Technical Readout

SIZE: 9.8 m long

MAXIMUM SPEED:
4500G/20,000 kph

PRIMARY MANUFACTURER:
Huppla Pasa Tisc
Shipwrights Collective

AFFILIATION:
Geonosians

Nantex-Class Territorial Defense Starfighter

As Count Dooku began organizing the Confederacy of Independent Systems, he chose his allies with utmost care. One of Dooku's most loyal supporters was the Geonosian archduke, Poggle the Lesser, whose people produced an endless supply of battle droids for the Confederacy's army. Dozens of battle droid factories sprung up on Geonosis, protected by fierce Geonosian warriors and a fleet of powerful *Nantex*-class starfighters, also known as beak-wings.

Like many Geonosian starships, the Geonosian starfighter's frame is built from strands of pliable laminasteel. During production, the heated laminasteel is wrapped around the ship's components; when the laminasteel hardens, it creates a strong yet flexible aerodynamic frame that can withstand tremendous impact.

Once the starfighter's frame is complete, Geonosian engineers outfit the vehicle with special magnetic sockets holding weapons and engines orbs. The sockets and orbs are completely modular, permitting engineers to modify a starfighter for a specific mission by integrating various additional components, such as engine boosters or advanced sensors.

In standard configuration, a Geonosian fighter has a single laser cannon turret. One hundred small tractor beam projectors arrayed in front of the laser cannon guide laserfire to provide incredible accuracy, especially during short-range firefights.

The Geonosian starfighter is often considered a stealth vehicle because the engine and weapons system produce very little ambient glow, enabling the vehicle to move and attack without giving away its position. The Geonosians rely on this feature when ambushing opponents in the asteroid field that surrounds their homeworld.

The beak-wing's cockpit is uniquely adapted to the Geonosian physiology. The multiple control yokes require innate Geonosian dexterity. In addition, communication between the starship and the pilot is achieved through a scent stimulator located in the pilot's mask, which relies on the Geonosians' uncanny sense of smell to impart vital status updates. Flight controllers can also alter a pilot's objectives remotely by releasing pheromone signals through the mask.

The efficiency of the starfighter is further increased by the Geonosians' rigid caste system, which includes a specific pilot caste. Fighter pilots are actually raised in massive hives, where they are molded from birth to fly headlong into battle. During this training, each developing pup creates a bonds with a specific starfighter's flight computer. This allows the pilot and starfighter to forge a lifelong bond that increases reaction time during combat.

When the Republic invaded their homeworld, the Geonosians scrambled thousands of starfighters to defend their hives. The invaders routed the confederate forces, but the attack only fueled Poggle the Lesser's hatred of the Republic. The Geonosians remained staunchly loyal to Count Dooku's Confederacy, and their starfighters were used in numerous engagements across the galaxy.

> **"The last human who tried to fly one of our ships crashed into the N'rakti Lava Fields. Your pilots would fall out of the sky like damp moths."**
>
> *—Archduke Poggle the Lesser to Count Dooku*

1 Laser Cannon: The laser cannon fires along the neutral space in between the prong shields.

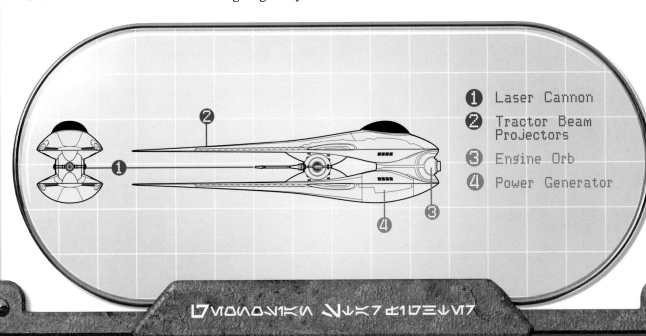

1 Laser Cannon
2 Tractor Beam Projectors
3 Engine Orb
4 Power Generator

GIAN SPEEDER

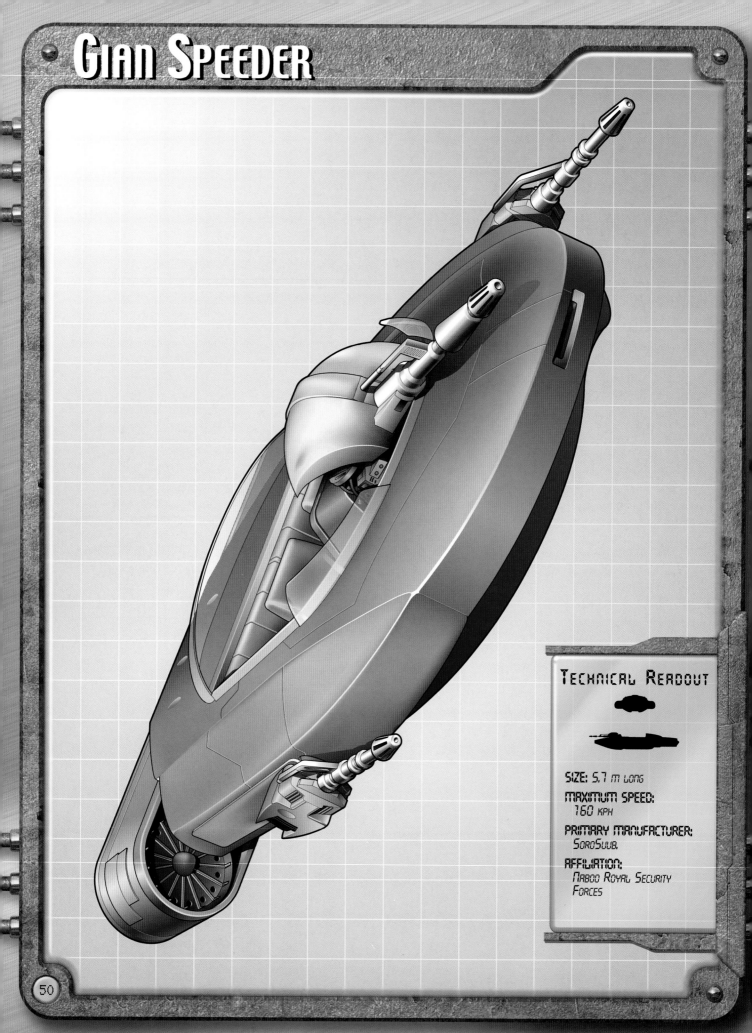

TECHNICAL READOUT

SIZE: 5.7 m LONG

MAXIMUM SPEED:
160 KPH

PRIMARY MANUFACTURER:
SoroSuub.

AFFILIATION:
Naboo Royal Security
Forces

Modified SoroSuub V-19 Landspeeder

Centuries before the Battle of Naboo, the human populace of that verdant planet lived in several fractured kingdoms that were constantly at war with one another. Eventually, the Naboo peoples became disgusted by the heavy losses caused by these endless battles, and united as one nation. They rejected their long history of warfare and became ardent pacifists. As the Naboo reinvented their civilization, they founded the Royal Security Forces to preserve peace and tranquillity on the planet.

In an attempt to prevent future outbreaks of violence, the RSF established a small fleet of military vehicles that would dissuade criminals or other malcontents from causing trouble. Central to this motor pool was a large landspeeder designed for diverse situations to include crowd control, wilderness excursions, and urban battles. Over the decades, the exact make and model of this combat-ready landspeeder have changed, with the Gian speeder representing the most recent version of the craft.

The Gian speeder is a modified SoroSuub V-19 landspeeder. Unlike the Seraph, which forms the basis for the Naboo's Flash speeder, the V-19 was actually designed by SoroSuub to serve as both military and civilian transport. The V-19's medium-grade hull plating and reinforced body have made it popular on congested urban worlds, where collisions are common. The RSF favors the craft because of its narrow silhouette and well-protected thrust pods. The vehicle can also carry up to four armed RSF officers, usually more than enough personnel to quell any disturbance.

> **"Hit them low, hard, and fast. Then get ready to run."**
> —*Captain Panaka, briefing Gian speeder pilots before an attack on Trade Federation AATs*

Once the V-19s reached Naboo, the RSF installed three forward-facing light repeating blasters to the vehicle. Each blaster has its own dedicated auxiliary power unit to ensure that the weapons can continue to operate even if the speeder's primary power generator is damaged. The RSF also upgraded the speeder's underside plating to withstand land mines, explosions, and natural hazards. Command versions of the Gian boast holographic projection systems for tactical planning and additional communications equipment.

At the time of the Battle of Naboo, the RSF had 36 Gian speeders in operation. When the Trade Federation launched its invasion, the RSF quickly readied the speeders, but the vehicles proved unsuited for direct combat with AATs. A handful of RSF officers escaped with intact Gian speeders, which then became part of the Naboo resistance movement. When the RSF sought to reclaim Theed, the remaining Gian speeders were carefully deployed to ambush lone AATs, allowing Queen Amidala and her allies to rush the Theed Palace.

5 Holographic Planning System: Amidala and her allies used a Gian speeder's tactical display to plan the recapture of Theed.

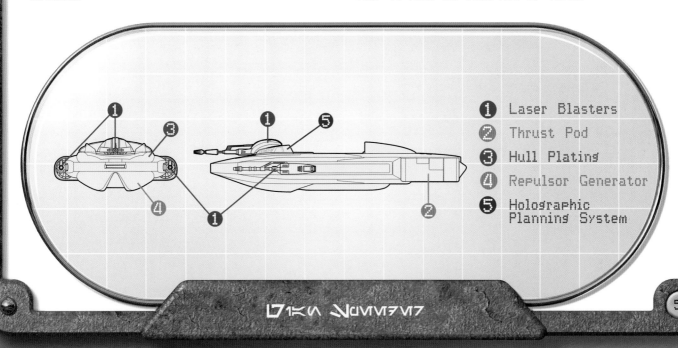

1 Laser Blasters
2 Thrust Pod
3 Hull Plating
4 Repulsor Generator
5 Holographic Planning System

HAILFIRE

TECHNICAL READOUT

SIZE: 8.5 m TALL

MAXIMUM SPEED:
45 KPH

PRIMARY MANUFACTURER:
Haor Chall Engineering

AFFILIATION:
Confederacy of
Independent Systems

InterGalactic Banking Clan *Hailfire*-Class Droid Tank

In many ways, the InterGalactic Banking Clan is similar to a Hutt criminal syndicate. Both organizations are happy to loan you credits, provided you agree to hefty interest rates. And when you default on the loan, both groups will attempt to recoup their perceived losses through acts of violence. In order to collect on bad debts, the Hutts usually rely on bounty hunters. The InterGalactic Banking Clan, in contrast, rolls out heavily armed droid vehicles.

The *Hailfire*-class droid tank is the most powerful of the InterGalactic Banking Clan's armed-response units. Ostensibly built to protect the clan's holdings on outlaw worlds, the tank has been more useful during land foreclosures and battles with rival credit lenders.

The hailfire is technically a large tank with two enormous hoop wheels. The wheels are covered by a high-traction tread most useful on paved streets. The vehicle is very light and mobile, allowing it to function in several other environments, including rocky Geonosis. The magpulse drive units, located low on each wheel, propel the vehicle to predetermined coordinates using a series of preprogrammed routes. Scanners located in the drive units determine whether routes are free of obstacles. During combat, the drive units often pause while reassessing the surroundings, bringing the vehicle to a sudden halt. When the hailfire's drive motors reactivate, the vehicle accelerates to its top speed within seconds. This system makes the hailfire appear erratic, although the droid is always fully aware of its final destination.

The bulk of the hailfire's sensors are packed into a single photoreceptor on the craft's armored body. The photoreceptor includes infrared imaging devices, range finders, and a targeting system. Because the hailfire's targets are usually preprogrammed, the vehicle doesn't need an advanced logic circuit; it merely rolls into battle and blasts anything identified as an enemy unit. This does prevent the tank from prioritizing its targets, but droid controllers can override the hailfire's programming to compensate for this drawback.

The hailfire's weapons system is designed for rapid strikes. Two missile racks mounted on the central unit carry a total of 30 hailfire missiles configured for maximum destruction. Hailfire missiles are short-range guided warheads that cause severe collateral damage when they strike a target. Against mobile units, such as gunships, the hailfire tank typically fires missiles in groups of three or four to ensure that at least one warhead strikes its target. When all 30 missiles have been launched, the hailfire tank must return to a hangar or base to replenish its ordnance.

The hailfire has a single, retractable antipersonnel blaster, but the vehicle generally relies on ground troops for protection during combat. In some cases, an entire squad of super battle droids or three Corporate Alliance tank droids must be assigned to protect a single hailfire. The vehicle is especially vulnerable when retreating to reload.

> ## "We've come to repossess the planet."
> *—InterGalactic Banking Clan commander Horgo Shive*

❺ Armored Command Module: The command pod on the hailfire bears a striking resemblance to the "cockpit" of the droid starfighter because the InterGalactic Banking Clan hired Haor Chall Engineering, creators of the droid starfighter, to design the vehicle.

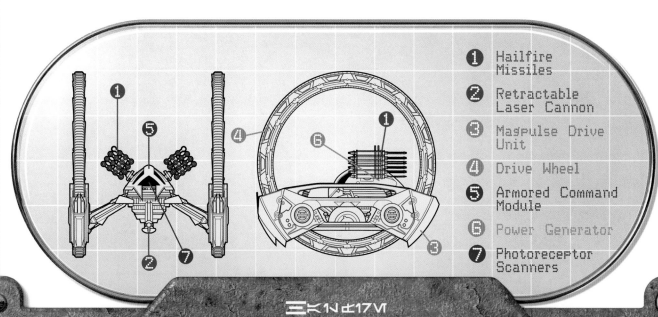

1. Hailfire Missiles
2. Retractable Laser Cannon
3. Magpulse Drive Unit
4. Drive Wheel
5. Armored Command Module
6. Power Generator
7. Photoreceptor Scanners

HAVOC

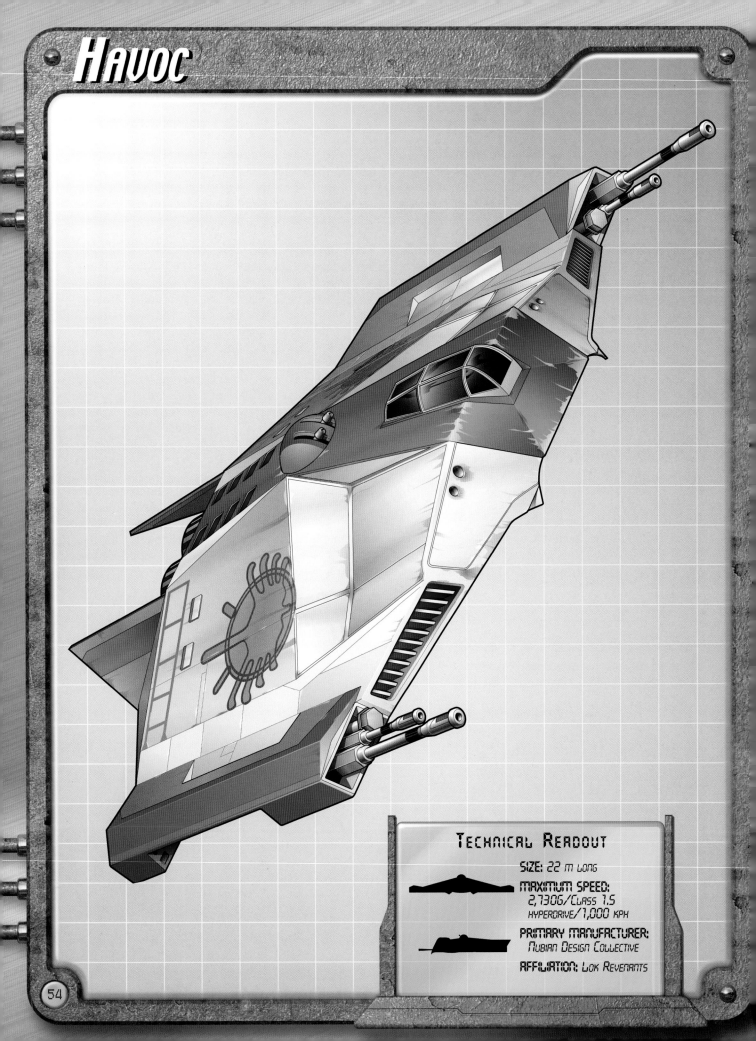

TECHNICAL READOUT

SIZE: 22 m long

MAXIMUM SPEED:
2,730G/CLASS 1.5
HYPERDRIVE/7,000 KPH

PRIMARY MANUFACTURER:
Nubian Design Collective

AFFILIATION: Lok Revenants

Modified Nubian Scurrg H-6 Prototype Bomber

The life of a pirate is exceedingly dangerous, and any self-respecting pirate captain requires a deadly personal starship. The Feeorin pirate Nym, who leads the band of mercenaries known as the Lok Revenants, embodies this philosophy: his *Havoc* bomber is one of the deadliest, and most experimental, starfighters in the galaxy.

The *Havoc* is a one-of-a-kind prototype originally built by the Nubian Design Collective in the hope of selling an entire line of the bombers to the Naboo. However, the peaceful Naboo rejected the excessively armed bomber, then dubbed the "Scurrg H-6." The bomber's chief designer, a Bith named Jinkins, continued to champion the project, but the Nubian Design Collective ultimately abandoned the expensive research, and the prototype was placed into storage.

Frustrated, Jinkins sought out Nym, and the two plotted to steal the bomber. In the years following, Jinkins made numerous modifications to the bomber, and the *Havoc* participated in many important conflicts, including the Battle of Naboo and the Battle of Geonosis.

While the *Havoc*'s speed, armor, shields, and onboard systems are impressive, the vehicle's weapons set her far apart from all other starfighters. Six forward-facing laser cannons, arranged three to a wing, provide the foundation of this arsenal. The cannons on each wing are fire-linked to allow all three to fire at a single target. An extremely powerful rotating laser cannon turret is mounted on top of the bomber. During firefights, the turret can coordinate with the other laser cannons or act independently to cover the starfighter's rear and flanks.

> **"Sometimes, I get the feelin' the *Havoc* is alive. She sometimes fires before I pull the trigger, an' when we're in hyperspace, I swear her engines sing me to sleep."**
>
> *—Nym*

The *Havoc*'s most formidable weapon is her "bomblet generator," a device capable of producing devastating energy bombs. Originally, the *Havoc* carried proton bombs, which were released via two bomb chutes. Nym and Jinkins later installed the highly experimental—and very unstable—bomblet generator to provide a continuous supply of explosives. Each bomb chute can hold up to five bombs, but the bomblet generator draws power from the main generator to replenish the energy bomb supply over time. The bomblet generator is also easily removed, allowing Nym and his crew to mount the device onto another vehicle if necessary.

Shortly before the Battle of Geonosis, Nym and his crew upgraded all of the *Havoc*'s weapons. They added devastating missiles, explosive proximity mines, and ionized cluster missiles that can tear through an enemy's shields.

The *Havoc* was originally intended for a crew of five, including a pilot, a dedicated turret gunner, a secondary gunner, a navigator, and a demolition specialist. To allow Nym to fly the starfighter alone, Jinkins equipped each weapons system with an independent targeting computer. Two astromechs housed inside the starfighter provide additional support.

❶ Pirate Symbol: The logo on Nym's *Havoc* mirrors a tattoo the pirate captain received after winning a violent free-for-all in the Blood Pits of Nar Shaddaa. The formerly meaningless symbol has since become the flag for the Lok Revenants, Nym's resourceful band of mercenaries.

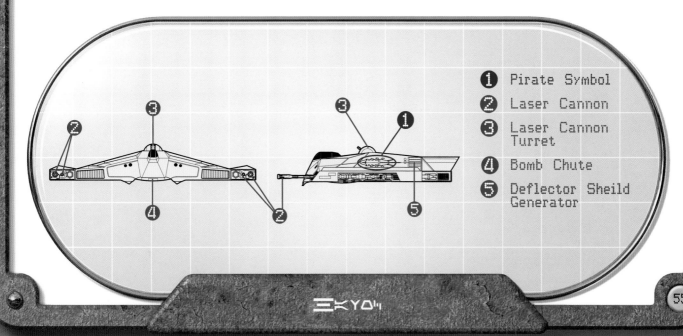

❶ Pirate Symbol
❷ Laser Cannon
❸ Laser Cannon Turret
❹ Bomb Chute
❺ Deflector Sheild Generator

HOUND'S TOOTH

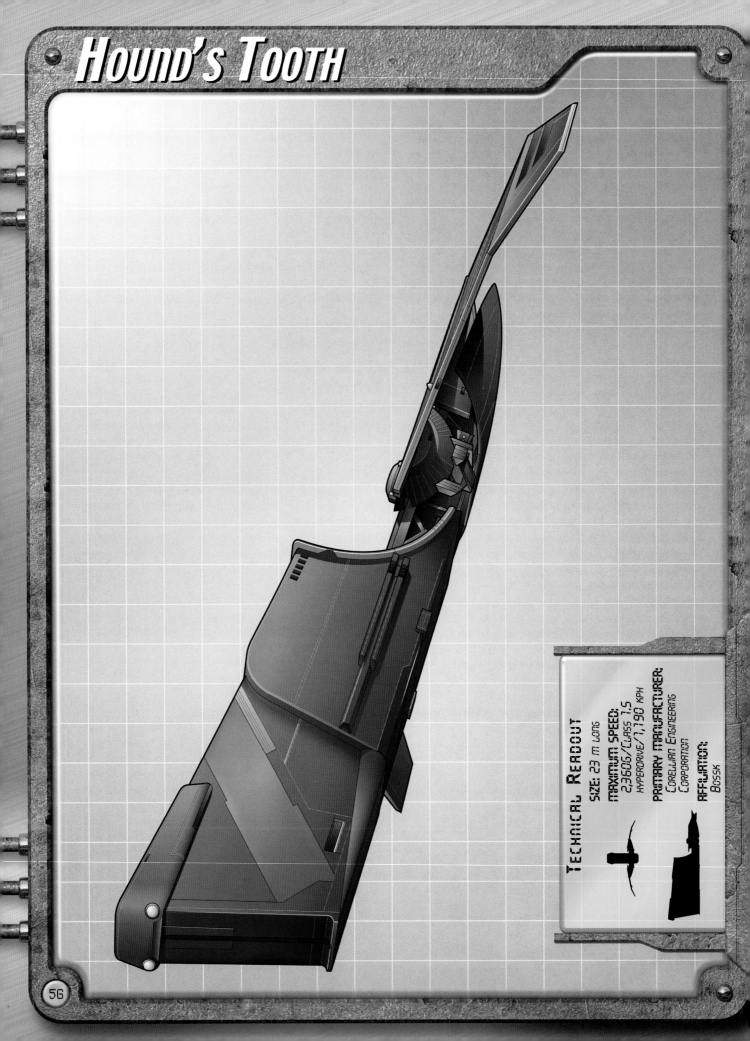

TECHNICAL READOUT

SIZE: 23 m LONG

MAXIMUM SPEED:
2,360G/CLASS 1.5
HYPERDRIVE/1,190 KPH

PRIMARY MANUFACTURER:
CORELLIAN ENGINEERING
CORPORATION

AFFILIATION:
BOSSK

Modified Corellian YV-666 Light Freighter

The *Hound's Tooth* is the personal transport of Bossk, a Trandoshan bounty hunter and slaver who has clashed with Han Solo and Chewbacca on numerous occasions. Like all YV-666 freighters, the *Hound's Tooth* has an elongated body originally meant for cargo transport. Bossk has modified much of the interior for personal use, although the vehicle still maintains a "three-deck" design.

The starship's main deck contains Bossk's private quarters, a training room, an armory, and an advanced medical bay. The aft section has been converted into a prison with several magnetically reinforced holding cages; these cells are connected to a force-field generator activated by motion sensors in the event of a breakout. The prison also sports a skinning table, interrogation devices, and Bossk's trophy collection.

The command deck, which rests atop the main deck, provides access to all systems. The cockpit's monitor bank relays information from concealed sensor screens, allowing Bossk to observe every corner of his vehicle. Other security measures include an interior scanning system that analyzes cargo, as well as motion sensors linked to neural stunners, sub-q injectors, and shock panels. Voice-recognition technology prevents unauthorized use of the vehicle.

The power core, weapons systems, life support, and virtually all other systems are located in the starship's lower deck. A small docking bay holds Bossk's scout ship, the *Nashtah Pup,* which is released via a hatch on top of the craft. The two-person scout ship is strictly a short-range craft with limited life support capabilities.

The *Hound's Tooth*'s propulsion system is simple in design, but provides a great deal of maneuverability despite the starship's size. Thrust is generated by standard ion engines. Long maneuvering fins connected to the engine block allow vertical movement, while two main drive nozzles located between the fins control turning.

The *Hound's Tooth*'s primary weapon is a retractable quad laser cannon that can rip through most starfighters. A secondary ion cannon can be deployed to disable fleeing quarry. Bossk attacks battleships with forward-firing concussion missile launchers, each with a magazine of six missiles. Shields and reinforced armor protect the *Hound's Tooth* during combat.

Because Bossk typically works alone, he has installed an X-10D droid brain aboard the *Hound's Tooth*. The droid brain responds to verbal commands and controls many of the shipboard systems, including security and weapons. Bossk can issue commands to the X-10D brain from virtually anywhere in the ship; direct datalinks are located on the bridge and in Bossk's cabin.

> **"The stench onboard was horrible. Between drying Wookiee pelts, a rotting corpse on the skinning table, and Bossk's own repellent scent, it was worse than a slaughterhouse on a sewage planet."**
> —*Rebel agent Jan Ors*

⑦ Boarding Ramp: The ramp is protected by several voice-controlled security measures, including conventional antipersonnel blasters, an electrocution array, and a durasteel net.

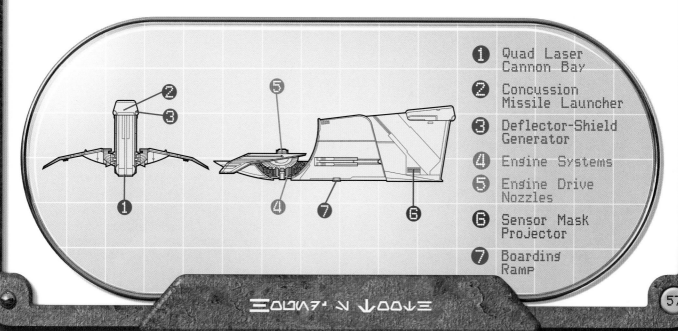

1. Quad Laser Cannon Bay
2. Concussion Missile Launcher
3. Deflector-Shield Generator
4. Engine Systems
5. Engine Drive Nozzles
6. Sensor Mask Projector
7. Boarding Ramp

HOWLRUNNER

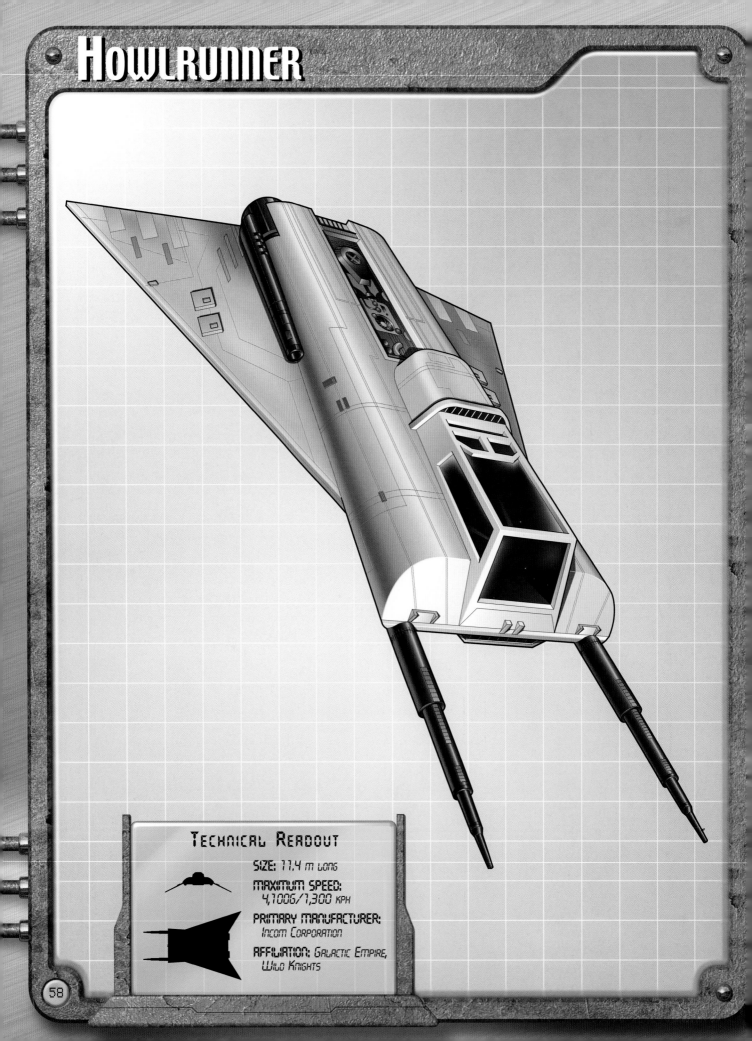

TECHNICAL READOUT

SIZE: 11.4 m LONG

MAXIMUM SPEED:
4,100G/1,300 KPH

PRIMARY MANUFACTURER:
Incom Corporation

AFFILIATION: Galactic Empire,
Wild Knights

Incom Corporation I-7 "Howlrunner"

The Howlrunner is a short-range, all-purpose attack starfighter first used by one of the dominant Imperial factions during the Imperial Civil War. Howlrunners remained part of the Imperial fleet after the return of Emperor Palpatine, and later became one of several starfighters used by Jedi Saba Sebatyne's Wild Knights.

The I-7 was designed by engineer Jo Ewsli, who was inspired by the hunting tactics of howlrunners, dangerous omnivores native to Kamar. The predatory howlrunners attack in packs and relentlessly pursue their prey, both traits that Ewsli believed could be adopted by a starfighter squadron. Thus, the engineer created the I-7 "Howlrunner"—which, like its namesake, is fast, agile, and well suited to blitz-style attacks.

The Howlrunner is built around a streamlined fixed-wing design. Two stabilizer fins with rudimentary maneuvering flaps sprout from the body of the craft. Despite its basic design, the Howlrunner is well adapted for both atmospheric and space flight. The rudimentary piloting system ensures that nearly anyone can fly the craft, although only truly experienced pilots can push the Howlrunner to its limits. The Howlrunner is faster than older X-wing and Y-wing starfighters, but can't match the top speed of more advanced craft, such as the E-wing and TIE interceptor.

I-7 starfighters have one distinct advantage over TIE fighters and other Imperial short-range fighters: a dedicated shield generator. The shield generator, along with

> **"As I sat watching the howl-runners, the walls of the safari dome seemed to melt away. For a brief moment, I was part of the pack, hunting and howling with these magnificent predators. I have spent the rest of my life trying to recapture that feeling, from the cockpit of a starfighter."**
>
> —*Excerpt from* THE ANTHROPOLOGY OF ENGINEERING *by Jo Ewsli*

the I-7's lean profile and low mass, make the Howlrunner difficult to destroy. Still, the Howlrunner is not designed for prolonged battles or one-on-one combat. Its weapon system consists of two very accurate but fairly weak fire-linked laser cannons and a low-end targeting system. Ewsli also ensured that the I-7 is inexpensive to manufacture, allowing the Empire to assemble large Howlrunner squadrons. As with TIE fighter attacks, the Empire deploys Howlrunners in huge numbers to overwhelm opponents. Smaller groups can be used for hit-and-run ambush attacks.

The I-7 was the first starfighter built after Incom was nationalized by the Empire. It was a very real attempt by the corporation to overshadow the X-wing, designed by ex-Incom engineers. Although considered only an "average" fighter, the Howlrunner soon became a common sight at many Imperial planetary bases, where its speed allowed for rapid reconnaissance and emergency response. While the Empire's TIE fighter squadrons were decimated during the Galactic Civil War, many Howlrunners escaped destruction and later rose to prominence as a key component of the Imperial Remnant's fleet. The Howlrunner continues to be favored by many Imperial pilots stationed along the fringes of the galaxy.

3 Power Generator: The Howlrunner's exposed power generator makes a good target for accurate starfighter aces.

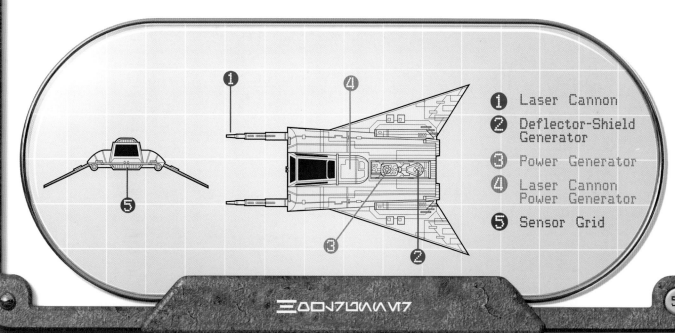

1 Laser Cannon
2 Deflector-Shield Generator
3 Power Generator
4 Laser Cannon Power Generator
5 Sensor Grid

IG-2000

TECHNICAL READOUT

SIZE: 20 m LONG

MAXIMUM SPEED:
2,500G/CLASS 2
HYPERDRIVE/7,200 KPH

PRIMARY MANUFACTURER:
TRILON, INC

AFFILIATION: IG-88

Modified Trilon, Inc., Aggressor Assault Fighter

A heavily modified assault starfighter used by the maniacal IG-88, *IG-2000* enabled the ruthless assassin droid to pursue his quarry to the ends of the galaxy. Designed for intense combat, *IG-2000* secured IG-88's reputation as one the most relentless bounty hunters in the galaxy.

IG-2000 helped IG-88 chase down nearly any prey and outmaneuver even the most brilliant pilots. The starship's sublight speed was provided by a Kuat Galaxy-15 ion engine, which IG-88 stole from a decommissioned Nebulon-B escort frigate. Energy from three converted Quadex power cores was fed directly into the engine, while eight bleed-off vents on the engine cowling prevented overloads.

Once IG-88 had a victim cornered, he began a terrifying assault with *IG-2000*'s two fire-linked laser cannons. This initial attack would be followed by blasts from a long-range ion cannon mounted below the cockpit. Both weapons were bolstered by an advanced targeting computer programmed by IG-88 himself. The assassin droid could also interface directly with all weapons systems, further enhancing the starship's accuracy.

After disabling his prey, IG-88 employed a pair of tractor beams to collect the helpless starship, pulling it toward *IG-2000*'s air lock. Four assault drones housed in the air lock would cut through the captured starship's hull, wipe out any opposition, and scout the vessel before IG-88 boarded to collect his prize.

IG-88's victims would be transported to a small prisoner hold located on *IG-2000*'s middle deck. The prisoner hold could secure up to eight captives and was the only part of the starship with life support systems. It also contained a simple medbay operated by an outdated FX-7 medical assistant droid, as well as an oft-used interrogation room. A single stasis tube could sustain a critically injured victim until IG-88 collected his bounty.

Aside from the small prisoner hold, the starship's interior was dominated by the massive engine systems, a powerful shield generator, and other key components. A cockpit situated between the forward mandibles contained IG-88's pilot's station, which provided direct datalinks to the ship's onboard computers. The cockpit also held a weapons locker and a small maintenance area.

Despite *IG-2000*'s amazing abilities, the starship was eventually destroyed by Boba Fett. While battling IG-88 above Tatooine, Fett captured *IG-2000* in *Slave I*'s tractor beams, then decimated the vehicle and its pilot with a barrage of concussion missiles. Because IG-88 could transfer his programming and memory between computers, however, it is quite possible that he could resurface, perhaps piloting a new and even more deadly version of *IG-2000*.

> **"You want me to describe the inside of *IG-2000*? It's cold and metal and a little bit evil. Just like its pilot."**
> —*Dash Rendar*

4 Magnetic Locking Pads: The magnetic locking pads allow IG-88 to capture prey between the *IG-2000*'s menacing mandibles.

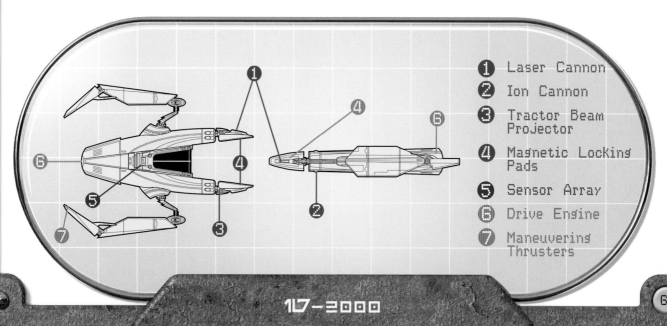

1. Laser Cannon
2. Ion Cannon
3. Tractor Beam Projector
4. Magnetic Locking Pads
5. Sensor Array
6. Drive Engine
7. Maneuvering Thrusters

Imperial Landing Craft

Technical Readout

Size: 20 m long

Maximum Speed:
2,400G/Class 1
Hyperdrive/1,000 kph

Primary Manufacturer:
Sienar Fleet Systems

Affiliation: Galactic Empire

Sienar Fleet Systems/Cygnus Spaceworks *Sentinel*–Class Landing Craft

The *Sentinel*-class landing shuttle is one of many transport vessels used by the Empire to convey troops into battle. Introduced shortly before the Battle of Yavin, the Sentinel remains one of the most pervasive landing craft in the Imperial fleet and is most often used to carry stormtroopers between Star Destroyers and planetside conflicts. The *Sentinel*-class starship also makes an excellent atmospheric transport; many Imperial garrisons, including those on Tatooine, utilize at least one of these vehicles.

In its standard configuration, the *Sentinel*-class shuttle carries 54 armed stormtroopers, 12 E-Web repeating blasters, and 6 speeder bikes. At least one of these speeder bikes is reserved for reconnaissance duty and is equipped with a slave communications terminal. Because the shuttle's seats are easily removed and installed, many other configurations are also possible. If all seats are removed, the shuttle can be used to transport 36 speeder bikes, 12 compact assault vehicles, or 180 metric tons of cargo.

In order to clear landing zones, the Imperial landing craft uses eight retractable laser cannons, two concussion missile launchers, a retractable ion cannon turret, and two rotating repeating blasters. Three gunners are responsible for operating these weapons, all of which are linked to the shuttle's precise targeting computers. Because it is so heavily armed, the Sentinel often serves as a combat support vehicle during battles.

The *Sentinel*-class transport is built around a folding tri-wing design popularized by the *Lambda*-class shuttle. The landing craft's exterior, however, is encased in armor plating 25 percent heavier than the armor

"Look, sir! Droids!"
—Imperial stormtrooper Davin Felth, after disembarking from an Imperial landing craft during the search for the Death Star plans

aboard the Lambda. The vehicle carries four deflector shield projectors. Despite the Sentinel's size and weight, it is surprisingly fast and agile due to a Cygnus HD7 engine array.

The Sentinel's cockpit supports a pilot and sensor officer, along with the three dedicated gunners. The ship's sensor suite, allowing navigation in almost all conditions, includes infrared imaging, motion detectors, and life-form indicators. The onboard computer has an automatic mapping function and a rudimentary autopilot that can fly the starship toward an Imperial garrison or homing beacon during emergencies. The shuttle's extremely powerful communications array allows contact with all Imperial vessels and units within a given system.

The Empire had often used the Sentinels in conjunction with the much larger Theta-class AT-AT barges for combined infantry/armor assaults. In response, the New Republic developed its own Bantha-class assault shuttle, which carried significantly more armor than the Imperial craft.

After the fall of the Empire, Sienar and Cygnus continued to produce the *Sentinel*-class shuttle despite the loss of its primary buyer. Because of their adaptability and strength in combat, these shuttles are still in heavy use throughout the galaxy by mercenary groups, Imperial Remnant forces, and the New Republic.

⑦ Folding Wings: The Imperial landing craft's folding-wing design is a hallmark of Sienar Fleet Systems shuttles.

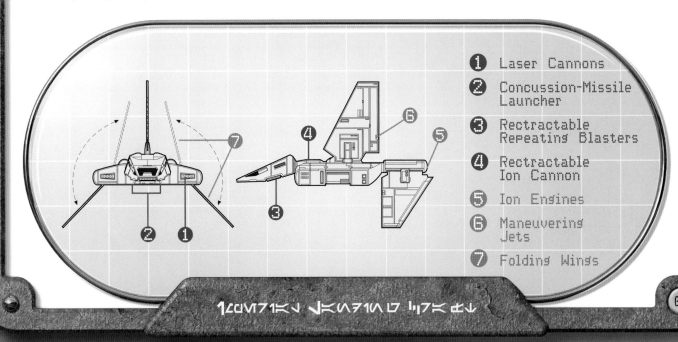

① Laser Cannons
② Concussion-Missile Launcher
③ Rectractable Repeating Blasters
④ Rectractable Ion Cannon
⑤ Ion Engines
⑥ Maneuvering Jets
⑦ Folding Wings

IMPERIAL SHUTTLE *(TYDIRIUM)*

TECHNICAL READOUT

SIZE: 20 M LONG

MAXIMUM SPEED:
1,400G/CLASS 1
HYPERDRIVE/850 KPH

PRIMARY MANUFACTURER:
SIENAR FLEET SYSTEMS

AFFILIATION: GALACTIC EMPIRE

Sienar Fleet Systems *Lambda*–Class Shuttle

Sienar Fleet Systems has always endeavored to remain on the cutting edge of starship design. One example of this philosophy is the *Lambda*-class shuttle, more often known as simply the "Imperial shuttle" because of its nearly exclusive use by the Galactic Empire. The Lambda has a tri-wing design with a central, stationary wing flanked by two folding wings. When in flight, the starship's wing configuration resembles an inverted Y; when landing, the lower wings fold upward.

The *Lambda*-class shuttle is both a cargo and passenger transport. It can carry up to 20 troops or 80 tons of cargo. The vehicle supports a crew of six: a pilot, copilot, navigator, gunner, communications officer, and engineer responsible for power distribution. The ship can be piloted by a single officer in an emergency.

The Lambda's primary mission profile involves transporting key Imperial personnel or cargo to virtually any location in the galaxy. The shuttle is equipped with a Class One hyperdrive for travel between systems. In the event of an attack, the starship can defend itself with two double laser cannons and two double blaster cannons. A third, retractable rear-mounted double blaster cannon is deployed to dissuade pursuing craft. The Lambda is encased in one of the Imperial fleet's most formidable deflector shields, powered by multiple generators. In the event the shields fail, the shuttle is still protected by a heavily reinforced hull. The Lambda shuttle is so well armed that it is quite capable of traversing the galaxy without an official escort, making it ideal for covert missions.

Because of its competency, the Lambda shuttle is favored by Imperial officers and was even used by the Emperor. High-ranking officers often convert the cargo space into lavish personal quarters. For key personnel such as Darth Vader, the Empire commissioned special shuttles with secure HoloNet transceivers directly linked to Imperial City on Coruscant. New Republic forces suspect that the Emperor's personal shuttle was equipped with experimental technology, such as a cloaking device.

The *Lambda*-class shuttle was first manufactured by Sienar Fleet Systems, which later subcontracted Cygnus Spaceworks to produce variations on the basic design. Among these new models is a military-grade shuttle with ten laser cannons. Since the fall of the Empire, Cygnus has continued to manufacture a version of the shuttle nearly identical to the original *Lambda*-class transport.

Although important to the Imperial war effort, the Lambda is probably best known for its unlikely role in aiding the Rebel Alliance. Shortly before the death of the Emperor, Han Solo's strike team used a stolen *Lambda*-class shuttle called the *Tydirium* to sneak past the Imperial blockade surrounding the forest moon of of Endor.

> **"I don't think the Empire had Wookiees in mind when they designed her, Chewie."**
> —*Han Solo*

⑤ Transponder: An Imperial shuttle's transponder sends coded messages to nearby Star Destroyers in order to prove the vehicle's authenticity. The Rebels' stolen shuttle transmitted an outdated code to an Imperial blockade around Endor; after a tense few moments, the Imperial controllers accepted the code and allowed the *Tydirium* to pass.

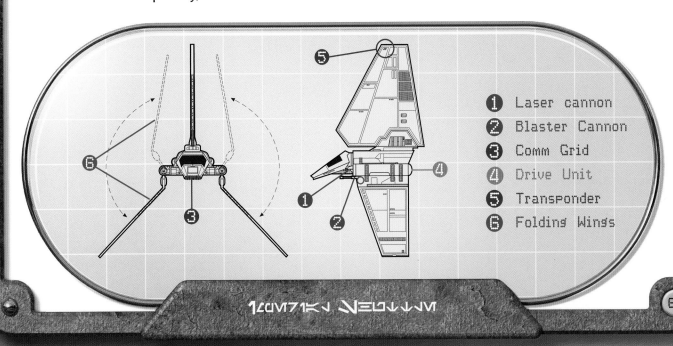

1. Laser cannon
2. Blaster Cannon
3. Comm Grid
4. Drive Unit
5. Transponder
6. Folding Wings

INFERNO

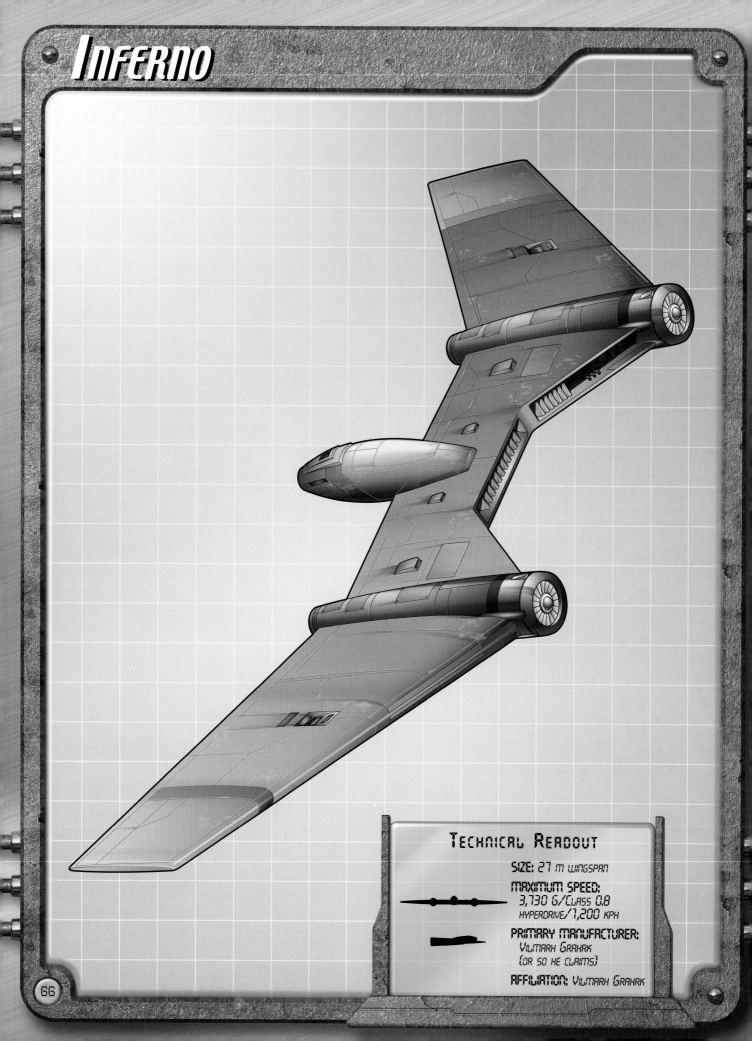

TECHNICAL READOUT

SIZE: 27 M WINGSPAN

MAXIMUM SPEED:
3,730 G/CLASS 0.8
HYPERDRIVE/1,200 KPH

PRIMARY MANUFACTURER:
VILMARH GRAHRK
(OR SO HE CLAIMS)

AFFILIATION: VILMARH GRAHRK

Custom-Built "Villie Special" Big Wing

It is a common belief among starship engineers that these vehicles, with their complex logic circuits and onboard computers, often develop personalities of their own. Such is definitely the case with the *Inferno*, a scout starship owned by Devaronian smuggler and mercenary Vilmarh "Villie" Grahrk.

The *Inferno* is a fairly large vessel resembling a massive, rust-colored gackle bat. A narrow cockpit, positioned high and toward the rear of the craft, overlooks a pair of long wings, each graced by a slender ion engine. When the *Inferno* takes flight, she casts a long shadow, but the craft's narrow frame makes her very difficult to target from the front or rear.

Because the vessel is meant for smuggling, Villie prefers to keep a low profile. Three laser cannons are concealed in each wing, and a small, short-range ion cannon remains hidden in the *Inferno*'s belly. The ship's weapons are hardly remarkable. Villie must rely on the vehicle's speed, maneuverability, and powerful deflector shields to flee enemy starfighters.

Despite her ominous name, the *Inferno*'s personality is largely defined by a pleasant NT 600 astronavigation droid. The droid, which Ville cleverly named "NT," is hardwired directly into the *Inferno*'s systems to provide constant assistance and serve as a copilot during flights. NT remotely controls a small probe droid, which cruises through the *Inferno* to inspect the ship, scan any passengers or cargo, and keep an eye on Villie. The probe droid can leave the *Inferno* as well, ensuring that NT's voice is never far from Villie's pointed ears.

> **"The bet I made on you dying—I bet the ship. You didn't die. If you had just died I not be in this mess!"**
> —*Villie Grahrk, explaining to Quinlan Vos why he had temporarily lost ownership of the* INFERNO

Because NT is programmed with a detailed ethics circuit, the droid also serves as the perfect counterpart to the immoral Devaronian. In fact, NT is often the voice of Villie's conscience. NT's moral code is so strong that the droid's programming forced it to rescue Grahrk on several occasions. Despite the droid's loyalty, Villie remains frustrated by NT's annoying morality and has spent several years searching for the computer's ethic circuits.

The *Inferno*'s other equipment includes a full-color holoprojector that can receive messages from across the galaxy. A precise tractor beam allows the smuggler to capture small cargo modules, starship components, and other stellar debris. The *Inferno* also has an escape pod and other emergency devices.

Villie, NT, and the *Inferno* have undertaken numerous missions together. They once aided Jedi Master Quinlan Vos in a quest to recover his memories, and escorted Princess Foolookoola to Dur Sabon. Although Villie remains deceitful and murderous, he has often managed to become a hero despite himself.

5 Hyperdrive Generator: The *Inferno*'s hyperdrive unit, considered state-of-the-art before the Battle of Naboo, has never truly recovered from a run-in with a trio of pit droids, so Villie must constantly repair the device.

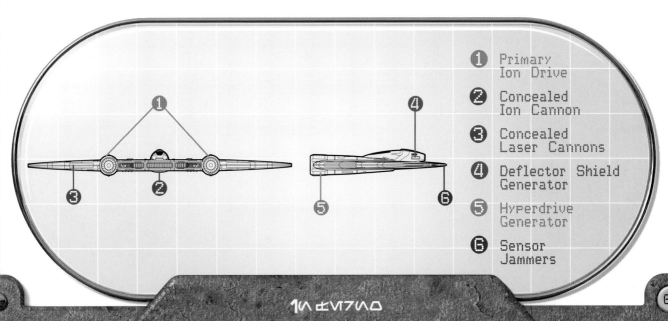

1 Primary Ion Drive

2 Concealed Ion Cannon

3 Concealed Laser Cannons

4 Deflector Shield Generator

5 Hyperdrive Generator

6 Sensor Jammers

INTERDICTOR CRUISER

Sienar Fleet Systems Immobilizer 418

During large space engagements, escape into hyperspace is often the last recourse for wounded starships. However, the Empire removed this tactic from the Rebel Alliance protocols by creating the formidable Interdictor cruiser. The Interdictor has four gravity-well projectors that can mimic a mass in space, thereby interrupting hyperspace travel. Nearby vessels are automatically prevented from engaging hyperdrive engines, and any starships passing through the area via hyperspace are suddenly forced into realspace.

Sienar Fleet Systems manufactured the first Interdictor cruisers two years before the Battle of Yavin, but the costly starships were produced in very limited quantities prior to the Battle of Hoth. Because the starships were rare, Imperial tacticians deployed them carefully, most often positioning the valuable cruisers along the perimeter of battles to keep Rebel starships from escaping. The cruisers could also be used to blockade planets or moons, such as Yavin 4. Alliance pilots quickly realized that the Interdictor's gravity-well projectors required more than 60 seconds to recharge, providing a small escape window, though this was rarely enough time for an entire fleet to make the jump into hyperspace.

When pressed, Rebel forces tried attacking Interdictors directly, only to be met by a devastating assault from the cruiser's 20 quad laser cannons. The all-purpose hull, which is nearly identical to that of the *Vindicator*-class heavy cruiser, can support a number of additional weapons depending upon mission profile. Enemy fire is absorbed by more than a dozen shield generators.

Producing a fleet of Interdictor cruisers proved a time-consuming and delicate project. By the Battle of Endor, Sienar had manufactured only a handful of the starships, most of which were under the command of Grand Admiral Thrawn in the Outer Rim. The vessels did not realize their full potential until several years after the Emperor's death, when the Interdictors became a key component in Thrawn's personal bid for power. Thrawn deployed the Interdictors to ambush New Republic forces. He also used an Interdictor, in conjunction with the Star Destroyer *Chimaera*, in an attempt to capture Luke Skywalker. After the Interdictor cornered Luke, the *Chimaera* trapped Skywalker's X-wing in its tractor beams. The Jedi reversed the X-wing's acceleration compensators and simultaneously fired a pair of proton torpedoes, creating a momentary distraction. When the *Chimaera*'s tractor beams focused on the incoming torpedoes, Luke made a quick microjump into hyperspace, eluding both battleships.

After Thrawn's defeat, the New Republic confiscated the remaining Interdictors. New Republic technicians redesigned the starship's gravity-well projectors, improving their range and recharge rate. These new Interdictors, designated "Immobilizer 418A," became one of the New Republic's secret weapons in the war against the Yuuzhan Vong. The New Republic also provided four Interdictor cruisers to the Hapan battle fleet for use at the Battle of Fondor.

> **"Never again will the Rebels leave you behind, looking flat-footed and foolish. The Immobilizer will see to that."**
> —*Unnamed Sienar official*

1 Gravity-Well Projector: The single most important system on the Interdictor cruiser, gravity-well projectors prevent nearby ships from escaping into hyperspace.

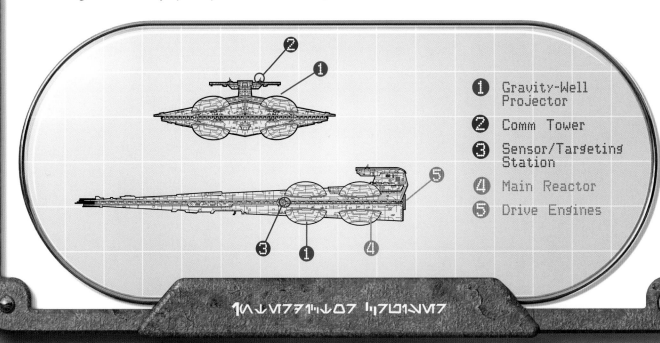

1 Gravity-Well Projector
2 Comm Tower
3 Sensor/Targeting Station
4 Main Reactor
5 Drive Engines

Jabba's Sail Barge *(Khetanna)*

Technical Readout

Size: 30 m long

Maximum Speed: 100 KPH

Primary Manufacturer: Ubrikkian

Affiliation: Jabba the Hutt

Ubrikkian Luxury Sail Barge

In many parts of the galaxy, simply owning a vehicle is a status symbol. However, major manufacturers produce a number of specialized luxury craft for the wealthiest individuals. Luxury starships, airspeeders, and even landspeeders are all available for those with enough credits. Among the most popular luxury vehicles are sail barges—repulsorlift vehicles well suited to long pleasure cruises on temperate worlds. The wealthy Hutts, in particular, favor sail barges.

Like many luxury craft, no two sail barges are exactly alike. Most utilize three-chambered repulsorlift engines to cruise over a planet's surface at about 100 kilometers per hour. The term *sail barge* is derived from the fact that many of these luxury liners utilize huge, retractable sails capable of catching the wind for more leisurely trips. Civilian sail barges generally lack armor and weapons.

Jabba the Hutt's sail barge, the *Khetanna*, was used for lavish parties and tours of Tatooine's desert. The pleasure cruises often culminated with executions of Jabba's enemies, who were unceremoniously pushed into the voracious Sarlacc. The sail barge hosted dozens of guests, along with Jabba's court of servants, slaves, and sycophants.

The *Khetanna* was divided into three decks. The topmost main deck was reserved for Jabba's crew and contained all of the vehicle's control systems. A large, heavy blaster cannon and numerous antipersonnel blasters were mounted on the main deck for confrontations with Tusken Raiders. An advanced sensor suite allowed Jabba and his crew to avoid Imperial entanglements.

> **"A Hutt without a sail barge is like a smoke moth without wings."**
> —*Translated from the Huttese*

Sail barges are meant to provide temporary living quarters for extended trips, and the passenger deck on Jabba's sail barge held a huge banquet room, fully stocked kitchen, and private quarters for the obese crimelord. To impress his guests, Jabba decorated the passenger deck with expensive tapestries, sculptures, and other trappings of wealth. Retractable viewports provided sweeping desert vistas.

The sail barge's lower deck consisted of engines, redundant steering systems, and holding cells for prisoners. A droid storage closet, small machine shop, and holding tanks for Jabba's live food filled out the rest of the lower deck.

Jabba planned his most extravagant party for the executions of Han Solo and his allies. Fortunately, Luke Skywalker had concocted an elaborate plan to topple the crimelord. As Luke dealt with Jabba's cronies, Princess Leia rigged the barge's mounted laser cannon to fire directly into the deck. The resulting chain reaction consumed the *Khetanna* and most of the criminals aboard.

1 Main Deck Mounted Blaster Cannon: Princess Leia used Jabba the Hutt's own laser cannon to destroy the criminal's sail barge in order to facilitate the rebels' escape.

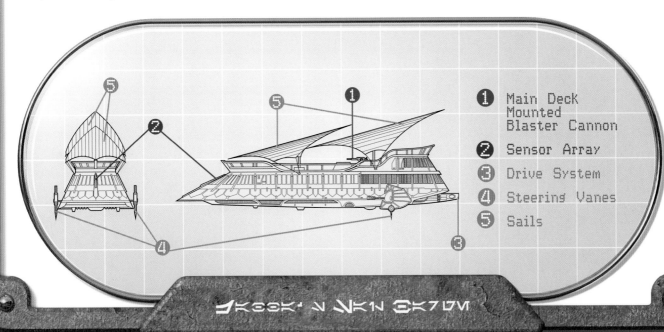

1. Main Deck Mounted Blaster Cannon
2. Sensor Array
3. Drive System
4. Steering Vanes
5. Sails

JABITHA

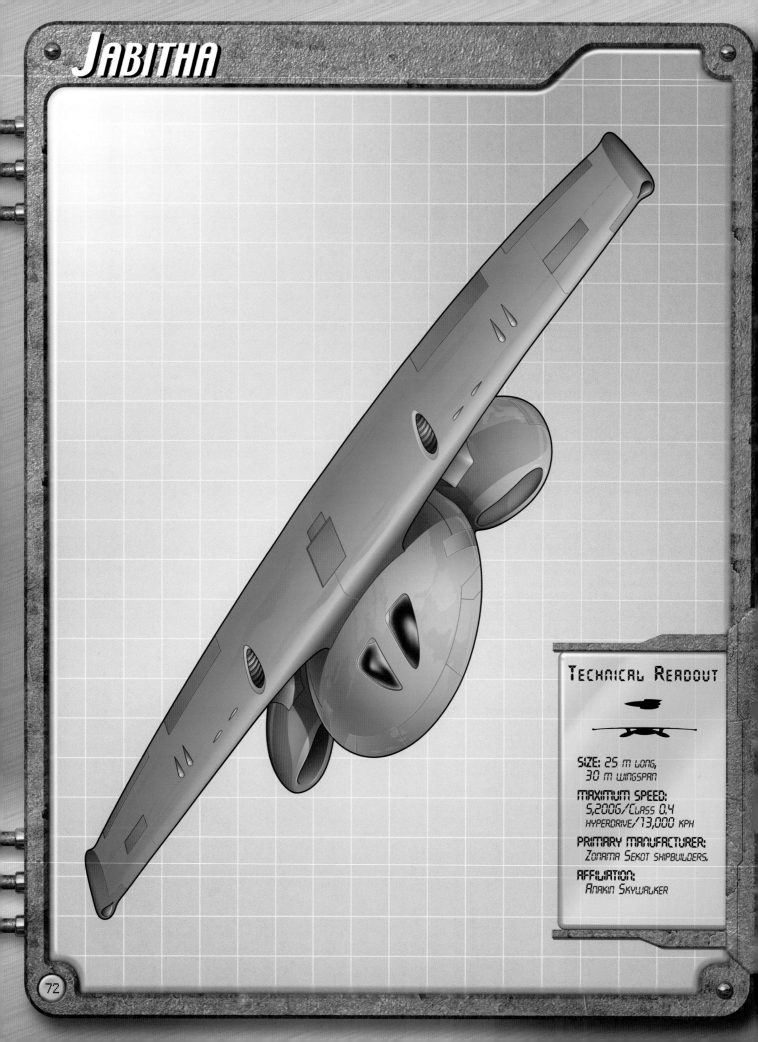

TECHNICAL READOUT

SIZE: 25 m long,
30 m wingspan

MAXIMUM SPEED:
5,200G/Class 0.4
hyperdrive/13,000 kph

PRIMARY MANUFACTURER:
Zonama Sekot shipbuilders.

AFFILIATION:
Anakin Skywalker

Handcrafted Sekotan Personal Starship

Three years after the Battle of Naboo, Obi-Wan Kenobi and his young Padawan, Anakin Skywalker, traveled to the mysterious world of Zonama Sekot, rumored to be home to the fastest starships in the galaxy. The two Jedi discovered that not only were Sekotan craft extremely fast, but they were also wondrous and beautiful *living* vehicles. The Sekotans presented the two Jedi with one of these starships, which Anakin named the *Jabitha* in honor of the Sekotan Magister's daughter.

As with all Sekotan ships, the *Jabitha*'s life began when Anakin and Obi-Wan were ushered into a large chamber for a special ceremony. The chamber was filled with thousands of tiny spikeballs, thorny spheroids with some degree of consciousness. These spikeballs, known as "seed-partners," quickly buried Obi-Wan and Anakin. When they recovered, Obi-Wan and Anakin learned that 15 of the seed-partners had "chosen" the Jedi, agreeing to become part of their new vessel.

Days later, Anakin and Obi-Wan were placed inside a handcrafted starship frame, as the *Jabitha* was literally built around them. The final result was an ingenious combination of their seed-partners, precious organoform circuits, and mechanical components purchased from standard manufacturers.

Because of the sheer number of seed-partners involved in the *Jabitha*'s creation, she was one of the most remarkable Sekotan ships ever produced. The hull consisted of three lobes fused together beneath a green, faintly glowing skin. Into this frame, the Sekotan shipbuilders incorporated two modified Haor Chall *Silver*-class light starship engines, fuel tanks, and a hyperdrive system. The vehicle also contained a typical shield array, but had no weapons.

Inside, the starship lived and breathed with a vibrant display of pulsing red, green, and blue lights. The unmarked controls were arranged in a standard configuration, and Anakin had little trouble intuiting how to pilot the ship. He was aided by the *Jabitha*, too: thanks to his strong bond with the seed-partners, Anakin could communicate with the starship telepathically.

Shortly after the *Jabitha*'s birth, Zonama Sekot fell under attack by Republic commander Tarkin. The *Jabitha* was badly damaged in the battle, which ended when the living world of Zonama Sekot unveiled its own massive hyperdrive system and escaped into hyperspace. Anakin piloted the *Jabitha* to the outpost world of Seline, but the wounded ship would not survive for long. Far from her nurturing homeworld, the *Jabitha* quietly died.

> **"You're not the brain, young owner, not in literal truth. The ship does think for herself, after a fashion, but she needs you while she's still young, and while she's being finished, or she gets, let's say, confused. Like a baby. You're her guardians now."**
> —*Zonama Sekot shipbuilder Fitch, to Anakin Skywalker*

7 Hyperdrive: Although the *Jabitha*'s HCE hyperdrive generator is technically a Class 1 device, the starship's unusual nature and her connection to Anakin allowed the vehicle to achieve a Class 0.4 speed far beyond her engine systems' standard capabilities.

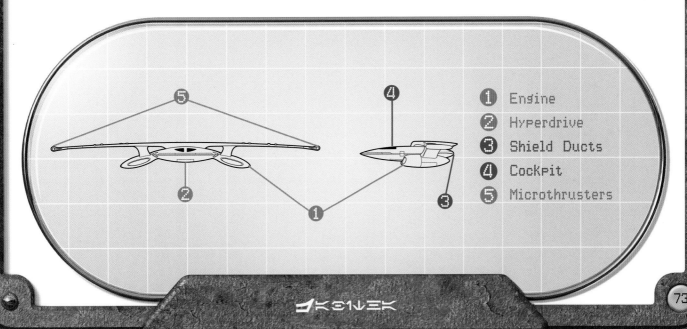

1 Engine
2 Hyperdrive
3 Shield Ducts
4 Cockpit
5 Microthrusters

JADE SHADOW

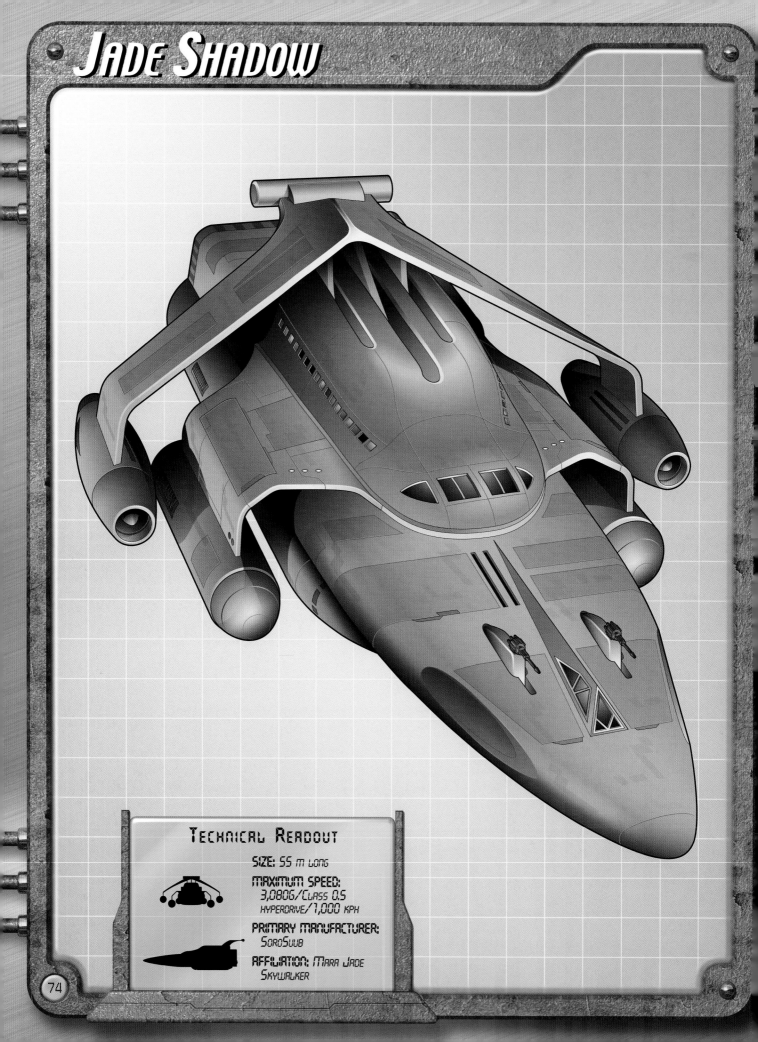

TECHNICAL READOUT

SIZE: 55 m long

MAXIMUM SPEED:
3,080G/Class 0.5
HYPERDRIVE/7,000 KPH

PRIMARY MANUFACTURER:
SoroSuub

AFFILIATION: Mara Jade
Skywalker

Modified SoroSuub *Horizon*-Class Star Yacht

The *Jade Shadow* is the most recent starship owned by New Republic hero Mara Jade, the wife of Luke Skywalker. Mara's previous vessel, the *Jade Sabre*, was destroyed during the Yuuzhan Vong invasion of Dantooine. Soon after, she received a generic star yacht from Lando Calrissian, who had purchased the vehicle from spice merchants. Lando's wife, Tendra, dubbed the yacht the *Jade Shadow* because of its nonreflective gray hull.

Like many star yachts, the *Jade Shadow* is built around a sturdy frame that begins fairly wide at the engines and tapers forward until reaching the narrow, triangular cockpit. Mara Jade's allies have combined forces to transform the utilitarian vessel into a powerful tool in the New Republic's war against the Yuuzhan Vong.

Lando and Talon Karrde took responsibility for the starship's weapons systems by installing retractable AG-1G laser cannons. The laser cannons are mounted on small turrets with a wide firing arc. Lando's engineers integrated two concealed Dymex HM-8 concussion missile launches, each with a magazine of eight high-yield torpedoes. All of the vehicle's weapons are connected to a targeting computer with multiple options. A "shoot-back" setting, for example, directs the targeting computer to automatically shoot down any craft that opens fire on the *Jade Shadow*.

To increase the *Jade Shadow*'s speed, Han Solo fine-tuned the twin ion drives and reworked the hyperdrive engines to emulate those aboard the *Millennium Falcon*. He donated an advanced long-range sensor suite complete with port and starboard visual scanners, jamming devices, sensor decoys, false transponder codes, and a remote-controlled slave circuit that can summon the starship over short distances.

Mara added a costly holographic communications array that can send and receive messages from Coruscant to the Outer Rim. With Luke's aid, Mara integrated a tractor beam projector and reconfigured the aft docking bay to contain a modified starfighter. Husband and wife again joined forces to add an autopilot programmed with a variety of evasive maneuvers. The *Jade Shadow* can host an astromech connected to a droid station on the flight deck. Many of the systems are voice-activated. System data is displayed on unobtrusive holograms synced to a retinal tracker, which positions these readouts just outside the pilot's forward line of sight.

Although the *Jade Shadow*'s many support features allow Mara to operate the starship without a crew, the bridge is designed for a pilot, copilot, and navigator. The crew sits beneath a massive, transparisteel canopy that provides breathtaking views of space—and a crystal-clear image of enemy starships.

> **"By the time we're through with her, the *Jade Shadow* will put the *Falcon* to shame."**
> —*Lando Calrissian*

❼ External Hatch Release: This hatch release is strictly cosmetic; the true release is hidden inside the bulkhead and can be activated only by using the Force.

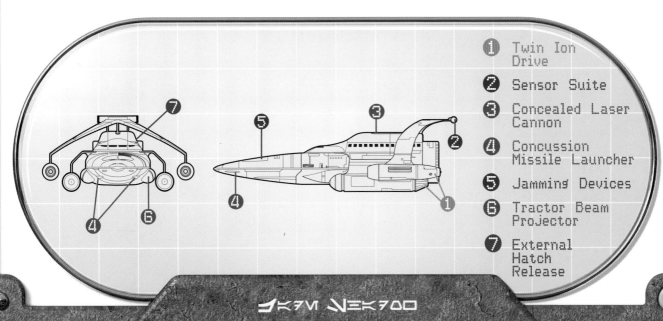

1. Twin Ion Drive
2. Sensor Suite
3. Concealed Laser Cannon
4. Concussion Missile Launcher
5. Jamming Devices
6. Tractor Beam Projector
7. External Hatch Release

Jedi Starfighter

TECHNICAL READOUT

SIZE: 8 m long

MAXIMUM SPEED:
5,000G/Class 1 hyperdrive module (Class 3 integrated hyperdrive for modified Delta-7s)/12,000 KPH

PRIMARY MANUFACTURER:
Kuat Systems Engineering

AFFILIATION:
Old Republic/Jedi Order

KSE Delta-7 *Aethersprite*-Class Light Interceptor

During the height of the Old Republic, the Jedi Temple maintained a large fleet of vehicles for emergencies. When assigned a mission, members of the Jedi Order would requisition starships, airspeeders, and other craft as necessary. Shortly before the Battle of Geonosis, the Jedi Council sought to bolster this motor pool with a new starfighter. Commissioned from Kuat Systems Engineering, this starfighter was meant to serve as a medium-range reconnaissance vehicle. KSE quickly produced the Delta-7 Aethersprite for the Council's approval. A short time later, the vehicles were being flown on dangerous missions to far-flung systems.

The original Delta-7 is a light, high-performance starfighter with a small profile and powerful engine systems. Offensively, it relies on a pair of forward-facing dual laser cannons. The weapons system has an impressive recharge rate and a state-of-the-art targeting computer. When combined with Jedi reflexes, it can prove devastating. The vehicle's shield system automatically distributes energy to areas that are under fire, strengthening the rear shields when the starfighter is being pursued or reinforcing the forward shields during a head-on assault. A standard astromech can be hardwired into the ship's frame to provide additional support.

As specified by the Jedi Council, the Delta-7 is not designed for deep-space flight, but KSE had enough foresight to contract a dedicated hyperdrive ring for the starfighter. TransGalMeg Industries provided KSE with the Syliure-31 long-range hyperdrive module, which KSE sold to the Jedi Council for a sizable profit. In order to travel between systems, the Delta-7 merely docks with a hyperspace transport ring that has its own dedicated Class 1 hyperdrive system. The Delta-7's interface has been specifically created with the Syliure-31 module in mind, allowing the Aethersprite to activate the hyperdrive manually. When the starfighter disengages from the ring, the device remains anchored in space until the Delta-7's return.

The Delta-7 was well received by the Jedi Knights. Several pilots, including Obi-Wan Kenobi, began using them immediately. Only Saesee Tiin, the Jedi Council's resident starfighter ace, was dissatisfied with the craft. He subjected the Delta-7 to rigorous testing, then personally modified a pair of the starfighters. Tiin increased the starfighter's firepower by adding four quad-pulse laser cannons. The additional weapons remain concealed behind breakaway panels until they are absolutely necessary. He also integrated a compact, Class 3 hyperdrive of his own design and replaced the standard pilot's seat with a more comfortable meditation chair. Adi Gallia took one of Saesee Tiin's modified Delta-7s to the Karthakk system shortly before the Battle of Geonosis. When her mission proved a resounding success, many of the existing starfighters were upgraded to Tiin's specifications.

> ## "I'd consider the Delta-7 combat capabilities well tested, Master Tiin."
>
> *—Obi-Wan Kenobi, after surviving the Battle of Geonosis*

7 **Hardwired Astromech:** The Delta-7 is too thin to house a full astromech, so an astromech unit, such as Obi-Wan's R4-P17, must be hardwired directly into the starfighter. Although the astromech's dome remains intact, all of its internal components are plugged directly into the Delta-7's astromech socket.

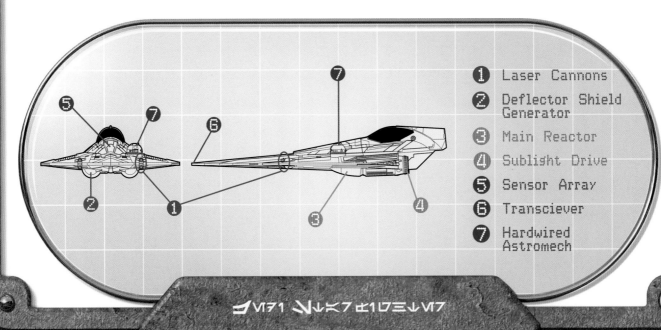

1. Laser Cannons
2. Deflector Shield Generator
3. Main Reactor
4. Sublight Drive
5. Sensor Array
6. Transciever
7. Hardwired Astromech

JUGGERNAUT

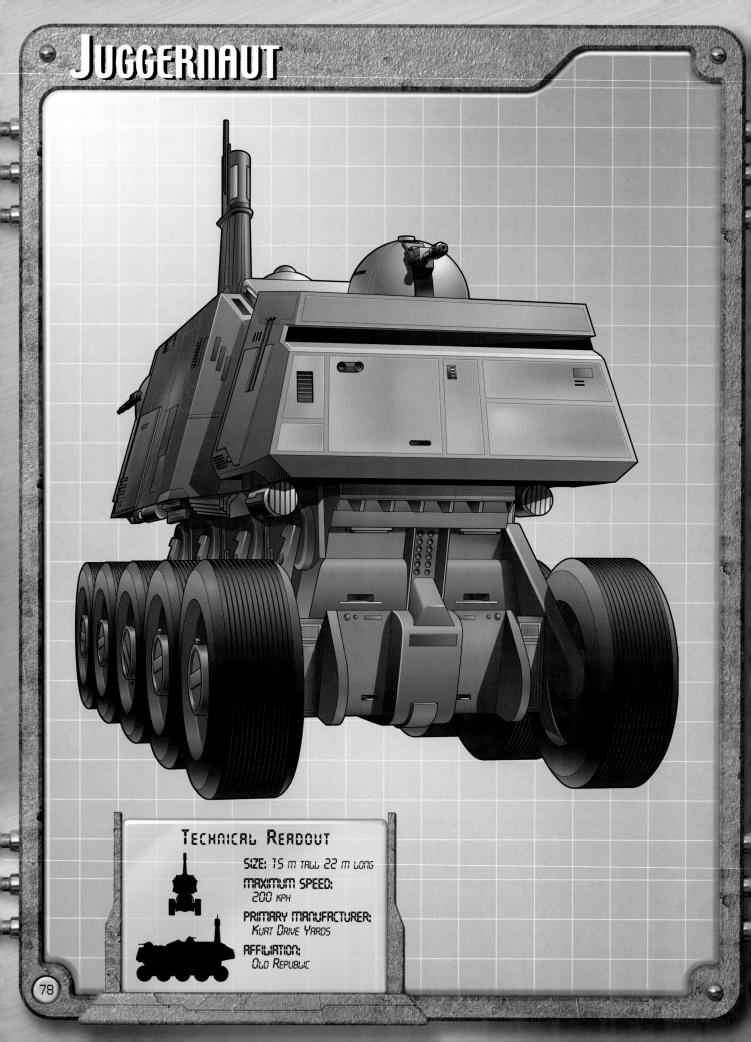

TECHNICAL READOUT

SIZE: 15 m TALL 22 m LONG

MAXIMUM SPEED:
200 KPH

PRIMARY MANUFACTURER:
KUAT DRIVE YARDS

AFFILIATION:
OLD REPUBLIC

Kuat Drive Yards HAVw Juggernaut Troop Carrier

During the Clone Wars, the Old Republic took drastic steps to repel the Confederacy of Independent Systems. Realizing that demilitarized systems would be wiped out by confederate forces, the Galactic Senate passed a resolution that allowed planets to create their own defense forces with the Republic's full support and financial backing. The Republic contracted Kuat Drive Yards to supply vehicles for these local armies, and the juggernaut was born.

Designed to be a larger version of AT-TE, the juggernaut shares a great deal of technology with its predecessor. The vehicle's heavy armor plating is nearly identical to the armor covering the AT-TE, and the secure command cabin is similar in design to the AT-TE's cockpit. Rather than rely on a walker configuration, however, the juggernaut has ten durable drive wheels connected to a flexible system of shocks and servos. The juggernaut excels when crossing rocky, uneven, or broken terrain and can reach top speeds of 200 kilometers per hour, although it must slow to nearly 25 kilometers per hour in order to turn. Because the juggernaut has forward and rear command cabins, it can travel in reverse at maximum speed. Relatively easy to pilot, the juggernaut requires only one driver in each command cabin.

Like the AT-TE and the later AT-AT, the juggernaut is primarily a troop transport. The vehicle can carry 50 troops with all necessary gear. As with the Imperial landing craft, the juggernaut can be reconfigured to carry speeder bikes, assault speeders, or other small repulsorlift craft.

During the last days of the Old Republic, the juggernaut was among the most powerful ground-based vehicles in operation. Aside from its tough hide, the juggernaut (nicknamed the "rolling slab") includes three rotating laser cannons with two-thirds the effective range of an AT-AT's more advanced cannons. A turret-mounted blaster cannon provides protection from aircraft, while two concussion grenade launchers supply covering fire as troops unload. The grenade launchers are entirely retractable, and each contains a magazine of ten grenades. A sentry in the vehicle's observation tower relays targeting information to six gunners responsible for the juggernaut's weapons.

The juggernaut served its purpose well for several years, but was eventually eclipsed by the AT-AT. The Empire considered the juggernaut's drive system primitive, largely because it could not traverse dense terrain. As the juggernaut fell out of favor with the military, suppliers stopped offering replacement parts for the vehicle. As of the Yuuzhan Vong invasion, very few juggernauts remained operational. Those that are still running require constant maintenance by skilled mechanics.

> **"DAY 17: Forward drive shaft on juggernaut-11 has snapped. Requesting replacement drive shaft. DAY 22: Resubmitting request for replacement drive shaft. DAY 38: Drive shaft still has not arrived. Please advise. DAY 50: Awaiting drive shaft. DAY 123: Awaiting drive shaft."**
> —*Excerpt from log of Imperial machinist stationed on Dathomir*

6 Sentry Tower: The highly visible sentry tower provides the Juggernaut with a wide field of view, but also serves as a perfect target for enemy sharpshooters.

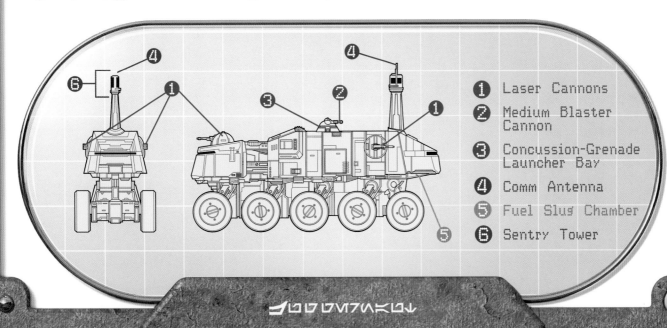

1. Laser Cannons
2. Medium Blaster Cannon
3. Concussion-Grenade Launcher Bay
4. Comm Antenna
5. Fuel Slug Chamber
6. Sentry Tower

K-WING

TECHNICAL READOUT

SIZE: 16 m LONG

MAXIMUM SPEED:
2,700S/1,000 KPH

PRIMARY MANUFACTURER:
KOENSAYR

AFFILIATION:
NEW REPUBLIC

Koensayr BTL-S8 K-Wing Assault Starfighter

The K-wing is one of the most recent starfighters produced by Koensayr for the New Republic's ongoing conflicts with Imperial Remnant forces and other threats. Descendants of the Y-wing, K-wings first appeared during the Black Fleet Crisis 16 standard years after the Battle of Yavin, and have been mobilized for nearly every subsequent conflict.

Like the X-wing and other New Republic starfighters, the K-wing was designed to fulfill a specific combat role while maintaining some degree of versatility. The K-wing's ideal mission profile involves close-range, precision bombardment of planetary targets, space stations, or slow-moving capital ships. However, it is also a competent escort fighter and short-range reconnaissance vehicle.

The distinctive K-wing consists of two maneuvering wings connected to a large, fixed stabilizer. Primary thrust turbines located at the junction between the stabilizer and maneuvering wings provide sublight speed's equivalent to a Y-wing's top velocity despite the K-wing's greater mass. A secondary ion engine mounted near the rear of the main stabilizer allows extremely rapid acceleration for short bursts. The starfighter lacks a hyperdrive and must be transported throughout the galaxy by large fleet carriers, such as the *Endurance*.

As befitting its role in the New Republic fleet, the K-wing supports an unprecedented arsenal for a vehicle of its size. Eighteen hard points spread across the three wings allow New Republic engineers to arm the

> **"We're the heavy hitters. When you need a command bridge leveled or a convoy of tanks wiped out, the K-wings get the call."**
> —*New Republic pilot Miranda Doni shortly before her death at Doornik-319*

vehicle with a variety of physical weapons, including concussion missiles, flechette missiles, sublight torpedoes, thermal warheads, and floating mines. The drawback to this system is obvious: once a K-wing fires its last weapon, it is without heavy firepower and must return to a docking bay to rearm. When attacked by starfighters, the K-wing can open fire with a short-range quad turbolaser turret and a medium-range twin laser cannon turret, both mounted on its command module. The craft is equipped with deflector shields as well.

Due to its proliferation of weapons, the K-wing requires a dedicated gunner. The pilot and gunner sit in small cockpits on either side of the command module. The entire command module can detach from the wing assembly to serve as an escape pod, although the pod has a very low sublight speed and makes for an inviting target.

2 Flechette Missile Launchers: The Fifth Fleet's K-wings deployed flechette missiles in order to destroy a hypervelocity gun during the fleet's first adventurous live-fire training exercise at Bessimir.

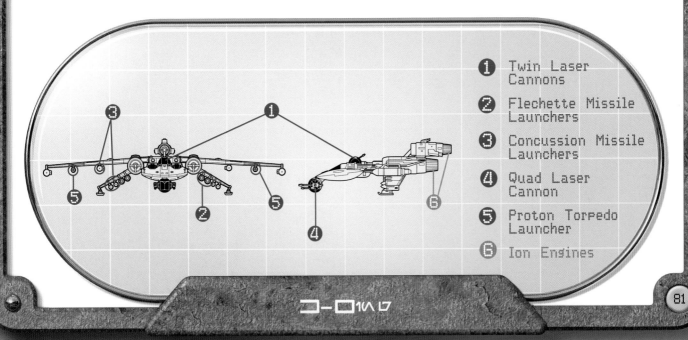

1 Twin Laser Cannons

2 Flechette Missile Launchers

3 Concussion Missile Launchers

4 Quad Laser Cannon

5 Proton Torpedo Launcher

6 Ion Engines

LADY LUCK

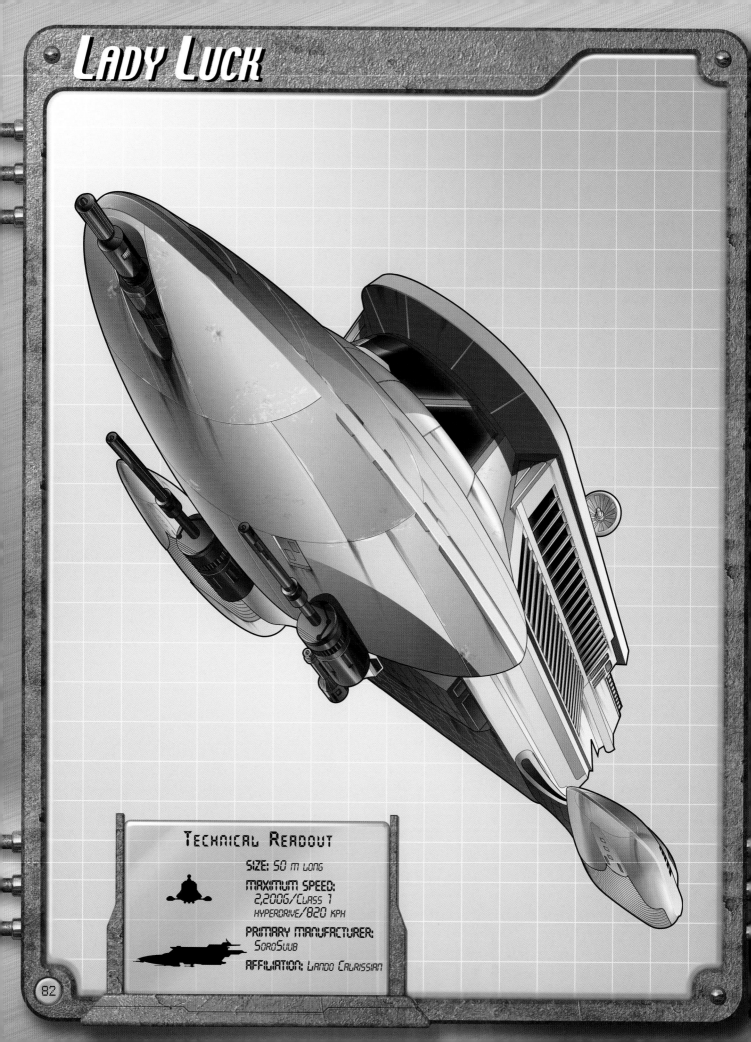

TECHNICAL READOUT

SIZE: 50 m long

MAXIMUM SPEED:
2,200G/Class 1
HYPERDRIVE/820 KPH

PRIMARY MANUFACTURER:
SoroSuub

AFFILIATION: Lando Calrissian

Modified SoroSuub Personal Luxury Yacht 3000

Lady Luck is the personal starship of gambler and New Republic hero Lando Calrissian. Lando has owned numerous starships throughout his long career, but the Lady Luck has been the most durable. Calrissian purchased her from an Orthellin royal mistress after the Battle of Endor. At the time, Lando's involvement with the mining operation known as Nomad City kept him from tinkering with the starship, but in the years since then he has repeatedly modified and upgraded the Lady Luck.

Lando initially planned to transform the Lady Luck into an advanced luxury cruiser, but his near-constant involvement with the New Republic has forced him to convert the Lady Luck into a competent combat vehicle. At first glance, the 50-meter-long starship appears to be an unarmed pleasure yacht, but this placid exterior conceals five retractable laser cannons and a small ion cannon turret. A pair of powerful Chempat-6 deflector shield generators provide moderate protection from enemy fire.

The Lady Luck's engines are housed in two long engine pods connected to the main hull. Although the starship's sublight and hyperdrive speeds can't match those of the Millennium Falcon, the Lady Luck can still outrace nearly any other luxury vehicle in the galaxy.

The Lady Luck's secondary systems truly set her apart. She has a highly sophisticated sensor system allowing Lando to detect, identify, and scan approaching vessels at great range. When the Lady Luck is scanned by customs officials or enemy forces, the ship's transponder can be programmed with up to three separate false identities, which include aliases, fake cargo manifests, and modified system specs. Lando frequently changes these identities, although he has used the alias "Stardream" on more than one occasion. A droid brain aboard the starship can pilot the starship in emergencies and direct her toward a summoning unit that Lando always keeps on his belt; this feature proved especially helpful when Lando, Luke Skywalker, and Han Solo were forced to flee the mining city of Ilic. The starship also has concealed smuggling compartments.

Although the Lady Luck is now useful in combat, she is still a lavish luxury starship. An entire observation level includes an exterior deck and numerous viewports. Lando's private suite and the five visitor cabins are decorated with rare art from around the galaxy. Conform couches can be found throughout the starship; the main deck contains a jet-stream meditation pool and a small crystal garden. Even the Lady Luck's escape pods are furnished with state-of-the-art grav couches covered in the finest Corellian leather.

> "Her name says all you need to know. The *Lady Luck's* fickle, but when she's smiling down on you, you're bound to win. She hasn't given up on me yet."
> —*Lando Calrissian*

7 **Exterior Observation Deck:** Lando and his female friends have spent many long hours observing the stars from this observation deck, which can be protected from the vacuum of space via an invisible force field.

1 Laser Cannon
2 Ion Engine
3 Hyperdrive Engine
4 Long Range Sensor Transceiver
5 Sensor Array
6 Comm Transceiver
7 Exterior Observation Deck

Luke's Landspeeder

Technical Readout

Size: 3.4 m long

Maximum Speed:
250 KPH

Primary Manufacturer:
SoroSuub

Affiliation: Luke Skywalker

SoroSuub X-34

If airspeeders are among the most common atmospheric craft in the galaxy, then landspeeders are certainly the most widespread ground vehicles. Small, repulsorlift craft that float about a meter above the ground, most landspeeders are designed as short-range civilian transports. An excellent alternative to the more expensive airspeeders, landspeeders (also known as "skimmers" or "floaters") are especially useful on sparsely populated worlds such as Tatooine.

As with airspeeders, landspeeders are relatively simple in design. A low-grade repulsorlift engine provides a small amount of lift. A variety of devices, from air thrusters to engine turbines, can be installed to generate forward thrust. The controls, which generally just include a steering wheel and a series of foot pedals, are easy to master. A rudimentary onboard computer-and-scanner system provides navigational aid. These scanners can be configured to detect life-forms, obstacles, or even a runaway astromech droid.

Countless companies manufacture landspeeders, although SoroSuub and Mobquet Swoops and Speeders are among the leaders in this category. Shortly before the Battle of Yavin, future Jedi Knight Luke Skywalker owned a SoroSuub X-34 landspeeder. While the X-34 was considered outdated at that time, it was nevertheless a popular choice on temperate worlds due to its open cockpit and retractable duraplex windscreens. The X-34 is also favored by younger pilots who value speed over comfort: It has three turbine engines that provide maximum speed of 250 kilometers per hour. Originally designed for a pilot and

"He says this is the best he can do. Since the XP-38 came out, they just aren't in demand."
—*Luke Skywalker, lamenting the low resale value of his X-34 landspeeder*

passengers, the X-34 also has magnetic clamps behind the seats for securing droids or small cargo modules.

While the X-34 has very limited storage and passenger space, the V-35 Courier was designed as a family vehicle. Owen and Beru Lars, Luke's foster parents, owned one of these practical landspeeders, which they used for trips into Anchorhead or visits with other moisture farmers. The Courier is inexpensive and reliable, but Luke frowned upon the vehicle because of its low top speed of only 100 kilometers per hour. The V-35 has an extremely large repulsorlift engine that dominates the craft. A series of three rectangular thrust turbines are mounted atop the vehicle and remain open to the air for cooling purposes. Capable of carrying three humanoids in relative comfort, the V-35 also has a large cargo hold located behind the passenger seats. The V-35 was actually introduced several decades prior to its use by the Lars family; Qui-Gon Jinn and Obi-Wan Kenobi used one of the vehicles during a mission to Ord Mantell, for instance, about five standard years before the Battle of Naboo. Despite the V-35's age, Luke and Owen were able to keep the Lars family speeder in excellent condition through routine maintenance and occasional upgrades.

Both the V-35 Courier and the X-34 had fallen out of favor by the Battle of Yavin, as Luke discovered

5 Scanning Device: Luke used his landspeeder's onboard scanners to search the Tatooine wastes for R2-D2, who had fled Skywalker in search of Obi-Wan Kenobi.

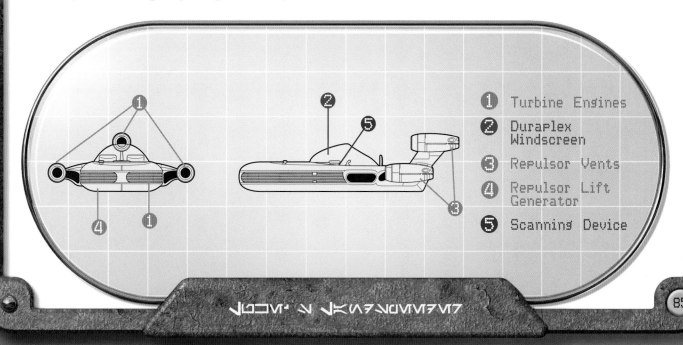

1 Turbine Engines
2 Duraplex Windscreen
3 Repulsor Vents
4 Repulsor Lift Generator
5 Scanning Device

when he tried to sell his battered landspeeder to buy passage off Tatooine. At that time, the most popular landspeeder models included the Bespin Motors Void Spider TX-3, the Ubrikkian 9000 Z001, and the highly advanced Mobquet Deluxe. On Tatooine, Luke's X-34 had been largely replaced by SoroSuub's newer model, the XP-38.

The XP-38 is one of SoroSuub's most successful designs. The target audience includes young consumers who dream of becoming fighter pilots or adventurers. The vehicle's sleek and stylized frame is reminiscent of many airspeeders. An autopilot built into the vehicle has been designed to resemble a starfighter's astromech unit. The engine and control systems are a huge leap forward from the X-34, offering much greater acceleration and the tighter turning radius needed for urban racing. The XP-38 can also be purchased with several options, including an advanced sensor array and a HoloNet transceiver.

Although extremely expensive when initially released shortly before the Battle of Yavin, the XP-38 became one of the most sought-after landspeeders in the galaxy. However, it soon became clear that the XP-38's rigid repulsorlift system is difficult to recalibrate and prevents travel over rough terrain. Newer versions of the XP-38, such as the XP-38 All-Terrain Roughrider, have been produced for sale on rural worlds.

Manufacturers such as SoroSuub are frequently looking to capture new markets and often create mod-ified landspeeders for use in specific environments. SoroSuub's recent Duneblaster series is designed for desert worlds, like Tatooine, and features sand filters and dedicated cooling systems. The Mobquet Deluxe can be outfitted with internal and external heaters, defrost devices, and a forward-mounted "icebreaker" laser cannon to become the Mobquet ArcticExplorer-4. On water worlds, locals frequently pilot water skimmers, which are built using basic landspeeder technologies.

Because of the landspeeder's versatility and accessibility, it has always been part of military motor pools. The Naboo Royal Security Forces use both the agile Flash speeder and the sturdy Gian speeder, both military versions of SoroSuub civilian vehicles. During the Galactic Civil War and Grand Admiral Thrawn's campaign, Imperial officers orchestrated battles from the Chariot LAV command speeder. The Rebel Alliance deployed the fairly large Arrow-23 transport landspeeder, which carries two crew and five passengers.

> ## "Don't be left in the dust!"
> *—Tatooine-specific advertisement for the*
> *XP-38 circa the Battle of Yavin*

⑥ Cargo Compartment: Cargo space on landspeeders is rare, and the Lars family valued this cargo compartment because it allowed them to transport goods between their farm and Anchorhead.

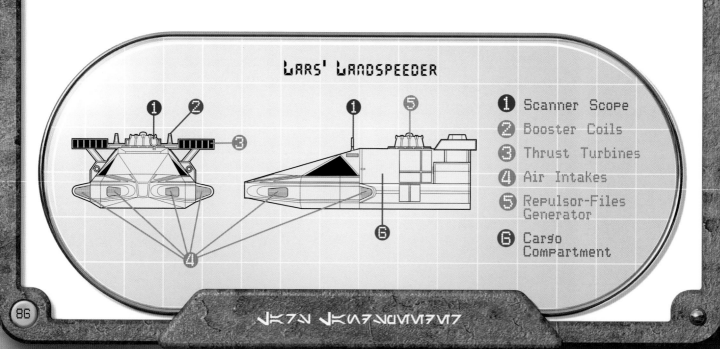

Lars' Landspeeder

① Scanner Scope
② Booster Coils
③ Thrust Turbines
④ Air Intakes
⑤ Repulsor-Files Generator
⑥ Cargo Compartment

Watto's Landspeeder

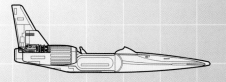

SoroSuub V-35 Courier

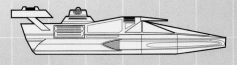

Trast A-A5 Speeder Truck

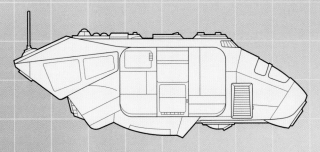

Arrow-23 Speeder

zZip I Motor Concepts Astral-8

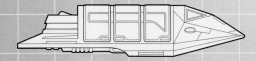

Tantive IV Landspeeder

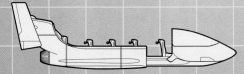

JG-8 Landspeeder

MandalMotors LUX-3 Landspeeder

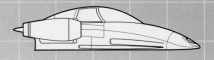

XP-38A Sport Landspeeder

Luke's Landspeeder

Gian Speeder

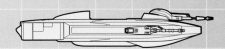

Flash Speeder

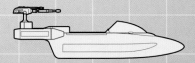

Lars' Landspeeder

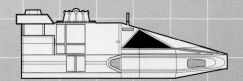

MILLENNIUM FALCON

TECHNICAL READOUT

SIZE: 27 m LONG

MAXIMUM SPEED:
3,000G/CLASS 0.5
HYPERDRIVE/1,050 KPH

PRIMARY MANUFACTURER:
CORELLIAN ENGINEERING
CORPORATION

AFFILIATION: HAN SOLO

Modified Corellian Engineering Corporation YT-1300 Transport

Few starships are as legendary as the *Millennium Falcon,* the personal starship of New Republic hero Han Solo. At first glance, the starship appears to be just another battered freighter. This unassuming exterior conceals the fact that the *Falcon* is among the fastest—and most unusual—vessels in the galaxy.

The *Millennium Falcon* is the product of years of constant modifications and upgrades. Soon after acquiring the starship, Solo and his Wookiee copilot Chewbacca installed a military-grade rectenna as part of a versatile (and highly illegal) long-range sensor suite. For combat, the pair incorporated two quad laser cannon turrets, which Wookiee Jowdrrl later connected to autotracking fire controllers in the cockpit. To protect the starship, Shug Ninx macrofused a sheet of Star Destroyer armor plating just aft of the starboard docking arm, while outlaw mechanics provided augmented deflector shields stolen from Imperial maintenance facilities.

The *Millennium Falcon's* speed is achieved through a heavily modified Class 0.5 hyperdrive engine. The sublight engines are formidable as well, and the agile *Falcon* can dodge Imperial TIE fighters or weave through a thick asteroid field. The engines have also been redesigned with a rapid, three-standard-minute start-up sequence to allow quick getaways; a retractable, rotating repeating blaster provides covering fire during these escapes. Because they are so advanced, the engine systems are extremely delicate and temperamental; the hyperdrive, in particular, requires constant repair and maintenance.

Among the *Falcon's* many other modifications are high-tech acceleration compensators, oversized thruster ports, and transparent optical transducer panels to enhance port and aft visibility. Three droid brains allow seamless communication among all systems. Finally, concealed smuggling compartments throughout the starship enable the transport of illegal goods. Han, Luke Skywalker, and their allies hid inside these compartments to elude Imperials after the *Falcon* was captured by the Death Star.

The *Millennium Falcon's* history is tangled. Gambler Lando Calrissian won the starship in a game of chance about four years before the Battle of Yavin. Lando piloted the *Falcon* on numerous adventures but lost her to Han Solo while playing sabacc. Solo used the *Falcon* to further his smuggling career until he aided the Rebel Alliance. At the Battle of Yavin, Solo rescued Luke Skywalker from Darth Vader. Three years later, Lando returned to the *Falcon's* cockpit to lead the attack on the second Death Star. During the early days of the New Republic, the *Falcon* proved instrumental in the war against Grand Admiral Thrawn and the reborn Emperor. Sadly, the *Falcon* bore witness to the death of Chewbacca during the Yuuzhan Vong invasion. Princess Leia has since become the *Falcon's* new copilot.

> *"It's the ship that made the Kessel Run in less than twelve parsecs! I've outrun Imperial starships, not the local bulk cruisers, mind you. I'm talking about the big Corellian ships now."*
>
> —Han Solo

7 Concealed Smuggling Compartments: These compartments allowed Han and his newfound allies to hide from an Imperial boarding party after the *Falcon* was captured by the Death Star.

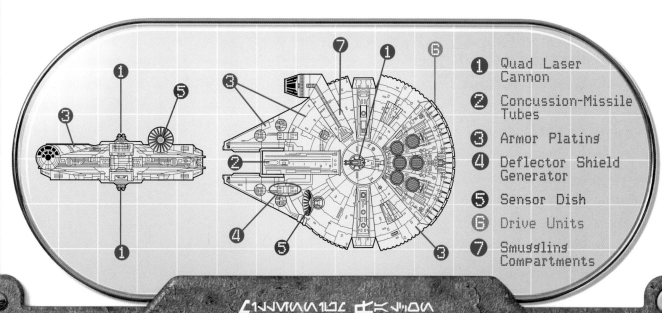

1. Quad Laser Cannon
2. Concussion-Missile Tubes
3. Armor Plating
4. Deflector Shield Generator
5. Sensor Dish
6. Drive Units
7. Smuggling Compartments

Mon Cal Cruiser (Home One)

Technical Readout

SIZE: 1,200 m long

MAXIMUM SPEED:
1,550G/Class 1 Hyperdrive

PRIMARY MANUFACTURER:
Mon Calamari

AFFILIATION:
Rebel Alliance/New Republic

Mon Calamari MC80 Star Cruiser

When the Mon Calamari entered the Galactic Civil War as allies of the Rebel Alliance, they donated a modest fleet of large, durable starships to the war effort. Dubbed "Mon Cal cruisers" by the Rebels, these versatile vessels proved a major factor in the Emperor's defeat.

Originally designed for colonization and civilian transport, Mon Cal cruisers are surprisingly adaptable. When modified for combat duty, a typical MC80 star cruiser can support 20 ion cannons, 48 turbolasers, and 6 tractor beam projectors. The MC80's docking bay can hold up to 36 starfighters.

Aside from thick hull plating, Mon Cal cruisers have unusually powerful overlapping deflector shields created by dozens of bulbous shield generators. Because a cruiser's shields overlap, damaged shield arrays can be quickly replaced during combat without exposing the vehicle to enemy fire.

Mon Cal cruisers represented the majority of the Rebel battleships at the Battle of Endor. During that engagement, the vessels were used as medical frigates, starfighter carriers, and support craft. Mon Cal cruiser *Home One* served as the headquarters frigate and Admiral Ackbar's personal flagship. *Home One*'s arsenal focused on ion attacks, with 36 ion cannons bolstered by 29 turbolasers. The ship also carried 120 starfighters, arranged into 10 full squadrons.

While many other Rebel starships have been designed for ease of use, the command stations aboard a Mon Cal cruiser are specifically engineered

> **"Make no mistake, the Mon Calamari saved the galaxy. Their cruisers protected our fleet at the Battle of Endor, allowing the starfighters to penetrate the second Death Star's core. Without Admiral Ackbar and his people, we would all be the Emperor's slaves."**
>
> —*Excerpt from Mon Mothma's memoirs*

for the Mon Calamari anatomy. The starships are controlled through both a standard computer interface and precise body movements, which most other species have difficulty simulating. The bridge display monitors are designed for the Mon Cals' wide vision spectrum, producing holodisplays that appear distorted to other creatures. Moreover, because of their unique design, Mon Calamari cruisers are not easy to repair.

After the Battle of Endor, the Mon Calamari continued to produce new and improved Mon Cal cruisers. The MC80B, typified by the *Mon Remonda*, was introduced a standard year after the Battle of Endor, and the MC90 followed shortly after. The first Mon Cal cruiser designed specifically as a battle cruiser, the MC90 has greater firepower than the MC80, with 75 turbolasers, 35 ion cannons, and 6 proton torpedo tubes. MC90s such as the *Galactic Voyager* are ideal for other species as well. The Mon Calamari have also produced the much larger *Viscount*-class Star Defender battleships, which can engage Imperial Star Destroyers. At the other end of the spectrum are small, fast Mon Cal light cruisers. Light cruisers such as the *Poesy* make quick strikes against larger battleships or starfighter squadrons using 14 turbolasers, 18 ion cannons, and 6 heavy tractor beams.

⑥ Modular Pod: The bulbous pods on the Mon Cal cruisers can hold deflector shield generators, turbolasers, sensor arrays, and ion cannons.

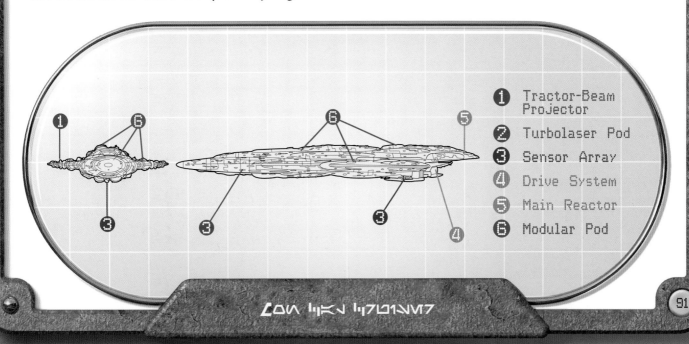

① Tractor-Beam Projector
② Turbolaser Pod
③ Sensor Array
④ Drive System
⑤ Main Reactor
⑥ Modular Pod

MTT

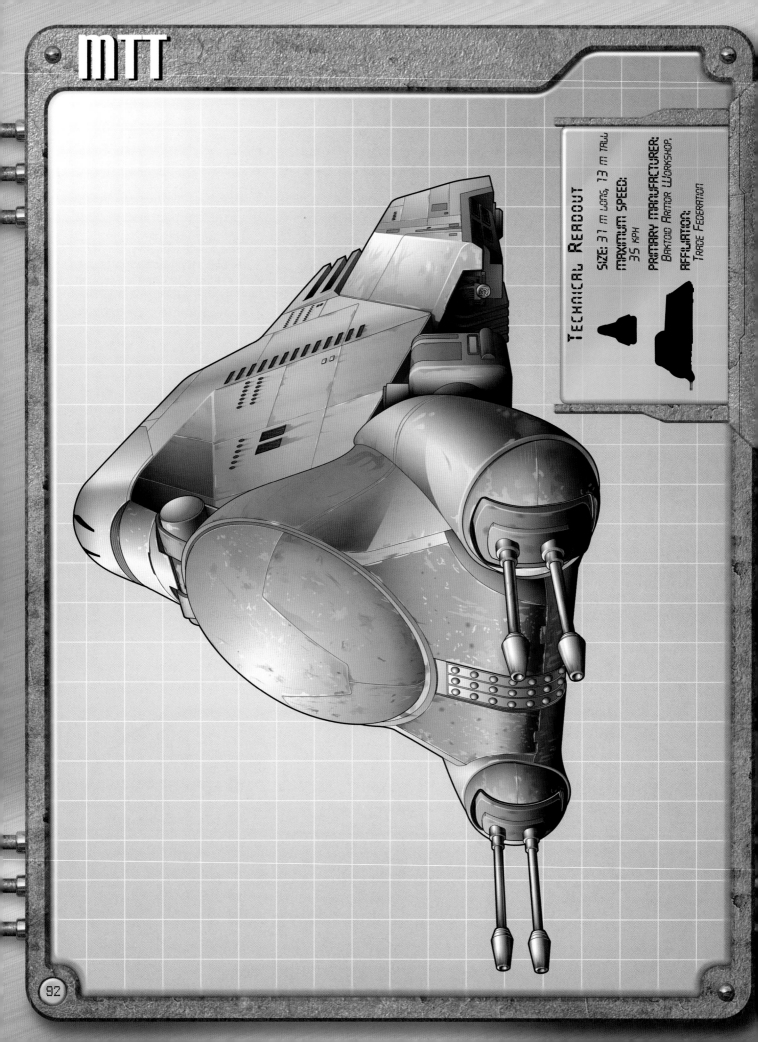

Technical Readout

SIZE: 31 m LONG, 13 m TALL

MAXIMUM SPEED:
35 KPH

PRIMARY MANUFACTURER:
Baktoid Armor Workshop.

AFFILIATION:
Trade Federation

Trade Federation Multitroop Transport

A well-designed troop transport is capable of delivering a large number of soldiers into combat quickly, safely, and efficiently. The truly exceptional troop transports are combat vehicles unto themselves, with the ability to defend troops during deployment and retrieval. The Trade Federation's MTT (also known more generally as a Trade Federation "large transport") is an exceptional vehicle. Integral to the Trade Federation's secret army, the MTT allowed the company to move a staggering number of battle droids at a moment's notice.

At first glance, the MTT is a relatively simple vehicle. While obviously armored, the dull brown exterior hides a number of innovative features. Chief among these is the inclusion of a long, extendable deployment rack. The engineers at Baktoid Armor Workshop, designers of the MTT, took full advantage of the fact that the Trade Federation's troops would be flexible droids. The deployment rack carries up to 112 battle droids, all folded into a compact "transport" configuration to conserve space. When the MTT enters battle, its forward hatch opens and the deployment rack extends. The activated battle droids then unfold into a default combat stance and are ready for attack. Due to the deployment rack, the MTT's carrying capacity is nearly three times that of any other transport of similar size. The rack can be completely removed and placed atop a repulsorsled troop carrier. These unarmored troop carriers, which are much faster than the MTT, can be used to move battle droids through Trade Federation bases, occupied cities, or other safe areas.

> **"We were hiding in the armory and then *bam*! The whole wall just fell down. Three tons of duracrete reduced to rubble by the business end of an MTT... I'm not ashamed to admit that we surrendered."**
>
> *—Hexler Pend, Naboo Royal Security Forces officer stationed in Keren*

When deploying battle droids into the thick of a conflict, MTTs must enter chaotic and dangerous environments. To survive such missions, the MTT is adorned with heavy frontal armor reinforced by case-hardened metal alloy studs. As with the AAT and other Baktoid craft, the MTT's most vital components, including the power converter grids, are located toward the rear of the transport for added protection. When faced by opposition, the MTT clears its path using four independent-fire antipersonnel blaster cannons. The cannons have a limited arc of fire, but MTTs are usually supported by a pair of AATs when traveling through hot zones.

Like the AAT, the MTT is piloted by a specially programmed battle droid. A second droid serves as a gunner. When deployed on Naboo, the MTTs followed preprogrammed routes, but the pilot may alter such rigid directions after conferring with the Droid Control Ship's central command computer.

Because of the MTT's impressive frontal armor, the Trade Federation often used MTTs as battering rams. Once an MTT has crashed through a structure or wall, it can unload its battle droids directly inside an enemy installation. This tactic caught many Naboo by surprise, ensuring easy victories at several small outposts near Theed.

② **Kuat Premion Mk. II Power Generator:** The heavy MTT requires a formidable generator to power its repulsorlift engines. Exhaust from the engine is channeled through vents under the AAT, creating a threatening cloud beneath the vehicle.

1. Twin Blaster Cannons
2. Power Generator Housing
3. Control Center
4. Repulsor Thrusters
5. Armored Hull
6. Exhaust Vents
7. Droid Hatch

Naboo Royal Cruiser

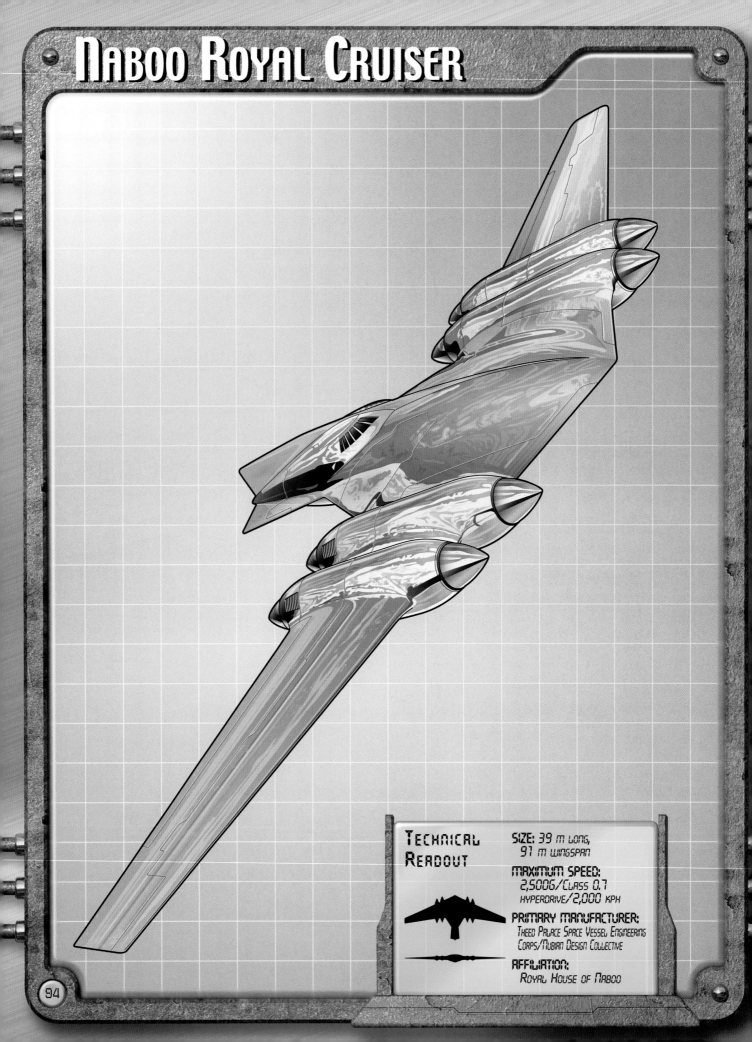

Technical Readout

SIZE: 39 m long, 91 m wingspan

MAXIMUM SPEED: 2,500G/Class 0.7 Hyperdrive/2,000 kph

PRIMARY MANUFACTURER: Theed Palace Space Vessel Engineering Corps/Nubian Design Collective

AFFILIATION: Royal House of Naboo

J–Type Custom–Built Diplomatic Barge

When Padmé Amidala left her post as Queen of Naboo, she continued to serve her people as a member of the Galactic Senate. The attractive and strong-willed young woman fought against the Senate's growing corruption and traveled the galaxy on a variety of relief missions. To aid Padmé on her diplomatic journeys, the Royal House of Naboo gave the Senator a gleaming, custom-built starship handcrafted by the Theed Palace Space Vessel Engineering Corps.

The Naboo Royal Cruiser was extremely similar to the Naboo Royal Starship used by Padmé during her reign as Queen, and the cruiser embodied the Naboo's pacifist policies by eschewing weapons of any kind. The craft also bore a familiar chromium coat that had previously been reserved for royal starships. When Amidala became Senator, the Royal House insisted that she continue to fly a chromium craft to signify Naboo's gratitude for her service; in many ways, Padmé will always be a member of the Royal House.

As with many Naboo starships, the Naboo Royal Cruiser incorporated several Nubian components. The hyperdrive system, sensor array, deflector shield generators, and sublight engines are all based around Nubian technology. These systems have received complete upgrades and a variety of modifications to allow seamless integration into the Naboo starship frame.

While the Theed engineers used the Naboo Royal Starship as a template for many of the cruiser's fea-

> **"When I think of all the dangerous missions we attempted in that starship, I'm amazed it wasn't destroyed sooner. Of course, there was the time it was stolen on Maramere."**
> —*Captain Typho*

tures, they also improved upon the previous design when creating Padmé's new vessel. The Royal Cruiser's shield generator is much more powerful and efficient than was its predecessor. To ensure that Padmé is never forced to stop for hyperdrive repairs, the cruiser actually has two separate but identical Nubian S-6 hyperdrive generators.

As a high-profile Senator, Padmé's life was often in danger. Because she could never travel without protection, the Royal Cruiser had spacious quarters for ten passengers, including Padmé's loyal bodyguard, Captain Typho. A pilot and copilot could handle the vehicle without additional crew, although the cockpit was designed to also accommodate a navigator, communications officer, and shield operator. Five astromechs performed repairs and monitor duty.

Despite its advanced features, the Naboo Royal Cruiser fell victim to a vile assassination plot. When Padmé and her entourage arrived on Coruscant shortly before the Battle of Geonosis, a well-placed explosive device ripped the cruiser apart. In the days and weeks that followed, Padmé was forced to rely on a much smaller Nubian yacht for transport.

⑤ Fighter Recharge Sockets: Recharge sockets built into the cruiser's wings enabled it to carry up to four escort starfighters on long-distance hyperspace journeys.

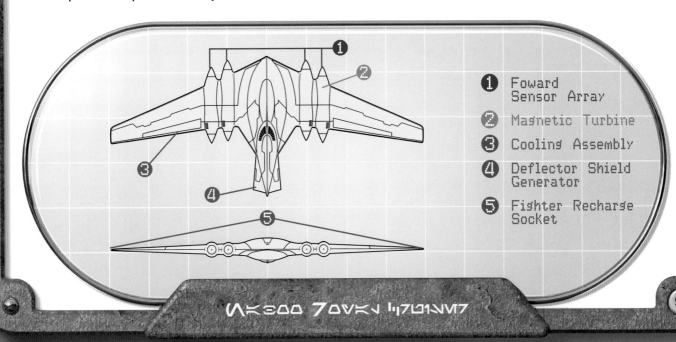

① Foward Sensor Array

② Magnetic Turbine

③ Cooling Assembly

④ Deflector Shield Generator

⑤ Fighter Recharge Socket

Naboo Queen's Royal Starship

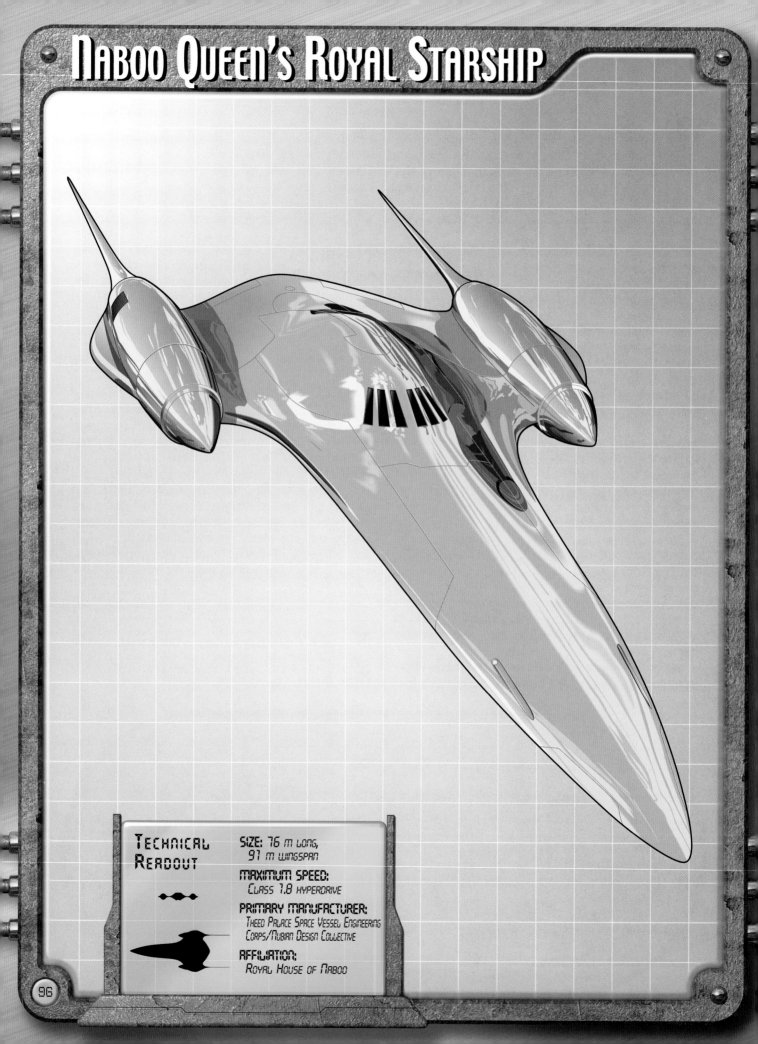

Technical Readout

Size: 76 m long, 91 m wingspan

Maximum Speed: Class 1.8 hyperdrive

Primary Manufacturer: Theed Palace Space Vessel Engineering Corps/Nubian Design Collective

Affiliation: Royal House of Naboo

Modified J-Type 327 Nubian Starship

The Naboo like to make a good first impression. When residents of Coruscant look toward the sky to see the elegant, chromium-covered Naboo starship descending to land, they can't help but feel inspired. The Naboo Royal Starship, a vehicle reserved for use by the Naboo sovereign, is a shining example of the marriage between art and design.

Naboo engineers claim that the Royal Starship is really composed of two major components: (1) the spaceframe, and (2) everything else. The spaceframe, created by the Theed Palace Space Vessel Engineering Corps, is a single long, supple hull. The frame is covered in chromium, once necessary to protect such starships from radiation but now included as a time-honored tradition.

The rest of the starship, from the engines to the life support systems, was provided by the Nubian Design Collective. Most impressive is the 327 Nubian hyperdrive, which, even when damaged, is powerful enough to take the starship from Naboo to Tatooine in a single jump. Unlike many other larger, complex hyperdrive units, the 327 is compact and accessible. The generator itself can be raised from a compartment in the floor to allow easy repairs, diagnostic checks, or even complete replacement.

The Royal Starship is strictly a diplomatic vessel and lacks weapons of any kind, though it is not without resources. The Headon-5 sublight engines, which have been modified by the Naboo for ecological protection, can exceed the speed of many small attack starfighters. Its strong shields can withstand a great deal of punishment, including an all-out assault by multiple turbolaser emplacements. Intricate sensors built into the starship report any damage instantly, allowing the crew to pinpoint trouble spots immediately. When the ship is damaged, up to eight loyal astromech droids rush to make repairs. The astromechs will even venture onto the starship's surface, braving the vacuum of space and enemy fire to protect the Naboo royalty.

Whenever the starship travels, it is always accompanied by a small wing of Naboo N-1 starfighters. This escort squadron, known as Bravo Flight, is handpicked by the Naboo sovereign's bodyguard from only the most dedicated and talented pilots in the Royal Security Forces.

During Queen Amidala's time in office, her starship was piloted by Ric Olié and a crew of well-trained technicians, engineers, navigators, diplomatic aides, scientists, and bosuns. The vehicle was furnished to accommodate the Queen's entire entourage, including her handmaidens and bodyguards. Large, climate-controlled wardrobe containers provided Amidala with clothing for any and all occasions. After Amidala left office, her starship was retired and another vessel was handcrafted for the new monarch, Queen Jamillia.

> ### "This is not a warship! We have no weapons. We're a nonviolent people....That is why the Trade Federation was brave enough to attack us."
> *—Captain Panaka to Qui-Gon Jinn*

6 327 Nubian Hyperdrive: When the Royal Starship's hyperdrive was damaged while fleeing Naboo, the vehicle was forced to stop on Tatooine to find a replacement. While on the desert planet, Queen Amidala first met her future husband, Anakin Skywalker.

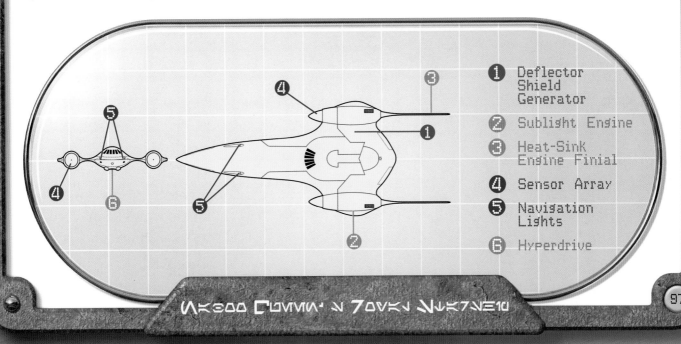

1. Deflector Shield Generator
2. Sublight Engine
3. Heat-Sink Engine Finial
4. Sensor Array
5. Navigation Lights
6. Hyperdrive

Naboo Starfighter

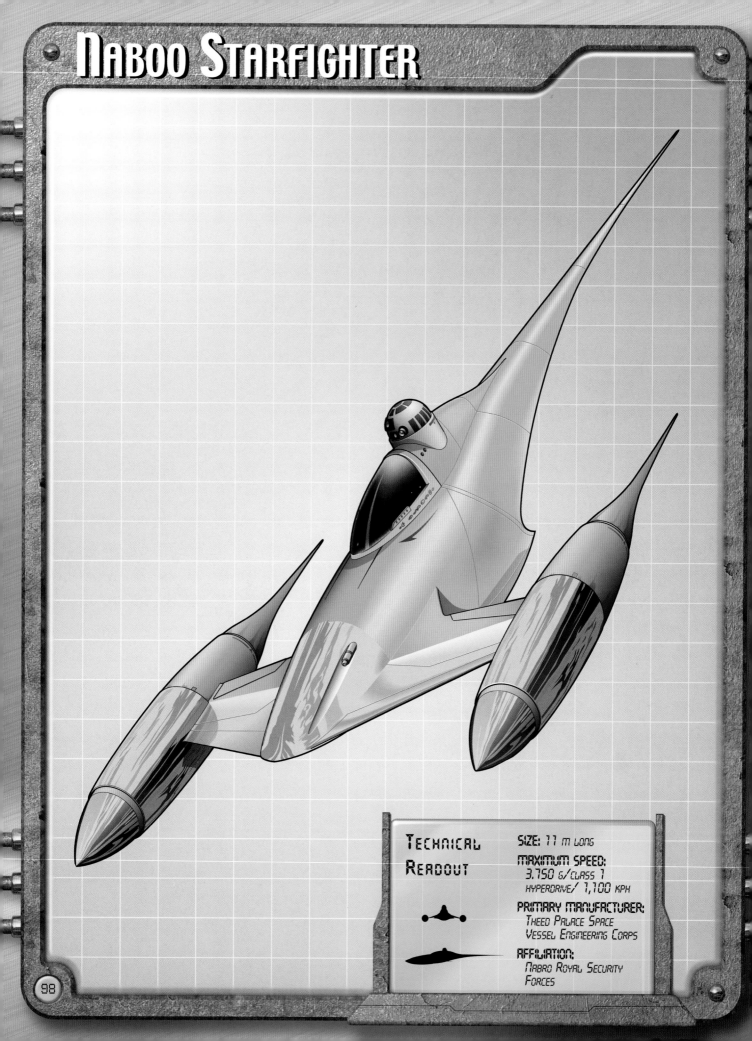

Technical Readout

Size: 11 m long

Maximum Speed:
3,750 g/class 1
hyperdrive/ 1,100 kph

Primary Manufacturer:
Theed Palace Space
Vessel Engineering Corps

Affiliation:
Naboo Royal Security
Forces

Naboo Royal N-1 Starfighter

Although a peaceful people, the Naboo have always recognized the need to patrol their borders. For ensuring the safety of Theed, the Naboo Royal Security Forces use the Flash speeder and other vehicles. When scouting their system, the Naboo rely on the nimble N-1 starfighter.

The sleek N-1 exemplifies the best elements of Naboo design. The craft is aesthetically sound, adhering to the Naboo's love of curves and aerodynamic shapes. A chromium finish on the front end of the vehicle gleams in the sunlight during parades and celebratory fly-bys. The chromium is purely decorative and reserved for starships assigned to the Royal House.

The Naboo are dedicated to protecting their ecologically sensitive planet, and the Naboo starfighter is a great example of this commitment. The N-1's specialized engine configuration ensures that fuel burns hotter in order to reduce harmful emissions. An advanced cooling system, which includes numerous heat sinks located along the engine finials, prevents overheating. The rear finial can be connected to specialized outlets in Naboo hangars that recharge the starfighter and transmit important data, including encoded mission profiles.

Prior to the Battle of Naboo, the N-1 was reserved for reconnaissance missions, escort duty, and ceremonial functions. In order to accompany the Queen's starship to Coruscant, the N-1 was equipped with a Nubian Monarc C-4 hyperdrive with a range of 1,000 light-years. Advanced life support systems and shields protect the pilots in most conditions, while a standard astromech assists with performance adjustments and repairs. The N-1 also has a relatively intelligent autopi-

"I'll try spinning. That's a good trick."
—*Anakin Skywalker, in an N1, during the Battle of Naboo*

lot computer that receives navigational data from hangar outlets or Naboo flight control. During a crisis, the autopilot can bring the N-1 directly to the site of an emergency, or see the pilot home safely.

N-1 pilots receive extensive training, part of which involves logging hundreds of standard hours inside the cockpit of a "police cruiser." A blue starfighter that bears a striking resemblance to the N-1, the police cruiser is used extensively by the RSF for atmospheric missions. The weapons and shields are less powerful than the N-1's systems, but the cruiser remains a formidable craft. Echo Flight, a squadron composed of RSF rookies, uses police cruisers almost exclusively.

The N-1 was never intended as a dedicated combat starfighter, but it does function well in small skirmishes against space pirates or outlaws. The vehicle's armaments are fairly standard, consisting of twin laser cannons and a full complement of ten proton torpedoes. The weapons are powerful enough to allow a squadron of N-1 starfighters to confront the Trade Federation Droid Control Ship at the Battle of Naboo. While Bravo Flight eliminated swarms of droid starfighters, Anakin Skywalker used the N-1's proton torpedoes to destroy the Droid Control Ship's central reactor.

7 **Astromech Unit: When** Bravo Flight prepared to launch its attack on the Droid Control Ship, R2-D2 positioned himself inside one of the N-1s to assist in the mission. Coincidentally, Anakin used that same starfighter as a hiding place, and the two friends soon found themselves battling the Trade Federation together.

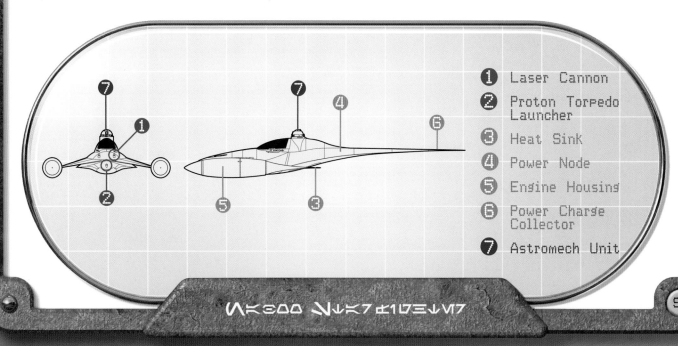

1. Laser Cannon
2. Proton Torpedo Launcher
3. Heat Sink
4. Power Node
5. Engine Housing
6. Power Charge Collector
7. Astromech Unit

OUTRIDER

TECHNICAL READOUT

SIZE: 27 m LONG

MAXIMUM SPEED:
2,860G/CLASS
0.75 HYPERDRIVE/1,000 KPH

PRIMARY MANUFACTURER:
CORELLIAN ENGINEERING
CORPORATION

AFFILIATION: DASH RENDAR

Corellian Engineering Corporation YT-2400 Freighter

The smuggler Dash Rendar relied on the *Outrider*, a heavily modified Corellian freighter, to commit crimes against the Empire during the height of the Galactic Civil War. A sometime ally of the Rebel Alliance, Rendar flew his personal starship at the Battle of Hoth and continued to aid the Rebels in their conflict with Prince Xizor's Black Sun criminal empire. When Darth Vader destroyed Xizor's skyhook, the *Outrider* was caught in the explosion and seemingly destroyed.

The *Outrider* was a modified YT-2400 transport, a vehicle originally intended as a medium-range stock cargo hauler. Similar in design to other YT freighters, the YT-2400 has a rounded hull and an elongated, tubular cockpit. The cockpit is connected to the body of the starship by a pair of reinforced bracing arms and includes a primary escape pod with seating for six. The crew quarters and living areas are located in the bracing arms. The freighter's oversized hull is capable of supporting the market's most advanced engines and weapons systems. A secondary escape pod can be found in the cargo area, directly opposite from the primary escape craft. The starship's speed, resilience, and adaptability have made it attractive to many mercenaries.

Like Han Solo's *Millennium Falcon,* the *Outrider* had been drastically altered from its original specifications for use in Rendar's smuggling operations. During the campaign against Xizor, the *Outrider*'s weapons system included two illegal Dymex double laser cannons located on the dorsal and ventral surfaces of the starship. The cannons, which were mounted on Corellian

> ## "I owe the *Outrider* the best. She's brought me home when any other ship would have scattered me across space."
> —*Dash Rendar*

1D servo turrets, had been personally altered by Rendar for increased range. They were generally staffed during combat, but could be controlled remotely from the cockpit as well. The laser cannons were complemented by a pair of concussion missile launchers installed on the cockpit.

Rendar replaced the transport's original engine systems with three stolen KonGar KGDefender military-grade ion engines. The vehicle's Class 0.75 hyperdrive was provided by a modified SoroSuub Griffyn/Y2TG hyperdrive engine. Like the engine systems, the *Outrider*'s weapons, deflector shields, and sensor stealth system were all considered quite illegal during the Galactic Civil War. Every time Dash activated the *Outrider*, he was breaking dozens of Imperial Laws.

Although the *Outrider* had saved Rendar's life on countless occasions, the vehicle was not fast enough to escape the destruction caused by Darth Vader's attack on Prince Xizor. Debris from Xizor's faltering skyhook slammed into the *Outrider*, and the starship apparently exploded. In the years since, there have been sporadic sightings of the *Outrider* and her infamous pilot, but these reports remain unconfirmed by New Republic sources.

5 Escape Pod: The *Outrider*'s primary escape pod is easily accessible from the cockpit. Dash's allies believed that the rogue managed to reach the escape pod moments before the *Outrider* exploded, but his closest friends are fairly certain that he would have never abandoned the starship.

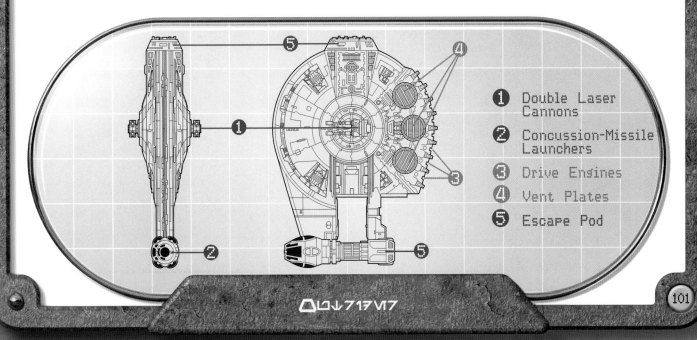

1. Double Laser Cannons
2. Concussion-Missile Launchers
3. Drive Engines
4. Vent Plates
5. Escape Pod

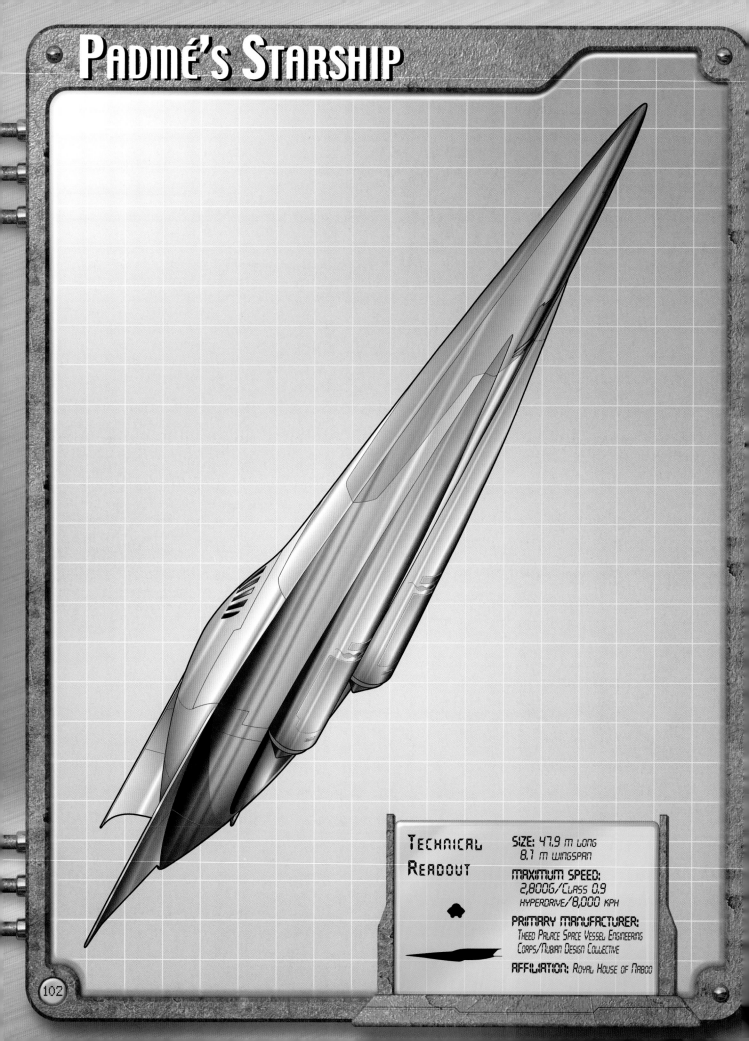

Technical Readout

SIZE: 47.9 m long
8.7 m wingspan

MAXIMUM SPEED:
2,800G/Class 0.9
Hyperdrive/8,000 kph

PRIMARY MANUFACTURER:
Theed Palace Space Vessel Engineering
Corps/Nubian Design Collective

AFFILIATION: Royal House of Naboo

Customized H-Type Nubian Yacht

The Trade Federation's occupation of Naboo was a defining moment in the planet's history. It forced the peaceful human residents of Naboo to re-evaluate their defenses and combat capabilities. In an effort led by Captain Panaka of the Royal Security Forces, the Naboo began building a number of discreet defenses, ranging from planetary shield generators to ion cannons. One of the most important defense initiatives provided funds for a steady supply of new starships designed for transporting Naboo dignitaries throughout the galaxy.

Among the many transport craft developed by the Naboo is the Royal Yacht, reserved for streaking across the galaxy without attracting undue attention. The vehicle's tremendous speed is combined with a narrow silhouette and sheltered engines, to provide the smallest possible sensor signature. In addition, the yacht is equipped with the most powerful shields available to the Naboo, ensuring that the starship can endure tremendous punishment before losing power. Formidable communications devices, including a long-range transmitter, can send and receive signals into the remote reaches of the Outer Rim. A robust hyperdrive system linked to the most updated navicomputer charts allows for quick retreats into hyperspace, while a handful of sophisticated electronic countermeasures and an escape capsule serve as a last line of defense.

Although the Royal Yacht does support a full crew, which that can include a pilot, co-pilot, navigator, com-scan/shield technician, and two astromech droids, the vehicle was explicitly designed for solo operation. The

> **"We wanted to give the Senator an N-1 escort wherever she went, but . . . we just couldn't keep up with the Royal Yacht, especially with Padmé at the controls."**
> *—Ric Olié*

yacht is extremely low-maintenance, with elegant yet simplified systems. A series of well-placed repair panels are spread throughout the ship, allowing easy access to power sources, wiring nodes, computer terminals, and other key components. A redundant power generator, secondary engines, and a layered shield system ensure that the yacht is never completely helpless.

Like the Naboo Royal Starship, the Royal Yacht is covered in a skin of mirrored chromium. Generally, such chromium finish is reserved for the ruling monarch's personal fleet. However, upon its completion the Royal Yacht was not immediately assigned to any single individual. Due to her role in the war against the Trade Federation, Padmé Amidala had earned the undying admiration of all the Naboo and was considered a part of the monarchy, regardless of her title. As a result, she was often allowed to use the yacht for low-profile personal missions. After the destruction of her Naboo cruiser, the Royal Yacht essentially became Padmé's personal starship. On the eve of the Clone Wars, Padmé commandeered the vehicle to take Anakin Skywalker to Tatooine; the pair later used the starship to journey to Geonosis in order to rescue Obi-Wan Kenobi.

① Shield Generator: When approaching Geonosis, Padmé, and Anakin lowered the ship's shields to reduce the starship's energy signature in the hopes that the Geonosian monitors would assume the small vehicle was a meteorite hurtling into the atmosphere. The ploy worked and allowed the yacht to land without incident.

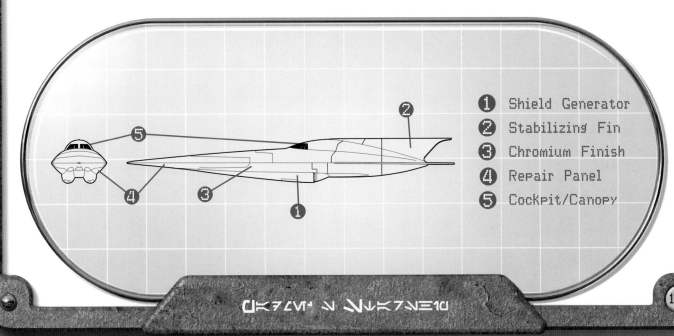

①	Shield Generator
②	Stabilizing Fin
③	Chromium Finish
④	Repair Panel
⑤	Cockpit/Canopy

Podracer (Anakin's)

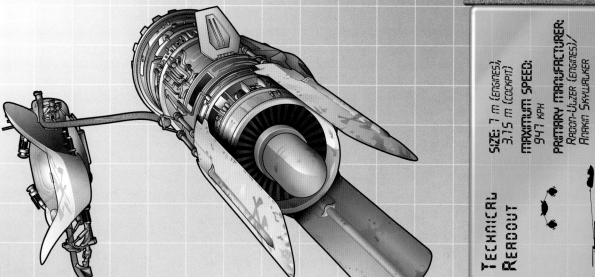

TECHNICAL READOUT

SIZE: 7 m (engines),
3.15 m (cockpit)

MAXIMUM SPEED:
947 KPH

PRIMARY MANUFACTURER:
Radon-Ulzer (engines)/
Anakin Skywalker

AFFILIATION:
Anakin Skywalker

Modified Radon-Ulzer 620C

Even under the benevolent rule of the New Republic, there are portions of the galaxy where life is filled with hardships. On Outer Rim worlds, in particular, each standard day can be spent toiling away for little or no gain. On these planets, entertainment comes in the form of exciting and often deadly sports such as Podracing.

A Podracer is a high-speed vehicle consisting of two large engines connected to a repulsorlift cockpit by flexible cables. Podraces involve up to several dozen of these craft careening through winding courses at speeds in excess of 900 kilometers per hour. During the event, Podracers collide with the terrain and one another—often with lethal results.

Despite the inherent risks in Podracing, young Anakin Skywalker yearned to become a champion Podracer pilot. To achieve this goal, the boy rebuilt a custom Podracer using spare parts scrounged from Watto's junk shop. When he finished working on the vehicle, it proved to be the fastest Podracer on Tatooine, with a top speed of around 950 kilometers per hour.

Anakin built his Podracer around a pair of competent Radon-Ulzer 620C engines. He modified the engines by adding an innovative fuel atomizer and distribution system to increase performance. Three bright yellow air scoops attached to each engine gave the Podracer phenomenal maneuverability, and a series of well-placed air brakes enabled sudden stops and improved cornering ability.

With the support of Qui-Gon Jinn, Anakin entered his custom-built Podracer in Tatooine's Boonta Eve Classic. To win, however, he would need to beat his nemesis: the crafty Dug Sebulba.

Although Sebulba's Podracer was not custom-built, it was no less impressive. Built around a pair of greatly modified Collor Pondrat Plug-F Mammoth racing engines, his Podracer was known to exceed 800 kilometers per hour over open ground. The strength of the orange Collor Pondrat was not in its speed, but its size: the large engines, fitted with split-x intakes, were perfect for ramming opponents and driving them off course. Sebulba used this tactic liberally throughout his Podracing career. Sebulba's Podracer also concealed several illegal modifications, including flamethrowers and a nail gun.

During the Boonta Eve Classic, Sebulba took an early lead, using his trademark treachery to force other pilots out of the race. Anakin eventually caught the Dug, however, and the two tussled as they screamed through the Tatooine desert. After years of tormenting his opponents, Sebulba finally met his match in the willful Anakin. During the final lap of the race, Sebulba lost control of his Podracer and crashed in Hutt Flats.

> **"Amazing . . . a controlled thrust and he's back on course! What a move! That little human is out of his mind!"**
>
> *—Podracing announcer Fode and Beed commenting on Anakin Skywalker's performance at the Boonta Eve Classic*

⑤ Paint Job: The paint job on Anakin's Podracer was applied by R2-D2 and C-3PO the night before the Boonta Eve Classic. Ironically, Sebulba later purchased the Podracer and repainted it with his signature orange-and-black color scheme.

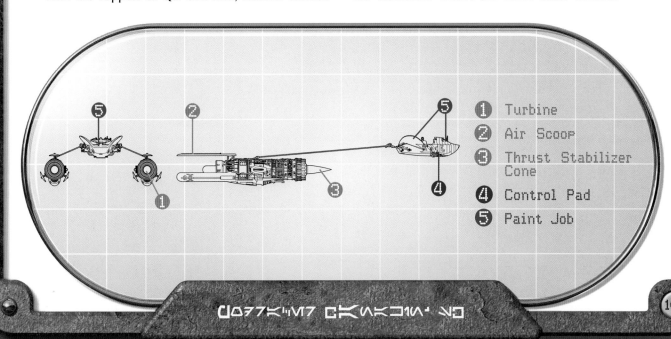

① Turbine
② Air Scoop
③ Thrust Stabilizer Cone
④ Control Pad
⑤ Paint Job

Podracer Classification

Scale in Meters
(5m = 16.5 ft)
0
5
Ben Quadinaros
Ratts Tyerell
Boles Roor
Dud Bolt
Anakin Skywalker
Mars Guo
Sebulba
Teemto Pagalies
Aldar Beedo
Neva Kee

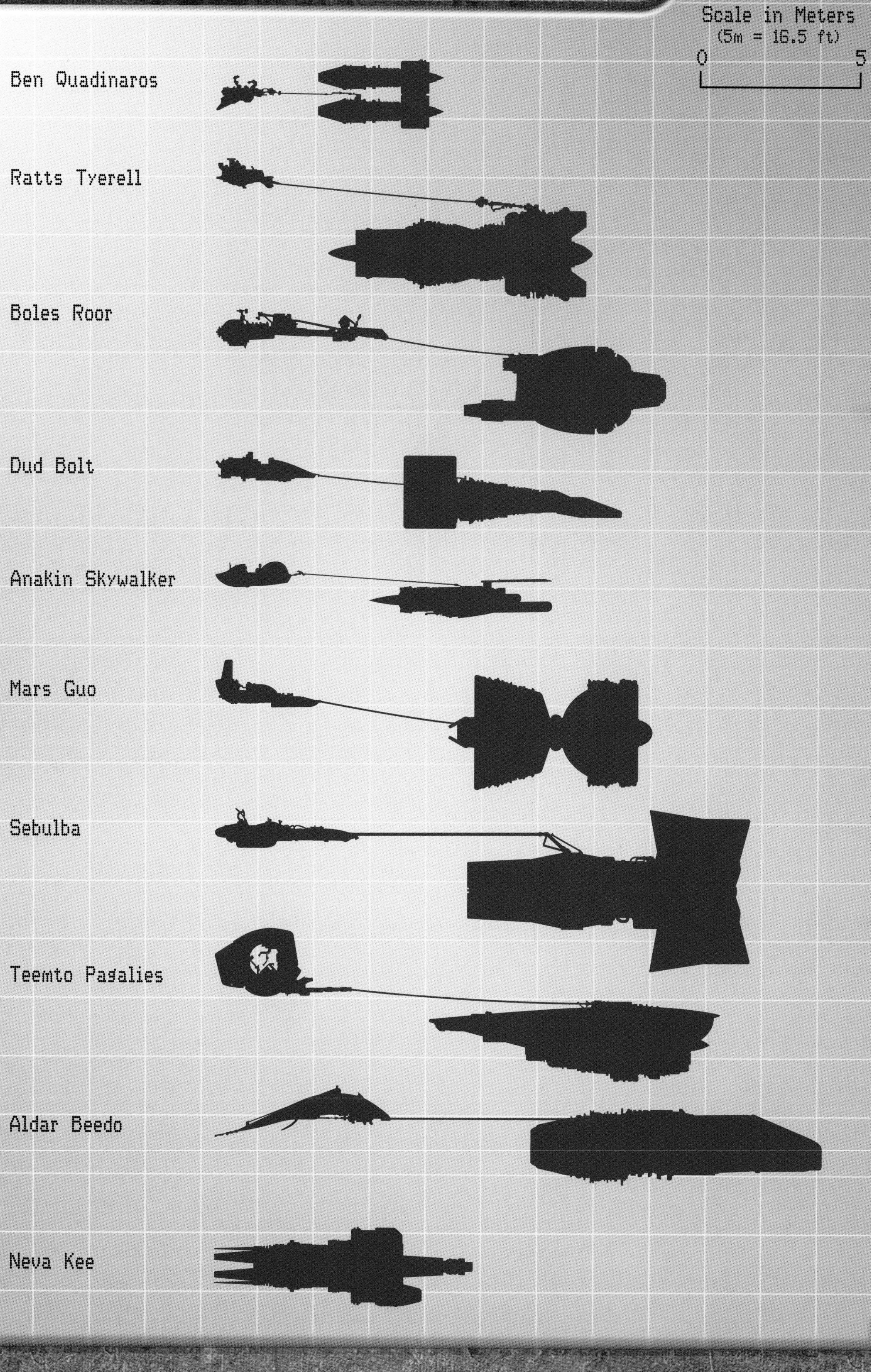

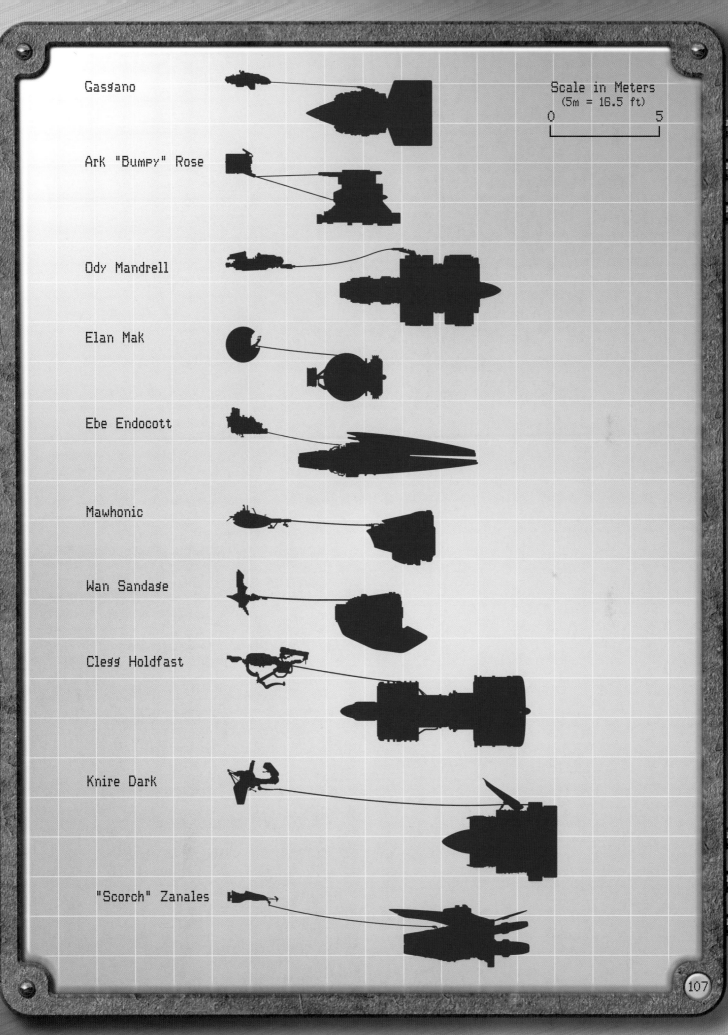

Gasgano

Ark "Bumpy" Rose

Ody Mandrell

Elan Mak

Ebe Endocott

Mawhonic

Wan Sandage

Clegg Holdfast

Knire Dark

"Scorch" Zanales

Scale in Meters
(5m = 16.5 ft)
0   5

REBEL BLOCKADE RUNNER *(Tantive IV)*

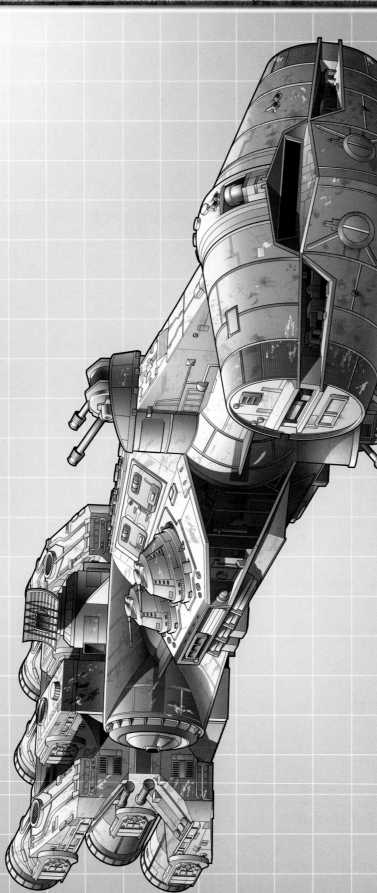

TECHNICAL READOUT

SIZE: 150 m LONG

MAXIMUM SPEED:
2,100G/CLASS 2
HYPERDRIVE/950 KPH

PRIMARY MANUFACTURER:
CORELLIAN ENGINEERING
CORPORATION

AFFILIATION:
REBEL ALLIANCE

Corellian Engineering Corporation Corvette

After Princess Leia intercepted the plans to the original Death Star, she attempted to flee Darth Vader in a Corellian corvette called the *Tantive IV*. Vader's forces destroyed the *Tantive IV*. In the years that followed, Corellian corvettes would become an important component of the Rebel Alliance's fleet. In fact, the corvettes became so strongly associated with the Alliance's ability to elude Imperial capture that many historians have referred to them as "Rebel blockade runners."

A Corellian corvette is an older-model, multipurpose capital ship. The vehicle can serve as a troop carrier, light escort vehicle, cargo transport, and even passenger liner. The original Corellian corvette is still in wide use throughout the galaxy, a testament to its quality design and durability.

Although the corvette was not designed for illegal activity, it does have features that make it appealing to pirates and smugglers. The starship has a very fast sublight drive coupled with an efficient hyperjump calculator. The combination of these two technologies allows the starship to escape into hyperspace very quickly. Corellian pirates found this useful for escaping CorSec authorities, while the Rebels relied on the corvette's hyperjump capabilities to flee Imperial Star Destroyers.

Corellian corvettes are manufactured without weapons installed, but they do possess several modular weapons emplacements. Princess Leia's *Tantive IV* carried six Taim & Bak H9 turbolaser cannons. Rebel blockade runners could support as many as eight tur-

> ## "I'm a member of the Imperial Senate on a diplomatic mission to Alderaan…"
> —*Princess Leia*
>
> ## "You are part of the Rebel Alliance, and a traitor. Take her away!"
> —*Darth Vader*

bolasers, six laser cannons, and four ion cannons. Standard shield generators provide enough protection for short skirmishes, but they are no match for the weaponry aboard a Star Destroyer.

The corvette *Tantive IV* was a consular ship registered to the Royal House of Alderaan. Because the starship's diplomatic status allowed her to travel the galaxy freely, Princess Leia often used her for relief missions to worlds under Imperial control. As the Empire grew more oppressive, Leia began using the *Tantive IV* to secretly aid the Alliance. During a "mercy mission" to Ralltiir, Leia acquired the Death Star plans.

The *Tantive IV* met her tragic end soon after. Darth Vader tracked the *Tantive IV* to Tatooine, where the Star Destroyer *Devastator* caught the corvette in its tractor beams. Stormtroopers boarded the *Tantive IV*, captured Princess Leia, and executed Captain Antilles. The *Devastator* then demolished the corvette with a barrage of turbolaser fire. Darth Vader later claimed that the *Tantive IV* had been destroyed in a deep-space disaster. Fortunately, Leia had already entrusted the Death Star plans to R2-D2, who escaped to Tatooine in one of the corvette's escape pods.

6 Escape Pod: A Corellian corvette's escape pod is often credited with saving the galaxy from Imperial tyranny. After receiving the plans to the Death Star, R2-D2 fled Imperials aboard one of the *Tantive IV's* escape pods. The plans would later ensure the Alliance's victory at the Battle of Yavin.

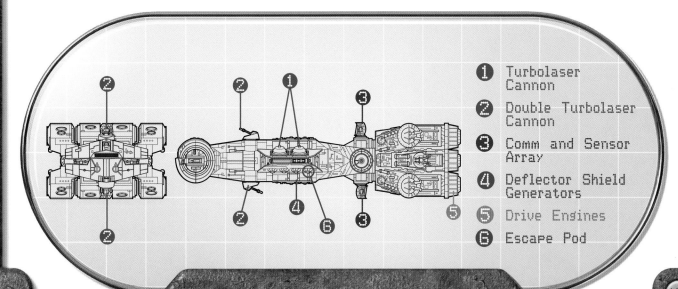

1. Turbolaser Cannon
2. Double Turbolaser Cannon
3. Comm and Sensor Array
4. Deflector Shield Generators
5. Drive Engines
6. Escape Pod

REBEL CRUISER (REDEMPTION)

TECHNICAL READOUT

SIZE: 300 m LONG

MAXIMUM SPEED:
1,200G/CLASS 2
HYPERDRIVE/800 KPH

PRIMARY MANUFACTURER:
KUAT DRIVE YARDS.

AFFILIATION: REBEL ALLIANCE

Kuat Drive Yards Nebulon-B Frigate

During its battle with the Empire, the Rebel Alliance was truly a ragtag organization. The Rebels would use virtually any vehicle they could find, from modified T-47 airspeeders to older-model Corellian corvettes. The so-called Rebel cruiser is, in actuality, a modified Nebulon-B escort frigate that the Alliance used for a variety of missions.

The Rebel cruiser is notable because most of the Nebulon-B frigates were originally commissioned by the Empire. Kuat Drive Yards designed the Nebulon-B to protect larger Imperial starships during attacks. The frigate includes twelve laser cannons with precision tracking servos and advanced targeting computers capable of acquiring fast-moving starfighters. The Nebulon-B frigates have twelve turbolaser batteries for use against capital ships. Small warships can attach to the Nebulon-B's central docking tube. The bay can hold up to twenty-four starfighters. Tough shields and a reinforced armor hull round out the vessel's combat capabilities.

To add some versatility to the craft, the Nebulon-B frigate is often equipped with two tractor beam projectors that can be used to rescue crippled friendly starfighters or capture disabled enemy ships. The Empire often used Nebulon-B frigates as long-range scouts because of the craft's sophisticated sensors and long-range, multifrequency communications transceivers. Some Imperial officers shunned the Nebulon-B because it is sluggish at sublight speeds, but other tacticians realized the benefit of using the frigate to launch short-range attacks on unsuspecting enemies.

Ironically, Rebel agents acquired several of the

> ## "Just once, I'd like to destroy a starship that *we* didn't pay for!"
> —*Imperial admiral Hurkk at the Battle of Oovo IV*

Nebulon-B frigates during defections or through outright theft. Early in the Galactic Civil War, the Nebulon-B frigates were the Alliance's primary assault ships. As newer and more powerful starships entered the Rebel fleet, many of the Nebulon-B frigates were converted into search-and-rescue starships, command vessels, and long-range reconnaissance vehicles.

After his confrontation with Darth Vader on Cloud City, Luke Skywalker recovered from his injuries aboard the *Redemption*, a Nebulon-B modified to serve as a medical frigate. The *Redemption* and other medical frigates have facilities for up to *700* wounded soldiers and include a full staff of medical droids and Alliance specialists. Sixteen bacta tanks and other equipment consume much of the medical frigate's docking bay space, forcing the vessel to rely on support ships when attacked. In addition, about half of the medical frigate's weapons have been removed and replaced with redundant systems, such as back-up power generators, shield projectors, and life support systems.

9 Sick Bay: After his battle with Darth Vader, Luke Skywalker received a prosthetic hand while recuperating aboard the *Redemption*, a Nebulon-B frigate modified for medical duty.

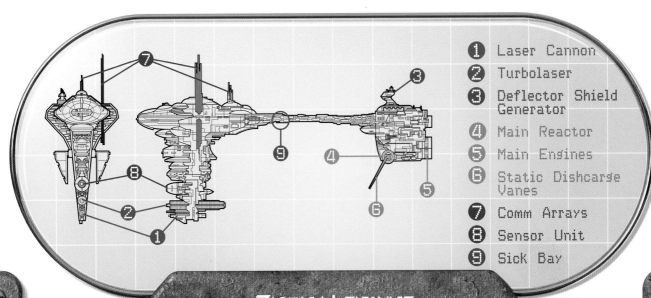

1. Laser Cannon
2. Turbolaser
3. Deflector Shield Generator
4. Main Reactor
5. Main Engines
6. Static Dishcarge Vanes
7. Comm Arrays
8. Sensor Unit
9. Sick Bay

REBEL TRANSPORT (BRIGHT HOPE)

TECHNICAL READOUT

SIZE: 90 m LONG

MAXIMUM SPEED:
9005/CLASS 4
HYPERDRIVE/650 KPH

PRIMARY MANUFACTURER:
GALLOFREE YARDS, INC.

AFFILIATION:
Rebel Alliance

Gallofree Yards Medium Transport

When Imperial forces led by Darth Vader attacked the hidden Rebel base on Hoth, it seemed as if the Alliance would soon be crushed. AT-AT walkers advanced on the Rebel positions, and snowtroopers soon infiltrated Echo Base. As they rushed into the Rebel facility, however, the Imperials discovered that the key Alliance personnel had eluded capture. This dramatic escape was made possible by a small fleet of Gallofree Yards medium transports, forever after known more generally as "Rebel transports" because of the important role they played at the Battle of Hoth. (Ironically, the "last transport" to leave Hoth was called the *Bright Hope*).

The Rebel Alliance exploited a wide range of starships as transports, including converted passenger liners, stolen Imperial vessels, and captured pirate ships. The most common starship used in this capacity was a true transport manufactured by Gallofree Yards and sold to the Rebel Alliance at an incredible discount. The Gallofree starships have a cargo capacity of 19,000 metric tons and allowed the Rebels to transport food, ammunition, medical supplies, weapons, troops, and even vehicles to all corners of the galaxy. The transport is easily identified by its outer hull, which consists of a series of durasteel plates carefully arranged to create a thick, protective shell. Hundreds of modular cargo pods with their own repulsorlift devices allow rapid loading and unloading. The cargo pods are locked into place and protected from the vacuum of space and atmospheric elements via an invisible magnetic shield. The transport is further protected by a very rudimentary deflector shield system.

Like many Rebel starships, the Gallofree Yards transports were relatively outdated vehicles modified by the Alliance. Variants included troops transports equipped with small medical bays, and weapons transports that functioned like mobile armories. Some medium transports became fuel tankers equipped with docking facilities to allow starships to refuel in space during long journeys.

Although an important part of the Rebel fleet, the Gallofree transports were by no means perfect. The ships are prone to malfunctions and are slow moving. Rebel engineers have been forced to add long-range sensors and advanced countermeasure systems to help the transport escape from Imperial pursuit.

Rebel transports are rarely armed. The Gallofree Yards vessel uses all available space for cargo or passengers. The only weapons are four retractable twin laser cannons. Because Rebel transports are not combat vessels, they must travel in convoys protected by X-wing squadrons or land-based ion cannons, as was the case during the evacuation of Hoth.

> ## "Your Highness, we must take the last transport! It's our only hope!"
> *—C-3PO, to Princess Leia during the evacuation of Hoth*

3 Command Pod: Although protected by a shield generator, the command pod aboard a Rebel transport is an easy target. When the command pod is destroyed, the transport is rendered helpless.

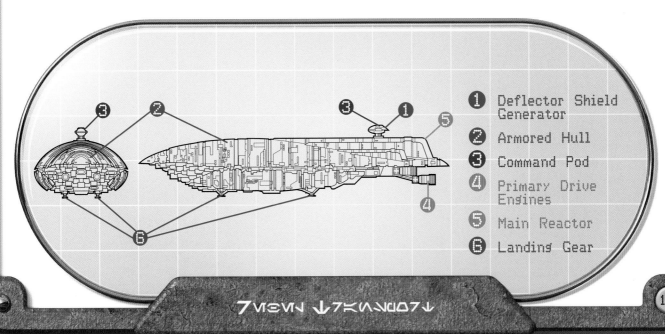

1. Deflector Shield Generator
2. Armored Hull
3. Command Pod
4. Primary Drive Engines
5. Main Reactor
6. Landing Gear

REPUBLIC ASSAULT SHIP

TECHNICAL READOUT

SIZE: 752 m LONG

MAXIMUM SPEED:
3,500G/CLASS
0.6 HYPERDRIVE

PRIMARY MANUFACTURER:
ROTHANA HEAVY ENGINEERING
(SUBSIDIARY OF KDY)

AFFILIATION: OLD REPUBLIC

RHE *Acclamator*-Class Transgalactic Military Assault Ship

When Count Dooku's separatist movement first formed, the Old Republic was woefully unprepared for a large-scale conflict. At that time, the Republic had no standing army and few military vehicles. Fortunately, Obi-Wan Kenobi soon discovered a clone army, complete with weapons, armor, and vehicles. As the Republic prepared to invade Geonosis, Master Yoda collected this clone army, which was transported to the battlefield in a fleet of large *Acclamator*-class battleships. According to many historians, the arrival of the new Republic assault ships marked the true beginning of the Clone Wars.

The Republic assault ship was produced by Rothana Heavy Engineering, a KDY subsidiary subcontracted by the Kaminoans. Each assault ship is meant to land a full invasion force consisting of 16,000 clone troopers, 320 speeder bikes, 48 AT-TE walkers, 80 gunships, and 36 self-propelled heavy artillery units. The assault ship's Class 0.6 hyperdrive, unusually fast for a craft of the *Acclamator*'s class, enabled the clone army to reach Geonosis soon after Obi-Wan's capture.

Once troops are released, the assault ship's mission profile changes to provide ground support. Scanning systems, including an extremely powerful radar array, gather data on enemy positions to assist in ground campaigns. The assault ship can also unleash a terrible orbital bombardment, launching high-yield proton torpedoes at slow-moving targets and opening fire with its 12 turbolasers to destroy buildings and emplacements. During the Clone Wars,

> ## "Master Sifo-Dyas requested the most powerful army in the galaxy. We have worked with only the best shipbuilders to fulfill that request."
>
> —*Kamino prime minister Lama Su*

tracking devices in every clone trooper's helmet allowed controllers aboard the assault ship to monitor troop movements and coordinate attacks.

While the Republic assault ship was not designed specifically for ship-to-ship battle, it is more than capable of destroying smaller starships and defending itself from attack. Redundant shield arrays crisscross the starship's body, although these devices place great strain on the vehicle's generators and are rarely activated. During space combat, the assault ship's 24 laser cannons are brought to bear on starfighters, while both the turbolasers and torpedo launchers can be repositioned to strike at capital ships. The assault's ship's planetary focus has undoubtedly affected its design: the ship-to-ship weapons are not incredibly accurate, and repositioning the weapons emplacements requires several minutes. As the Clone Wars progressed, many Republic assault ships traveled with starfighter and battleship escorts to protect against ambushes.

The Republic assault ship was both a deciding factor at the Battle of Geonosis and a sign of things to come. In later years, the Empire would rely on Star Destroyers modeled on the assault ship. In fact, Star Destroyers eventually made the *Acclamator*-class starship obsolete.

⑤ Clone Troopers: The Republic assault ship transported thousands of clone troopers throughout the galaxy during the Clone Wars, one of the most critical conflicts in galactic history.

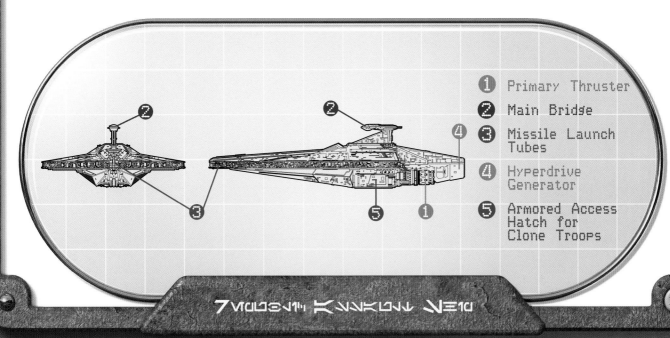

① Primary Thruster
② Main Bridge
③ Missile Launch Tubes
④ Hyperdrive Generator
⑤ Armored Access Hatch for Clone Troops

REPUBLIC CRUISER *(Radiant VII)*

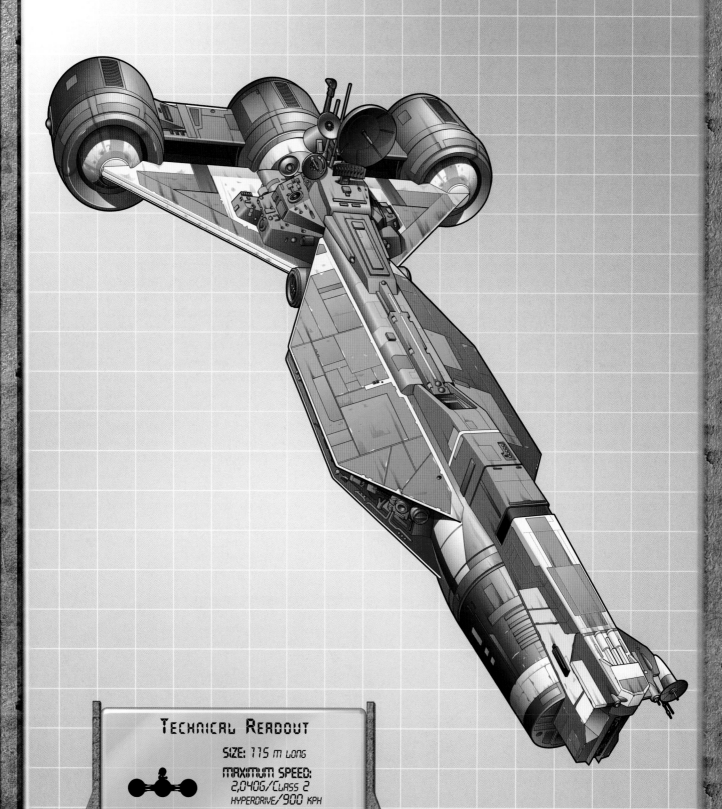

TECHNICAL READOUT

SIZE: 115 m long

MAXIMUM SPEED:
2,040G/Class 2
Hyperdrive/900 kph

PRIMARY MANUFACTURER:
Corellian Engineering
Corporation

AFFILIATION: Old Republic

CEC *Consular*-Class Space Cruiser

Although the Old Republic had little in the way of a military, it did maintain vehicles for use by diplomats, Republic security forces, and even the Jedi Order. One of the stalwart starships in this fleet was the Republic cruiser, a Corellian vessel manufactured specifically for use by Republic dignitaries.

Republic cruisers first saw flight during the Old Republic's final years. Predicated by cost cutbacks, the cruiser is meant to be efficient and utilitarian. While previous Senatorial transports contained spacious climate-controlled living quarters and other amenities, the *Consular*-class cruiser is relatively plain and unassuming. For this reason, it was often used by the Jedi, who preferred the simple transport over more extravagant vessels. Obi-Wan Kenobi and Qui-Gon Jinn used a Republic cruiser called the Radiant VII to travel to Naboo in a vain attempt to negotiate with the Trade Federation.

> **"Don't they know that painting the ship red only makes it a better target?"**
> —*Trade Federation gunner Jull Dremon, shortly before firing upon the* RADIANT VII

Most Republic cruisers were painted scarlet to identify them as diplomatic starships. To allow for a wide variety of passengers and dignitaries, each cruiser carried a modular salon pod capable of supporting various atmospheres and environments. A salon pod could be reconfigured between missions to serve as living quarters for alien Senators. The salon pods were also armored, insulated, and protected against surveillance devices, making them the perfect setting for delicate negotiations. Since the fall of the Republic, mechanics have discovered that a cruiser's salon pod can be replaced by cargo modules, specialized rooms, and even a docking bay for a small fighter.

During diplomatic missions, negotiations and peace talks could be handled through the starship's versatile communications suite, which is designed to receive and transmit messages to almost any type of vehicle or installation in thousands of Republic languages. Such diplomatic vessels lacked weapons and relied on an array of deflector shields and starfighter escort for protection. In the event a Republic cruiser was badly damaged, the dignitaries aboard could escape in a pair of escape pods.

As the Old Republic began to crumble, its Senators became increasingly paranoid. As a result, most *Consular*-class cruisers maintained a minimal crew for security and secrecy. A typical crew included two communications officers, three engineers, two pilots, and a captain, along with several utility droids.

As the Old Republic shifted funds to fight the Clone Wars, the Republic cruisers began undertaking a wider variety of missions. Many were equipped with double turbolaser cannons and two concussion missile launchers to serve in the Republic Navy. A handful of these armed cruisers are still in operation throughout the galaxy; the smuggler Rif Taranu aided the Rebel Alliance by transporting contraband aboard his modified Corellian cruiser, the *Dead Reckoning*.

7 Cockpit: During the sensitive mission to Naboo, the *Radiant VII* was assigned a skeleton crew of one pilot and a captain. Both were killed when the Trade Federation destroyed their cruiser.

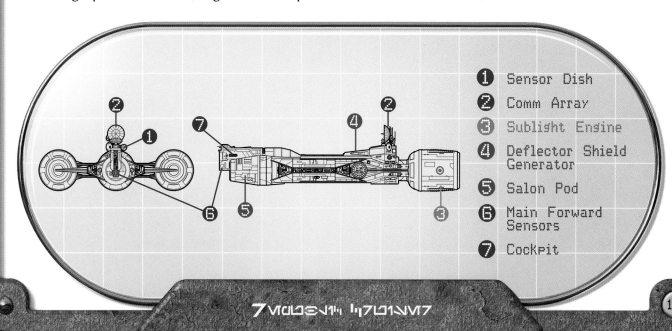

1. Sensor Dish
2. Comm Array
3. Sublight Engine
4. Deflector Shield Generator
5. Salon Pod
6. Main Forward Sensors
7. Cockpit

REPUBLIC GUNSHIP

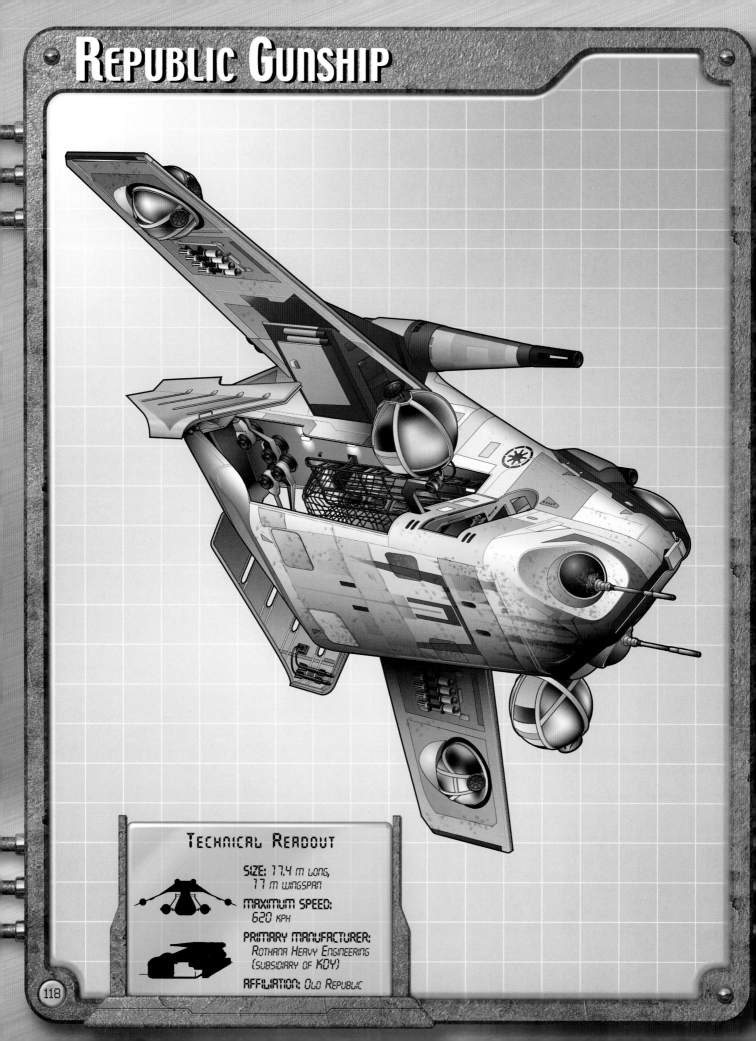

TECHNICAL READOUT

SIZE: 17.4 m long,
17 m wingspan

MAXIMUM SPEED:
620 kph

PRIMARY MANUFACTURER:
Rothana Heavy Engineering
(subsidiary of KDY)

AFFILIATION: Old Republic

RHE Low-Altitude Assault Transport/Infantry (LAAT/i) Repulsorlift Gunship

The army that invaded Geonosis on the eve of the Clone Wars proved amazingly effective. Its success was due, in large part, to its diverse array of military vehicles. While AT-TE walkers conveyed troops into the thick of the battle, a fleet of heavily armed assault gunships carried soldiers to key locations for tactical strikes.

Like many of the Republic's clone army vehicles, the LAAT/i gunship is designed to perform primary and secondary functions. The gunship's first duty is the transport of troopers: the vehicle holds 30 soldiers in the passenger compartment and four military speeder bikes in a rear hangar. The vehicle's armored hull is meant to absorb a great deal of punishment, but in the event the gunship is disabled, the vehicle's cockpit ejects as a separate escape pod.

The LAAT/i's secondary functions include reconnaissance, fire support, search-and-recovery missions, and low-altitude combat against ground units, airspeeders, and even starfighters. Two mass-drive missile launchers can fire a variety of ordnance. Short-range homing missiles are most often used to destroy armored vehicles and installations. Four air-to-air rockets tucked under each wing target starships and airspeeders. Three antipersonnel turrets blast any enemy soldiers and other small, fast-moving targets that approach the gunship. Finally, the craft's four ball turrets fire synchronized tributary beams with frightening precision. The ball turrets are positioned to provide tremendous field of fire, allowing them to shoot at targets above and below the gunship. With their tremendous array of firepower, gunships are often

> **"These gunships fly like butcherbugs and cut into us like Blood Carvers. We must have one."**
> *—Archduke Poggle the Lesser*

called upon to clear a deployment zone before troops are released.

Republic gunships were used on countless worlds during the Clone Wars because of their great maneuverability and atmospheric speed. Gunships can weave between large rock formations, dive into canyons and valleys, hover over a forest, and cruise between structures in sprawling urban areas—all while flying at more than 600 kilometers per hour. Only the most mobile enemy craft can keep a gunship in its sights. Even skilled pilots find it nearly impossible to avoid the craft's multiple weapons.

The LAAT/i gunship was one of several vehicles in the LAAT series. The basic gunship design is extremely versatile, and the vehicle has been modified to transport a wide variety of cargo. The LAAT/v is slightly larger than the standard troop transport and lacks a passenger compartment; instead, the rear hangar has been expanded to allow the vehicle to carry up to 16 speeder bikes or eight military landspeeders. At the Battle of Geonosis, the clone army deployed LAAT/c gunships to deposit AT-TE walkers at key sites across the battlefield.

6 Clone Pilot: Many of the Kaminoan clones were specially trained for specific military roles. Gunship pilots, identified by yellow markings on their helmets, underwent several years of training to master a range of military craft.

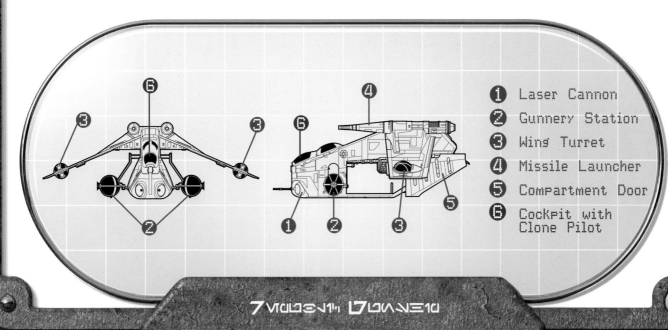

1 Laser Cannon
2 Gunnery Station
3 Wing Turret
4 Missile Launcher
5 Compartment Door
6 Cockpit with Clone Pilot

Sandcrawler

Technical Readout

Size: 20 m tall, 36.8 m long

Maximum Speed:
30 kph

Primary Manufacturer:
Corellia Mining

Affiliation:
Tatooine's Jawas

Modified Corellia Mining Digger Crawler

Tatooine is an extremely harsh world, and surviving on the desert planet is difficult even under the best of circumstances. Many galactic anthropologists are stunned to learn that the diminutive Jawas not only survive in Tatooine's wastes but actually manage to thrive while wandering the Dune Sea. Part of this success can be attributed to their massive sandcrawlers, the lumbering hulks used by the Jawas to travel the desert.

Sandcrawlers are actually sturdy ore haulers originally transported to Tatooine by early colonists who hoped to find valuable resources on the desert world. When this plan failed, the Corellian mining vehicles were abandoned. The Jawas quickly adopted the leviathans, which have since become known as "sandcrawlers" by Tatooine locals. Sandcrawlers are extremely important to Jawas because they provide a home and a method for scouring the desert in search of the droids, downed starships, and scrap metal that form the basis of Jawa economy.

The ancient sandcrawlers are powered by outdated and cumbersome steam-powered nuclear fusion engines. Giant treads enable sandcrawlers to roll over any number of obstacles. Sandcrawlers must be extremely stable to prevent the vehicle from toppling when caught in violent sandstorms.

An entire clan of several hundred Jawas lives inside each sandcrawler, where they remain protected from the elements and Tusken Raiders by the vehicle's thick armor plating. While precision blaster rifle fire can destroy a sandcrawler's drive motors, very few weapons on Tatooine can even slow the vehicle.

The sandcrawler's bridge is located high atop the vehicle. The clan's chieftain can usually be found in the command center, which provides a breathtaking view of the desert. Scouts keep watch for telltale glints of metal that might indicate a hidden treasure. Scanners and simple metal detectors aid in this search. Captured droids and small pieces of equipment can be pulled into the sandcrawler through an extendable magnetic suction tube originally designed to load ore. A retractable front-loading hatch allows the Jawas to claim larger machinery. Any reclaimed materials are added to the maze of junk strewn throughout the sandcrawler's belly.

Because of their age, the sandcrawlers require constant repairs. Aside from the Jawas themselves, no one knows for certain how many sandcrawlers are still in operation—but the Jawas seem quite capable of keeping the vehicles running forever. The vehicles are rarely seen traveling together, although they do convene once a year at a secret location in the Dune Sea. At this gathering, the Jawas open their sandcrawlers to share their finds.

> **"Why would Imperial troops want to slaughter Jawas?"**
> —*Luke Skywalker*

⑤ Interior Storage: After landing on Tatooine in an escape pod, R2-D2 and C-3PO were briefly imprisoned in the heart of a Jawa sandcrawler, amid barely functioning droids, broken machinery, and assorted junk.

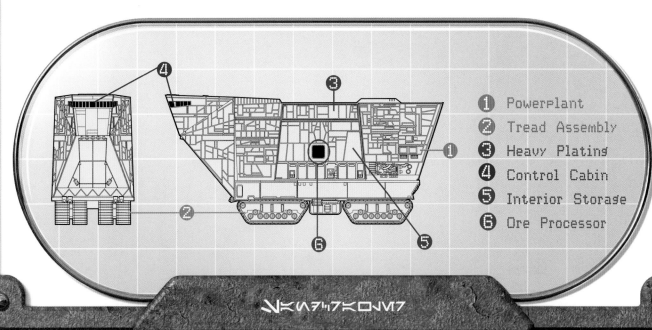

① Powerplant
② Tread Assembly
③ Heavy Plating
④ Control Cabin
⑤ Interior Storage
⑥ Ore Processor

SHARP SPIRAL

Modified SoroSuub Cutlass-9 Patrol Fighter

During the height of the Old Republic, Jedi were trained to handle any situation. Because many missions required long-distance space flights and starfighter combat, every Jedi needed at least a basic grasp of starship technology. With the rise of the New Republic, Luke Skywalker has revived this tradition, and his Jedi students are among the most competent pilots in the galaxy. Jedi pilots outperform peers with similar training because of the Jedi's strong connection to the Force. When flying, a Jedi can use the Force to sense events before they happen, thus dramatically increasing reaction time. But even among the Jedi, the piloting prowess of Iktotchi Jedi Master Saesee Tiin remains unrivaled. Tiin's legacy is due, in part, to his specialized starship, the *Sharp Spiral*.

Although Jedi avoid personal possessions, Saesee Tiin cherished the *Sharp Spiral*. He received the SoroSuub Cutlass-9 patrol starfighter from grateful Duros diplomats after he rescued their convoy from pirates. The vehicle was competent from the start, but Tiin drastically redesigned the craft to suit his own unique abilities. He removed the starship's deflector shields to make room for a handcrafted hyperdrive and later replaced the vehicle's blaster cannons with military-grade lasers confiscated from a Hutt arms dealer. A small proton torpedo launcher was concealed beneath the starfighter.

Each Jedi connects to the Force in his or her own way, and Tiin's Force abilities allowed him to focus his thoughts to control his starfighter even while traveling through hyperspace. While flying at lightspeed, Tiin had no need of a nav computer. He increased the

Sharp Spiral's performance by taking hyperspace shortcuts and flying dangerously close to mass shadows. Tiin's piloting skills earned him the respect of the Freedom's Sons, a militant civilian security corps that frequently aided the Jedi Master.

The *Sharp Spiral*'s aerodynamic design and powerful ion engine array also made her one of the fastest atmospheric craft in the Jedi fleet. Tiin honed his skills and the vehicle's performance on Iktotch, where the tumultuous winds could easily down lesser pilots. Such diligent practice prepared Tiin for virtually any environment, and the *Sharp Spiral* rarely faltered in even the most chaotic atmospheric conditions.

The *Sharp Spiral*'s most dramatic mission pitted the starfighter against three warships piloted by rogue members of the Freedom's Sons. Although the *Sharp Spiral* lacked deflector shields, Tiin was able to fly rings around the trained soldiers. With Jedi precision, he destroyed every key component on the warships, including the deflector shield generators and control towers. The disabled ships were left floating in space until Republic authorities arrived to arrest the mercenaries.

> ## "He talks more to that starship than he does to me."
> —*Adi Gallia, fellow Jedi Council member, on Saesee Tiin's relationship with the* SHARP SPIRAL

1 Laser Cannons: The laser cannons on the *Sharp Spiral* could be cycled down to become "training lasers," enabling Tiin to train other Jedi pilots.

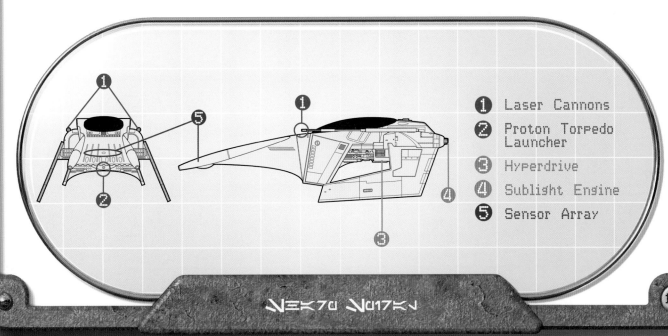

1 Laser Cannons
2 Proton Torpedo Launcher
3 Hyperdrive
4 Sublight Engine
5 Sensor Array

SITH INFILTRATOR (SCIMITAR)

TECHNICAL READOUT

SIZE: 26.5 M LONG

MAXIMUM SPEED:
3,730G/CLASS 3
HYPERDRIVE/1,180 KPH

PRIMARY MANUFACTURER:
SIENAR DESIGN SYSTEMS

AFFILIATION: SITH

Modified SDS Armed Star Courier Prototype

The nefarious Sith have a long history utilizing strange and experimental technology to achieve their evil ends. They have relied on a series of terrifying starfighters, also known as Sith Infiltrators for their ability to operate unseen. About six months before the Battle of Naboo, Darth Sidious presented a magnificent starfighter to his apprentice, Darth Maul, in preparation for the coming battle with the Jedi. Maul dubbed the starship *Scimitar* and used it in his relentless pursuit of Queen Amidala.

The origins of Maul's Sith Infiltrator remain mysterious. Old Republic authorities, who captured the vessel on Naboo after Maul's death, believed that the starship was somehow linked to Raith Sienar and his experimental Sienar Design Systems laboratory. Shortly before the Battle of Naboo, SDS had been designing an armed star courier that bore a striking resemblance to the Infiltrator. Raith denied any connection to the vehicle, but the *Scimitar*'s bent wings and round cockpit would resurface in Sienar's TIE fighter series. Even the ion drive proved to be a prototype for future Sienar vehicles, and the Infiltrator's hyperdrive was an unmodified Sienar SSDS 11-A system.

The Infiltrator's history may be muddled, but its legacy is clear: it remains one of the most complex and foreboding vehicles ever encountered by Old Republic forces. The *Scimitar*'s ominous reputation stems from its built-in cloaking device, technology that is rarely found on starships of the Infiltrator's size. Fueled by rare stygium crystals, the cloaking device allowed

> **"That ship is alive with the dark side, Master Yoda. I can feel it clinging to my robes. And worse, it still tempts me, calling me back with promises of fantastic journeys to the far reaches of the galaxy."**
>
> —*Jedi Master Saesee Tiin*

Darth Maul to travel anywhere undetected by conventional sensors.

As Republic engineers continued to explore the craft, they discovered that it contained a host of unpleasant surprises. Six concealed laser cannons could extend and fire several laser bursts in an eye blink. The first engineers to enter the vehicle were gunned down by security probe droids, forcing the Republic to call in Jedi Master Saesee Tiin to help secure the craft. Inside, Tiin uncovered dozens of hidden compartments with a wide range of malevolent Sith equipment, including surveillance gear, bombs, mines, poisons, torture devices, and interrogator droids. A small garage held Maul's Sith speeder, *Bloodfin*. Unfortunately, Tiin also discovered that the starship's onboard computers had been completely erased and yielded no new clues about Darth Maul or the Sith.

Tiin recommended that the Infiltrator be placed in the Jedi Council's care, but Kuati Senators successfully lobbied for an opportunity to study the starfighter. Before the *Scimitar* could be transported to a Kuat Drive Yards facility, it mysteriously disappeared. Whether it was stolen by Darth Sidious's agents, acquired by Raith Sienar or another competitor, or taken by the Jedi for safekeeping remains unknown.

④ Cloaking Field Generator: The Infiltrator was one of the very few Old Republic vehicles to possess a cloaking device.

① Laser Cannon
② Radiator Panel
③ Sublight Engine
④ Cloaking Field Generator
⑤ Folding Wings

SITH SPEEDER _(Bloodfin)_

TECHNICAL READOUT

SIZE: 1.64 m LONG

MAXIMUM SPEED: 650 KPH

PRIMARY MANUFACTURER: DARTH MAUL

AFFILIATION: SITH

126

Custom Razalon FC-20 Speeder Bike

Every assassin needs a fast, quiet vehicle for pursuing quarry and ambushing prey. For Darth Maul, this role was fulfilled by a sleek, custom-built speeder bike. As is traditional for Sith warriors, Maul named his vehicle for a predator with which he strongly identified: the speeder bike's name was *Bloodfin*, in reference to a vicious aquatic hunter Maul once encountered on an ocean world in the Outer Rim.

Like all speeder bikes, *Bloodfin* was a small repulsorlift vehicle with a powerful rear thrust engine. The engine systems were designed to provide quick acceleration, allowing the vehicle to reach its maximum open-ground speed in a matter of seconds. *Bloodfin* is unusual in that is has a strange, curved body. This design actually provides the vehicle with a very low center of gravity, which dramatically improves the speeder bike's cornering ability. The compact design also presents a very small target.

Maul used *Bloodfin* to chase down his enemies. Once he caught up with them, he preferred to deal with victims personally. The speeder bike lacked weapons of any kind. Maul became skilled at leaping from the vehicle and entering directly into combat, proving that he did not need a laser cannon or similar weapon to achieve his goals. An auto-brake feature slowly brought *Bloodfin* to a safe stop whenever the handlebars were released, ensuring that the speeder bike did not crash or topple over after one of Maul's sudden dismounts.

The speeder bike was bereft of shields and sensors, additional devices that Maul considered a sign of weakness. Maul equipped *Bloodfin* with a remote piloting system. He could use a wrist-mounted comlink to summon and pilot the speeder from up to eight kilometers away. When within the visual range of the vehicle, Maul learned to employ his telekinetic Force abilities to adjust the speeder's controls and pilot it through sheer force of will.

Like Maul's Infiltrator, the Sith speeder is a traditional vehicle of the villainous Sith Order. All Sith speeders throughout history have been similarly agile craft. Maul's preference for hand-to-hand combat is not unique, and most of his ancestors also shunned armed speeder bikes. The ancient Sith did decorate their vehicles with a variety of mystic runes, gruesome trophies, and stolen artifacts.

The Bloodfin was actually one of several Sith speeders used by Darth Maul. Shortly before the invasion of Naboo, Maul owned a T-shaped speeder that was destroyed during a battle with Jedi Master Anoon Bondara. It is rumored that Maul also possessed an armed attack speeder equipped with laser cannons and a personal deflector shield generator—but those rumors have never been substantiated.

Maul's speeder bike, perhaps the last of its kind, was confiscated by the Republic after his death on Naboo. The vehicle later vanished, along with Maul's Sith Infiltrator, seemingly lost forever.

> **"Stealth is the greatest tool of the Sith assassin."**
> —*Darth Sidious*

⑤ Curved Seat: The Sith speeder's curved seat allowed Darth Maul to launch himself from the vehicle by merely rocking forward. He used this tactic to attack Qui-Gon Jinn on Tatooine.

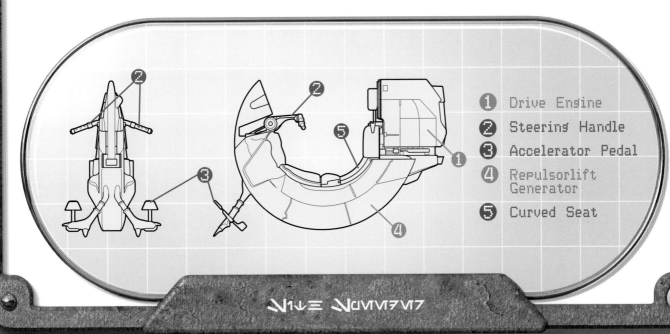

① Drive Engine
② Steering Handle
③ Accelerator Pedal
④ Repulsorlift Generator
⑤ Curved Seat

SKYHOPPER

TECHNICAL READOUT

SIZE: 10.4 m TALL

MAXIMUM SPEED:
1,200 KPH

PRIMARY MANUFACTURER:
Incom Corporation

AFFILIATION: Luke Skywalker

Incom Corporation T-16 Skyhopper

While growing up on Tatooine, Luke Skywalker held fast to a dream of becoming a starfighter pilot. Unfortunately, Tatooine is a remote Outer Rim world where the young moisture farmer had virtually no access to X-wing starfighters or similar craft. Luke's only alternative was a battered T-16 skyhopper, a high-speed transorbital craft used as a personal transport on many worlds. Luke and his friends spent much of their youth racing the vehicles through the winding corridors of Beggar's Canyon. It was during these contests that Luke honed valuable piloting skills that would one day save the Rebel Alliance.

The skyhopper is a common sight across the galaxy, with versions of the craft found on nearly every settled world. The T-16, a particularly successful model, is identified by its tri-wing design and triangular cabin. The three wings, which have been reproduced in countless Imperial transports, provide great stability. The central airfoil does segment the canopy and block the pilot's starboard view, but computer displays and a holographic mapping system compensate for this decreased field of view.

One of the few atmospheric craft with both repulsorlift and ion engines, the skyhopper is able to reach low orbit and cover huge distances in record time. The vehicle receives its name from its ability to quickly "hop" from one settlement to another; after takeoff, the skyhopper ascends rapidly to a height of about 300 kilometers, cruises through the thin upper atmosphere at the E-16/x ion engine's top speed of nearly 1,200 kilometers per hour, and then drops suddenly toward its destination.

Young pilots prefer the skyhopper over more traditional airspeeders because of the craft's amazing maneuverability. The skyhopper includes an advanced system of gyrostabilizers that work in conjunction with the two DCJ-45 repulsorlift generators to allow for tight turns, steep dives, and daredevil stunts. Luke mastered the T-16 and once flew the vehicle through the Stone Needle, a spire in Beggar's Canyon with a very narrow opening at its peak.

As a civilian vehicle, the skyhopper lacks conventional weapons. However, many skyhoppers are manufactured with stun cannons to protect pilot and passenger from any local predators or other threats. The skyhopper does have modular weapons emplacements, and owners are free to replace the stun cannons with pneumatic projectile cannons and targeting lasers. When used by local militias or police forces, the skyhopper can be armed with a single heavy laser cannon.

> **"It's not impossible. I used to bull's-eye womp rats in my T-16 back home. They're not much bigger than two meters."**
> —*Luke Skywalker, expressing his confidence in the plan to destroy the Death Star by targeting its two-meter-wide exhaust port*

8 Cockpit With Control Panels: The controls on a skyhopper are nearly identical to those found aboard an X-wing starfighter, allowing young bush pilots such as Luke Skywalker and Jek Porkins to easily adapt to the more powerful X-wing.

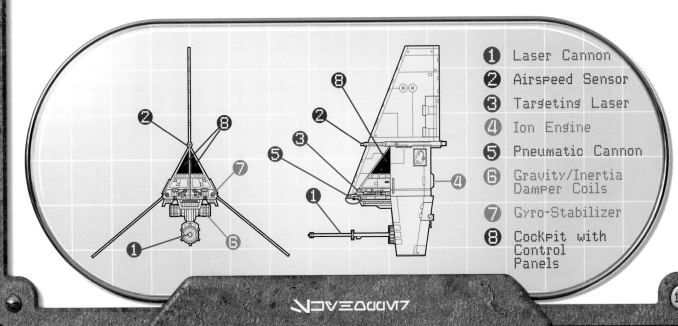

1 Laser Cannon
2 Airspeed Sensor
3 Targeting Laser
4 Ion Engine
5 Pneumatic Cannon
6 Gravity/Inertia Damper Coils
7 Gyro-Stabilizer
8 Cockpit with Control Panels

Slave I

Technical Readout

Size: 21.5 m long,
21.3 m wingspan

Maximum Speed:
2,500G/Class 1
hyperdrive/1,000 kph

Primary Manufacturer:
Kuat Systems Engineering

Affiliation: Jango and
Boba Fett

Modified Kuat Systems Engineering *Firespray*-Class Patrol and Attack Ship

The life of a bounty hunter requires constant travel. Wanted criminals hide in every corner of the galaxy, and searching for such quarry necessitates a powerful and well-equipped starship. The notorious bounty hunter Jango Fett, who became the template for the clone soldiers used by the Confederacy of Independent Systems, pursued his prey in a modified starship called *Slave I*. After Jango's death at the Battle of Geonosis, Boba Fett used the starship to follow in his father's footsteps.

Jango Fett first acquired *Slave I* during a dramatic escape from the prison planet Oovo IV. As he fled authorities, Fett stumbled across a hangar full of prototype *Firespray*-class attack ships on loan to the prison for testing. Without hesitation, the bounty hunter stole one of the starships and turned her weapons on the remaining Firesprays before they could leave the hangar. For many years, *Slave I* was the only surviving Firespray, although KSE eventually revived the line around the time of the Battle of Yavin.

After stealing *Slave I*, Jango subjected the vehicle to a long series of modifications, most focusing on the weapons systems. The vehicle's standard twin blaster cannons received an enhanced targeting computer and variable power regulator. Jango added concealed laser cannons; these weapons were less accurate than the blaster cannons, but they had a rapid recharge rate that allowed Jango to envelop his enemies in a hailstorm of energy blasts. A naval minelayer and retractable torpedo launcher armed with guided projectiles completed the early *Slave I*'s arsenal.

> **"There's no star system *Slave I* can't reach, and there's no planet I can't find. There's nowhere in the galaxy for you to run. Might as well give up now."**
> —*Boba Fett*

Four Kuat X-F-16 power generators and F-31 drive engines consume much of the *Slave I*'s interior. Jango completely remodeled the interior, adding small crew quarters for long journeys and installing additional navigational equipment in the cockpit. The patrol craft was originally equipped with standard prisoner cages, but Jango replaced these with narrow wall cabinets for up to six prisoners.

While in Boba Fett's care, *Slave I* evolved still further. Boba replaced the concealed laser cannons with ion cannons for disabling valuable starships. Proton torpedoes or tracking devices frequently supplanted the guided missiles used by Jango. Boba also integrated a turret-mounted tractor beam projector and an illegal sensor-jamming system. Boba even redesigned one of the coffinlike cells to hold Force-wielding prisoners.

During the Galactic Civil War, *Slave I* was often in relentless pursuit of Han Solo. After Boba fell into the Sarlacc on Tatooine, Alliance forces captured *Slave I* and impounded the starship on Grakouine. Boba piloted a second starship (*Slave II*) for a short time, but he eventually recaptured *Slave I* and renewed his hunt for Solo.

⑦ Cargo Hold: A small, climate-controlled cargo hold located just beyond the boarding ramp allowed Boba Fett to store dead prisoners, or a block of carbonite.

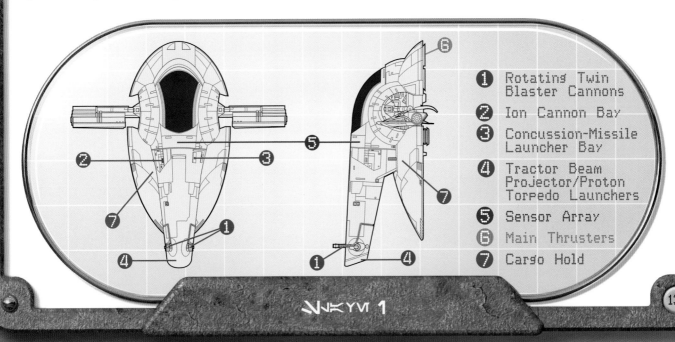

1 Rotating Twin Blaster Cannons
2 Ion Cannon Bay
3 Concussion-Missile Launcher Bay
4 Tractor Beam Projector/Proton Torpedo Launchers
5 Sensor Array
6 Main Thrusters
7 Cargo Hold

SNOWSPEEDER

TECHNICAL READOUT

SIZE: 5.3 m long

MAXIMUM SPEED: 1,100 kph

PRIMARY MANUFACTURER: Incom Corporation

AFFILIATION: Rebel Alliance

Modified Incom T-47 Airspeeder

When the Rebel army relocated to Hoth, Alliance technicians spent many months modifying the motor pool for use on the frozen world. Among the vehicles eventually adapted to Hoth's climate was the T-47 airspeeder, which the Rebels had previously used for reconnaissance on Dantooine and other planets. After extensive modifications, the T-47 proved extremely useful on Hoth and has since become known more generically as the Rebel "snowspeeder."

The T-47 is a fairly basic airspeeder, with a conventional repulsorlift engine and high-powered afterburners. The drive units are easily accessible, allowing the Rebels to easily install repulsor coil heaters to keep the engines from freezing. The mechanics also added deicing nozzles to the braking and turning flaps to prevent ice from forming on these delicate components.

Incom Corporation initially designed the T-47 for industrial use as an atmospheric cargo handler. In the original design, the airspeeder's cockpit was configured for a forward-facing pilot and rear-facing "cargo manager." The cargo manager was responsible for securing repulsorlift cargo modules using the airspeeder's magnetic harpoon gun and durasteel tow cable.

The Alliance adopted the T-47 early in the Galactic Civil War. To prepare the vehicle for combat, the Rebels armed the airspeeder with twin laser cannons and transformed the cargo manager into a gunner. The gunner utilizes computerized targeting systems and holographic projection displays to control the laser cannons and the harpoon gun, although the pilot can assume responsibility for the weapons if necessary. To ensure the T-47's survival, the Rebels added armor plating to the vehicle's hull. The T-47 lacks shields, but its small frame and exceptional maneuverability allow it to dodge enemy fire. Pilots also rely on the vehicle's great speed: the T-47 has a maximum velocity in excess of 1,000 kilometers per hour, with an ideal combat speed of about 600 kilometers per hour.

Rebel snowspeeders proved critical at the Battle of Hoth, delaying the advancing AT-ATs just long enough for Alliance personnel to evacuate the hidden Echo Base. While the snowspeeders proved no match for the armored AT-ATs in a direct firefight, Wedge Antilles and Luke Skywalker devised a unique tow-cable attack that toppled at least one of the massive walkers.

Based on the success of the snowspeeder, the Rebels continued to modify the T-47 for use on other worlds. Swampspeeders incorporate flotation devices, water-sealed thrust nozzles, and watertight cockpits. Sandspeeders are equipped with advanced filters that prevent sand buildup in the engines and steering flaps; cockpit and engine cooling systems to eliminate overheating; and a long-range radar system for navigating in sandstorms. Finally, skyspeeders have more powerful repulsorlift engines and pressurized cabins for high-altitude flights.

> **"That armor's too strong for blasters. Rogue Group, use your harpoons and tow cables. Go for the legs. It might be our only chance of stopping them."**
> —*Commander Luke Skywalker*

5 Harpoon Gun: Rebel pilot Wedge Antilles used the snowspeeder's harpoon and tow cable to entangle the legs of an AT-AT walker at the Battle of Hoth. The AT-AT stumbled over the cable and collapsed to the ground.

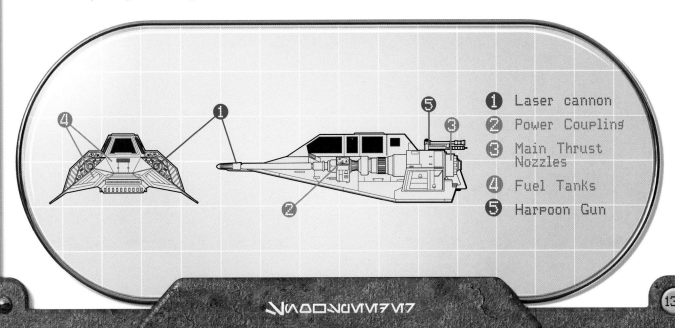

1 Laser cannon
2 Power Coupling
3 Main Thrust Nozzles
4 Fuel Tanks
5 Harpoon Gun

Solar Sailer

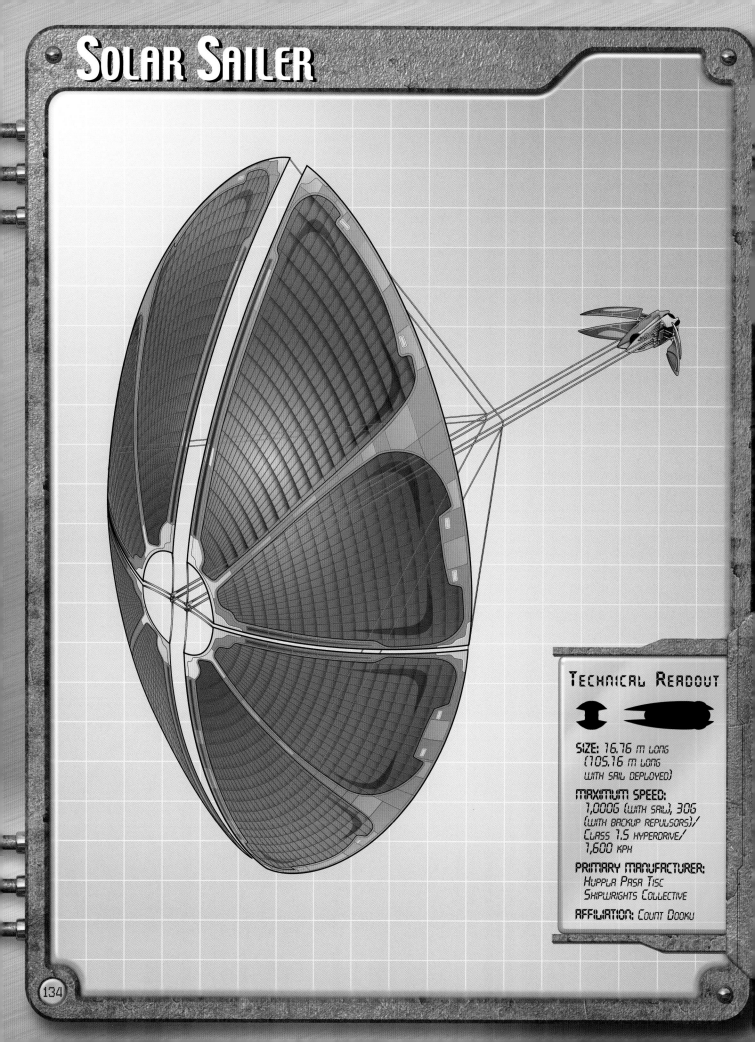

Technical Readout

SIZE: 16.76 m long
(105.16 m long
with sail deployed)

MAXIMUM SPEED:
1,000G (with sail), 30G
(with backup repulsors)/
Class 1.5 hyperdrive/
1,600 kph

PRIMARY MANUFACTURER:
Huppla Pasa Tisc
Shipwrights Collective

AFFILIATION: Count Dooku

Punworcca 116–Class Interstellar Sloop

nearly ten years before the start of the Clone Wars, Count Dooku traveled to Geonosis to forge a partnership with the Geonosian Archduke, Poggle the Lesser. A collector of rare antiquities and a student of vehicle design, Dooku impressed Poggle with his knowledge of ancient Geonosian sailing vessels. To honor the new partnership and encourage Dooku's fascination with Geonosian technology, Poggle and his engineers agreed to build a magnificent interstellar sloop for the former Jedi. Dooku supplied an unusual sail for the vehicle, and the solar sailer was complete.

The solar sailer's key component was, of course, its large stellar sail, which Dooku purchased from an antiques dealer near the Gree Enclave. When the sail was deployed, it reflected unidentified forms of energy to pull the vehicle through space at rather leisurely sublight speeds. The inclusion of the sail removed the need for cumbersome power generators, although the starship still possessed repulsorlift engines, a hyperdrive, and emergency sublight engines for use in the event the sail was damaged.

Aside from the magnificent sail, Dooku's starship was very similar to other Geonosian vessels. The hull displayed the distinctive oval shape shared by the Geonosian starfighter. A modular orb served as the cockpit, typically occupied by an FA-4 pilot droid. A collection of shield generators hidden beneath the hull provided a revolving triple-layer deflector shield, a Geonosian innovation that allowed the starship to endure prolonged enemy fire.

Many Geonosian craft utilize a system of minute tractor beam and repulsor field projectors for increased maneuverability and short-range offensive attacks. The system functions by pushing off from or pulling against nearby objects, such as the asteroids surrounding Geonosis. Count Dooku's solar sailer was equipped with 84 of these emitters, so the Confederacy leader quickly learned to use the devices to push asteroids and stellar debris into the path of pursuing starships.

The solar sailer's narrow interior had been furnished to provide a comfortable living space during the long trips between Geonosis and the Core Worlds. A library aboard the starship contained galactic maps, databooks on virtually every subject, and a HoloNet transceiver.

When the tide turned against the Confederacy at the Battle of Geonosis, Dooku used his solar sailer to escape the planet and head into deep space. Pursuing Jedi starfighters were stymied by the asteroid field, which Dooku expertly navigated before launching into hyperspace.

> ## "The human's starship, it flies as if by magic. If Poggle crosses him, the human might use his magic against us."
> —*Anonymous Geonosian guard*

6 Retractable Sail Release: The solar sailer's propulsion system relies on a rare and mysterious sail that reflects energy in order to produce forward motion.

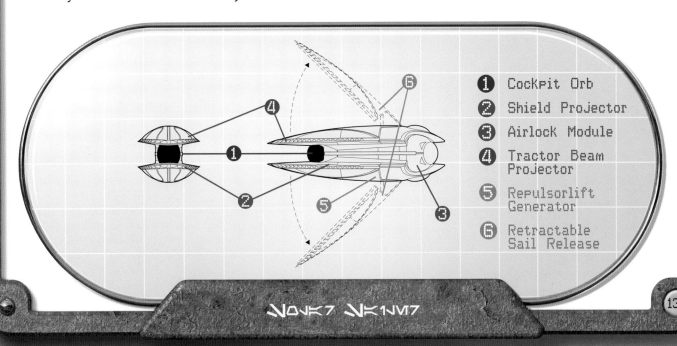

1. Cockpit Orb
2. Shield Projector
3. Airlock Module
4. Tractor Beam Projector
5. Repulsorlift Generator
6. Retractable Sail Release

Speeder Bike

Technical Readout

SIZE: 4.4 m long

MAXIMUM SPEED: 500 KPH

PRIMARY MANUFACTURER: Aratech Repulsor Company

AFFILIATION: Galactic Empire

Aratech 74-Z Military Speeder Bike

At the Battle of Geonosis and subsequent conflicts, the Republic's clone army often employed exceptional tactics to defeat enemy forces. Successful battle plans, however, required detailed reconnaissance, intense coordination of troop movements, and constant communication between the clone troopers and their Jedi commanders. In order to quickly gather data on enemy positions and to relay important information to squads, the clone army utilized military speeder bikes capable of quickly covering huge tracts of land. Speeder bikes serve as excellent scout vehicles because they can reach speeds of up to 500 kilometers per hour and are far more maneuverable than landspeeders or airspeeders.

> **"What's the last thing to go through an Imperial scout trooper's head when he hits a tree? His afterburner."**
>
> —*Joke told by Rebel forces on Endor*

A standard speeder bike is a single-occupant repulsorlift vehicle. Handlebars located near the front of the chassis are used to steer the craft, while foot pedals adjust both speed and altitude. Controls for sensors, communications devices, and weapons can be found between the handlebars.

The speeder bikes used by the clone army were donated by Aratech Repulsor Company, a staunch supporter of the Republic. The compact vehicles were favored by the Republic tacticians because they could be loaded into virtually any transport, including AT-TE walkers and Republic gunships. They fly low to the ground and present a small profile, allowing the 74-Z to go unnoticed when patrolling a battlefield's perimeter. If the speeder should run across enemy troops, it can open fire with a rotating blaster cannon located under the chassis.

Once Emperor Palpatine assumed control of the galaxy, Aratech began supplying speeder bikes to Imperial forces. Even after the fall of the Empire, Aratech has maintained a strong relationship with rogue Imperial factions, although the company now sells vehicles to the New Republic as well.

In the Empire's service, speeder bikes are usually issued to specialized stormtroopers, known as scout troopers, who are trained to pilot the speeder bikes in every conceivable environment. Advanced sensors in a scout trooper's helmet scan upcoming terrain to provide greater reaction time. The speeder bikes typically travel in small packs for protection. Scout troopers are assigned to reconnaissance missions, perimeter defense, and surgical strikes against small enemy forces.

The Empire eventually began using other speeder bikes, including the Aratech 64-Y Swift 3 Repulsorlift Sled, the Mobquet TrailMaker III, and the Ikas-Adno Starhawk, but none of these has displaced the 74-Z among scout troopers. The 74-Z remains the Imperial speeder bike of choice in part due to its reliability: the vehicle can travel several thousand kilometers without maintenance. This long-range capability enables scout troopers to operate independently for weeks at a time.

③ Steering Vane: All control over the speeder bike stems from four directional steering vanes connected to two outriggers. Without them, the speeder bike will spin wildly until it crashes. While on Endor, Luke Skywalker exploited this weakness when he used his lightsaber to sever an enemy speeder bike's outriggers.

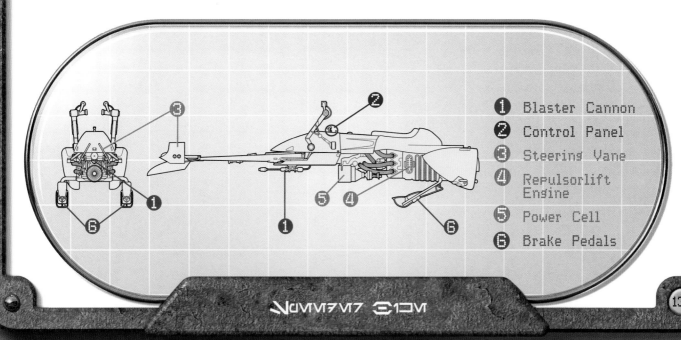

1. Blaster Cannon
2. Control Panel
3. Steering Vane
4. Repulsorlift Engine
5. Power Cell
6. Brake Pedals

SPHA-T

TECHNICAL READOUT

SIZE: 20.6 m TALL

MAXIMUM SPEED:
35 KPH

PRIMARY MANUFACTURER:
Rothana Heavy Engineering

AFFILIATION:
Old Republic

Rothana Heavy Engineering Self-Propelled Heavy Artillery—Turbolaser

When the Confederacy of Independent Systems fell under heavy attack at the Battle of Geonosis, the Trade Federation attempted to launch several massive core ships from the planet's surface. The core ships were filled with thousands of battle droids, super battle droids, heavy weapons, and assorted vehicles. Every core ship that escaped would provide the Confederacy with a large and powerful army for use in future conflicts. In order to destroy the behemoth core ships before they could reach the upper atmosphere, the clone army deployed several self-propelled heavy artillery units armed with large turbolasers. The artillery pieces lumbered across the Geonosis battlefield until they had the core ships in range; when the artillery units opened fire, core ships sank back into the dirt and exploded, reducing the battle droids to slag.

Any self-propelled heavy artillery unit is a relatively simple vehicle consisting of two parts: the locomotive drive unit and the primary weapon. In most cases, the weapon is developed first; the drive unit is simply a method for transporting the experimental or especially powerful weapon to strategic positions during a battle. Most conventional SPHA units utilize repulsorlift platforms to carry ion cannons, antivehicle laser cannons, or concussion missile launchers.

The Rothana Heavy Engineering (RHE) SPHA-T is typical of a self-propelled artillery unit in that the turbolaser, the key component of the vehicle, was designed first. The turbolaser utilizes a large focusing array to produce a beam of potent energy. The tur-

> **"Using this weapon against droids is a necessary evil. But what if such destructive power should be turned against living creatures? A sad thought, indeed."**
> —*Jedi Master Mace Windu*

bolaser has tremendous range and is capable of penetrating deflector shields. Unfortunately, the turbolaser requires a gargantuan reactor core. The sheer size of the turbolaser and its attendant equipment prevented the weapon from being installed on any known RHE vehicle.

To provide the turbolaser with some degree of mobility, RHE produced a large, well-armored drive unit. The drive unit consists of several treads that can roll over uneven terrain, crush roadblocks or other obstacles, and send enemy units running in terror. The turbolaser is fixed on top of the vehicle and does not rotate like a normal turret. Instead, the vehicle itself turns to provide the turbolaser with a clear line of fire. The turbolaser can elevate to enable it to target airborne craft, such as core ships. When the turbolaser is moved into position for firing, four stabilizing struts extend to provide support as the weapon unleashes its devastating beam.

The SPHA-T requires a crew of 15 clone troopers to operate the turbolaser, pilot the drive unit, and monitor the reactor core. The SPHA-T can also be equipped with 12 retractable antipersonnel blasters, which necessitate 10 dedicated gunners. A small staging below the turbolaser allows the vehicle to carry an additional 20 clone troopers.

2 Focusing Dish: The SPHA-T uses a large focusing dish to create a devastating turbolaser. The same basic technology will be used on a much larger scale to build the Death Star's superlaser.

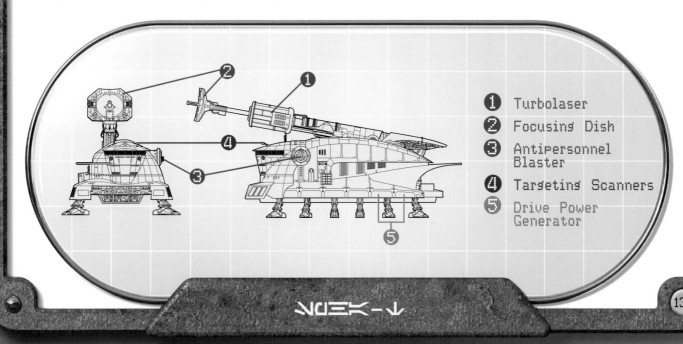

1 Turbolaser
2 Focusing Dish
3 Antipersonnel Blaster
4 Targeting Scanners
5 Drive Power Generator

STAP

Technical Readout

SIZE: 2 m TALL

MAXIMUM SPEED: 400 KPH

PRIMARY MANUFACTURER: Baktoid Armor Workshop

AFFILIATION: Trade Federation

Baktoid Armor Workshop Single Trooper Aerial Platform

The STAP is a slender low-atmosphere repulsorlift reconnaissance vehicle designed to carry a single soldier. Most recently used in large numbers on Naboo by the Trade Federation's secret army, STAPs display great agility and can be piloted through dense terrain, such as thick forests and swamps.

The STAP is a military version of a civilian craft commonly known as the airhook. An airhook generally consists of a rounded control module connected to a long airfoil. Repulsorlift engines located near the bottom of the airfoil provide lift, although an airhook's maximum altitude is generally limited to 25 meters. Two drive turbines propel the vehicle forward. Some models include stun cannons for use against local wildlife. Civilian airhooks are susceptible to violent weather patterns and are most often found on temperate worlds with stable atmospheric conditions.

The Trade Federation STAP improves upon a civilian airhook manufactured by Longspur & Alloi by replacing the stun cannons with lethal twin blasters designed to take down small targets, including fleeing Naboo civilians. The vehicle is coated in light armor plating, although this protects only the craft from handheld blasters.

Like all Trade Federation vehicles, STAPs are piloted exclusively by battle droids. The droid stands on a long foot panel, while gripping a pair of handles that control the vehicle's velocity, weapons, and heading. High-voltage energy cells sustain the vehicle at maximum power for short periods of time; when the cells

are depleted, the STAP must return to a Trade Federation facility for recharging. On Naboo, STAPs undertook short-range reconnaissance missions in search of resistance and provided air support for ground units.

As of the Battle of Naboo, the Trade Federation had also developed the Heavy STAP. The armored Heavy STAP supports larger laser cannons and a missile launcher for its more direct role in small battles. The Heavy STAP is generally deployed to scout dangerous areas or eliminate retreating enemy forces, but it is less agile than its predecessor and has difficulty crossing some types of terrain, including rivers.

The Trade Federation STAP is not the first combat-ready airfoil. Many local defense groups employ small fleets of modified airfoils, and military-grade airfoils were used by Empress Teta's forces 5,000 years before the Battle of Yavin. Even the Jedi have used airfoils as personal transports, deploying them during rescue missions at the Battle of Ruusan and other conflicts. Rebel forces maintained a small number of military airfoils on Dantooine, but these vehicles were abandoned when the Alliance relocated to frozen Hoth.

> **"We could have stayed hidden in the swamps forever, if not for those accursed STAPs. They rooted us out of the trees like Gungans searching for gumbols."**
> —*Royal Security Force officer Tobias Pall*

❶ Twin Blasters: The STAP's twin blasters were brought to bear on Qui-Gon Jinn, but the Jedi Master easily deflected the bolts to destroy his attacker.

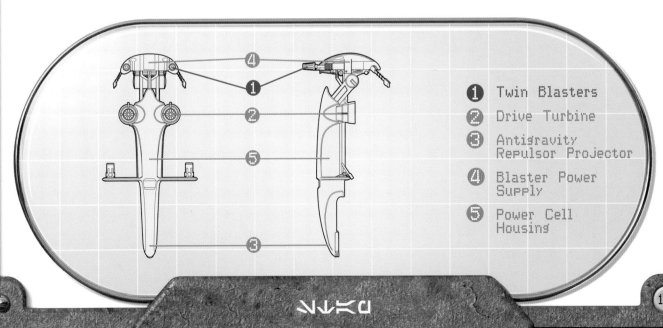

❶ Twin Blasters
❷ Drive Turbine
❸ Antigravity Repulsor Projector
❹ Blaster Power Supply
❺ Power Cell Housing

STAR DESTROYER

TECHNICAL READOUT

SIZE: 1,600 M LONG

MAXIMUM SPEED:
2,300G/CLASS 2 HYPERDRIVE

PRIMARY MANUFACTURER:
KUAT DRIVE YARDS

AFFILIATION:
GALACTIC EMPIRE

Kuat Drive Yards *Imperial I*–Class Star Destroyer

The dark soul of the Imperial Navy, the Star Destroyer is a massive vessel designed to terrorize local systems. The *Imperial I*–class Star Destroyer served as the most prominent symbol of the Empire's strength during much of the Galactic Civil War.

With the aid of Rendili StarDrive, Kuat Drive Yards began producing Star Destroyers during the final days of the Old Republic. The first Star Destroyer, designated *Victory*-class, was an extension of the Republic assault ship. Victory destroyers, and all subsequent models, share the assault ship's wedge-shaped frame and elevated command bridge. At 900 meters long, the Victory destroyer is larger than the Republic assault ship and carries heavier firepower. While the Victory destroyer is considered slow, the starship did enjoy heavy use prior to the Galactic Civil War. Grand Admiral Thrawn later restored many Victory destroyers, and the New Republic continues to use the vessels against the Yuuzhan Vong invasion.

When the Emperor came to power, Kuat Drive Yards developed the next wave of galactic assault vessels: the *Imperial I*–class Star Destroyer. Nearly twice the size of its predecessor, the Imperial Star Destroyer's primary weapons system includes 60 Taim & Bak XX-9 turbolasers equipped with advanced targeting technology for use against fast-moving starfighters. Sixty Borstel NK-7 ion cannons disable enemy starships for capture by one of Star Destroyer's 10 Phylon Q7 tractor beam projectors. Two giant deflector shield generators atop the bridge protect the vessel from all but the most powerful capital ship weapons.

> **"Yes! I said *closer*! Move as close as you can and engage those Star Destroyers at point-blank range... We'll last longer than we will against that Death Star, and we might just take a few of them with us!"**
>
> —*Lando Calrissian at the Battle of Endor*

The Imperial Star Destroyer's power generator has yet to be surpassed. The Sienar Fleet Systems I-a2b solar ionization reactor can fuel the starship's weaponry, sublight drives, and other systems at maximum levels while retaining a substantial reserve. The reactor is encased in a shielded dome, constructed of durasteel and carbonite, located on the Destroyer's ventral surface.

The Star Destroyer is both a deep-space combat vessel and a transport. The *Imperial I*–class Star Destroyer carries 9,700 soldiers, 72 TIE fighters, 20 AT-ATs, 30 AT-STs, and an assortment of barges, gunboats, transports, shuttles, and Skipray blastboats. The Destroyer also holds a prefabricated garrison base for long-term planetary occupations.

After the Battle of Yavin, KDY continued to improve upon the Star Destroyer by manufacturing an *Imperial II*–class starship with more powerful turbolasers and ion cannons. The Imperial II was soon followed by the Super Star Destroyer, one of the most terrifying capital ships ever produced. Years later, the Republic Engineering Corporation designed the Defender–class Star Destroyer for the New Republic. The Defender is smaller and faster than the traditional Imperial Star Destroyers, but carries nearly as many weapons emplacements. The first New Republic Defender was named the Obi-Wan in honor of Luke Skywalker's mentor.

6 Central Hangar: The Imperial Star Destroyer's tractor beams draw enemy starships, like Princess Leia's *Tantive IV*, into a large docking bay capable of holding vessels up to 150 meters long.

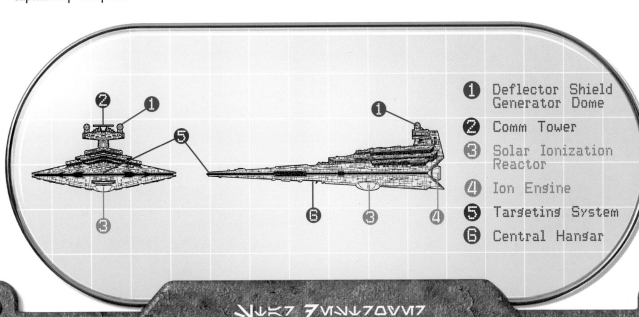

1 Deflector Shield Generator Dome

2 Comm Tower

3 Solar Ionization Reactor

4 Ion Engine

5 Targeting System

6 Central Hangar

Swoop Bikes

Technical Readout

Size: 3 m long

Maximum Speed:
600 kph

Primary Manufacturer:
Mobquet Swoops and
Speeders

Affiliation:
None

TaggeCo. Air-2 Swoop

Swoop is a generic term for an entire class of small, high-speed repulsorlift vehicles that have become one of the most common forms of personal transport in the galaxy. Little more than repulsorlift engines with seats, the crude and noisy swoops are exceedingly fast. Like skyhoppers, they are often favored by young and adventurous pilots who wish to test their mettle in dangerous swoop races. Han Solo was a champion swoop racer in his youth. Outlaw swoop gangs also plague many planets, including Tatooine.

Swoops are among the fastest ground vehicles, with top speeds exceeding six hundred kilometers per hour. They are notoriously difficult to control and offer no protection to the pilot. Even at modest speeds, a swoop crash often proves fatal.

A generic swoop, such as the TaggeCo. Air-2 model used by Han Solo to escape slavers on Bonadan, consists of a very lightweight alloy frame surrounding powerful ion and repulsorlift engines. Only a seat and simple controls are added to this crude design. The maneuvering flaps and steering vanes used to control the vehicle are adjusted through the hand-grips, but the pilot must also shift his weight in order to make tight turns. Changes in speed and altitude are made through the knee pegs and foot pegs. Few swoops have weapons, and virtually none provide any type of armor.

Because of their simple design, swoops are relatively inexpensive and very easy to build, modify, upgrade, and repair. Through small modifications, swoops can be adapted for a number of environments: swoops on the island-world of Bestine typically have engines encased in water-proof housings, while Tatooine's swoops are fitted

with sand filters to protect the engines from grit. In rare instances (and at great expense), a swoop can been equipped with a sealed canopy to protect the rider from the elements, but this is not the norm; as a result, swoops are seldom found in areas with extreme temperatures or violent weather conditions. And although accessible for repairs, the engine systems can be temperamental, breaking down often and at the worst possible moments.

The origin of the swoop is unknown, but the vehicles have been in heavy use across the galaxy for hundreds of thousands of years. Some historians theorize that swoops first appeared on the planet Taris, where swoop racing captured the imagination of the galaxy roughly four thousand years before the Battle of Yavin. Using an intricate network of hyperspace beacons, Taris race organizers broadcast the results of the dangerous swoop races throughout the galaxy, which eventually gave rise to an immense - and lucrative - gambling operation. Taris remained a hub for swoop racing for decades, despite incursion by the Hutts and other criminal organizations.

As swoop racing grew more popular and began attracting less reputable elements, numerous swoop gangs emerged. Bearing frightening names such as the Dark Star Hellions, the Nova Demons, and the Bloodsniffers, these gangs have long terrorized numerous worlds, mostly in the Outer Rim. Over the cen-

> ## "Swoop jockeys have the brains of a blister gnat—and about the same life expectancy."
> *—Han Solo to Anakin Solo when the latter expressed an interest in swoop racing*

⑤ **Engine Intake:** Most swoops have very noisy engines, thanks in part to overly-large engine intakes. On Tatooine, these loud engines frequently startle skittish beasts of burden called rontos.

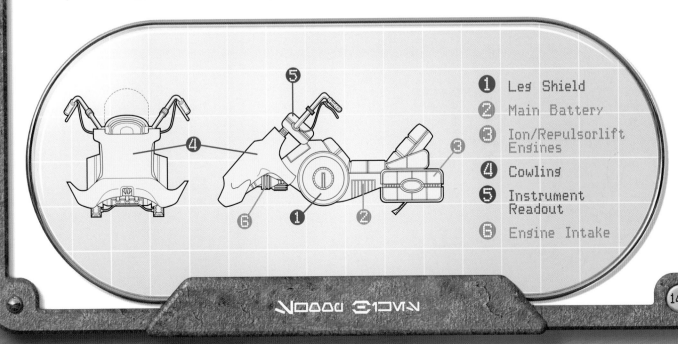

❶	Leg Shield
❷	Main Battery
❸	Ion/Repulsorlift Engines
❹	Cowling
❺	Instrument Readout
❻	Engine Intake

turies, swoop gangs have evolved from bands of petty thugs to hired muscle for the Hutts to viable criminal empires in their own right. Perhaps the most notorious swoop gangs are found in the Shesharile system, where the inhabited moons of Shesharile 5 and 6 are largely at the mercy of swoop gangs like the Raging Banthas, the Spiders, and the Rabid Mynocks. Swoop gangs have elevated swoop culture by creating new brands of repulsorlift vehicles: the Cloud Riders on Aduba-3 pilot "skyspeeders," which are actually heavily-modified and stripped-down Aratech Peregrine 240s sporting Mobquet Nebulo-Q thruster jets. No longer quite swoops, but not yet considered airspeeders, the skyspeeders are among the most powerful personal ground vehicles in the galaxy enabling them to reach higher altitudes than most other standard models. Fortunately, the vast majority of swoop owners are respectable citizens who use their vehicles for personal transportation. Around the time of the Battle of Geonosis, Owen Lars owned a modest Mobquet Zephyr-G swoop. Used for patrolling his father's moisture farm and inspecting far-distant moisture vaporators, Owen's swoop had a top speed of about 350 kilometers per hour, slow by swoop standards. The weather-beaten vehicle was twenty years old when purchased by Owen, and yet it was still considered state-of-the-art on backwater Tatooine. The swoop was favored over other vehicles on the Lars' farm because it was fuel-efficient and could be repaired easily using parts purchased from Jawa traders. The swoop enabled Anakin Skywalker to track down the Tusken Raiders who had kidnapped his mother, Shmi.

As the swoop market has grown, a variety of companies have introduced new and more powerful models. The Flare-S Swoop, produced by Mobquet Swoops and Speeders, combines elements from both speeder bikes and traditional swoops. It features a heavier, curved and reinforced chassis for greater stability while advanced control vanes add maneuverability. Despite these design upgrades, the s-swoop is still more difficult to pilot than a traditional speeder bike, as Dengar discovered when he crashed his Flare-S during a race against Han Solo in Corellia's Agrilat swamps. The accident disfigured Dengar, who became a bounty hunter and vowed revenge against Solo.

Although it's uncommon, swoops can be outfitted for combat. While speeder bikes are used for reconnaissance, battle-ready swoop bikes can be used on the frontlines of skirmishes, especially when facing infantry units. Combat swoops typically have some sort of forward-facing armor plating, although their flanks and rear remain largely unprotected. The bounty hunter Aurra Sing, for example, piloted a menacing swoop with a skull-like armor shield. The most advanced combat swoops sport small deflector shields, but the power generators required for such devices usually slows top speed to under 350 kilometers per hour. Combat swoops have limited armaments, such as a single blaster cannon, but these are meant to supplement the pilot's own weapons. Control pegs may be modified to allow the pilot to steer the vehicle by shifting his weight alone, freeing his hands to hold blasters, a rifle, or other weapons. The CIS mercenary Durge owned a durable swoop, which he used to charge enemy clone troopers while wielding a deadly energy lance. In more recent years, New Republic technicians have experimented with adding targeting computers, more robust weapons, and even small droid co-pilots to swoops, but few of these modifications have proved worth the expense, effort, or negative effect on the swoop's speed and handling.

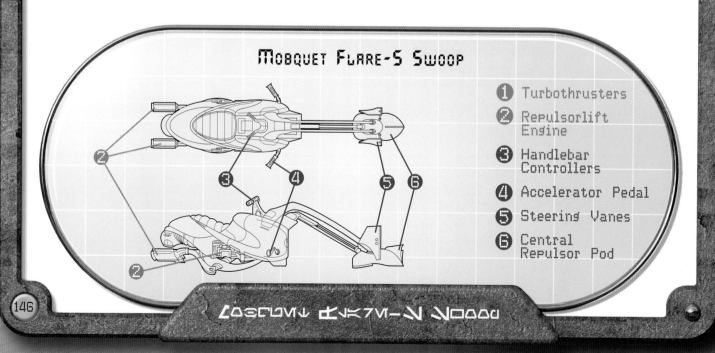

MOBQUET FLARE-S SWOOP

1. Turbothrusters
2. Repulsorlift Engine
3. Handlebar Controllers
4. Accelerator Pedal
5. Steering Vanes
6. Central Repulsor Pod

Swoop Classification

TaggeCo. Air-2 Swoop

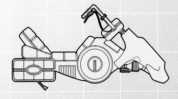

INCOM MVR-3 Speeder Bike

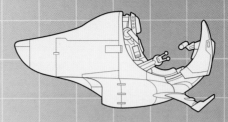

Mobquet Overracer

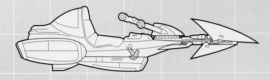

Aratech 74-Z Military Speeder Bike

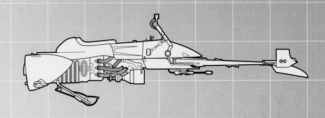

Mobquet Flare-S Swoop

Geonosian Speeder Bike

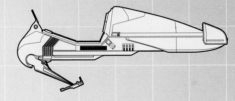

Razalon FC-20 Speeder Bike

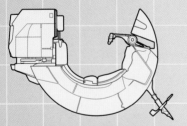

Owen Lars's Zephyr-G Swoop

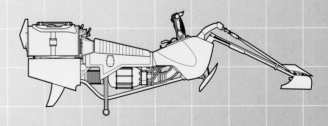

Bespin Motors JR-4 Swoop

Keluda's Speeder Bike

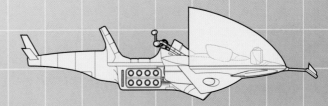

Techno Union Starship

Technical Readout

SIZE: 220 m tall

MAXIMUM SPEED:
400G/Class 7 Hyperdrive

PRIMARY MANUFACTURER:
Techno Union

AFFILIATION:
Confereracy of Independent
Systems

Hardcell-Class Interstellar Transport

Throughout the galaxy, the most common types of starships are generic transports designed solely for the purpose of conveying passengers or cargo. Passenger transports range from small vehicles meant to take a handful of beings on short journeys to large cruisers capable of carrying hundreds of travelers on voyages that last many standard years. Cargo transports are equally diverse, with design dictated by the exact nature of cargo being hauled.

The Techno Union, one of the galaxy's most powerful organizations in the years leading up to the Clone Wars, maintained an impressive fleet of dual-purpose transports that would eventually be used for a wide variety of missions in support of the Confederacy of Independent Systems. Regardless of appearance and design, all of the Techno Union transports were employed to travel between star systems in order to strike business deals, scout resources, or collect payments from financial partners. All had hyperdrive systems, standard defenses, dedicated life support systems, and many creature comforts, such as fully-stocked kitchens and zero-gravity sleep chambers. Because the Techno Union was created and operated by a huge contingent of Skakoans—humanoid aliens who wear pressurized suits when visiting most worlds—nearly every Techno Union transport had pressurized cabins which allowed Skakoans to comfortably remove their bulky suits.

The Techno Union's most visible transport was the rocket-shaped *Hardcell* starship. In its base configuration, the vehicle utilized a series of six large thrusters that enabled it to quickly exit planetary atmospheres.

> **"The *Hardcell* will get you noticed as you travel the space-lanes. Even Corellian cruisers will get out of your way. And if they don't, you can run them over."**
>
> *-Internal Techno Union memo written to increase orders of the* HARDCELL *transport*

Because of their size and energy output, the thrusters wreaked havoc on surrounding environments, but the Techno Union seemed unconcerned about any ecological impact or noise pollution caused by the starship. In addition to being loud, the *Hardcell*'s engines were amazingly fuel *in*efficient, consuming hundreds of concentrated fuel slugs during every planetary exit. Despite the starship's shortcomings, it became a status symbol among Techno Union officials.

The Techno Union was one of the first organizations to declare allegiance to Count Dooku and his dream of a Confederacy of Independent Systems. In fact, the Techno Union owned and operated the foundries on Geonosis where many of the Confederacy's weapons of war were constructed. When Dooku called a meeting on Geonosis to officially form the Confederacy, the Techno Union sent foreman Wat Tambor to the rocky planet as their representative. He arrived on Geonosis in his own, personalized *Hardcell* transport. The paranoid Tambor installed powerful deflector shields and a series of synchronized scanners that continually swept the interior of the starship for bugs (perhaps planted by his Techno Union rivals). Although the starship retained its original subspace engines, the hyperdrive system was extremely advanced and could calculate hyperspace jumps in seconds. This ability was vital to Wat Tambor, who fled Geonosis when the Republic army arrived.

1   **Engine Ring:** The Hardcell's engine ring has several modular engine supports, allowing drastic reconfiguration of the entire engine system.

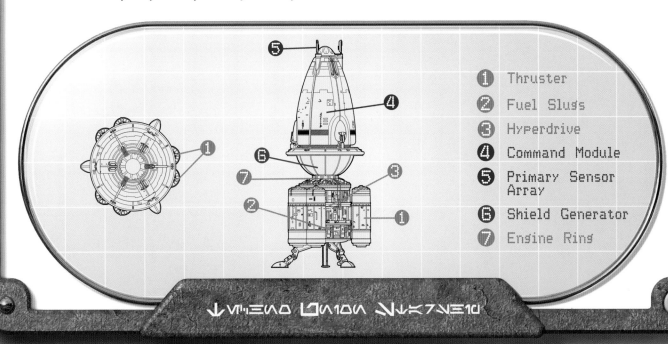

1. Thruster
2. Fuel Slugs
3. Hyperdrive
4. Command Module
5. Primary Sensor Array
6. Shield Generator
7. Engine Ring

TIE Advanced (Darth Vader's TIE Fighter)

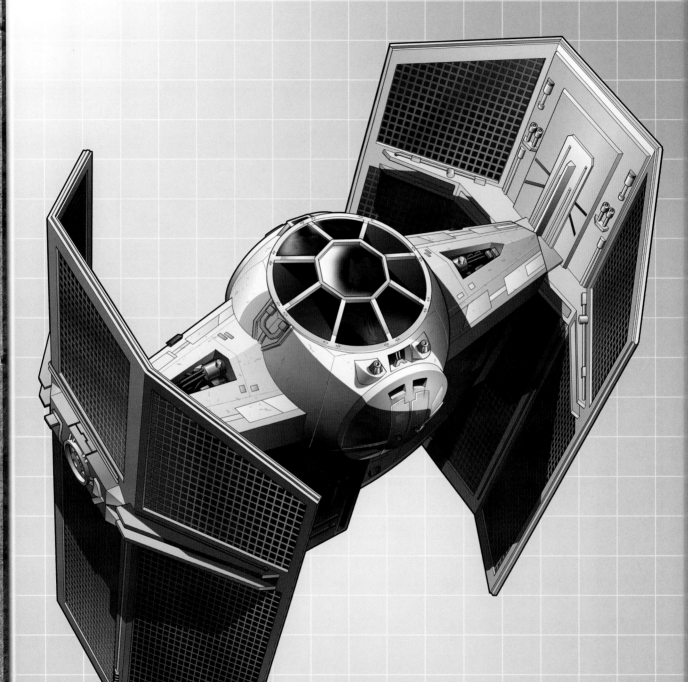

Technical Readout

SIZE: 9.2 m long

MAXIMUM SPEED:
4,150G/Class 4
Hyperdrive/7,200 kph

PRIMARY MANUFACTURER:
Sienar Fleet Systems

AFFILIATION: Galactic Empire

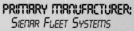

Sienar Fleet Systems TIE Advanced x1 Prototype

The TIE Advanced was the prototype TIE fighter flown by Darth Vader at the Battle of Yavin. An experimental craft combining TIE fighter technology with more conventional starfighter components such as a hyperdrive and deflector shield generators, the TIE Advanced eventually became the template for the incredibly efficient TIE interceptor.

Based on original Sienar TIE fighter designs, the TIE Advanced consisted of a rounded cockpit connected to two solar array wings. The vessel featured a durasteel-alloy hull, elongated rear deck, and powerful twin laser cannons located just below the large canopy.

As in all TIE starfighters, the prototype's propulsion system revolved around twin ion engines, although its solar ionization reactor was much more powerful than those on standard TIE fighters. Despite the improved power supply, Vader's TIE proved only slightly faster than the previous TIE models due to inefficient shield generators, which consumed a great deal of power, and the increased mass created by the addition of heavy armor plating. The hyperdrive was very slow and the prototype lacked long-term life support, ensuring that Vader could make only very short jaunts through hyperspace.

With Darth Vader at the controls, the TIE Advanced proved a devastating starfighter. While piloting the prototype, Vader very nearly thwarted the Rebel Alliance's attempt to destroy the Death Star. Only the last-minute arrival of Han Solo and the *Millennium Falcon* prevented the Sith Lord from firing on Luke Skywalker's X-wing. After being clipped by the *Falcon*'s quad laser cannons, the prototype spun into space. Vader eventually regained control of the craft and fled to the nearest Imperial facility. The prototype was repaired and remained one of Vader's most prized possessions. At the Battle of Endor, the starfighter was stowed aboard the *Executor* but was obliterated when the Super Star Destroyer crashed into the second Death Star.

Despite the original prototype's obvious strengths, the Galactic Empire ordered very few of the costly TIE Advanced starfighters. Unfazed, Sienar designers simply incorporated the TIE Advanced's best qualities into the TIE interceptor. At the time of the Battle of Endor, Sienar had ceased producing the TIE Advanced x1 altogether; over the course of the next several years, most of the remaining starfighters were destroyed. As of the Yuuzhan Vong invasion, Lando Calrissian owned a modified TIE Advanced x1, although this starfighter is likely the last of its kind.

> ## "I have you now."
> —*Darth Vader as he prepared to destroy Luke Skywalker's X-wing*

5 **Deflector Shield Generator:** During the climactic Battle of Yavin, the TIE Advanced's powerful deflector shield generator allowed the starfighter—and Darth Vader—to survive a brush with the *Millennium Falcon*'s lethal quad laser cannon.

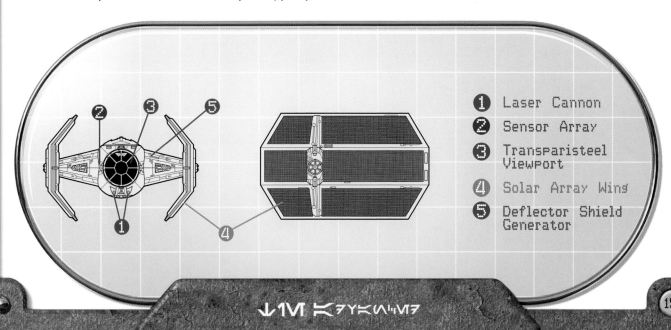

1 Laser Cannon
2 Sensor Array
3 Transparisteel Viewport
4 Solar Array Wing
5 Deflector Shield Generator

TIE Bomber

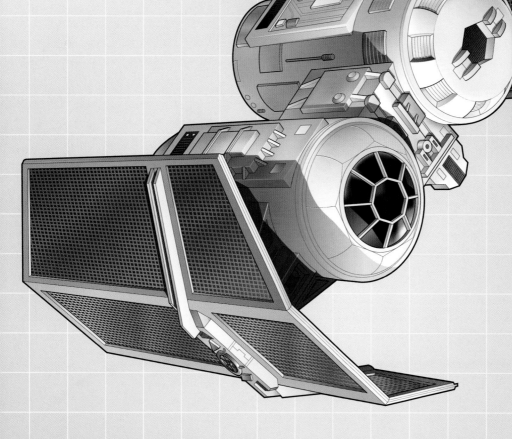

Technical Readout

SIZE: 7.8 m long

MAXIMUM SPEED:
2,380G/850 KPH

PRIMARY MANUFACTURER:
Sienar Fleet Systems

AFFILIATION:
Galactic Empire

Sienar Fleet Systems TIE Bomber

Of all the TIE fighter variants produced by Sienar Fleet Systems for the Galactic Empire, the TIE bomber was one of the most effective. The heavy assault ship, designed for strategic strikes against surface and deep-space targets, proved one of the most heavily armed starships in the Imperial fleet. It contributed to the capture of Yavin 4, aided in the search for the *Millennium Falcon* near Hoth, and made direct attacks on Alliance capital ships at the Battle of Endor and other conflicts.

TIE bombers utilize the distinctive bent wings found on the TIE Advanced prototype. These solar array panels frame a rounded TIE cockpit and a large ordnance pod that can be configured to carry a wide array of destructive weapons. While not nearly as fast or agile as the original TIE fighter, TIE bombers are much more destructive. A single TIE bomber's payload can include a volatile combination of proton torpedoes, guided concussion missiles, orbital mines, and free-falling thermal detonators. A complex targeting and delivery system ensures that these weapons always hit their mark. When up against starfighters, the TIE bomber opens fire with two forward-facing laser cannons identical to those aboard the standard TIE fighter.

The starboard command module houses the pilot, flight computers, communications systems, and a vaunted life support system. The life support system, which is found on very few other TIE starfighters, enables the pilot to operate the vehicle without a sealed flight suit.

TIE bombers are deployed against space stations, orbital docking platforms, and orbital facilities, but they are especially effective against capital ships. After standard TIE fighters weaken the target's defenses, the bombers swoop in to disable vital areas such as the shield generators and engines. Once the enemy ship is crippled, Imperial boarding parties take control of the vessel and capture the enemy troops for interrogation.

While certainly competent during space combat, TIE bombers truly excel when sent on bombing runs against ground targets. The TIE bomber's incredibly precise targeting computers allow the pilot to completely destroy a specific building without damaging surrounding structures. The vehicle's fair maneuverability and small size enable it to cruise between buildings, drop into canyons, and thread other dangerous terrain.

Like standard TIE fighters, TIE bombers can be found aboard almost every Imperial space station and capital ship. A Star Destroyer typically carries one squadron of 12 TIE bombers, and most ground installations maintain a small complement of these craft. Despite its widespread use, the TIE bomber was largely replaced after Emperor Palpatine's death by a more efficient and destructive TIE variant known as the Scimitar assault bomber.

> **"When the TIE bombers first started shelling Yavin 4, I thought the planet would crack wide open. Those egg layers leveled the jungle."**
> —*Rebel controller Tigran Jamiro*

❷ Ordnance Pod: The ordnance pod often carries glowing proton bombs. These explosive bombs were dropped onto asteroids near Hoth as the Imperials searched for Han Solo's *Millennium Falcon*.

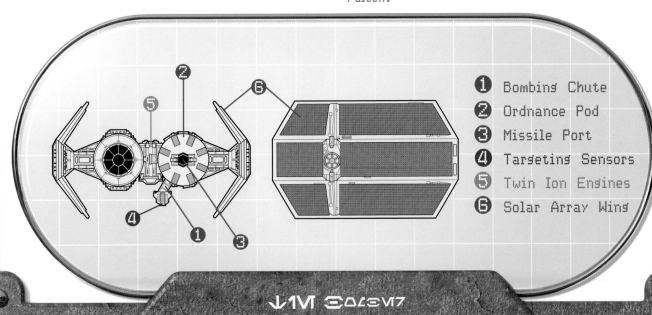

1. Bombing Chute
2. Ordnance Pod
3. Missile Port
4. Targeting Sensors
5. Twin Ion Engines
6. Solar Array Wing

TIE Defender

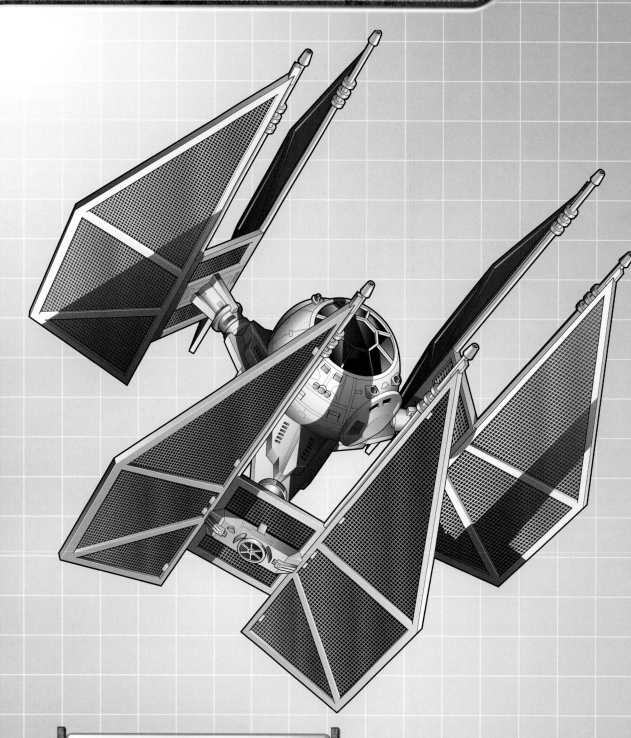

Technical Readout

SIZE: 6.6 m

MAXIMUM SPEED:
4,220G/Class 2
HYPERDRIVE/7,680 KPH

PRIMARY MANUFACTURER:
Sienar Fleet Systems

AFFILIATION: Galactic Empire

Sienar Fleet Systems TIE Defender

Another prototype TIE series starfighter, the TIE defender was first produced by Sienar Fleet Systems shortly before the Battle of Endor. The vehicle is perhaps the most experimental of the TIE craft, incorporating an unusual tri-wing design and slightly elongated cockpit. This design enables the TIE defender to perform steep dives, a variety of spins and twists, and tight turns.

The TIE defender project was conducted in utmost secrecy, and the vehicles were initially deployed in only very small numbers. The basic philosophy behind the starfighter is actually a testament to the success of *Alliance* craft such as the X-wing and Y-wing; the TIE defender was designed specifically as a heavily armed, well-protected assault fighter with hyperspace capabilities. The TIE defender's first full-scale combat use came during the Empire's successful attempt to defeat rogue Imperial admiral Zaarin.

While standard TIE fighters rely on numbers to overwhelm enemies, the TIE defender's weapons systems allow it to confront powerful Y-wings, X-wings, and even small transports. The TIE defender's weapons include two cannon emplacements installed on each wing. In standard configuration, the wings flanking the cockpit possess laser cannons, while the top wing holds ion cannons. All of the cannons can be fire-linked into pairs or quartets. The vehicle also fires proton torpedoes and concussion missiles from launchers located on the cockpit.

> **"Imperial High Command decided that defender pilots would only be selected from TIE interceptor pilots who had flown at least twenty combat missions and survived. We're either the best pilots in the Imperial fleet or the luckiest."**
>
> *—Onyx Squadron leader*
> *Rexler Brath*

The TIE defender's basic engine design is unchanged from previous TIE models, but it does use more advanced P-sz9.7 engines and is about 40 percent faster than the TIE fighter in an atmosphere. Maneuvering jet arrays on the tri-wing assembly allow sublight acrobatics impossible in other TIE craft.

TIE defenders proved more than five times more expensive than standard TIE fighters and thus never received widespread use during the Galactic Civil War. At the Battle of Endor, the Empire deployed only a handful of the defenders as part of Onyx Squadron. After the Emperor's death, TIE defenders nearly disappeared. They resurfaced momentarily during Grand Admiral Thrawn's reign, but, even then, they were deemed too difficult to produce and maintain. They have yet to supplant TIE/ln starfighters and TIE interceptors within the Imperial fleet.

6 Deflector Shield Projector: Deflector shields are very rare on TIE craft, but these allow the TIE defender to face off against well-armed Alliance vehicles such as the X-wing.

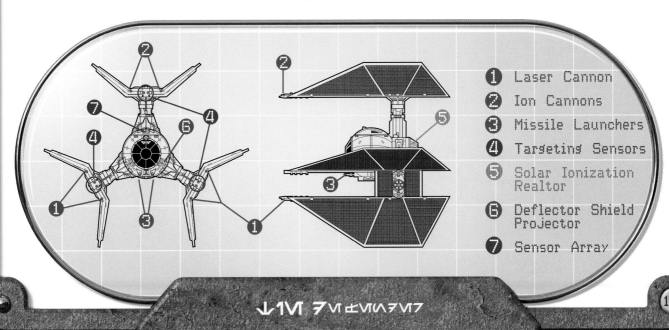

1 Laser Cannon
2 Ion Cannons
3 Missile Launchers
4 Targeting Sensors
5 Solar Ionization Realtor
6 Deflector Shield Projector
7 Sensor Array

TIE Fighter

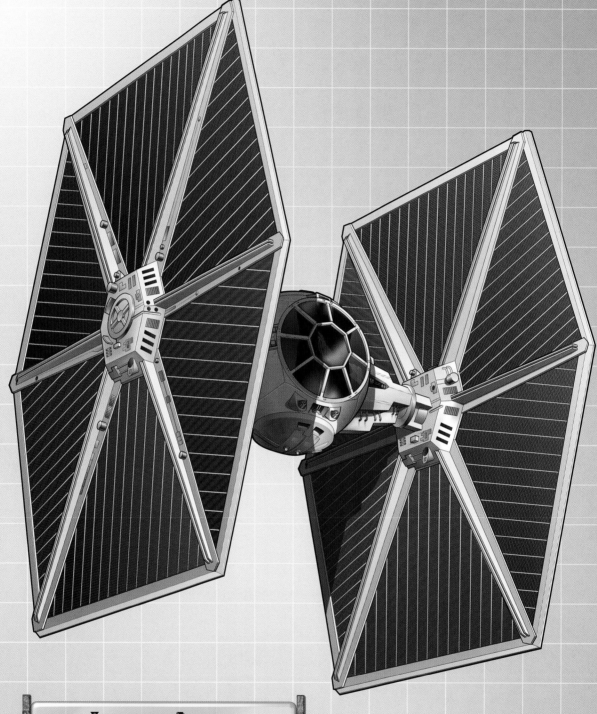

Technical Readout

SIZE: 6.3 m long

MAXIMUM SPEED:
4,100G/1,200 KPH

PRIMARY MANUFACTURER:
Sienar Fleet Systems

AFFILIATION: Galactic Empire

Sienar Fleet Systems TIE/ln Space Superiority Starfighter

From the beginning of the Galactic Civil War, the Emperor believed that the conflict would be a war of attrition. Nowhere is that philosophy more evident than in the design and tactics of the staple starfighter of the Imperial Navy, the TIE fighter. TIE fighters are meant to overwhelm enemy forces in huge numbers and have therefore been designed for speed and affordability.

The TIE fighter is built around twin ion engine technology. The twin ion engine was invented by Sienar Fleet Systems well before the Clone Wars, though the company did not perfect a compact and inexpensive version of the system until shortly before the Battle of Yavin. These new ion engines were built into a spherical cockpit connected to two large solar array wings to produce the familiar TIE fighter.

To minimize the TIE fighter's mass and thus increase its speed, the starfighter lacks anything deemed "excessive" by Imperial tacticians. The TIE fighter is without a hyperdrive, deflector shields, and life support systems. While other starfighters have a variety of weapons, the TIE fighter's only armaments are two L-s1 laser cannons on the round cockpit.

Because it lacks so many essential starfighter technologies, the TIE fighter may seem inadequate. Yet, while it is clearly without adequate defenses and versatility, the TIE fighter is among the fastest and most maneuverable craft in the galaxy. The TIE fighter can outrun virtually any Alliance or New Republic vehicles, save the A-wing and E-wing starfighters. And because it is so inexpensive, even Imperial Remnant forces can afford entire squadrons of the vehicles.

The TIE fighter's laser cannons are not very powerful on their own, but when dozens of TIE fighters attack simultaneously, as is often the case, they can demolish anything in their path.

The TIE fighter's small size makes it easy to store and transport. The starfighters can be found aboard all Imperial vessels, ranging from relatively compact cruisers to leviathans like the *Executor*. They are also stationed at planetary installations and orbital platforms.

Like their ships, TIE fighter pilots are often considered expendable. Because the TIE fighter lacks a life support system, its pilots must wear fully sealed flight suits with self-contained oxygen supplies and atmosphere converters. The pilot is strapped into a small high-g shock couch and is further protected by a crude repulsorlift antigravity field and crash webbing—but these devices offer little defense against enemy cannon fire.

Based on the success of the TIE fighter, Sienar produced numerous TIE variants for specific mission profiles. TIE bombers, TIE interceptors, reconnaissance TIE fighters, and even the TIE crawler tank are all extensions of the original TIE fighter design.

> ## "For every TIE fighter you shoot down, a thousand more will take its place."
> —*Imperial TIE fighter pilot Baron Fel*

④ **Solar Array Wing:** The cockpit provides a very small target for enemy starfighters approaching from the front or rear. However, most Alliance pilots learned to flank TIE fighters and target the vehicle's large solar array wings.

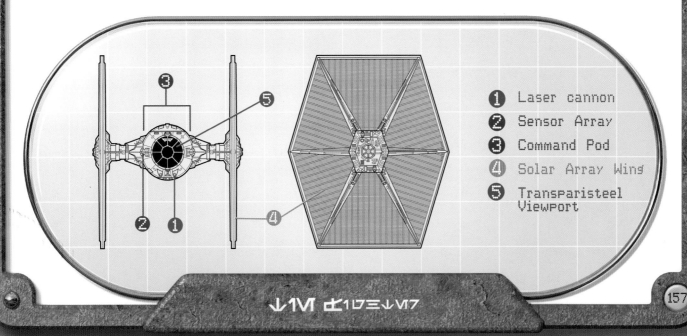

1. Laser cannon
2. Sensor Array
3. Command Pod
4. Solar Array Wing
5. Transparisteel Viewport

TIE Interceptor

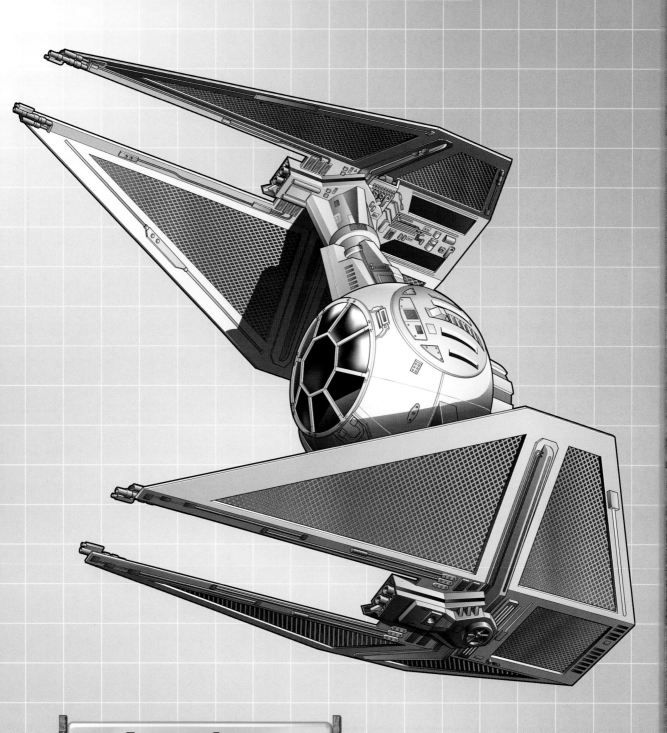

Technical Readout

SIZE: 9.6 m long

MAXIMUM SPEED:
4,240G/1,250 kph

PRIMARY MANUFACTURER:
Sienar Fleet Systems

AFFILIATION: Galactic Empire

Sienar Fleet Systems TIE Interceptor

Sienar Fleet Systems was never idle during the Galactic Civil War. After producing the effective TIE fighter, the Sienar design team began work on the TIE Advanced x1 prototype. When the TIE Advanced proved too costly for the Empire's tastes, Sienar transferred many of the prototype's features to its newest TIE design: the TIE interceptor.

The TIE interceptor was a direct response to the Rebel Alliance's development of faster and more dangerous starfighters. Hoping to develop a vehicle that could compete with the A-wing in both speed and maneuverability, Sienar invested huge sums into improving upon the standard TIE fighter's existing twin ion engines. Sienar engineers quickly developed a breakthrough ion stream projector that allows TIE interceptors to execute tight turns and rolls not possible in most other starfighters. Steering port deflectors can be manipulated individually for fine control and counterbalancing during especially trying maneuvers. This complex engine system makes the TIE interceptor the fastest starfighter in the Imperial fleet. And while the TIE interceptor is still slightly slower than the A-wing, it outperforms nearly every starfighter in the galaxy during dogfights.

The TIE interceptor's bent wings, an element lifted directly from the TIE Advanced prototype, give the starfighter a smaller profile and increased power. Four laser cannons, mounted two to a wing, are paired with targeting sensors to create the most accurate weapons on any Imperial starship save the TIE defender. The fire-linked cannons are arranged to provide the greatest possible field of fire.

The TIE interceptor does not represent a huge stride forward in terms of secondary systems. Like the TIE fighter, the interceptor is without armor, deflector shields, a hyperdrive, or life support. Interceptor combat tactics are therefore nearly identical to the "strength-in-numbers" approach used by standard TIE fighters.

The Empire intended to replace the standard TIE fighters with TIE interceptors. By the Battle of Endor, when TIE interceptor production reached its peak, the vehicles represented about 20 percent of the Imperial starfighter fleet. The valuable starfighters were stationed aboard Star Destroyers, on the second Death Star, and at key bases, such as the starship yards near Kuat and Fondor.

The Emperor's death and subsequent collapse of the Empire derailed further production of the interceptors. As Imperial funds dwindled, remnant forces found it increasingly difficult to acquire interceptors. Grand Admiral Thrawn eventually realized that the starfighters were not expendable, and he began equipping them with deflector shields.

> **"Your generic TIE grunt is just plain suicidal. And the TIE defender jockey is bloodthirsty. But the TIE interceptor pilot, he's suicidal *and* bloodthirsty. When you see a squad of those maniacs flying your way, you'd better hope your hyperdrive is operational."**
>
> —*New Republic operative Kyle Katarn*

5 **Bent Wings:** The TIE interceptor's bent-wing design is reminiscent of the Sith Infiltrator, which many believe Raith Sienar created for Darth Maul. The dagger-shaped wings give the interceptor a sinister appearance.

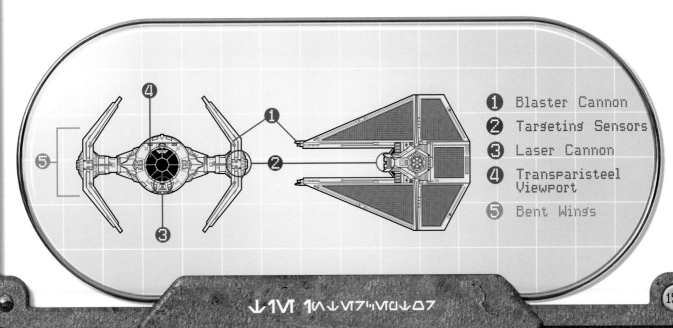

1. Blaster Cannon
2. Targeting Sensors
3. Laser Cannon
4. Transparisteel Viewport
5. Bent Wings

Vangaak

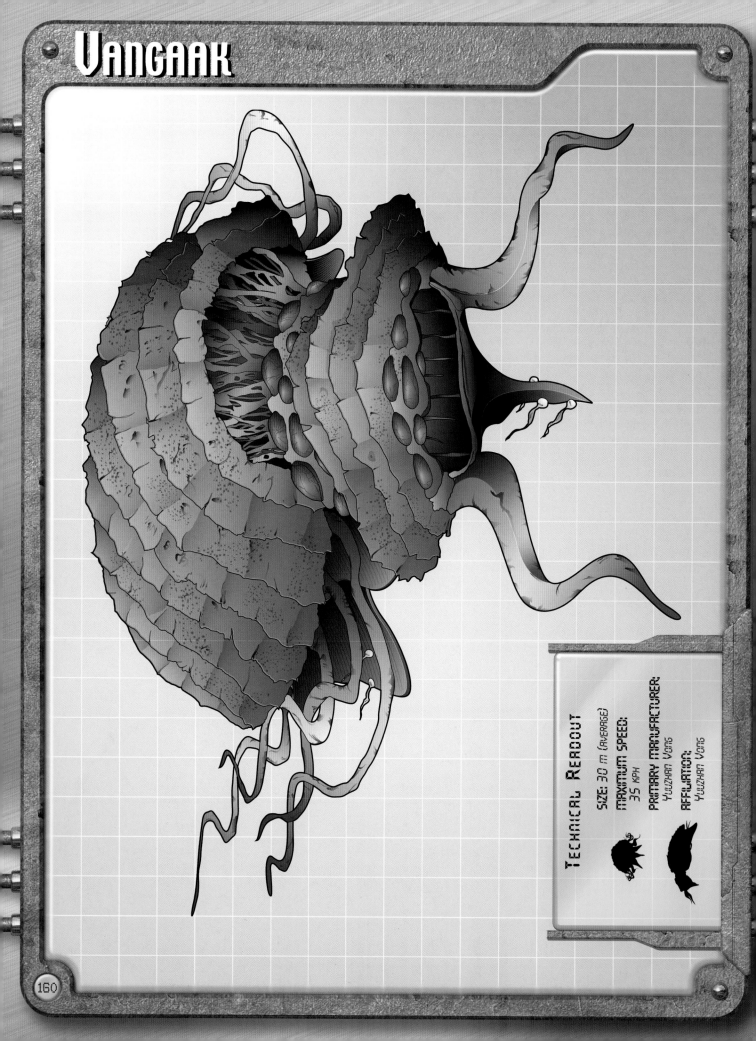

Technical Readout

Size: 30 m (average)

Maximum Speed:
35 kph

Primary Manufacturer:
Yuuzhan Vong

Affiliation:
Yuuzhan Vong

Yuuzhan Vong Vangaak

Yuuzhan Vong bioengineered vehicles display an amazing variety in both form and function. These craft range from starfighter analogs such as coralskippers to massive worldships to the aquatic trawlers known as vangaak.

Like many Yuuzhan Vong vessels, vangaak are grown from a variety of organic materials. The vehicle's interior frame is composed of hard and resilient yorik coral, the same living substance that forms the basis of the coralskipper. Once the frame matures, Yuuzhan Vong shapers seed the skeleton with a gelatinous organism called kera-boa. The kera-boa reproduces rapidly, creating a semisentient, protoplasmic colony. The colony sprouts millions of long, microscopic tendrils, which dangle below the vangaak. When the tendrils are compelled to move together, they can propel the vangaak forward or in reverse, or change the craft's heading.

After the vangaak's kera-boa system takes root, the vessel is covered with hundreds of long, chitinous scales. These dull green scutes are actually supplied by a giant dora-mu, an aquatic Yuuzhan Vong creature. Once removed from its dora-mu host, however, a scute does not die: instead, it can mold itself to the vangaak's skeleton and receive sustenance from the living craft. The vangaak's armored shell is very durable, able to withstand blaster bolts at close range. The scutes can also heal damage over time. As the scutes bond with the rest of the craft, knobby projections sprout from the carapace; when the vangaak is complete, these projections can be manipulated to control the entire vessel.

The vangaak trawlers on Yavin 4 are used to gather fish and other foodstuffs. A trawler travels largely submerged, with only a broad, flat dome visible. The dome serves as the vangaak's sensory device, allowing the craft to detect obstacles in its path. The vangaak trawler "feeds" by opening a large maw near the front of the craft. As the vangaak swims forward, water is filtered through thick, sticky strands of kera-boa. Large organisms are captured in the web, while smaller organisms pass through the kera-boa and into the vangaak's digestive membrane to fuel the craft. Yuuzhan Vong trawler operators regularly clear the kera-boa traps.

> ## "Feed the vangaak, feed yourself."
> —*Translated from the Yuuzhan Vong*

The former Yuuzhan Vong commander Vua Rapuung was reduced to being a vangaak tender after his love affair with shaper Mezhan Kwaad caused him to become a Shamed One. After Vua Rapuung joined forces with Anakin Solo, a Yuuzhan Vong Shamed One named Qe'u took Rapuung's place trawling the rivers of Yavin 4.

Large vangaak can be outfitted for combat with the addition of miniature plasma projectors, similar to those found aboard coralskippers. Immense dora-mu shells shield the crew from counterattacks. When a combat vangaak closes with an enemy ship, the kera-boa strands reach out to immobilize the target and allow a Yuuzhan Vong raiding party to board the unfortunate vessel.

6 Sensory Dome: On many vangaak, only the sensory dome is visible as the vehicle travels.

1. Propulsion Tendrils
2. Maw
3. Armored Shell
4. Filtering Membrane
5. Forward Kera-Boa Tendrils
6. Sensory Dome

VIRAGO

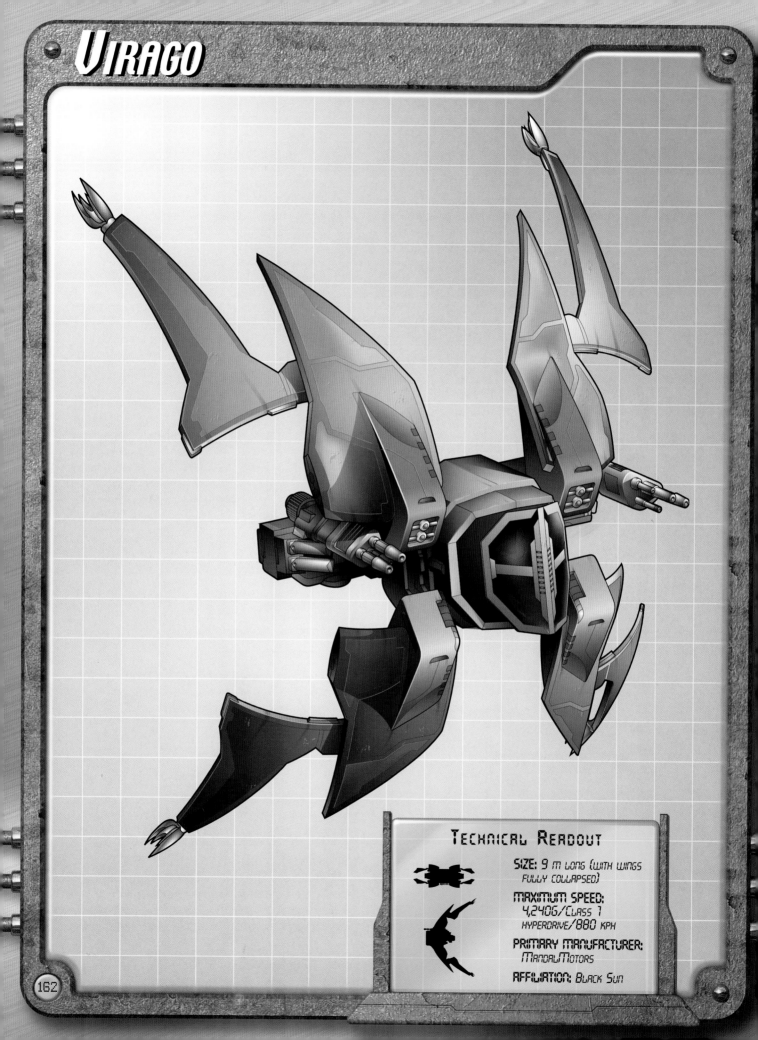

TECHNICAL READOUT

SIZE: 9 m long (with wings fully collapsed)

MAXIMUM SPEED: 4,240G/Class 1 hyperdrive/880 kph

PRIMARY MANUFACTURER: MandalMotors

AFFILIATION: Black Sun

Prince Xizor's MandalMotors *StarViper*-Class Attack Platform

Black Sun is one of the galaxy's largest and most powerful criminal organizations. As of the Battle of Hoth, the syndicate was ruled by Prince Xizor, a brilliant and ruthless Falleen. Although Xizor had access to numerous starships, his favorite vehicle was a custom-built heavy assault fighter known as *Virago*.

The *Virago* was a product of Xizor's egotism and the hard work of the entire MandalMotors design team. When Xizor decided he wanted a new starship, he contracted MandalMotors to develop the craft exactly to his specifications. Together, MandalMotors and Xizor created the *StarViper*-class attack platform, a vehicle that initially seems more akin to a mobile weapons station than a starfighter. Satisfied with the creation, Xizor named the ship *Virago* and promptly purchased all rights to the design to ensure that his personal starship would remain unique.

> ## "I think that's just about the most disturbing thing I've ever seen."
> —*Dash Rendar, upon seeing the* VIRAGO *for the first time*

When he first commissioned the *Virago*, Xizor demanded a starship that could rival the Imperial TIE interceptor in both speed and agility. MandalMotors succeeded here by providing the starship with four adjustable wings, each capped with two microthrusters. Both the wings and thrust nacelles constantly moved during flight, creating the illusion that the *Virago* was a bizarre, living creature. To achieve top speeds or travel in an atmosphere, the *Virago*'s wings folded closed behind the cockpit. In combat, however, the four wings expanded for greater maneuverability. Like the rest of the craft, the wings were extremely well armored. Each wing also contained one of the *Virago*'s four separate power generators, along with reserve fuel tanks for long-distance journeys.

Unlike many other craft, the *Virago*'s weapons system was not built around the weapons themselves, a tactic that would have required the development of new and likely illegal armaments. Instead, MandalMotors focused on creating an extraordinarily advanced targeting computer coupled with an experimental laser sighting system. Once the targeting computer was in place, any weapons installed on the *Virago* would perform far beyond their manufacturer specifications. Xizor's Black Sun engineers secured a pair of Taim & Bak Ht-12 double heavy laser cannons, each mounted on a forward-extending arm with a 180-degree field of fire. Two forward-facing Borstel proton torpedo launchers completed the weapons package.

It is widely believed that the *Virago* was destroyed when Darth Vader obliterated Prince Xizor's skyhook, but whether or not the starship—or her owner—actually perished remains conjecture. Soon after Xizor's apparent death, MandalMotors regained the rights to the StarViper design and began releasing less powerful versions of the *Virago*.

⑦ S-Foil Actuator: The *Virago*'s wings move using the same type of S-foil technology that allows the X-wing's airfoils to open and close.

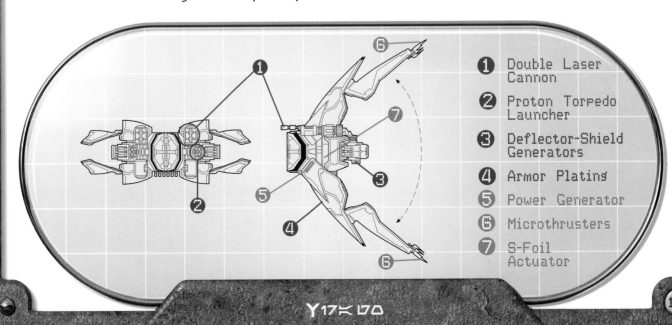

1. Double Laser Cannon
2. Proton Torpedo Launcher
3. Deflector-Shield Generators
4. Armor Plating
5. Power Generator
6. Microthrusters
7. S-Foil Actuator

V-WING

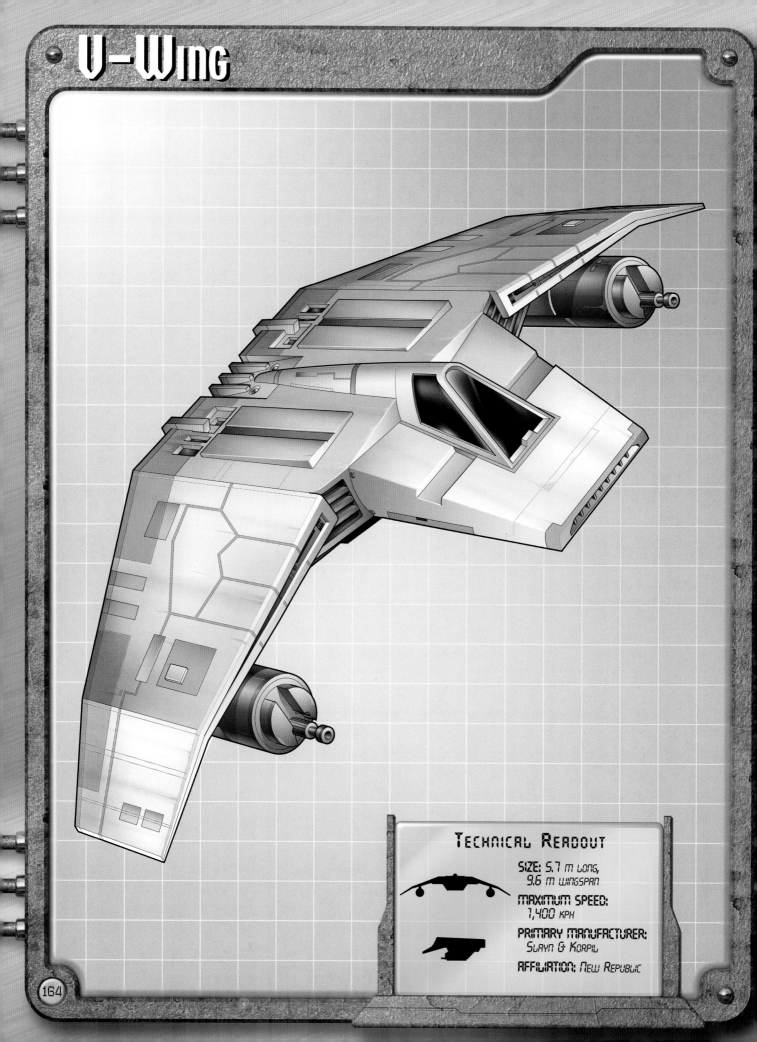

TECHNICAL READOUT

SIZE: 5.7 m long,
9.6 m wingspan

MAXIMUM SPEED:
1,400 kph

PRIMARY MANUFACTURER:
Slayn & Korpil

AFFILIATION: New Republic

Slayn & Korpil V-Wing Airspeeder

The V-wing airspeeder is the first New Republic vehicle designed specifically as a high-atmosphere combat fighter craft. New Republic forces previously relied on T-47 airspeeders and similar vehicles for air-to-air combat within a planetary atmosphere. As the struggle with the Imperial Remnant continued, Republic engineers addressed the need for a longer-range airspeeder with a greater flight ceiling to take on TIE bombers and other starfighters. The V-wing was completed just in time for the Battle of Mon Calamari.

Designed and constructed by the Verpine Slayn & Korpil colonies, developers of the B-wing starfighter, the V-wing is a drastic improvement over previous airspeeder designs. The V-wing's standard repulsorlift system is paired with efficient ion afterburners to provide the tiny craft with tremendous speed. The vehicle's top combat speed of 1,000 kilometers per hour is slightly slower than the T-47's maximum velocity, but its maximum altitude of 100 kilometers far outstrips the T-47's 250-meter flight ceiling. The V-wing's flight ceiling is nearly equal that of the cloud cars used on Bespin. In addition, the V-wing is equipped with a robust Chab-Ylwoum scramjet booster—which, when activated, increases the fighter's speed to 1,400 kph. Combat is not advised while traveling at such speeds, since any sudden maneuver can cause the airspeeder to break apart. The scramjet is therefore reserved for quick escapes from enemy craft.

When engaged in combat, the V-wing relies on two fire-linked blaster cannons with an effective range of about two kilometers. A V-wing pilot must use the vehicle's speed and size to its full advantage during confrontations with Imperial starfighters, because the airspeeder lacks deflector shields or other defenses.

V-wings are typically kept in docking bays at planetary bases and aboard large starships. When deployed from space, the V-wings must be transferred to a planetary atmosphere by Slayn & Korpil speeder transports. These large, unarmed vessels can carry between four and six airspeeders, which immediately release once the transport breaches the upper atmosphere.

V-wings are fairly versatile and can be used for many types of missions. They are excellent patrol craft and are often instructed to defend planetary installations from enemy starfighter attack. V-wings prove especially devastating to slower and less maneuverable TIE bombers. Because of their speed and their ability to remain hidden in an upper atmosphere, they are also instrumental in surprise raids and ambushes. At the Battle of Mon Calamari, V-wings ripped apart Imperial forces, destroying countless TIE/D fighters and water-based amphibins.

> **"We were told not to use the scramjets during combat, but it was just too tempting at Mon Cal. It doesn't get much more exciting than using the scramjet to overtake one of those droid TIE fighters."**
>
> —*Anonymous Rogue Squadron pilot*

⑤ Scramjet Intake: Air is forced through the scramjet intake to increase the V-wing's speed for short bursts.

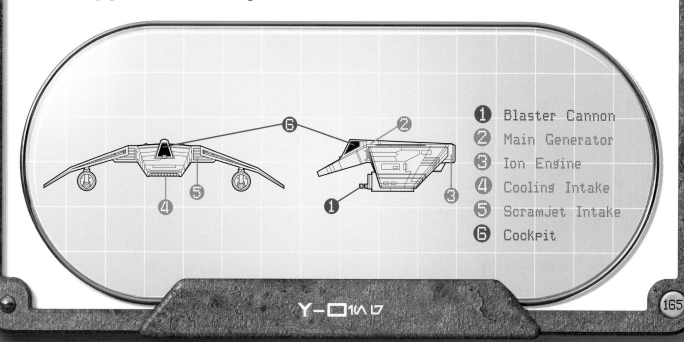

① Blaster Cannon
② Main Generator
③ Ion Engine
④ Cooling Intake
⑤ Scramjet Intake
⑥ Cockpit

WILD KARRDE

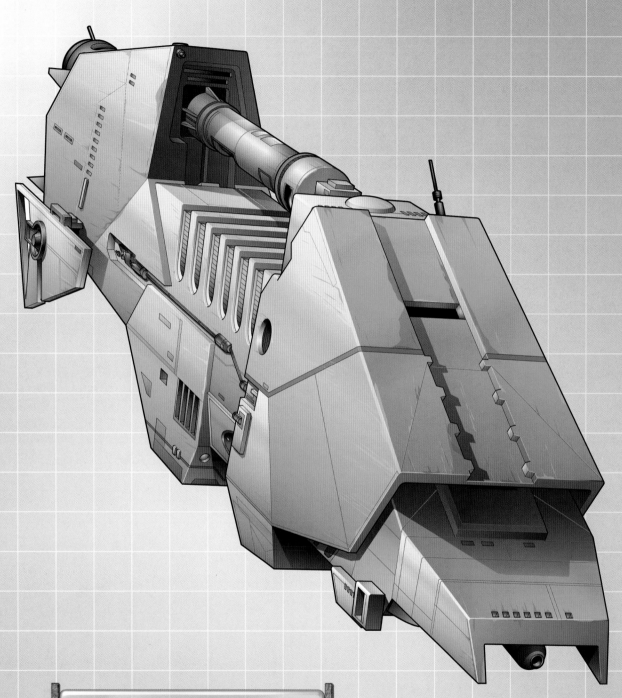

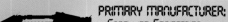

Modified Corellian Action VI Transport

A smuggler's best friend is often his or her starship. Han Solo would have been arrested or killed long ago if not for the *Millennium Falcon*. Dash Rendar's *Outrider* allowed him to fend off bounty hunters such as IG-88 and Boba Fett. Despite the abilities of these remarkable starships, from the outside they appear to be battered but benign freighters. Smugglers favor such vehicles because they are reliable, easy to modify, and rarely attract attention. Smuggling kingpin Talon Karrde is no exception to this rule: his personal transport, the *Wild Karrde*, seems to be an aging Corellian Action VI bulk freighter. But beneath the scratched and dented exterior hides one of the most comprehensive mobile communications bases in the galaxy.

A standard Action VI transport is a slow-moving, awkward vessel that lacks weapons but has tremendous carrying capacity of about 90,000 metric tons. The *Wild Karrde* is not a typical starship, and Karrde has made several modifications to the freighter. The most obvious alterations include the addition of three retractable turbolasers, all suitable for combat against capital ships. The hull is covered in reinforced plating, carefully selected to match the texture of the vessel's original light armor. Deflector shield generators with a dedicated power source have also been installed.

Talon Karrde prides himself on being well informed. He has contacts in nearly every part of the galaxy sending a steady stream of data to the *Wild Karrde*. To process this information, the vessel's passenger and crew quarters have largely been converted into a communications center. A sophisticated hyperradio array grants Karrde instant access to his spies, while HoloNet transceivers monitor countless broadcasts from around the galaxy. The sensor system includes a masking device that conceals the *Wild Karrde* from casual scans and sends false transponder information regarding the ship's cargo.

Alterations to the cargo hold include the addition of a life support system for transporting passengers or animals. Karrde carries at least one small repulsorlift vehicle aboard the ship as well. A small docking bay and extendable force tube allow the *Wild Karrde* to link to small ships while in space. The medical bay can treat nearly any humanoid species, while a droid hold contains assorted astromechs and GNK power droids. The starship even has kennels for Karrde's pet vornskrs.

Despite his shady past, Talon Karrde has become a valuable ally to the New Republic. After the initial Yuuzhan Vong invasion, Karrde and his starship raced to Yavin 4 to aid the Jedi academy. He has remained actively involved in the war with the Yuuzhan Vong ever since.

> **"You can't even call your wife on a comlink without Talon Karrde hearing about it."**
> —*Han Solo*

5 Hyperradio Comm Array: This small device is actually one of the most powerful components on the *Wild Karrde*, permitting Talon Karrde to send messages to all corners of the galaxy.

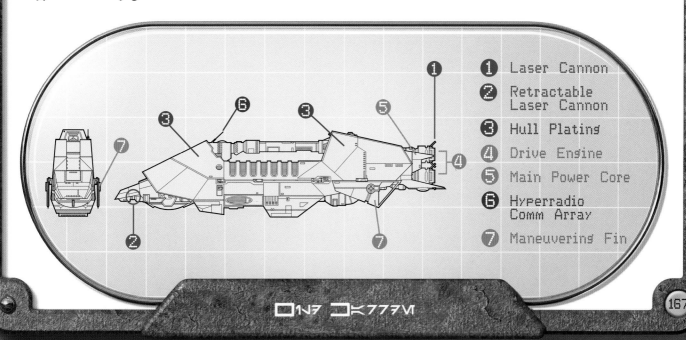

1. Laser Cannon
2. Retractable Laser Cannon
3. Hull Plating
4. Drive Engine
5. Main Power Core
6. Hyperradio Comm Array
7. Maneuvering Fin

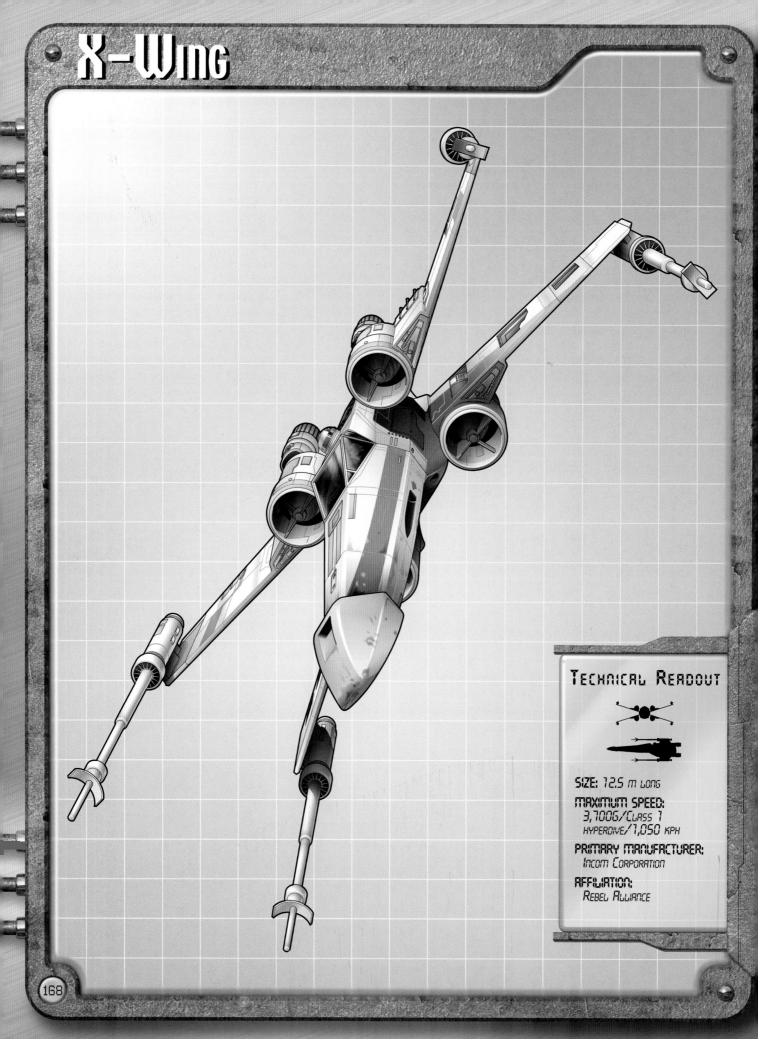

X-WING

TECHNICAL READOUT

SIZE: 12.5 m long

MAXIMUM SPEED:
3,700G/Class 1
HYPERDRIVE/1,050 KPH

PRIMARY MANUFACTURER:
Incom Corporation

AFFILIATION:
Rebel Alliance

Incom Corporation T-65 X-Wing Space Superiority Fighter

History will always report that the Rebel Alliance was saved from total annihilation by an X-wing starfighter. The X-wing played a pivotal role at the Battle of Yavin, enabling young pilot Luke Skywalker to fly into the Death Star's trench and target a small, two-meter-wide exhaust port. Luke was aided by the Force, but the mission would not have succeeded without the X-wing's superior capabilities. In fact, many students of technology claim that the X-wing is the most advanced single-pilot starfighter ever produced.

The X-wing receives its name from its double-layered wings, which separate into an X formation during combat to increase the starfighter's field of fire. Each wing is armed with a high-powered Taim & Bak KX9 laser cannon. The cannons can be fired individually, simultaneously, in pairs, or in any other combination. Proton torpedoes, such as those used to destroy the Death Star, are fired from Krupx MG7 launchers located near the bottom of the vessel.

Although the X-wing is designed for just one pilot and no passengers, the X-wing jockey is never truly alone thanks to the astromech socket located behind the cockpit. While in flight and during combat, the X-wing's astromech is responsible for astrogation, navigation, damage control, and flight adjustments. The unit can also pilot the fighter in an emergency. R2 astromechs assigned to X-wings carry up to ten jump coordinates for escapes into hyperspace.

One of the X-wing's greatest assets is its durability.

> ## "It's going to be like old times, Luke. We're a couple of shooting stars that'll never be stopped!"
>
> *—Biggs Darklighter moments before he boarded his X-wing to participate in the Battle of Yavin*

The fighter's reinforced titanium-alloy hull, Chempat deflector screen and deflector shield projectors, and transparisteel canopy ensure that it can withstand several hits without suffering serious damage. In the event of disabling damage, the pilot can deploy the ship's ejection system.

The X-wing's history is nearly as important as its capabilities. Designed by Incom Corporation in the early days of the Empire, the X-wing schematics found their way into Rebel hands when several Incom engineers defected to the Alliance. The Rebels began producing X-wings in modest numbers, and the vehicle quickly became one the most important weapons in the Alliance arsenal.

Since the Battle of Yavin, several X-wing variants have been produced. The T-65A3 is a simple upgrade with improved shields, laser cannons, and targeting computers. The T-65AC4 was designed for increased durability and can withstand more punishment than other X-wings. A reconnaissance X-wing, the T-65R or "snoop," lacks weapons and instead carries a host of sensors. The newest version of the starfighter, the T-65XJ3, was introduced shortly before the fall of Coruscant to the Yuuzhan Vong, and includes three proton torpedo launchers. The majority of XJ3 X-wings are operated by Jedi.

2 Proton Torpedo Launcher: Two proton torpedoes launched from Luke Skywalker's X-wing destroyed the Empire's first Death Star.

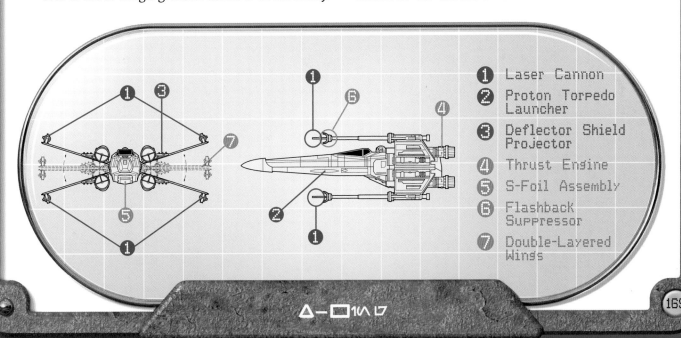

1 Laser Cannon
2 Proton Torpedo Launcher
3 Deflector Shield Projector
4 Thrust Engine
5 S-Foil Assembly
6 Flashback Suppressor
7 Double-Layered Wings

Yuuzhan Vong Transport Carrier

Technical Readout

SIZE: 48 m long (average)

MAXIMUM SPEED:
1,500G/3,000 kph (descent),
1,000 kph (ascent)

PRIMARY MANUFACTURER:
Yuuzhan Vong

AFFILIATION:
Yuuzhan Vong

Yuuzhan Vong Yorik-Trema

The Yuuzhan Vong invasion is terrifying in its efficiency. As the alien marauders sweep across the galaxy, they crush stellar opposition and then swiftly occupy target worlds with thousands of Yuuzhan Vong warriors. Planetary incursions are accomplished using highly mobile transports known as yorik-tremas.

The yorik-trema is a bio-engineered vessel that resembles a bloated mass of molting tissue. The vehicle is actually a complex organism composed of living yorik coral and undulating vastiv membranes.

When a planetary invasion begins, hundreds of yorik-trema transports are released from worldships, warships, and other Yuuzhan Vong vessels. The transports fall rapidly toward the target planet, descending in a straight line as if simply dropped. Because of the yorik-tremas' unusual landing pattern, New Republic forces have taken to calling the transports "crates."

Yorik-trema transports are escorted by several coralskippers, but they are not without weapons of their own. When attacked, a yorik-trema sprouts a pair of hornlike projections that are actually weapons. The projections can fire damaging plasma bolts at planetary weapons emplacements and are quite capable of targeting even small, fast-moving starfighters.

As it descends into an atmosphere, the yorik-trema is protected from anti-aircraft artillery by a thick shell covering its ventral surface. The shell is ablative and will wear away under prolonged fire; however, it also has regenerative properties and can replenish quickly,

"When the Yuuzhan Vong first invaded Ithor, I thought that some horrible creature had exploded in the upper atmosphere ... The transports were like giant gobs of flesh falling to the planet's surface."—

—Dirin Maj'o,
New Republic Relief Corps

even while under attack.

The yorik-trema possesses numerous sensors that track the movements of escort coralskippers and can quickly identify incoming enemy fighters. The scanners are unsettling—they resemble giant, alien eyes.

Each yorik-trema is divided into two sections. The forward compartment has enough room for only a pilot and commander. The spacious rear section, though, holds up to 30 armed soldiers led by 6 full-fledged Yuuzhan Vong warriors. The yorik-trema can also carry Yuuzhan Vong speeders and other vehicles.

The yorik-trema's landing gear consists of several sharp landing claws that can penetrate nearly any surface. The Yuuzhan Vong transports can secure purchase on rocky cliffs, snowy plains, or even armored buildings. Once the vehicle has landed, several hollow molleung worms extend from the yorik-trema's sides. These worms serve as debarking tubes for the soldiers, who pour out onto the battlefield in search of victims. The yorik-trema can also attach to enemy starships, where it literally chews a hole through the target's hull. Once the hull has been breached, the Yuuzhan Vong soldiers can easily board the enemy vessel.

④ **Molleung Worms:** The molleung worms are living creatures that can lash out at any enemy troops in order to clear a landing zone. Once the area is secure, the molleung worms allow Yuuzhan Vong soldiers to exit the transport.

① Sensor "Eyes"
② Cockpit Compartment
③ Cargo Section
④ Molleung Worm Valve
⑤ Plasma Projector
⑥ Primary Landing Claw

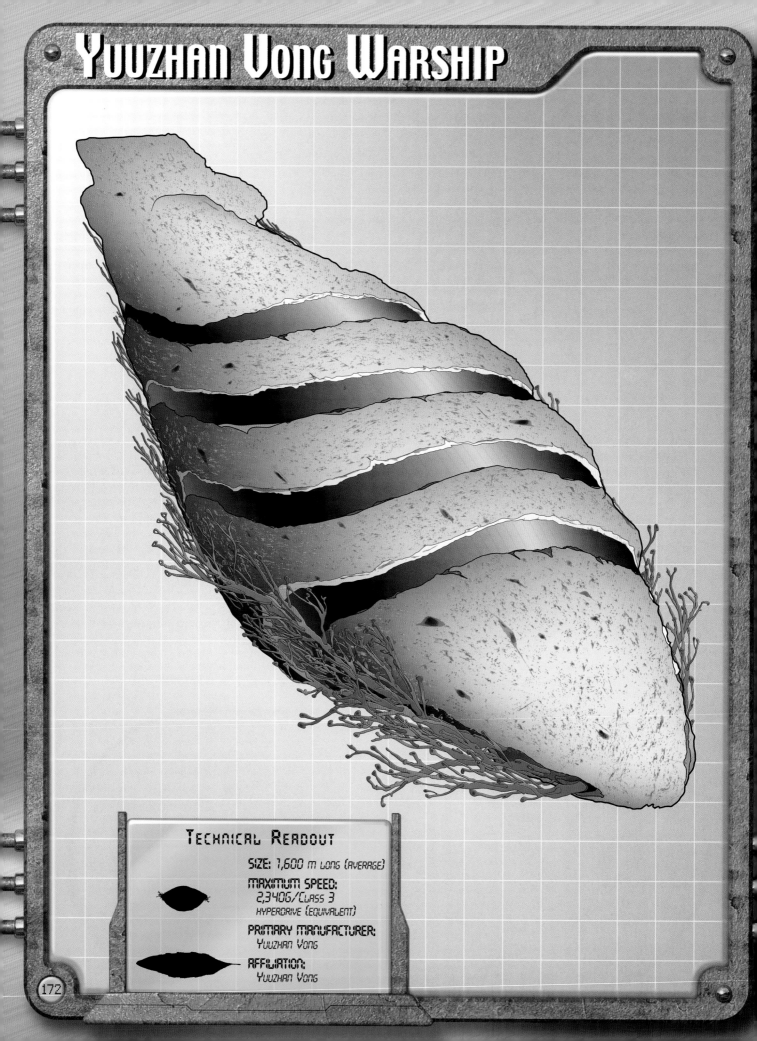

Technical Readout

SIZE: 1,600 m long (average)

MAXIMUM SPEED:
2,340G/Class 3
Hyperdrive (Equivalent)

PRIMARY MANUFACTURER:
Yuuzhan Vong

AFFILIATION:
Yuuzhan Vong

Yuuzhan Vong Miid Ro'ik

Perhaps the most powerful starship in the Yuuzhan Vong arsenal, the miid ro'ik warship is the rough analog to conventional capital battleships such as the Imperial Star Destroyer. The menacing ovoids serve as command ships, blockade vessels, and assault starships.

At its core, a miid ro'ik warship is similar to other Yuuzhan Vong vessels, with a core structure formed by yorik coral. The vehicle's propulsion system relies on dovin basals, which can lock onto gravitational fields in order to pull the warship through space. The warship is unique in its ability to recycle other Yuuzhan Vong starships. Whenever a coralskipper, kor chokk, or even a worldship begins to die, its organic material is fed to the miid ro'ik. The dying matter is converted into fuel for the warship's magma weapons and other systems. Some of this material is also transformed into viscous secretions that ooze onto the vehicle's hull and harden into glossy, black armored plates. These armored regions can reflect blasterfire and withstand collisions.

The warship's magma weapons, which disgorge streams of molten rock, are hidden in deep crags along the vessel's outer hull; a typical miid ro'ik can support up to 60 of these weapons. The critical dovin basals are likewise protected. Miid ro'ik have many hundred dovin basals, providing the vessel with greater speed than other Yuuzhan Vong starships, which is critical because the warships are often used as command craft and must move quickly between key locations during a battle. Miid ro'ik are responsible for securing a perimeter during a space engagement. To prevent enemy ships from escaping, the warship's dovin basals produce a unified gravity well to prevent hyperspace retreats.

> ### "From the dead, we grant life."
> —*Yuuzhan Vong shaper*

The Miid ro'ik's most terrifying feature is its so-called dread weapon: a grotesque, serpentine appendage, the retractable dread weapon can be several times longer than the length of the warship. The bioengineered device has rough skin covered in dark flecks. An opening at the end of the weapon creates a powerful vacuum that can consume small starships or individuals. When the warship is hungry, the Yuuzhan Vong have no qualms about using the dread weapon on a populated area. The dread weapon can also be used to convey troops between starships or onto a planet's surface.

As midsized Yuuzhan Vong transports, warships carry nearly 3,000 troops and various vehicles. The miid ro'ik is also a carrier, moving hundreds of coralskippers through space via several long coral arms growing from the main hull. These deep red and dark blue arms sprout from the warship's nose, spine, and posterior. Coralskippers can easily attach to these arms and then release again when combat is necessary.

⑤ Dovin Basal: Arguably the most powerful and important component of any Yuuzhan Vong starship, the dovin basal both seeks out and projects gravity wells.

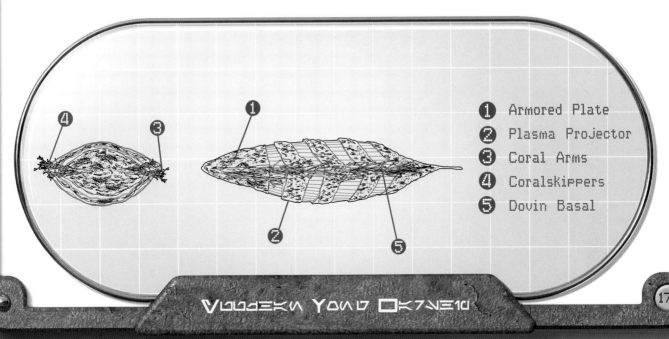

① Armored Plate
② Plasma Projector
③ Coral Arms
④ Coralskippers
⑤ Dovin Basal

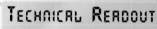

Technical Readout

SIZE: 10 km long

MAXIMUM SPEED
1,100G/Class 1.5
HYPERDRIVE (EQUIVALENT)

PRIMARY MANUFACTURER:
Yuuzhan Vong

AFFILIATION:
Yuuzhan Vong

Yuuzhan Vong *Koros-Strohna*

Perhaps the most mind-bending starship in the Yuuzhan Vong fleet, the terrifying worldship is a massive bioengineered vessel that serves as a staging ground for prolonged battles. Similar in function to a Super Star Destroyer, the living worldship is a transport, battleship, and psychological weapon all at once. In fact, the worldships carry the entire Yuuzhan Vong population. The Yuuzhan Vong are refugees from a destroyed home planet, and they use their worldships to locate new planets to conquer.

The basic worldship is composed of a single mass of yorik coral about 10 kilometers long. The yorik coral forms symbiotic relationships with dozens of other organic materials to provide weapons, propulsion systems, and defensive capabilities.

Like all Yuuzhan Vong starships, the worldship relies heavily on dovin basals—spherical organisms capable of projecting a gravity well. Worldships possess dozens of dovin basals ranging from one to three meters in diameter. The pulsating creatures are capable of locking onto a specific gravity field, regardless of distance, in order to pull the worldship through space.

In areas where gravitational pull is weak, including the region between galaxies, the worldship extends membranous tendrils called outrider ganglia. Each tendril is anchored by many piloted coralskippers, which help unfold the membranes. Once unfurled, the ganglia serve as cosmic sails.

Each worldship is equipped with hundreds of magma weapons that expel molten slag at enemy vessels. These magma weapons range from small openings, with the destructive capability of conventional blaster cannons, to larger emitters, which can shoot burning rocks the size of small freighters over great distances. The worldship's weapons are spaced sporadically and recharge slowly as new magma is produced, but they prove incredibly accurate despite their unconventional "technology."

The dovin basals can serve as weapons. When these organisms concentrate their gravity wells, they can cause a space station to collapse or force a moon to collide with its orbital partner. Dovin basals also wreak havoc with conventional shields, enabling the worldships to strip their enemies of defenses before an attack. The worldship's own defenses rely on the dovin basals' ability to use gravity wells to intercept incoming proton torpedoes and other weapons.

> **"The *Koros-Strohna* is all I've ever known. I have lived within the ship my entire life."**
> —*Anonymous Yuuzhan Vong warrior*

The sheer size of a worldship enables it to transport even a small Yuuzhan Vong army. Each worldship carries more than 5,000 deadly Yuuzhan Vong warriors and their coralskipper starfighters.

As living creatures, worldships have some rudimentary consciousness and can communicate with Yuuzhan Vong pilots. A typical worldship has a life span well over 500 years, and they continue to grow in size as they age. The *Baanu Miir,* the largest worldship yet encountered by the New Republic, is more than 1,000 years old. Aged worldships do eventually sicken and die. A dying ship can be identified by color variations in its dovin basals and the myogens that illuminate the vessel's hallways.

⑥ Gorros' Fen: The worldship carries a gigantic, tubular worm that can extend from the vessel to a planet's surface in order to collect nutrients for the worldship.

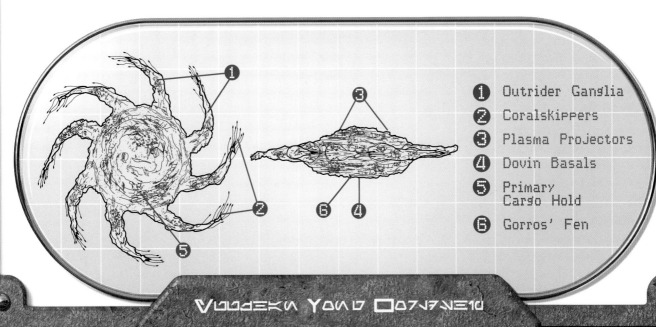

1. Outrider Ganglia
2. Coralskippers
3. Plasma Projectors
4. Dovin Basals
5. Primary Cargo Hold
6. Gorros' Fen

Y-Wing

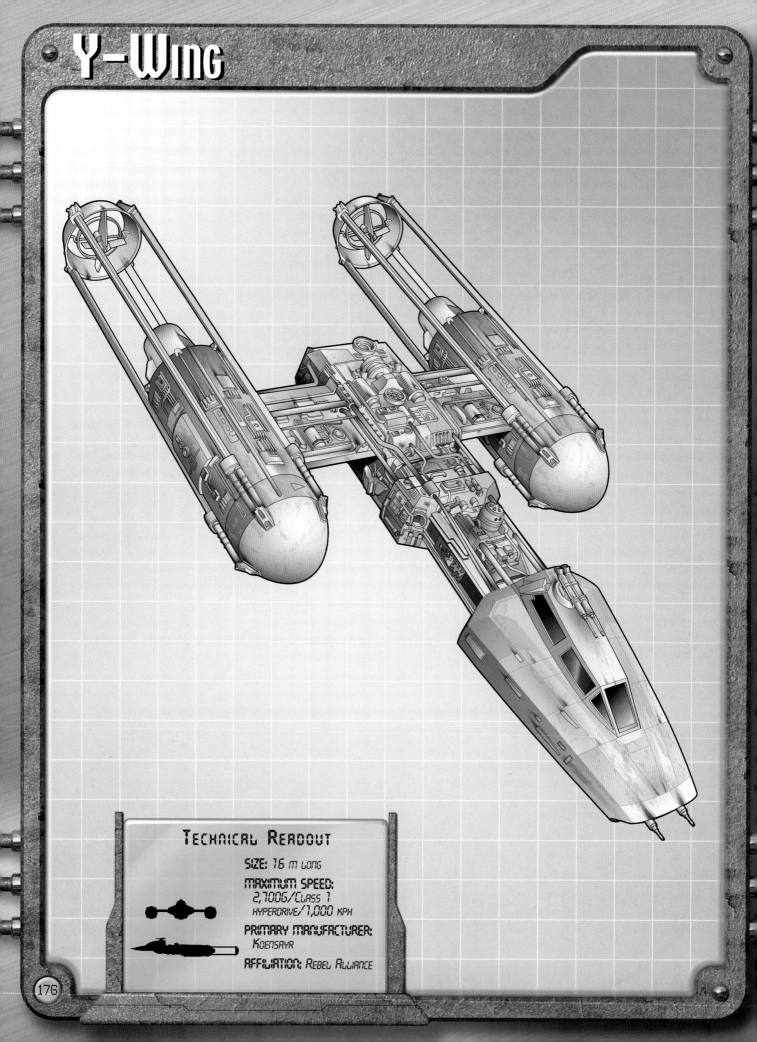

Technical Readout

SIZE: 16 m LONG

MAXIMUM SPEED:
2,700G/CLASS 1
HYPERDRIVE/1,000 KPH

PRIMARY MANUFACTURER:
KOENSAYR

AFFILIATION: REBEL ALLIANCE

Koensayr BTL-S3 Y-Wing Attack Starfighter

Prior to the advent of the X-wing, the Y-wing served as the Rebel Alliance's primary attack starfighter. The snubfighter, characterized by its triangular cockpit and two long engine pylons, was critical to many early battles, but ultimately proved less versatile than the X-wing. Although outdated by the time of the Battle of Yavin, the Y-wing's durability and heavy firepower ensured it a place in the New Republic fleet even well into the Yuuzhan Vong invasion.

While the Alliance relied on the Y-wing for everything from escort duty to reconnaissance, the starfighter was originally designed for close-quarters combat with space stations and large starships. Light bombing runs and surgical strikes are also part of the Y-wing's mission profile. The starfighter's weapons emplacements are fairly modular. Most Rebel Y-wings used a pair of laser cannons and a rotating ion cannon. The Y-wing can be equipped with proton torpedoes, concussion missiles, and proton bombs for more direct assaults.

As on the X-wing, an R2 or R4 astromech droid fits into a droid socket behind the cockpit and monitors all flight, navigation, and power systems. The droid can also handle fire control, perform in-flight maintenance, and reroute power as needed. Most importantly, the R2 unit stores several hyperspace jump coordinates to allow quick retreats.

Y-wings proved invaluable early in the Galactic Civil War. In particular, the starfighters were lauded for their role in holding TIE bombers at bay during the Siege of Ank Ki'Shor. As the civil war continued, it became apparent that the Y-wing could not be the Alliance's sole starfighter. The Y-wing lacked the payload capacity, speed, stealth, and maneuverability of many Imperial attack fighters and couldn't survive encounters with TIE interceptor squadrons. Fortunately, the arrival of the X-wing allowed the Y-wing to be used for more specialized combat roles. Y-wings were often used at major engagements to soften targets such as Star Destroyers before capital ships moved in.

Alliance engineers also mastered the Y-wing's design and found that it could be easily modified and reconfigured. Alliance technicians often stripped a Y-wing of bulky armor and generators before an assault on an Imperial convoy, or prepared the craft for bombing runs by adding more powerful shields and significantly increasing the vehicle's payload. Y-wings also serve on diplomatic escort missions and for long-range patrols: the BTL-A4 Y-wing (LP), or Longprobe, has extra provisions, more powerful sensors, and a sophisticated nav computer specifically for patrol and reconnaissance duty. A version of the Y-wing with an extended cockpit supports a copilot, who generally functions as a gunner.

> ## "They're the workhorses of this outfit, I can tell you that."
> *—Rebel Y-wing pilot Tiree, before the Battle of Yavin*

7 Detachable Cockpit: Some versions of the Y-wing include a detachable cockpit that serves as an emergency escape pod.

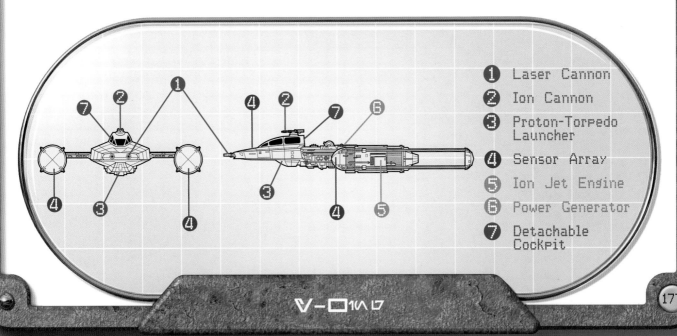

1 Laser Cannon
2 Ion Cannon
3 Proton-Torpedo Launcher
4 Sensor Array
5 Ion Jet Engine
6 Power Generator
7 Detachable Cockpit

Z-95 Headhunter

Technical Readout

SIZE: 11.8 m

MAXIMUM SPEED:
2,780G/1,150 KPH

PRIMARY MANUFACTURER:
Incom Corporation/
Subpro Corporation

AFFILIATION: None

Incom/Subpro Z-95-AF4 Headhunter

One of the oldest starfighters still in use by the New Republic, the Headhunter predates the Battle of Yavin by several decades and has experienced several revivals since its first appearance. The starfighter's longevity is based on its legendary resilience, and it remains an attractive option to mercenaries and security personnel throughout the galaxy.

The original Z-95 Mark I Headhunter was marketed as an atmospheric fighter craft, although Incom also pushed the fact that the vehicle could be easily modified for space travel. The basic design consisted of twin engines and two swing-wings. A bubble canopy, similar to the later X-wing's canopy, allowed for the clearest possible field of view. The Mark I was not manufactured with weapons initially, but the popularity of the craft among outlaw groups and police forces convinced Incom to add a set of triple blasters on each wing.

Despite Incom's claims to the contrary, the Mark I was not suitable for space combat. Incom quickly produced more advanced variations of the Headhunter with sublight travel in mind. The most drastic design change involved replacing the Mark I's swing-wings with fixed wings equipped with rear-mounted maneuvering jets. The revised Headhunters also boasted transparisteel canopies and vastly improved tactical displays. Incom increased the Headhunter's appeal by offering several aftermarket modification kits for both the weapons and engines.

As with many other starfighters, the Headhunter has spawned a number of variants. The military-grade Z-95-AF4 includes Incom 2a fission engines, Taim & Bak KX5 laser cannons, and a pair of Krupx MG5 concussion missile launchers, placing it on par with the Y-wing in terms of destructive capability. The Rebel Alliance was known to convert Headhunters for short-range bombing runs. The Rebels also used Headhunters for training missions because the vehicle's controls were nearly identical to those of the X-wing and Y-wing.

Because Headhunters are fairly common, it's no surprise that many of the galaxy's heroes have piloted the star-fighter on occasion. Mara Jade has been known to pilot a modified Headhunter equipped with a hyperdrive. During his days in the Corporate Sector, Han Solo hopped into a Mark I Headhunter to lead a group of outlaw mechanics against Corporate Sector Authority fighters. During the confrontation, Solo proved that the Headhunter's atmospheric capabilities far exceeded those of most conventional starfighters, including those of the Authority's IRD fighters.

> **"As long as mechanics keep finding ways to improve this baby, the Headhunter will never be outdated."**
> —*Outlaw mechanic Doc*

⑦ Maneuvering Jets: The maneuvering jets provide the Headhunter with surprising maneuverability during atmospheric combat.

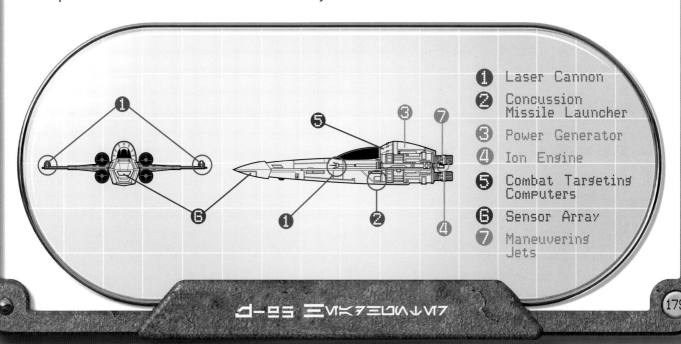

1. Laser Cannon
2. Concussion Missile Launcher
3. Power Generator
4. Ion Engine
5. Combat Targeting Computers
6. Sensor Array
7. Maneuvering Jets

A SHORT HISTORY OF WAR

The invention of the hyperdrive more than 25,000 years before the Yuuzhan Vong invasion marks a turning point in galactic history. Prior to the advent of hyperspace travel, worlds and systems developed in isolation from one another with no unified sense of a galactic community. The hyperdrive allowed the Core systems to build massive starships for plying the space lanes. They made first contact with other worlds, spreading goodwill and the vision of a single benevolent government. Soon the Republic was born.

The Old Republic's early days were not peaceful ones. As the Republic fleet spread out the far corners of the galaxy, its ships met countless warlike civilizations. The Republic realized the need for armed warships and other military vehicles. Innovations such as turbolasers, ion cannons, and proton torpedoes were discovered during the Republic's early years to help protect the galaxy's denizens from one another. The proliferation of vehicles and weapons only increased the use of violence throughout the stars.

Eventually, the Old Republic established peace and prosperity throughout the galaxy. Small, inconsequential conflicts would occasionally erupt on Outer Rim worlds or non-Republic systems, but it appeared that the Core Worlds had put war behind them. Although technological advances continued, they largely focused on noncombat applications. It required major military emergencies—such as the invasion of Sith armies—to encourage the continued development of mobile weapons of war.

From the Sith War to the Clone Wars and from the Galactic Civil War to the Yuuzhan Vong invasion, every new conflict has spurred major advances in vehicle technology and tactics. When the galaxy is embroiled in war, defense contractors continually push the boundaries of design, searching for innovations that will give their vehicles a distinct advantage during combat. For every superweapon there must be a countermeasure; for every Imperial starfighter, a New Republic counterpart.

Here we focus on five key conflicts from recent history, exploring the ways in which these battles capitalized on technological innovations and how certain vehicles turned the tide of battle.

THE BATTLE OF NABOO

Date: 32 Before the Battle of Yavin (B.B.Y.)
Factions: Trade Federation vs. Naboo/Gungans
Key Vehicles: Trade Federation Droid Control Ship, AATs, and droid starfighters; Naboo N-1 starfighters and Gian speeders

The Old Republic had been at peace for eons. Although fairly bloated and more corrupt than it should've been, the government managed to maintain harmony. With the aid of the Jedi Order, disputes were resolved and threats put down before they could escalate into full-scale war.

The Trade Federation shattered the galaxy's tranquillity, however, when it unleashed a secret droid army on pastoral Naboo. The army incorporated vehicles produced specifically for the Trade Federation, including deadly droid starfighters, unstoppable transports (MTTs), and devastating tanks (AATs). The Trade Federation converted their own cargo vessels into battleships.

The surprise invasion overwhelmed the Naboo. The Theed strike force alone included 342 battle tanks, which entered the city from all directions. The AATs proved more than a match for the Royal Security Forces (RSF) military speeders, while droid starfighters kept the N-1 fighters grounded.

Queen Amidala joined forces with the Gungans and a small RSF resistance movement to launch a counterattack. The offensive featured three separate fronts: a clash between the Gungans and the Trade Federation's droid army; Queen Amidala's assault on the Theed Palace; and a Naboo starfighter strike against the Droid Control Ship.

The Gungan army, with its relatively primitive weapons, was never meant to defeat the Trade Federation. Instead, the Gungan troop movements were designed to draw the Trade Federation army away from Theed. The plan worked well. As soon as the Gungans emerged from the swamps, the Trade Federation sent dozens of MTTs, AATs, and STAPs to the battlefield. Each MTT was protected by at least five AATs as troops were deployed. The AATs targeted the Gungan shield generators once the battle droids had entered the fray, allowing the tanks and other large units to advance. The Gungans were soon routed, but the "distraction" had allowed Amidala's forces to infiltrate Theed.

Naboo vehicles played an important role in the

BATTLE OF NABOO

Key
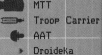

MTT
Troop Carrier
AAT
Droideka

Long Range Offensive

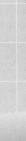

Battle
Droids

Battle
Droids

Battle
Droids

Shield

Gungan Grand Array

Battle Stage

Droid Army

Army A

Both views
not to scale

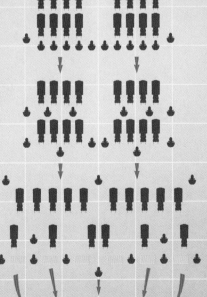

Army B

Army C

Nym

Royal Security Force

Gungan Grand Array

BATTLE OF GEONOSIS

Battle Stage

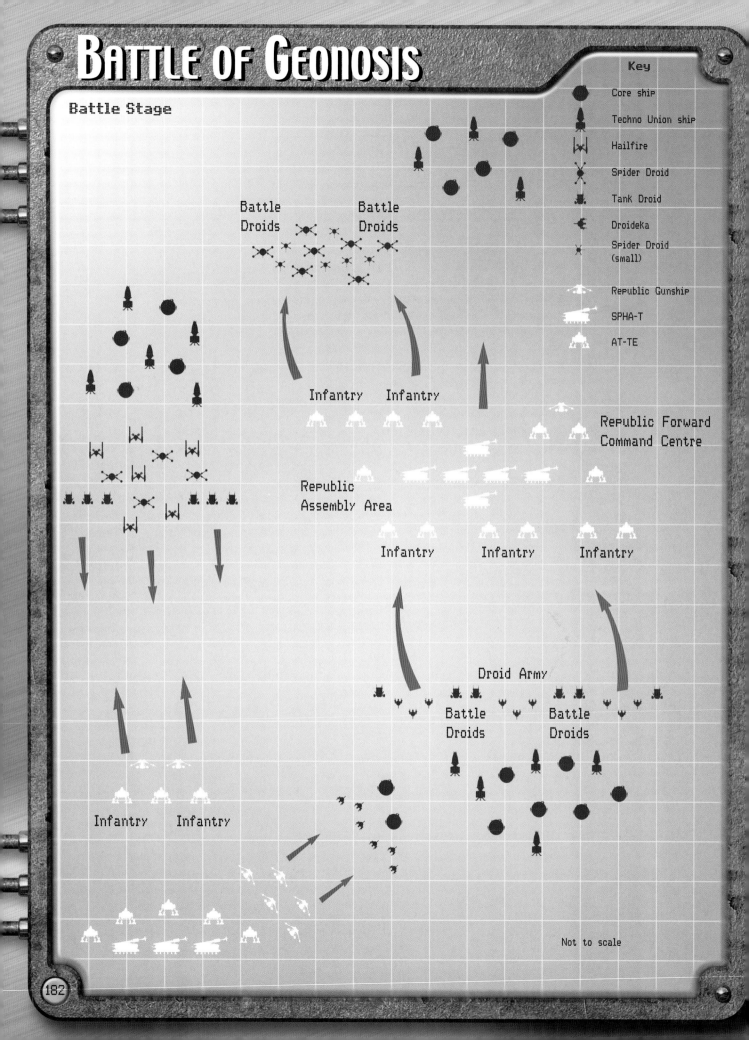

Key

Core ship	
Techno Union ship	
Hailfire	
Spider Droid	
Tank Droid	
Droideka	
Spider Droid (small)	
Republic Gunship	
SPHA-T	
AT-TE	

Battle Droids

Battle Droids

Infantry   Infantry

Republic Forward Command Centre

Republic Assembly Area

Infantry   Infantry   Infantry

Droid Army

Battle Droids   Battle Droids

Infantry   Infantry

Not to scale

recapture of Theed. While the RSF speeders had been ineffective in direct confrontations with AATs, Captain Panaka and his crew found that they could be used to ambush lone tanks. They cleared a path to the palace by destroying one AAT.

Once the palace hangar had been breached, Bravo Flight pilots secured Naboo N-1 starfighters and launched them against the Trade Federation's Droid Control Ship. Although the N-1 was never intended as a true assault fighter, the Bravo Flight pilots used exceptional tactics to survive. They quickly closed with the Droid Control Ship to elude the vessel's turbolasers, which could not target at such close range. When the Droid Control Ship launched its droid starfighters, the Naboo pilots continually altered their attack patterns and flew erratically to overload the droids' tactical processors. Regardless, the sheer number of droid starfighters would have overwhelmed Bravo Flight if not for Anakin Skywalker.

Skywalker inadvertently discovered the Control Ship's weakness when he flew a borrowed N-1 starfighter into the battleship's main hangar. Using the N-1's high-yield proton torpedoes, Anakin destroyed the Droid Control Ship's main reactor. The resulting explosion consumed the starship and ended the Trade Federation's invasion.

Although the Trade Federation was defeated at Naboo, the conflict caused major ripples throughout the galaxy. No longer could peaceful systems rely on the Republic for protection.

THE BATTLE OF GEONOSIS

Date: 22 B.B.Y.
Factions: Confederacy of Independent Systems vs. Old Republic
Key Vehicles: Confederacy homing droids, hailfires, and droid tanks; Republic gunships, AT-TEs, and SPHA-Ts

In the years preceding the Battle of Geonosis, a disturbing number of systems expressed dissatisfaction with the Galactic Republic. Ex-Jedi Count Dooku fueled this discontent by forming a small but vocal separatist movement. He allied with foundries on Geonosis to provide weapons and vehicles in the event of a war with the Republic. He also gained support from the Commerce Guild and other groups. They officially founded the Confederacy of Independent Systems at a meeting on Geonosis.

Meanwhile, the Republic had discovered a clone army on far-flung Kamino. Allegedly ordered by a mysterious Jedi, the clone army was fully trained and well equipped. When the situation on Geonosis became critical, the Republic assumed control of the clone army and launched an attack on Geonosis. The resulting battle marked the start of the infamous Clone Wars.

The Battle of Geonosis was primarily a ground campaign. The Republic planned the attack as a sudden, overwhelming assault that would stamp out the Confederacy before it could gain more power. After penetrating the upper atmosphere with huge military assault ships, the Republic dropped a fleet of gunships to the planet's surface. The transports carried thousands of clone troopers and dozens of AT-TE walkers. The army advanced on the Geonosian arena, where a Jedi strike team was surrounded, then attacked the core ships of the Trade Federation.

The Confederacy and its fierce Geonosian allies refused to surrender. Geonosian starfighters tried to stop the clone troopers, but the AT-TE walkers, gunships, and a handful of Jedi starfighters kept the Geonosians at bay. To counter the walkers and gunships, a variety of heavy assault platforms were rolled into position. Tank droids, hailfire units, and homing droids managed to slow the clone army temporarily, but the Jedi commanders spread their forces to flank the slow-moving droids. Reconnaissance troopers riding speeder bikes crisscrossed the battlefield, gathering vital information about enemy troop movements and capabilities.

Once the Confederacy leaders realized that the Republic would carry the day, the Trade Federation tried to launch several core ships to safety. The core ships contained an untold number of battle droids, weapons, and vehicles. Clone scouts spotted the core ships and warned Yoda and the other Jedi commanders. The Jedi knew that every core ship represented a small army; thus, destroying these vessels became a priority. The clone army rushed to reposition several powerful self-propelled heavy artillery units equipped with advanced turbolasers. The turbolasers, which required constant protection from gunships and AT-TE walkers, managed to down at least one of the behemoth core ships, crippling the Confederacy's army.

The Battle of Geonosis exacted a heavy toll on the Republic forces, resulting in the deaths of numerous Jedi and legions of clone troopers. And while the Republic's attack severely damaged the Confederacy's war effort, it also galvanized the Separatists. The Clone Wars escalated quickly, affecting every aspect of galactic life.

THE BATTLE OF YAVIN

Date: 0 B.B.Y.
Factions: Galactic Empire vs. Rebel Alliance
Key Vehicles: Death Star, Imperial TIE fighters, and Vader's TIE Advanced; Rebel X-wing starfighters, Y-wing starfighters, and the *Millennium Falcon*

BATTLE OF YAVIN

Typical Formations

Y-Wing

X-Wing

TIE Fighter

TIE Advanced

Attacks

Trench Run

TIE
Covering Squadron

Death Star
surface

Trench

Turret Attack

The Battle of Yavin was the first major engagement of the Galactic Civil War, pitting the incredibly powerful Galactic Empire against the underequipped Rebel Alliance. Prophetically, it was also the first significant tactical victory for the Rebels, who relied on superior planning, versatile starfighters, and the Force to destroy the dreaded Death Star.

During the early days of the Galactic Civil War, the Rebel Alliance tried to avoid conflict whenever possible. They learned of the Empire's Death Star, a secret weapon that could destroy a planet. Rebel spies stole the secret plans for the battle station, but the Empire eventually traced the Alliance to Yavin 4, a jungle planet near a large gas giant.

With only 30 standard minutes before the Death Star came within range of Yavin 4, the Rebels mustered a very small attack force of Y-wing and X-wing starfighters. The pilots were drawn from Rebel bases across the galaxy and included new recruits such as Luke Skywalker. Although many of the pilots had never been in combat before, they had flown small repulsorlift craft; the controls of the skyhopper, in particular, are nearly identical to those aboard the X-wing.

The Alliance's attack plan was bold: a Rebel pilot would need to reach the Death Star, dodging TIE fighters and turbolaser fire, then descend into a long trench and fire a proton torpedo into a two-meter-wide exhaust port. Scoring a direct hit against the unshielded thermal exhaust vent would start a chain reaction that could collapse the battle station's power core.

The Rebel starfighters were arranged into Red Squadron, composed of X-wings, and Gold Squadron, composed of Y-wings. The pilots approached the Death Star in tight wings, with a central starfighter flanked by two wingmates. As Gold Squadron's commander and his wingmates made their way toward the Death Star trench, the remaining starfighters occupied the TIE fighters and destroyed countless turbolasers. Once the Imperials uncovered the Alliance's plan, Darth Vader boarded his TIE fighter prototype to defend the trench. Vader was accompanied by two hand-selected wingmates.

At the battle's outset, it seemed as if the Rebels were doomed. Although the X-wing and Y-wing starfighters were able to avoid the turbolasers and their greater firepower enabled them to destroy many Imperial TIE fighters, the sheer numerical superiority of the Imperials began to take its toll.

The Death Star trench proved too narrow for the less-than-maneuverable Y-wings, and the first strike against the Death Star ended in failure. A trio of X-wings headed by Red Leader made the second run, but Darth Vader's TIE fighter easily overtook the Rebel starfighters. Only three X-wings remained, including that of Luke Skywalker. Luke descended into the Death Star trench

even as the Death Star prepared to destroy Yavin 4.

Luke used the X-wing's targeting computer to lead him toward the Death Star's exhaust port, but Vader's much faster TIE prototype was on him in moments. Vader was about to obliterate Luke's X-wing when the *Millennium Falcon* appeared on the scene. The *Falcon's* quad laser cannons opened fire. The attack would have demolished any other TIE fighter, but Vader's starship possessed deflector shields. Instead of exploding, the prototype spun out of control, leaving Luke free to continue down the trench. Using the Force, Luke unleashed the X-wing's proton torpedoes, and the energy missiles traveled into the exhaust port. As predicted, the attack caused a chain reaction in the Death Star's main reactor and the superweapon was destroyed.

THE BATTLE OF HOTH

Date: 3 A.B.Y.
Factions: Galactic Empire vs. Rebel Alliance
Key Vehicles: Imperial AT-ATs, AT-STs, and Star Destroyers; Rebel snowspeeders and transports

After the Battle of Yavin, the Rebel Alliance spent three years running from the Galactic Empire. The Rebels relocated to Hoth, but Darth Vader continued his relentless search for Luke Skywalker and the Alliance leaders. As he combed the galaxy in his Super Star Destroyer the *Executor*, Vader eventually located the Rebel base and launched one of the largest ground offensives of the Galactic Civil War. The Battle of Hoth would become the Rebel Alliance's most terrible defeat.

Vader's fleet moved on Hoth immediately. However, the *Executor's* commander, Admiral Ozzel, made a tactical blunder early in the offensive. The overconfident Ozzel emerged from hyperspace too close to the Hoth system and allowed the Rebels to detect the fleet's approach. Alerted to the invasion, the Alliance erected a planetary shield to prevent bombardment from space and began preparing a full-scale retreat.

The Imperial forces on Hoth were led by General Maximilian Veers, whose tactical brilliance would be pitted against the military pragmatism of Alliance general Carlist Rieekan. Veers's goal was simple: overrun the Rebel base and capture all Rebel personnel. Rieekan was dedicated to seeing the Rebels to safety. He ordered the Alliance to prepare the Rebel transports and sent Rogue Squadron onto the battlefield to delay the approaching Imperials.

Upon entering the Hoth system, Veers deployed several AT-AT landing barges and Imperial transports. The AT-AT squad, dubbed Blizzard Force, consisted of sev-

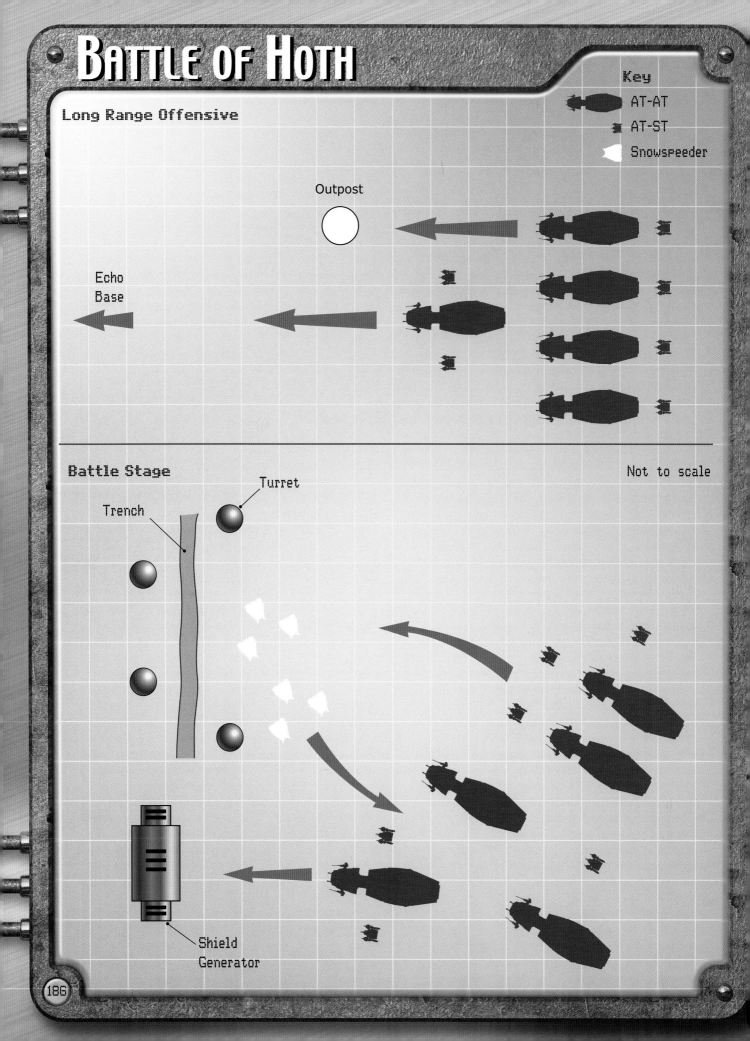

BATTLE OF HOTH

Long Range Offensive

Key
AT-AT
AT-ST
Snowspeeder

Outpost

Echo
Base

Battle Stage

Not to scale

Turret

Trench

Shield
Generator

eral AT-AT walkers, each commanded by a high-rank-ing Imperial officer. Several of the AT-ATs were modi-fied vehicles with unique features; Veers's own Blizzard One was more heavily armored than a standard AT-AT. AT-ST walkers protected the AT-ATs flanks as the attack force marched toward the Rebel base.

To stall the AT-ATs, Rogue Squadron flew modified T-47 airspeeders. These "snowspeeders" flew in a loose delta formation to draw AT-AT fire away from the Rebel ground troops. Unfortunately, the snowspeeders' laser cannons could not penetrate the AT-ATs' thick hides, forcing Wedge Antilles to resort to a daring tactic: using his airspeeder's harpoon and tow cable, Wedge entangled an AT-AT's legs, forcing it to the ground.

As Rogue Squadron struggled with Veers's Blizzard Force, Rebel transports began launching. Initially, each transport launched individually. An ion cannon provid-ed covering fire, slamming into Imperial Star Destroyers blockading the planet, while a pair of X-wings served as escort fighters. As the AT-ATs closed in, however, the Rebels were forced to launch the trans-ports in pairs. The final transport, the *Bright Hope*, was disabled as it fled Hoth, but the bounty hunters 4-LOM and Zuckuss eventually aided the vehicle's escape.

Although many Rebel transports escaped Hoth, the Alliance suffered heavy casualties. The defeat on Hoth severely weakened the Alliance, and Rebel forces remained understaffed for the remainder of the Galactic Civil War. A year later, still suffering from the aftereffects of Hoth, the Alliance was forced into its incredibly risky assault on the second Death Star at the Battle of Endor.

The Battle of Endor

Date: 4 A.B.Y.
Factions: Galactic Empire vs. Rebel Alliance
Key Vehicles: Imperial TIE fighters, TIE bombers, TIE interceptors, Star Destroyers, and AT-STs; Rebel X-wings, Y-wings, B-wings, A-wings, Mon Cal cruisers, and the *Millennium Falcon*

The most decisive, and final, engagement of the Galactic Civil War, the Battle of Endor included a major space battle and ground offensive. In contrast to the Battle of Hoth, the Battle of Endor was initiated by the Alliance as a last-ditch effort to stop the Emperor's ter-rible regime. The Alliance rallied to launch a strike on the second Death Star, which was still under construc-tion in orbit around the forest moon of Endor. Unfortunately, the shield generator on Endor projected a defensive screen around the Death Star, preventing a direct assault.

The first part of the Alliance's plan involved sending a Rebel strike team to Endor. The Rebels, led by Han Solo, were to destroy the shield generator moments before the Rebel fleet arrived in the system. After numerous misadventures, Solo's group reached the shield generator, where they discovered a squad of the Empire's finest troops waiting. The Imperials were armed with AT-STs and speeder bikes, which they used to quickly surround the Rebels.

Unaware of Solo's plight, the bulk of the Rebel fleet exited hyperspace near the Death Star. The fleet was led by a Mon Cal cruiser designated *Home One*, and including several starfighter squadrons composed of X-wings, Y-wings, A-wings, and B-wings. Lando Calrissian, aboard the *Millennium Falcon*, led the starfighter attack as Gold Leader. Once the Alliance fleet realized that the Death Star's shield was still active, Admiral Ackbar advised breaking off the attack, but Lando urged the Rebels forward. They were met by a massive fleet of TIE craft, including standard TIE fighters and the new TIE interceptors. The versatility of the Rebel fleet, which included powerhouse B-wings and agile A-wings, enabled the Alliance to form small wings capable of crashing headlong into this wave. While A-wings pur-sued the TIE interceptors, the B-wings and other craft provided covering fire.

On Endor, Solo and his squad were rescued by Ewoks, a species native to Endor. The Ewoks capital-ized on the AT-ST's inability to cross shifting terrain by rolling logs under the scout walker's metal feet. They also used primitive traps to down speeder bikes. The Wookiee Chewbacca later leapt out of the trees to cap-ture an AT-ST from above, turning the tide of the ground battle. Solo's team destroyed the generator, but the outcome of the space battle was still in doubt.

As the ground team fought to gain access to the Imperial facility, the Alliance fleet discovered that the Death Star's superlaser was fully functional. The space station destroyed one Mon Cal cruiser and was prepar-ing to fire again when Ackbar ordered a full retreat. Lando suggested that the Alliance ships close with the Imperial Star Destroyer; the Death Star wouldn't fire on any enemy ship in close proximity to the Star Destroyer fleet. During the fight, an A-wing barreled through the *Executor*'s bridge, and the ship crashed into the Death Star. The *Executor*'s demise was a major turning point in the battle.

When the shield dropped thanks to the land force's efforts, Lando and Wedge Antilles flew into the Death Star and directly attacked the main reactor core. Proton torpedoes were used to disrupt the reactor. As with the first Death Star, the destruction of the reactor caused an explosive chain reaction.

Battle of Endor

Typical Formations

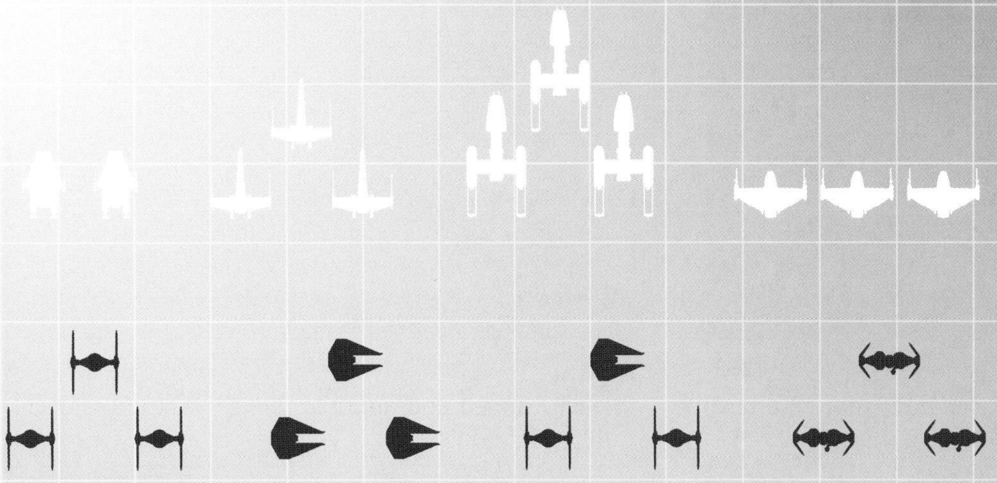

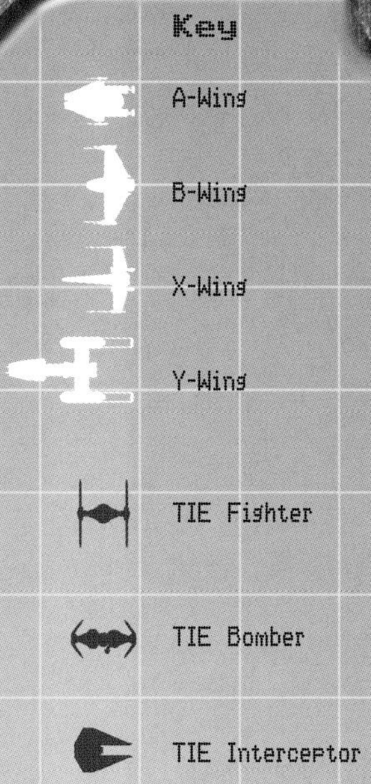

A-Wing

B-Wing

X-Wing

Y-Wing

TIE Fighter

TIE Bomber

TIE Interceptor

Battle Stage

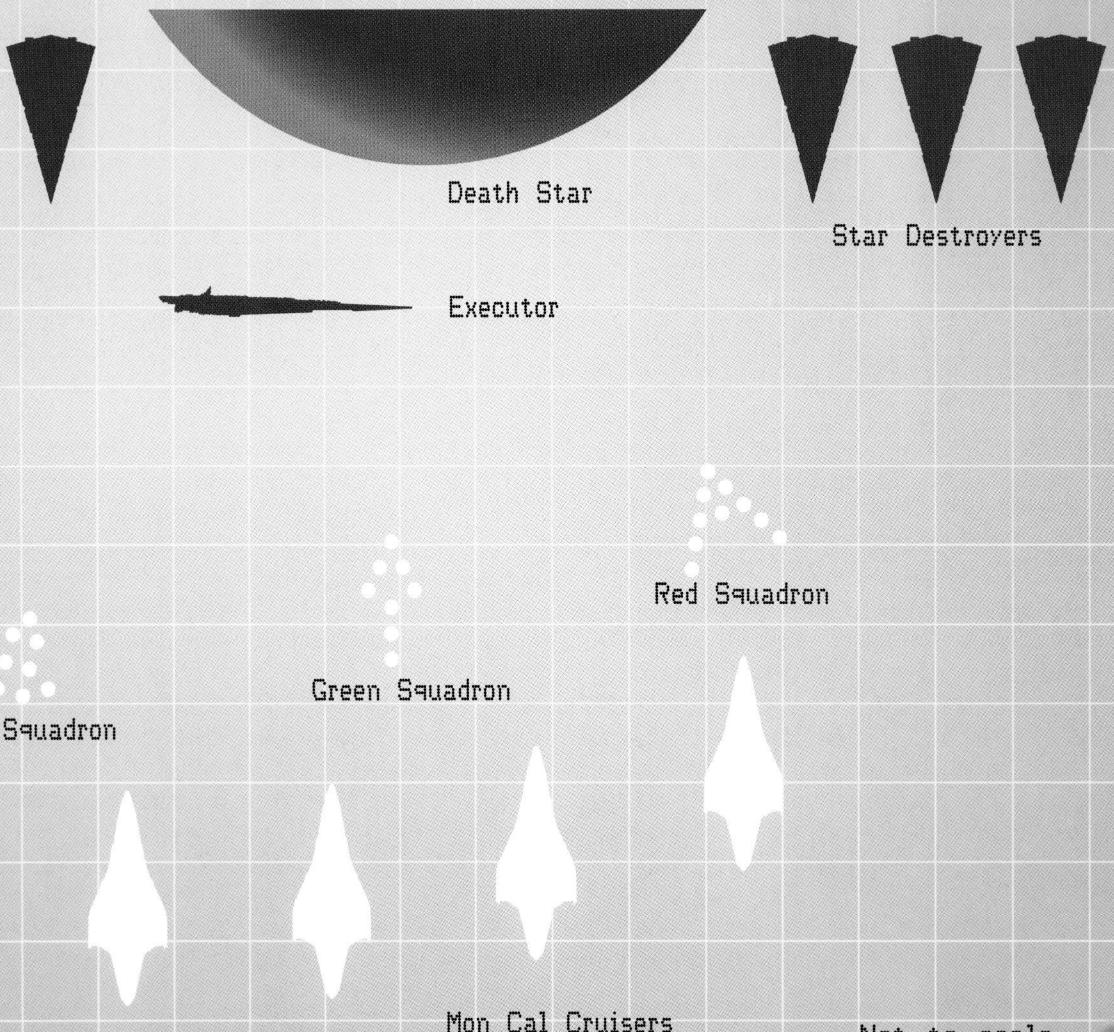

Death Star

Star Destroyers

Executor

Red Squadron

Green Squadron

Gold Squadron

Mon Cal Cruisers

Not to scale

188

Other Vehicles and Vessels of Note

The galaxy is replete with vehicles of every variety, ranging from simple single-person repulsorlift transports to massive starships that almost defy logic. A full account of every craft in existence since the earliest days of the Old Republic would fill volumes. This appendix—though not exhaustive—is meant to show the great range, in both function and form, of those many vehicles and vessels piloted by the galaxy's denizens.

A-9 Vigilance Interceptor

A short-range fighter used by Imperial Remnant forces. The starfighter, which appeared shortly after the defeat of Grand Admiral Thrawn, has two laser cannons. It lacks a hyperdrive and shields. The A-9 can match the A-wing's speed, but is less maneuverable. It is small, light, and designed for sudden strikes against enemy bases or capital ships.

Amphibion

A water assault craft used extensively at the Battle of Mon Calamari. Amphibions serve as troop transports and can travel over both land and water at speeds of up to 100 kilometers per hour. The vehicle boasts a rotating antipersonnel blaster cannon.

A-Vek Iiluunu

(Yuuzhan Vong Fighter Carrier)
A bioengineered capital ship used by the Yuuzhan Vong. Coralskippers attach to the vessel by branchlike projections. A standard carrier measuring nearly 800 meters long can hold 200 coralskippers.

Bria

A SoroSuub Starmite owned and piloted by Han Solo before he acquired the *Millennium Falcon*. The starship was named for Solo's first love.

Carrack Cruiser

A small combat cruiser integral to the Imperial fleet. Heavily armed and armored, the Carrack cruiser has 10 heavy turbolasers and 20 ion cannons. The starship has no docking bay and must carry five TIE fighters on external racks.

Chariot LAV

A modified military landspeeder designed to serve as a command vehicle during ground engagements. The Chariot Light Assault Vehicle (LAV) has minimal weaponry and relies rather on other craft for defense. Despite this drawback, the Chariot LAV was favored by Imperial commanders because of its low cost, sophisticated communications bay, and ability to navigate most terrain. Grand Admiral Thrawn upgraded several Chariot LAVs to make them more formidable combat vehicles.

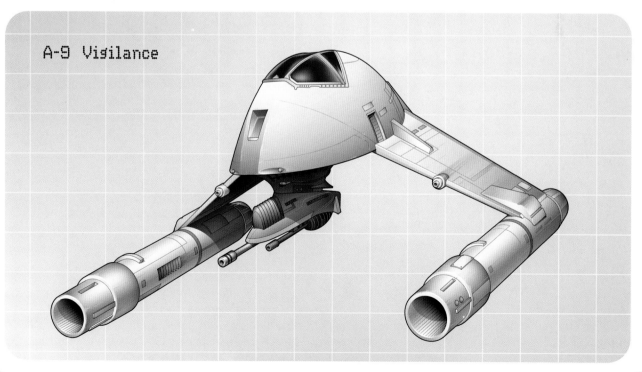

A-9 Vigilance

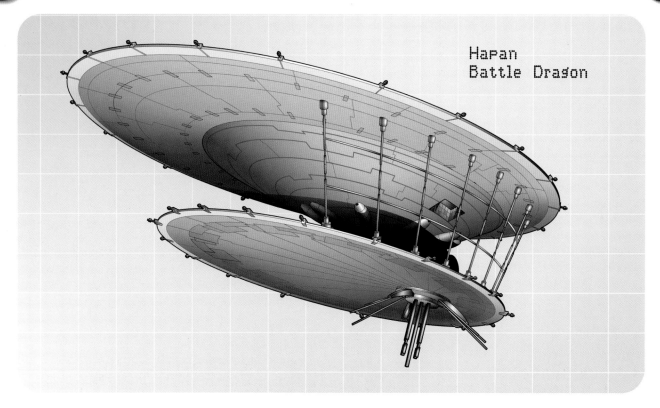

Hapan
Battle Dragon

CHU'UNTHOR

A massive cruiser that served as a mobile training academy for the Jedi Order. Built about 400 years before the Battle of Yavin, the *Chu'unthor* eventually vanished, along with the nearly 10,000 Jedi aboard. Luke Skywalker later discovered that the starship had crashed on the world of Dathomir, home to Force-sensitive "Witches" descended from a Jedi exile.

COMBAT CLOUD CAR

An armed cloud car designed to fill a niche between standard airspeeders and space-capable starfighters. Combat cloud cars have a maximum altitude of 100 kilometers.

CORAL VANDA

A subocean liner and pleasure cruiser that navigates the oceans of Pantolomin. The *Coral Vanda* boasts 8 decadent casinos, 16 luxury suites, cabins for 600 passengers, and 4 "adventure rooms" that use holographic technology to re-create exotic locales. Han Solo and Lando Calrissian boarded the *Coral Vanda* while searching for the lost *Katana* fleet during the Thrawn conflict.

DREADNAUGHT

Massive, ancient starships used as heavy cruisers by the Old Republic. Although fairly weak when compared to Star Destroyers, Dreadnaughts remain active throughout the galaxy because they can be refitted with more advanced weapons and other systems. Modified Dreadnaughts were used by both the Empire and Rebel Alliance during the Galactic Civil War, although the Rebels focused on increasing the Dreadnaught's speed and maneuverability.

ENFORCER ONE

Bogga the Hutt's flagship, which was in use thousands of years before the Battle of Naboo. *Enforcer One* was notable for a fixed heavy turbolaser that had a dedicated power core, advanced cooling systems, and a long barrel fitted with experimental galven circuitry to produce a tightly focused beam with tremendous range.

FLURRY

A carrier donated to the Rebel Alliance by sympathetic Virgillians, the *Flurry* was destroyed by the Imperial *Carrack*-class cruiser Dominant over Bakura. All hands were lost.

GUARDIAN MANTIS

A starfighter piloted by the mercenary Vana Sage, the *Guardian Mantis* has stealth capabilities, tracking devices, and modular weapons emplacements. Vana's R2 unit was hardwired into the ship, and the ship's torpedo launchers fired small nano-missiles.

HAPAN BATTLE DRAGON

Saucer-shaped starships used in the Hapes Cluster. Each Battle Dragon is about 500 meters in diameter. The heavily armed vehicles have nearly 100 weapons emplacements. The Hapans also deploy pulse-mass mines that simulate a mass shadow in space to prevent hyperspace jumps.

HAPES NOVA BATTLE CRUISER

A 400-meter-long patrol ship found in the Hapes Cluster. The vehicles are designed for swift, brutal attacks. Hapan Prince Isolder, who sought Princess Leia's hand in marriage, once offered Han Solo a *Nova*-class battle cruiser in exchange for ceasing his own pursuit of Leia. Han declined the offer.

HELL'S ANVIL

A dangerous starfighter used by bounty hunter and ex-Mandalorian Montross. *Hell's Anvil* had solar ionization cannons that ignored deflector shields and could melt durasteel. Montross used the vehicle in a failed attempt to kill Jango Fett around the time of the Battle of Naboo.

HEYBLIBBER

A luxury Gungan bongo. Jar Jar Binks crashed Boss Nass's heyblibber shortly before being exiled from Otoh Gunga.

HORNET INTERCEPTOR

A perfectly aerodynamic ship favored by pirates, smugglers, and other criminals. The Hornet has a thin, daggerlike body, with insectlike wings for atmospheric flight. It is more maneuverable than an X-wing.

HUTT CARAVEL

A short-range space transport used by Hutt crimelords, most often to travel between Nal Hutta and its spaceport moon, Nar Shaddaa.

HYPERSPACE MARAUDER

A converted freighter owned by the smuggler Lo Khan, who often allows the slow and unarmed vehicle to be overtaken by pirates. As the raiders prepare to board, Lo Khan uses the *Marauder*'s computer system to take control of the enemy ship's own systems for his personal use.

I'FRIIL MA-NAT
(YUUZHAN VONG CORVETTE)

Yuuzhan Vong analogs to the Corellian corvette, these vessels have a roughly pyramidlike shape and are constructed from jet-black yorik coral. The lightly armed starships typically strike quickly and retreat to the safety of a fleet before enemy forces can regroup. Two of these starships participated in a battle at Ord Mantell.

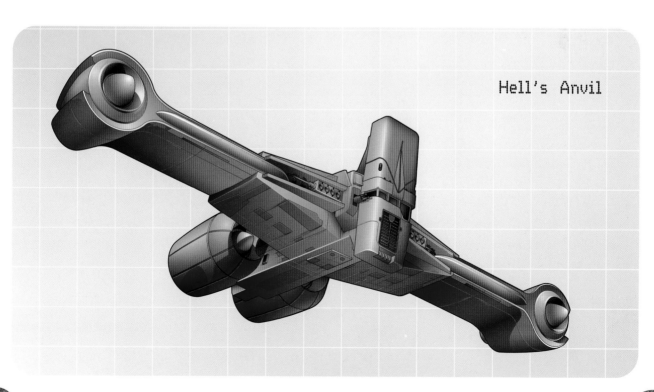

Hell's Anvil

Incom Y-4 Raptor Transport

A military transport shuttle used extensively by Warlord Zsinj during his bid for power. Raptors were designed to ferry troops and supplies between starships or bases. The vehicles allowed Zsinj's forces to quietly and quickly infiltrate planetary defenses for surgical strikes and other missions.

Ithullan Ore Hauler

An ancient vehicle constructed from the carapaces of kilometer-long Ithullan colossus wasps. The ore haulers were used to transport precious mutonium ore. Their main weapons were a pair of heavy turbolasers mounted in the forward section of the wasp's chest.

Jabba's Space Cruiser

A customized Ubrikkian starship used by Jabba the Hutt for his "personal business trips." The crimelord installed hidden gunports on the vessel as an unpleasant surprise for would-be pirates.

Jade's Fire

Mara Jade Skywalker's first shuttle. *Jade's Fire* was destroyed when Mara intentionally crashed the vehicle into the *Hand of Thrawn's* docking bay on Nirauan. One unique feature on her ship was the "shoot-back system." When laserfire hit the hull, a small turret blaster automatically fired in the general direction of the incoming shots. The feature has been replicated in her current ship, the *Jade Shadow*.

Jade Sabre

Mara Jade's second shuttle, constructed for her by Luke Skywalker. The green starship had an inertial compensator, etheric rudder, and expanded docking bay to carry Luke's XJ X-wing starfighter. The Yuuzhan Vong discovered the *Jade Sabre* on Dantooine and destroyed the vessel.

Jaster's Legacy

Jango Fett's first personal starship, which he named for his Mandalorian mentor. Jango lost the vehicle on Oovo IV and was forced to steal a *Firespray*-class patrol ship that eventually became known as *Slave I*.

Lancer Frigate

A 250-meter-long Imperial capital ship designed to combat Rebel starfighters. The frigates have 20 tower-mounted quad laser cannons, but little defense against other combat starships. Five years after the death of Emperor Palpatine, Grand Admiral Thrawn used *Lancer*-class frigates as a major component of Imperial raiding missions.

Legacy of Torment

A Yuuzhan Vong vessel destroyed at Ithor. Like the kor chokk, another Yuuzhan Vong capital ship or "grand cruiser," she was roughly the size of a Super Star Destroyer.

Marauder Corvette

A capital ship used extensively by the Corporate Sector Authority's Picket Fleet. The vessels are 195 meters long and streamlined for atmospheric combat. A stan-

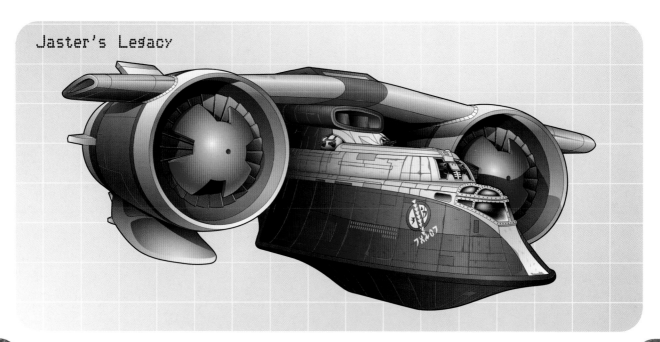

Jaster's Legacy

Legacy of Torment

Miy'til Fighter

The Hapes Consortium's fast, maneuverable starfighter. Designed as a patrol and attack craft, the Miy'til fighter has a hyperdrive, two fire-linked laser cannons, and a small concussion missile tube. The craft is frequently deployed for antipirate missions.

Moldy Crow

The starship used by Rebel operative Jan Ors and Kyle Katarn during their investigation into the Empire's Dark Trooper program. Jan often piloted the vehicle to rescue Kyle from Imperial forces.

Mon Remonda

An MC80B Mon Calamari star cruiser delivered to the New Republic about 18 months after the Battle of Endor. She was a major component in the New Republic's battle to retake Coruscant. She also served as the flagship of a New Republic fleet sent to repel the offensive of Imperial Warlord Zsinj.

MorningStar

A tri-winged starfighter often used by mercenaries in the Naboo system.

MT-AT

An Imperial walker designed to navigate steep inclines with independently articulated legs and clawed footpads. The MT-AT's eight-legged design has earned it the nickname "Spider Walker."

Naboo Bomber

A prototype vehicle seldom used by the Naboo Royal Security Forces. The Naboo bomber combines deadly Nubian technology with Naboo spaceframe design. The heavily armored vehicle carries devastating energy bombs for air-to-ground combat.

Nebulon Ranger

A large courier ship used by the Jedi brothers Ulic and Cay Qel-Droma and the Twi'lek Jedi Tott Doneeta, 4,000 years before the rise of the Emperor. The *Nebulon Ranger* had retractable wings that were extended for atmospheric flight.

dard Marauder carries eight double turbolasers and three tractor beam projectors, twelve fighters for long-range assault and patrol missions, and two platoons of forty troopers.

Marauder Starjacker

An ore-raiding ship commanded by pirate captain Finhead Stonebone some 4,000 years before the Galactic Civil War. The starship resembled an insect, although it was about 100 meters long.

Miy'til Assault Bomber

A powerful bomber used exclusively by the Hapes Consortium. The Miy'til bomber is faster and more agile than the Empire's TIE bomber. The Hapes Consortium reserves these starfighters for major offensives, and few outside of the Hapan Cluster understand the ship's capabilities.

NEIMOIDIAN SHUTTLE

A transport shuttle used by Neimoidian Trade Federation officials such as Nute Gunray and Rune Haako. The shuttle vaguely resembles a large insect and has pointed landing claws. The Neimoidian shuttle does not require a pilot. Nute Gunray's shuttle was a *Sheathipede*-class vessel called the *Lapiz Cutter*.

PHANTOM TIE

A secret weapon developed by the Empire. The Phantom TIE was a tri-winged TIE fighter with cloaking ability. The prototype was destroyed by Rebel agents.

PHOENIX HAWK LIGHT PINNACE

One of Kuat Systems Engineering's first starships, designed for a small group of passengers to make long-distance trips. Affordable and moderately armed but cramped and ugly, the *Phoenix Hawk*–class light pinnace has virtually disappeared during the New Republic era.

REPUBLIC INTERCEPTOR TX-130S FIGHTER TANK

A repulsor craft used extensively by Jedi generals during the Clone Wars. The TX-130S was developed to combat the Confederacy of Independent Systems' droid armies and lead Republic ground troops into battle. The vehicle was fast and agile, enabling the Jedi to quickly reach any area on a battlefield. It was also an effective front-line combat vehicle.

RO'IK CHUUN M'ARH

A Yuuzhan Vong frigate analog anywhere between 200 and 500 meters long. The size of the chuun m'arh frigates varies because they are designed to fulfill many roles, from cargo transport to combat support and even long-range reconnaissance. Five such vehicles participated in the Battle of Ord Mantell. The Yuuzhan Vong frigates also have boarding skiffs capable of carrying up to 100 warriors.

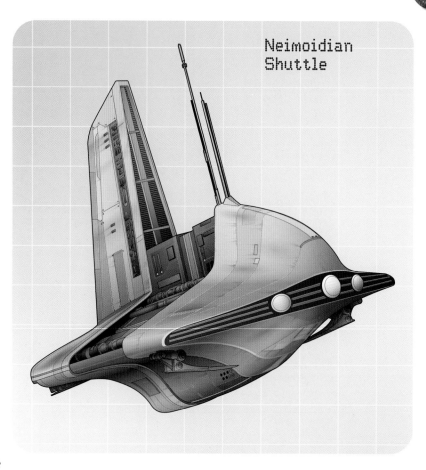

Neimoidian Shuttle

SABAOTH FIGHTER

Deadly starfighters used by Captain Cavik Toth's mercenary army around the time of the Battle of Geonosis. Jedi Master Adi Gallia tested her prototype Jedi starfighter against the sabaoth fighters in the Karthakk system.

SCARAB

Trade Federation starfighters used in a plot to explore and conquer lawless Outer Rim worlds.

SCIMITAR ASSAULT BOMBER

An Imperial bomber used by Grand Admiral Thrawn's forces. The Scimitar assault bomber is a dedicated atmospheric and space bomber with better performance than a standard TIE bomber. It was designed partly by members of the elite and highly decorated Scimitar bomber assault wing.

SHIELDSHIP

A custom-built escort vessel that protects ships traveling to the planet Nkllon in the Athega system. The system's sun emits dangerous rays that destroy any vessel not protected by a shieldship. Lando Calrissian later converted shieldships into war machines to battle the Yuuzhan Vong.

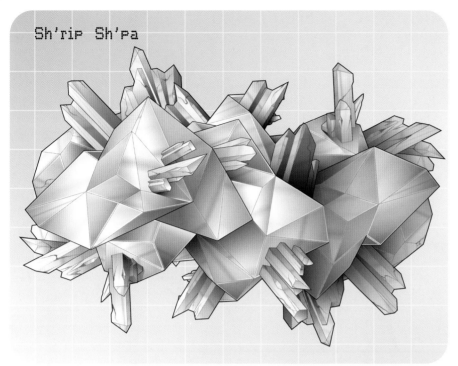

Sh'rip Sh'pa

SKIPRAY BLASTBOAT

An assault gunship used by the Empire. Blastboats are larger and more powerful than starfighters, yet still small enough to be carried aboard capital ships. The 25-meter-long vessel has an inordinate number of weapons for its size, including three medium ion cannons, a proton torpedo launcher, two laser cannons, and a concussion missile launcher.

SLAVE II

A starship owned by Boba Fett that served as his primary vessel after he escaped from the Sarlacc on Tatooine. *Slave II* is a *Pursuer*-class patrol starship that, decades earlier, had been popular with Mandalorian mercenaries. After *Slave II* was damaged over the world of Byss, Fett recovered his original starship, *Slave I*, from a New Republic impound.

SITH MEDITATION SPHERE

A large, round starship used by ancient Sith warlords to focus the Sith "battle meditation" technique and other abilities. The meditation sphere used by Sith Lord Naga Sadow about 5,000 years before the Battle of Yavin appeared as a giant, floating eye with batlike wings.

SPEEDER BUS

Large repulsorlift transports used in the skylanes of Coruscant. The largest speeder buses can carry up to 1,000 passengers.

SH'RIP SH'PA

(YUUZHAN VONG SPAWN SHIP)

A large Yuuzhan Vong cruiser that carries the supplies necessary for terraforming captured planets. The spawn ship resembles an enormous, faceted polyhedron with onyx skin.

SHRIWIRR

A large, customized Ssi-ruuvi battle cruiser. The flagship during the Ssi-ruuk's attack on Bakura, the *Shriwirr* was oval in shape and served as both a warship and transport carrying about 500 battle droids. The *Shriwirr* contained a disturbing "entechment lab" that allowed the Ssi-ruuk to steal living energy from prisoners in order to power their equipment.

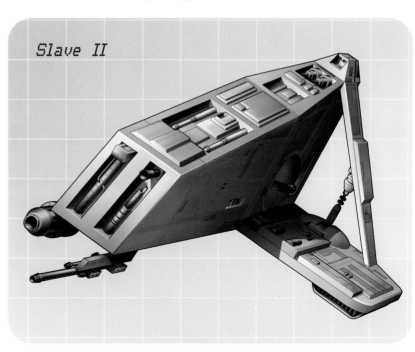

Slave II

Ssi-Ruuvi Assault Carrier

Sh'ner-class planetary assault carriers used by the reptilian Ssi-ruuk. The ovoid ships are nearly 750 meters long. The assault carrier is believed to be rare. Only one was used during the Ssi-ruuk's attack on Bakura.

Ssi-Ruuvi Picket Ship

Small Ssi-ruuvi Imperium combat ships. Picket ships are typically used to disable enemy vessels and guard the perimeters of Ssi-ruuvi fleets. The small attack vessels are fairly delicate and require inefficient shields. Because the vehicles are crewed by droids and P'w'eck slaves, the Ssi-ruuk consider the picket ships expendable and often send them on suicide missions.

Star Home

A four-thousand-standard-year-old transport vessel designed for the Hapes Cluster's Queen Mother. The vessel is unique because she perfectly replicates the Queen Mother's castle on the planet Hapes, all atop a giant basalt base housing traditional starship systems.

Starlight Intruder

Salla Zend's modified Mobquet transport. Converted for smuggling runs, the *Starlight Intruder* carried seven times the cargo of other light freighters and had four military-grade ion engines for quick escapes. The starship was captured by Imperial forces on Byss, who stripped the ship and used her to fuel furnaces.

Stinger

The personal transport of Prince Xizor's cyborg aide, Guri. Guri once used the modified Surronian Conqueror assault ship's proton torpedoes to single-handedly destroy an Imperial Star Destroyer.

Storm

Prince Isolder's starfighter, designed by the prince himself. The fighter uses miniaturized components to keep her size just over seven meters long. She is also extremely well armed with a set of triple-linked laser cannons, a mini concussion missile launcher, two ion cannons, and a thermal detonator bomb chute.

Sun Crusher

An Imperial superweapon with resonance torpedoes capable of destroying a star. The long, dagger-shaped vessel was protected from enemy starfighters by rotating laser cannons. The Sun Crusher was destroyed when it was trapped in a gravity well produced by the Maw's black holes.

Suuv Ban D'Krid

(YUUZHAN VONG CRUISER)

A Yuuzhan Vong capital ship similar to a cruiser. Yuuzhan Vong cruisers are multicolored vessels bio-engineered using yorik coral. During the Battle of Duro, the Yuuzhan Vong used a cruiser to ram an unshielded orbital city.

Tafanda Bay

An Ithorian herd ship. The Ithorians have lived in herd ships, which cruise slowly over the beautiful world of Ithor, for generations. Each herd ship is hundreds of meters tall and holds thousands of Ithorians. Shortly before the Battle of Ithor, *Tafanda Bay* hosted a reception for New Republic and Imperial Remnant forces. When the Yuuzhan Vong fleet arrived, Yuuzhan Vong warriors boarded the herd ship and clashed with Luke Skywalker and his Jedi allies. Soon after, Ithor was consumed in a fireball and the *Tafanda Bay* was presumably destroyed.

TIE Avenger

A TIE fighter design based on Darth Vader's prototype TIE fighter. Like Vader's TIE, the TIE avenger had deflector shields and a hyperdrive. The expensive vehicle was produced in very limited numbers and eventually replaced by the TIE interceptor.

TIE Crawler

A tank based on the TIE fighter design. The TIE crawler has a round cockpit connected to two large treads. Also known as the "century tank," the TIE crawler was essential to the Empire's efforts to retake Coruscant.

TIE/D Fighter

An automated TIE fighter with an integrated Cybot Galactica Ace-6 fighter unit. The computerized pilots can be programmed with the latest tactics and combat protocols. The starfighter also has distinctive rectangular wings and heavy armor.

TIE/fc Fighter

A modified TIE fighter that provides fire control and targeting aid for long-range naval artillery. The TIE/fc is equipped with protected comlinks and advanced targeting computers. The vessels can hover near a target and transmit precise aiming adjustments to an attacking fleet ship.

TIE/gt Fighter

The predecessor of the TIE bomber. The TIE/gt is essentially a standard TIE fighter with an expanded hull loaded with proton torpedoes and bombs.

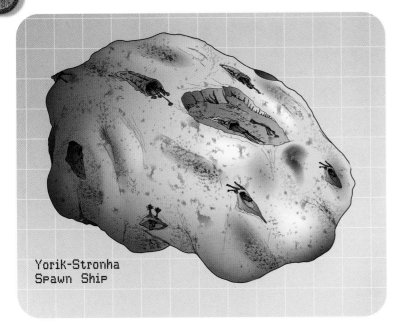

Yorik-Stronha
Spawn Ship

Tsik Vai

(YUUZHAN VONG FLIER)

An atmospheric, bioengineered flying vehicle. The Yuuzhan Vong used fliers to search for Anakin Solo on Yavin 4. The tsik vai looks like a winged sea creature with several tentacles for grasping prey. The vehicle's intake vents function like gills and create an audible whine.

Uro-Ik V'alh

(YUUZHAN VONG BATTLESHIP)

A massive Yuuzhan Vong vessel. The uro-ik v'alh is larger than the Yuuzhan Vong warship and resembles a long, rocky slab composed of hardened slag. The uro-ik v'alh carries up to 80 plasma projectors and is designed specifically for direct confrontations with capital ships.

Uumufalh

(YUUZHAN VONG GUNSHIP)

An escort starship used by the Yuuzhan Vong to protect cruisers and other larger starships, the uumufalh can spray volleys of plasma.

Yorik-Stronha

(YUUZHAN VONG SPY SHIP)

An asteroid-shaped scout ship used by the Yuuzhan Vong. The spy ship is usually sent into enemy territory well in advance of an attack fleet to gauge the enemy's capabilities. Built from yorik coral and covered with layers of rock, the yorik-stronha is often equipped with a cloaking shadow. Anakin Solo and his allies commandeered a spy ship called the *Stalking Moon*.

Yorik-Ta

(YUUZHAN VONG ESCAPE POD)

An escape pod constructed from black yorik coral. The escape pod incorporates a dovin basal for travel and protection. Roughly the size of a landspeeder, the yorik-ta has a transparent canopy and no weapons.

Zoomer

A salvage ship used by the Toydarian mechanic Reti around the time of the Battle of Naboo. The *Zoomer* retrieved Naboo pilot Rhys Dallows after he was ambushed by mercenaries hired by the Trade Federation. Several standard years later, Reti and his starship joined forces with pirate captain Nym.

TIE/rc Fighter

A reconnaissance TIE fighter with advanced sensor packages and communications devices. The TIE/rc was eventually replaced by the TIE vanguard.

TIE Shuttle

A personal shuttle used by high-ranking Imperials on high-priority missions. The shuttle is 7.8 meters long and can carry a pilot and two passengers. TIE shuttles were in heavy use around the time of the Battle of Hoth.

TIE Vanguard

A descendant of the TIE/rc starfighter, the TIE vanguard was designed for reconnaissance and spy missions. Deflector shields protected any data gathered by the starfighter.

TIE-Wing

A starfighter that combines a TIE fighter cockpit with a Y-wing's engine nacelle. Considered "ugly" because it is cobbled together from other vehicles, the TIE-wing was used by Kavil's Corsairs during their conflicts with Rogue Squadron.

Trade Federation Gunboat

A seaworthy vessel designed to explore swamps and other waterways. The Trade Federation used the gunboat's twin laser cannons and a rotating turret to battle the Royal Security Forces resistance fighters and Gungan warriors during the invasion of Naboo.

Hyperdrive Classification

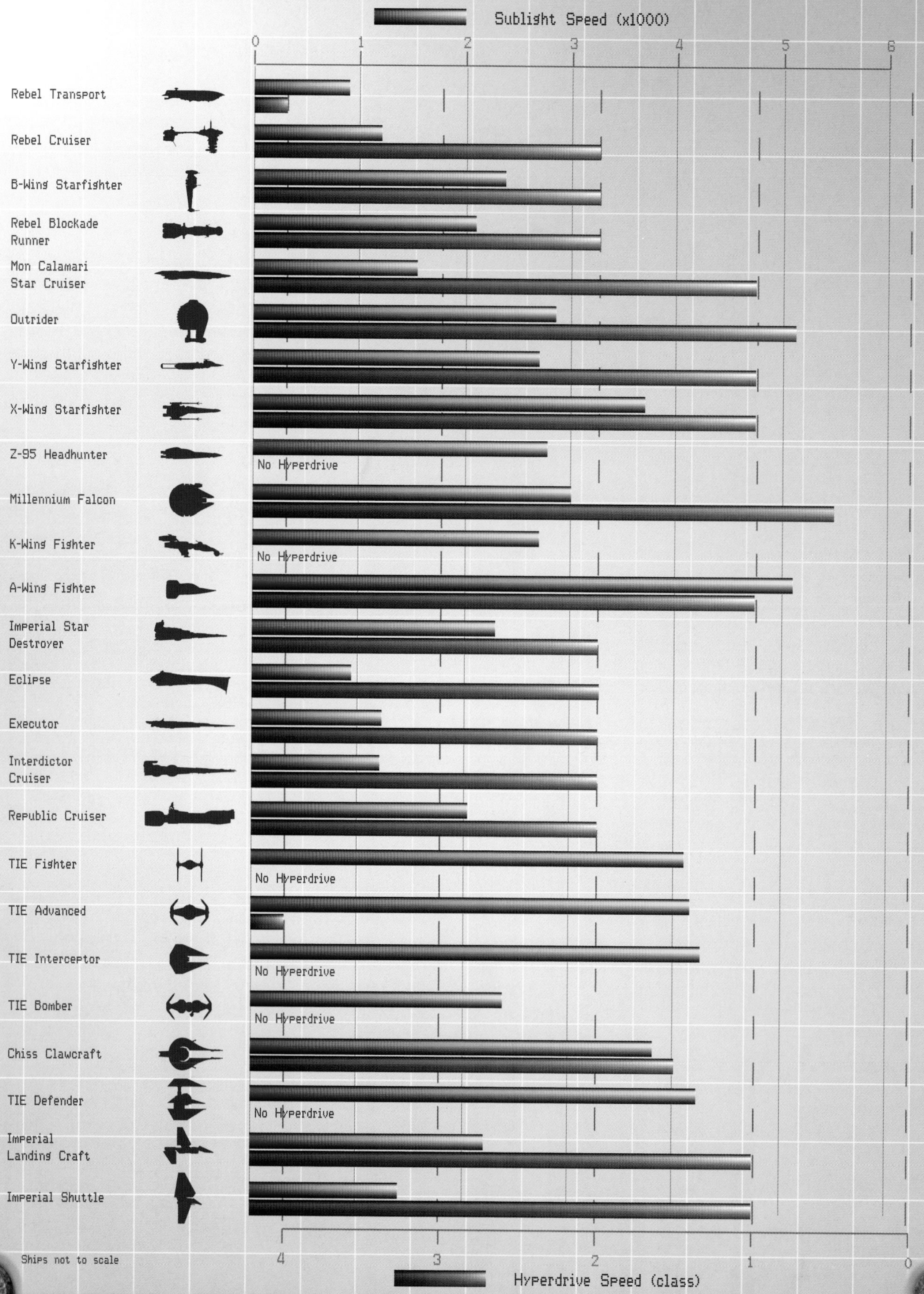

Sublight Speed (x1000)
0
1
2
3
4
5
6
Rebel Transport
Rebel Cruiser
B-Wing Starfighter
Rebel Blockade Runner
Mon Calamari Star Cruiser
Outrider
Y-Wing Starfighter
X-Wing Starfighter
Z-95 Headhunter
No Hyperdrive
Millennium Falcon
K-Wing Fighter
No Hyperdrive
A-Wing Fighter
Imperial Star Destroyer
Eclipse
Executor
Interdictor Cruiser
Republic Cruiser
TIE Fighter
No Hyperdrive
TIE Advanced
TIE Interceptor
No Hyperdrive
TIE Bomber
No Hyperdrive
Chiss Clawcraft
TIE Defender
No Hyperdrive
Imperial Landing Craft
Imperial Shuttle
Ships not to scale
4
3
2
1
0
Hyperdrive Speed (class)

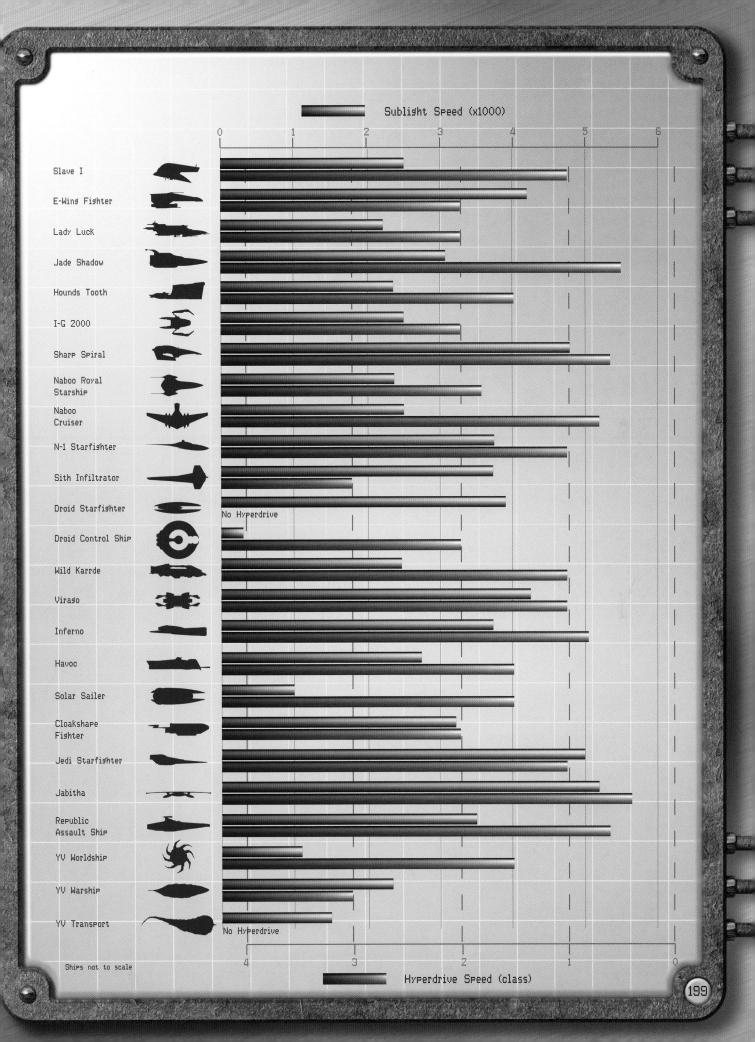

Sublight Speed (x1000)

Slave I	
E-Wing Fighter	
Lady Luck	
Jade Shadow	
Hounds Tooth	
I-G 2000	
Sharp Spiral	
Naboo Royal Starship	
Naboo Cruiser	
N-1 Starfighter	
Sith Infiltrator	
Droid Starfighter	No Hyperdrive
Droid Control Ship	
Wild Karrde	
Virago	
Inferno	
Havoc	
Solar Sailer	
Cloakshape Fighter	
Jedi Starfighter	
Jabitha	
Republic Assault Ship	
YV Worldship	
YV Warship	
YV Transport	No Hyperdrive

Ships not to scale

Hyperdrive Speed (class)

About the Author

W. Haden Blackman is the author of *The Field Guide to North American Monsters* and *The Field Guide to North American Hauntings*. He has also worked extensively "in" the Star Wars universe on a variety of video games and comic books, including LucasArts' *Star Wars Galaxies: An Empire Divided* and Dark Horse Comics' *Jango Fett: Open Seasons*. He thinks Lando is completely misunderstood.

About the Illustrator

Ian Fullwood lives and works in Herefordshire, England, and has clients both at home and in the USA.

With more than fifteen years' experience in technical illustration and commercial art, he works with a range of clients, who include publishing and engineering companies. He produces a variety of work ranging from science fiction to product visualizing and animation.

Ian uses traditional drawing skills combined with computer programs—Illustrator, Photoshop, and Lightwave 3D—to produce technically demanding and visually exciting pieces of work. Vist *www.if3d.com* for more visual indigestion!

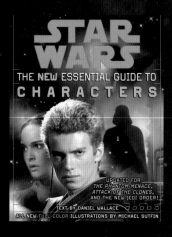
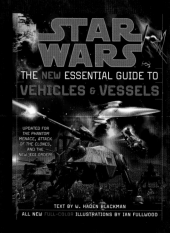

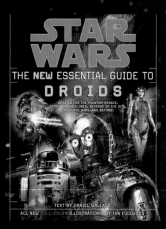
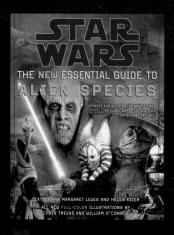
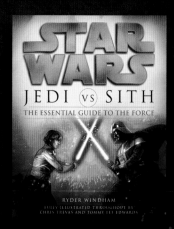